W9-BIR-415

OBSCURED

CHARLOTTE MILLS

ALSO BY CHARLOTTE MILLS

COPYRIGHT

Obscured
First Edition copyright 2022 Charlotte Mills.

All rights reserved. No part of this book may be reproduced in any form, in whole or in part, without the written permission of the author. The characters, incidents and dialogue are fictional and any resemblance to actual events or persons, living or dead is purely coincidental.

Editor Hayley Sherman
Cover MP Designs

For mum.

CHAPTER 1

DETECTIVE SERGEANT LUCY FULLER swallowed the last bite of her chocolate digestive, she needed something to wash it down now. Mug in hand she got to her feet ambling in the direction of the small kitchen on the far side of the room. The office was busy with most desks occupied by uniformed officers, she was enjoying the contrast of a slower pace of life without DCI Barrel standing over her, breathing down her neck all day.

A familiar face appearing in the kitchen doorway put pay to any quietude she'd been feeling. She wasn't exactly in PC Andy Tanner's good books after she had turned him down in the pub last week. She'd made it clear she didn't date people who worked at the same station, especially male colleagues, or men of any kind for that matter. Tanner had been polite about it, but she knew it would make waves. A panic swept over her as she met his eyes, the office seemed to fall silent around them.

Andy's eyebrows raised, his mouth opened but no words came or at least nothing that she heard.

Lucy's phone blared from her pocket jolting her to life. She answered it without even looking at the caller id. "DS Fuller," Anything to avoid interaction with Tanner.

"Stop trying to make out you're busy, Fuller. I know you miss me when I'm away."

Lucy squinted one eye in frustration as she turned back towards her desk. She hated the fact that he was always one step ahead of her. In his absence she'd been mainly tasked with tidying up the paperwork on the cases they'd been working on. The price of being a bagman, or woman in her case. "Boss. How's it going in court?" This was only the second day of the complex people-trafficking case he'd worked on just before she was transferred to his charge. It had taken the CPS over two years to get it to trial. She perched on her seat ready for his latest grievances.

"Shit, as expected. Anyway, I've got a job for you. A body's been found just outside Kingsford. It's our case apparently."

"What?" Lucy sat up a little straighter, was he on his way back. "Ours? Why are they giving it to us?" In the two years she'd worked with Barrel, she'd barely been trusted to tie her shoelaces let alone run a case on her own. As part of a small CID team they wouldn't be called in unless there was a question regarding the manner of death, which meant a possible murder case. She mentally rubbed her hands together then felt terrible about it.

"Stop complaining. At least you'll be sleeping in your own bed tonight. Kingsford's just up the road. I'll still be stuck in Slough of all fucking places."

"Why us, though? Why not DCI Thompson?" Lucy queried again. Kingsford was sandwiched between two much bigger towns which housed far larger police stations and CID teams. West Heath usually covered Kingsford. Officers from her station in Woodley were rarely called in.

"He's tied up with that drugs case. They're pretty stretched after Porter's heart attack last month."

Shit! The funeral they'd attended two weeks ago seemed so far away now; life moved on so quickly. Lucy made a mental note to ask about Porter's family when she got to the scene.

"Anyone would think you don't want to be a copper or something."

Barrels words echoed in her ear. "What-no-I just don't like stepping on people's toes, that's all."

"Get used to it." Barrel let out a breath down the phone. "Get over to Kingsford, I'm stuck here so I need you to start the leg work on this. I'll join you over there as soon as I can, hopefully in the next day or two."

"Okay, boss. Where am I going?" Lucy grabbed a pen to take down the information.

"Combe Farm, it's on the Stype Hill Road. Keep me updated with any developments."

Muffled conversation came down the phoneline but her thoughts were elsewhere at this point; she'd been left to her own devices and her mind went blank as she tried to figure out her next move. She'd worked cases involving death before, mostly drug and drink related. Thankfully, murders were still rare in the area.

"And, Fuller …"

Lucy blinked herself alert as she waited for the reprimand that was surely coming.

"Don't fuck this up."

His voice took on a familiar firm timbre. "Yes, boss." She bit down on her bottom lip to prevent her from saying anything else.

An hour later, she was driving under a police cordon, held aloft by a uniformed officer, several familiar faces from the local press glanced her way. The circus had already arrived, thankfully, they were being kept at bay.

She parked up alongside two other police vehicles in a small court-yard and held up a hand to shield her eyes from the sun as she got out of her car. Scanning the immediate area as she moved to the boot, she saw that there was no-one in sight. She took the opportunity to take a breath and get her head in the game. She hated to even think it, but this was an opportunity for her to prove herself, to finally step out of Barrel's shadow. Her mind fizzed as she pulled out her crime scene gear, grateful that the eyes of the media were in the distance outside the farm boundary.

Lucy threw her jacket in the boot before struggling into the clean white jumpsuit, unsure of what she was walking into. Barrel had given barely any details, probably on purpose, she thought now. She just hoped it wasn't a gory one. She'd had trouble eating after the last time. Who knew a dog walker colliding with a train could make quite so much mess? She swallowed down that unpleasant thought as she zipped up her protective suit.

"Hey, Fuller, when he said he was sending his best man, I didn't realise it would be you."

Lucy turned to glare at the uniformed PC before raising her middle finger in reply. "If you weren't so shit at your job, Laxton, I wouldn't need to be here!" She'd crossed paths with Laxton at several crime scenes over the years. He wasn't exactly backwards in coming forwards.

She closed her boot before turning to speak to him more formally, feeling the need to soften the blow of her arrival. "How's Porter's family doing?" .

Laxton pursed his lips, before letting out a breath. "Not great. We're trying to rally round where we can. It's a big adjustment for them."

Lucy let the words hang between them as she looked down at her wellies. She waited a few beats before asking, "We're outside?"

"Yeah, the field behind the main barn, there." Laxton indicated towards a large building edging the far side of the courtyard they were stood in.

As she looked around, Lucy realised Combe Farm was no longer a working farm. It had been gentrified somewhat. Muddy surfaces had been replaced with block paving and bark chippings. The double fronted farm house hand been extended and upgraded for pleasure rather than necessity with an extravagant sliding roof on the left-hand side. She glanced back towards the barn Laxton had indicated earlier, it too had been given a new lease of life with fresh hardwood cladding. New windows had been installed indicating a mezzanine floor inside.

She slipped off her shoes and left them under the shelter of her car. The wellies were cool inside as her feet half-filled the cavernous space.

"Pathologist's here," Laxton announced as they walked between the two buildings, nearing the scene, the top of a mini digger and a mountain of soil protruded over sloping land, three uniformed officers were milling about on the open scrubland beyond the buildings. Her wellies clunked as she walked; she needed to add a thick pair of socks to her scene-of-crime supplies.

"What have we got?" Lucy finally asked.

"Body was found in an old well, near the boundary over there," Laxton supplied.

Shit! She hoped they'd got it out already. She didn't fancy climbing into a well.

Lucy followed Laxton's nod, relieved when the tops of two white tents came into view. At least something had been set up. Barrel must have barked his orders from Slough. She hoped Dr Reed wasn't inside one of them, he always managed to set her on edge when he was at a crime scene. "Who found the body?"

"Contractor called it in when they dug into the side of the well. It was buried below the surface. Got out to have a look, saw the skull and freaked."

"Skull, as in skeleton? Not a body-body?" Lucy tried not to sound too grateful that there would be less gore, hopefully.

"Nope, sounds pretty old from what I've heard."

With her elevated view Lucy glanced back towards the bustling entrance. "We need to keep a lid on this."

"On it." Laxton replied.

Lucy considered the odds of it being an ancient find from hundreds of years ago and out of her remit. Typical; first solo job and she was already writing it off as ancient remains. Maybe Barrel's comment was right on the mark; she didn't want to be a copper. Six years in uniform had taught her one thing: she wanted to be a detective.

"What were the contractors digging for?"

"Owners wanted a new outbuilding, accommodation for some retreat or something. Contractors were digging out for the foundations."

Shouldn't existing features be noted on the plans? A question for the contractor.

"What about the property owners?" Lucy queried. There was a

distinct lack of civilians peeking out of windows, watching events unfold.

"The Carters. Away in London. They're on their way back now. Apparently they didn't know the well was there either."

Lucy heard the disbelief in Laxton's tone. Kingsford, like many surrounding towns, was roughly an hour's drive from London and overrun with semi-residential commuters. Depending on how much time they spent at Combe Farm, it was possible they knew nothing. Surely it would be the type of feature covered in a buyer's survey.

"How long have they lived here?" She unzipped her suit, taking out her notebook to scribble down a few items to follow up.

"Ten years."

"What about the previous tenants?" she asked without even looking up. Someone knew the well existed. Maybe they also knew it was the perfect place to hide a body.

"Jesus, Fuller, you know you're here to do all that shit now. PC Springer's on the phone getting you their details." Laxton's bluster was all bravado; he was just taking advantage of Barrel being off the scene.

"Okay. Good." She grinned, although she had no idea who PC Springer was.

Lucy was approaching the first tent when she noticed a large, almost circular object lying on the ground a few feet away from the tent. She stepped closer, crouching to take a better look. "Is this what was covering the well?"

"It's not true what they say is it? You really are a detective."

She glared at Laxton before returning her attention to the thick metal slab. The edge was coarsely cut, the exposed surface smooth and brown but not rusty. A thick layer of soil and roots from vegetation covered most of it. The contractors' gouging machinery had disturbed a section on one edge, leaving a deep scratch in the surface.

Lucy got to her feet. Leaving Laxton behind, she pulled aside the sheeting and stepped inside. It was empty except for a folding table on the far side. She spotted a box of latex gloves, grabbed two and quickly struggled into them, not wanting to be reprimanded by anyone.

The surface of the table was covered with bagged-up items. She figured they had been found in the well with the body or at least in the vicinity. At this point, it was impossible to say what was relevant. She stooped over the table to get a look at the contents. A pair of small, dirty, white trainers sat in one corner, maybe those of a woman or a child. She couldn't make out the brand, but they looked pretty scuffed up. She swallowed hard. She slowly closed her eyes as the realisation set in. Jesus, where was Barrel when she needed him? She wasn't ready for this. Murder cases involving children marred some careers and ended others. Any relief she'd felt at the news of skeletal remains disappeared.

She took a deep breath. *I still have a job to do here*, she reminded herself and considered some of the first questions to be answered. How did the victim get here? Were they lured here, considering the remote location? Were they killed here? If not, where? How did the perpetrator get here? With that in mind, she opened her eyes and moved further along the table, tattered clothing filled three more bags. She dragged her gaze over other bagged items, ending on a small, light-blue, oblong shape. An image of what looked like Tony the Tiger was just visible through the layer of dirt. Black print at one end confirmed her suspicions – *FROSTIES*. A red button was located next to the lettering. A treasured toy at one point. Maybe it could help identify the owner.

Lucy pulled out her phone and took a few pictures for her own reference. The label on the evidence bag stated that it had been found in the front-left pocket of the victims jeans.

"DS Fuller?"

Lucy jumped at the voice behind her, cringing at the sharp pain in her back as she straightened abruptly. She recognised the voice immediately before she turned around. "Dr Reed." She tried to keep her tone light despite being faced with his looming figure. His tall, usually slim frame, lost in the baggy white forensic suit, was stooped slightly under the restricted height of the forensics tent, making him a dead ringer for the Michelin Man. His bald head and round, metal-rimmed glasses certainly didn't help his case. They'd met a handful of times over the last year or so, mostly for accidental or drug related deaths. Each time he'd managed to unnerve her with his unwavering stare and hulking presence.

"DCI Barrel's case, is it?"

"It is." *When he can find the time to turn up, that is.* "What can you tell me so far?"

Reed looked down at the table in front of her. "As you can see, some of the clothing is pretty tattered and damp. We'll need to dry it out before we can get a good look at it."

Lucy waited a few beats before asking her next question. "And the identification of the body?"

Reed stood back from the table glaring at her as he adjusted the sleeve of his suit. "There's a lack of soft tissue due to decay. You'll need a forensic anthropologist to work on this one."

"You can't tell me anything?" Lucy pressed. Knowing full well Barrel would be on her case for information as soon as possible..

Reed looked at her for a moment as if weighing up his options. Reaching out a single gloved finger he pushed his glasses up his nose. "All I can tell you is it's a young male. There's some damage to the bones, which may or may not be the cause of death. There's at least one animal down there too."

Animal? Lucy refocussed on the human aspect … *may or may not be the cause of death.* "What sort of damage?"

"Fractures. There's too much surface debris to say if the damage was before or after he was put down there. Unfortunately, one of the stones on the edge was pushed down the well when it was discovered. I'll need to check but it may have caused some of the damage."

Lucy nodded as she made notes for her next conversation with Barrel. "What type of animal is it?"

"I'm pretty sure it's a dog. Could have gone in first, and he tried to rescue it."

Lucy said nothing. Someone had covered the well at some point, why would you do that if it was an innocent accident? Regardless the death would immediately be treated as suspicious as it was a child and there was no identification on the body.

"There's a Dr Chadwick just joined Reading University. I've worked with her before; she's exceptionally good. I'll give her a call when I get back to the office. Most importantly, she's worked with the police before."

Great! Another doctor. Reed was bad enough. "Thank you. Can I ask how long it'll take the forensic anthropologist to identify the victim?"

Reed's face scrunched up as he blew out a breath. "Well, it's a time-consuming process and Dr Chadwick does have teaching responsibilities." He pushed up his glasses again.

Lucy tuned out focussing on the artifacts on the table again as Reed continued to educate her on the intimacies of biological profiling, healed injuries and DNA extraction.

"Of course, they'll need something to compare them with to get a positive identification."

"Can't they just get DNA from the hair?" She knew there were numerous examples of old cases where hair had been used to identify a body and even exonerate suspects in old cases.

Reed took a deep breath. "The body has extensive decay, and the poor environmental conditions where it was stored are making it difficult to recover some items. Intermittent water, silt and soil have potentially removed some materials. If the hair was short, it may be difficult to find in these conditions I'm afraid."

"The well, it wasn't disused? Dried up?" Someone had to have noticed if a working well was suddenly covered over.

"According to one of the tecs, there was some evidence of different water level lines inside. The underground aquifer could have been compromised at some point before the body was inserted."

Lucy nodded and made a mental note to google how wells work when she got back to the office. "How deep is the well?"

"Oh, err, about twenty-five feet or so. Regarding the hair DNA, without the hair being intact, Dr Chadwick may prefer to use an alternative method of identification to prevent any mistakes."

"I see." Lucy nodded. "Can I take a look?" She didn't want to, but she knew she had to.

Dr Reed stepped back to the entrance. Separating the white sheeting, he indicated for her to go first. She walked the short distance to the second tent and pushed her way inside. A light mounted on a tripod dazzled her as she stepped into the enclosed space. Blinking as she looked away she noticed a yawning crater lay open in the ground to her left. Yellow cables trailed down into the abyss below, a soft white glow emanating from the aperture. The circular edge was ragged on one side. Deep cuts in the ground led to the well edge where some of the blocks had been disturbed. The wind pushed against the side of the tent making her shiver as the smell of mustiness filled her nostrils.

A second table was set up on the opposite side. The surface contained what she recognised as bones, laid out to create a reclining form. The figure was small, barely four feet tall by her estimation.

"The slight V-shape in the pelvis indicates it was a male. Young."

Lucy looked up, expecting more. Reed's mouth simply formed a straight line.

"Dr Chadwick will be able to tell you more," was all he offered, despite her raised eyebrows.

"How young?" It was the obvious question, and one she needed an answer to.

Reed's face flinched before he spoke. "It's difficult to be accurate at this stage, Dr Chad –"

"If you had to guess."

"I don't like to guess, DS Fuller," he fired back.

She pushed, despite his reluctance. "Ball park."

"The number of bones we have found would indicate a child of between maybe eight and twelve years old."

Just a kid. "Could it have been an accident?" The hopeful words were out of her mouth before she could stop them.

Reed's large figure appeared next to her. "The body had been partially covered with soil and plastic. So, the likelihood of them being alive and attempting to get out is slim. I'll need to do more work, but from the position of the body, it looks like he was probably dead before he was put down there."

"Where's the plastic?" Lucy asked.

Reed pointed to one of the opened boxes on the floor.

"This was covering the body?" she confirmed.

Reed nodded. "Partially."

Lucy crouched to look at the bagged-up, blue plastic.
a tarpaulin or something?"

"No. Smaller, thick plastic, more like a feed bag o
Opened out to make it bigger by the look of it. The lab sh
to tell you more."

A feedbag on a farm. Makes sense if it was a working farm in the
past. Repurposed to cover a body, to hide it or because they were
ashamed of what they had done. She got to her feet, mentally
preparing herself for the next part, and stared at the discoloured bones,
stained with dirt and debris. It looked like they had been carved from
wood, a linear grain almost visible on the surface of each piece.

"How long do you think he was down there?"

"Well, more than twenty and less than forty."

"Years?"

"Yes, DS Fuller, years. Of course, Dr Chadwick will be able to give
you more accurate information on that, but the wristwatch is a bit of an
indicator."

"Wristwatch?" Lucy dragged her gaze from the table. Reed looked
a little smug, eyebrows raised as he looked back at her. *Shit!* She'd seen
enough of the remains for now, they were out of her skillset, but the
personal effects were right up her street.

She stepped back from the table feeling his eyes on her again. In her
haste to get away from him to the other tent, her foot caught on the
corner of a plastic evidence box. A strong hand gripped her arm as she
stumbled.

"Steady, Detective, don't want you ending up down there too."

Lucy glanced around blood rushing to her cheeks as she staggered
upright; the well opening was only a few feet away. She swallowed
down the panic in her throat. "Thanks." Her voice was thick as she
spoke, taking a step closer, risking a look down the stone-lined shaft.
The light was directed towards the bed of the well. The silty floor was
broken up with debris and what she figured was one of the stone
blocks that Reed had mentioned earlier.

Reed was watching her as he finally let go of her arm. Not for the
first time, the hair on the back of her neck stood on end. Regaining
some composure she swiftly exited the tent.

She slipped through the opening of the first tent, not caring if Reed followed her as she approached the table of bagged-up contents. The black digital watch was at the far end of the table, the display long dead. A rainbow-like pattern covered the surface of the face, a crack on the left disjointing the pattern. She heard someone rustling behind her.

"Popular in the eighties and nineties," Reed said.

"Looks like it." She took out her phone to snap a quick image. She could recall childhood friends having similar watches while she had always preferred her prized Mickey Mouse analogue watch. "Can you send me through the details of Doctor Chadwick, and the photos of recovered evidence." She knew her first job would be to search missing persons reports. Hopefully, there would be details of what they were last seen wearing, which could help narrow down the ID for DNA comparison.

"I'll send them through as soon as I've finished here. I'll contact Dr Chadwick too."

Reed's imposing stature made her want to leave. "Thanks," she said, flipping her notebook shut. "I better check in with the boss," she added and stepped around Reed and out into the fresh air. She glanced around to get her bearings the only other buildings she could see apart from the Carters home were a small line of what looked like industrial units in the distance across the valley. She checked she was alone before dialling Barrel's mobile as she unzipped her suit. He answered on the first ring.

"What have we got?"

Lucy focused on the basics. "Young boy found in a well, skeletal remains, Dr Creepy estimates he's been down there twenty to forty years."

"Shit! Dr Creepy?"

"Dr Reed. Don't you find him creepy?" she asked, incredulous.

"Seriously, Fuller, anyone who spends that much time with dead people is meant to be creepy. Get over it."

Lucy ignored his comment as she continued back to her car.

"Okay. Check missing persons from the area and neighbouring counties for the last forty years. I know it's a long job, but you've got to start somewhere. Get Tanner to help you if you need it."

Lucy let out a long breath. "Yes, boss." She rolled her eyes at the thought of working with Tanner.

"Let me know if anything comes up."

"Will do." Lucy ended the call. With her suit unzipped, she slipped her arms free as she approached her car. As she made her way between the outbuildings, she noticed Laxton lurking around the boot of her car.

"It's got an alarm, Laxton."

He turned sharply at her words. "Don't worry, I'm not after your valuables."

"Good." Lucy dug around in her pocket for her key fob. Opening the driver's door, she dropped her notebook on the seat then moved towards Laxton, leaving the door open.

"Unlike Tanner," he mumbled under his breath as he looked away. It hadn't taken long for news to spread.

Lucy ignored him as she rested her hand on the boot of her car. She purposely avoided extricating herself from her suit in front of him in case she fell over in the process.

"Here are the details for the current and previous owners," Laxton told her, waving a piece of paper in her direction. "The Carters should be back tomorrow morning for interview, and the contractor Mark Irving's over there in his van." He pointed in the direction of a dark blue van.

Lucy blinked as she took in the information and stretched out her arm to take the offered paper. "Okay. Thanks."

"No problem. Let me know if you need anything else."

He sounded genuine, but he walked away before she could reply. In the two years she'd known him, she knew he liked the banter but as a copper when it came down to it he was a stand-up guy.

Lucy removed her white suit and dumped it in her car, along with her wellies. Redressed she made her way over to the blue van. There were no decals on the side, indicating that the owner was indeed a contractor. As she approached, a bulky figure unfolded as he exited the driver's side. A tall, solid white man, she estimated to be in his forties with windswept, dark hair turned towards her.

"Mr Irving?" she asked as she pulled out her notebook.

He nodded his reply.

"DS Fuller," she told him and offered her credentials. "You're the contractor for the Carters?"

Irving's thick coat rustled as he rammed his hands in his pockets. The action caused a shiver down Lucy's spine. Despite the bright sunshine, the October day was chilly. Mud was ground into the knees of his black work trousers, more mud covered the top of his boots.

"Yeah, I can't believe it. I've never seen anything like it. Well, I've dug up animals and stuff, but nothing like that. We only broke bloody ground yesterday."

His voice was shaky as he rambled.

"Broke ground?" she asked.

"Started clearing the ground, digging out for the foundations."

She had to admit that ordinarily Irving would have the perfect job to hide a body, but not this time, she doubted he even knew about the well. Over the next ten minutes she discovered that Irving hadn't worked in the area before and only took the job on because he had worked on the Carter's other home in Surrey. According to the plans he produced the well was not marked, he had even provided her with his latest copy produced by the architects, Stribbling & Co. marking exactly where they had been digging. Apparently there were earlier copies, she needed to follow that up with the architects.

Concluding the interview she reminded him he would need to make a statement and to keep away from the press as they weren't able to inform the victim's family yet. The cool breeze picked up around them as they traded business cards.

"Don't fancy your job this time of year," she added. Although the morning frost had gone, there was still an icy chill in the air.

Irving shrugged. "We were meant to start months ago. Got delayed with an environmental survey for GCNs. And now this."

"GCNs?" Lucy asked.

"Great Crested Newts. They're protected, so they had to get a survey done."

"I see." Something else she'd have to follow up with the Carters. "Okay. Thanks," she said, but as she turned to leave a thought occurred to her about the metal covering. "Oh, Mr Irving, the thick metal covering the well. What sort of tool would you need to cut through something like that?"

Irving looked surprised by her question.

"Err it, it looked pretty thick, so a plasma cutter or an oxy-acetylene torch. Something heavy duty."

Lucy nodded as she made a note. "Thanks."

CHAPTER 2

It was early evening when Lucy finally got back to the office. Thankfully, DC Tanner was nowhere to be seen.

Waking up her computer, she opened the MisPer database. The disappearance of children in the deceased's age range is still relatively rare. Although up to twenty thousand people do go missing every year in the UK, around sixty percent of that figure are children. Ninety-nine percent of these cases result in the child returning of their own volition or being traced alive and well. With modern alerts systems on hand as soon as a child is confirmed missing and considered high risk, the media is brought in to assist with national publicity. Unfortunately, when this kid disappeared, there were no such systems in place.

Lucy studied the search parameters. She had so little information to input right now. Undeterred, she began typing, largely because Barrel would probably on the phone in an hour or two. She had no idea of the ethnicity, height, or even distinguishing features at this stage. The only thing she knew for sure was the gender and a rough age. That and the fact that they had been dead for between twenty and forty years.

Reed had guesstimated the boy's age to be between eight and twelve. With the minimum details keyed in, she clicked on the search button.

"Fuck," she mumbled under her breath as she saw the number of matches appearing on the screen. Thousands of kids had gone missing in the twenty-year timeframe. She ploughed on and soon noticed that the database had been updated since she had last used it. After the initial search screen, she was now able to choose a location where the MisPer had been reported. Breathing a sigh of relief, she selected the south-west region of the UK, but the fact that some of the counties bordered London certainly didn't help, with many running away to the capital, making the number still in the hundreds.

She knew that decreasing the timeframe, would reduce the number of matches, and so she began to take a mental inventory of any information she might have to assist with that. She thought about the items recovered with the body. The clothing and shoes were too nondescript to search for without the manufacturers' information, but the watch might be useful. Lucy pulled her phone from her pocket and quickly opened the photo app, only to be disappointed a few moments later. The dirt and grime had built up over the years alongside the usual wear and tear made the exact details difficult to read on the photo even when she zoomed in.

Without the watch in front of her, she didn't have enough information to perform a search. The product number on the back would give them a year when the item became available. She swiped to the next picture, and the small plastic object from the boy's pocket filled the screen.

The Frosties game. It looked like the kind of thing that came free in a cereal box. *Kellogg's Frosties* was just visible at the bottom of the blue plastic shape. The image inside the transparent frame had worn over the years. A small hoop had attached itself to the inside surface. It was worth a try.

She clicked on Google; her hands hovered above the keys as she considered what to search for. She couldn't remember anything like that when she was a kid. Reed's outside estimate of forty years took her back to the late 1970s. Did they even have free gifts in cereal back then?

She typed in her question anyway, '*Free cereal gifts in the UK*' several hits looked positive. The third one down caught her eye: *Free cereal gifts every 80s and 90s kid will remember.*

She clicked on it, and familiar-looking bike reflectors flashed on the screen. She'd installed them on her own bicycle as a child along with the plastic caps from beer kegs to make it sound like a motorbike. She scrolled further down, past weird spoons and mini frisbees. Her hand stilled as three Tony the Tiger water games filled the screen. The red button at the bottom and the colour were consistent with her photograph, and the image in the centre vaguely matched the remaining outline on her decaying model. The hoop stuck to the inside sealed it. She looked for a date that they were issued. Apparently, you had to collect tokens to get one of these games in 1987. Energised by this new information, Lucy took a photo of the three water games on the screen and made a note to contact the company, although she doubted that they would still have any customer details on record. She had a starting point.

Returning to the MisPer search screen, she keyed in *1987-1998* to start with she could always widen the search parameters later if necessary. She'd managed to shave almost ten years off the timeframe and several hundred possibilities, but the result was still high with twenty-two matches. Now she needed to narrow down the geographical area, but instead of a region she decided to go with a county. Berkshire, as it was where the body had been discovered.

This time the results were vastly different: only three matches. She made a note of all three, circling them on her larger list. She couldn't explain it, but something in her gut told her he was local. Statistically it was more likely with a high proportion of offenders being known to the victims in some way plus the fact that offenders often live in the vicinity of their victims.

With the list was narrowed down as much as possible, considering the sparce information she had so far. She opened a new search window; she wanted to know the basics of how wells work.

All she could remember from geography lessons at school were oxbow lakes and something about swash and backwash at shorelines. She clicked on a link from Google. Aquifers. Reed had said something about them earlier. She scanned the text, talking to herself in the empty room.

"Water seeps through the rocks and loose materials, collecting deep below the surface. Manmade wells draw on this water." She looked further down the page to the next sub-heading. "They dry up when the water table lowers, due to other wells drawing up the water before it can be replenished."

She wanted to find out who knew about the location of the well and the current, and the previous owners were her first port of call. She pulled the piece of paper Laxton had given her from her pocket. Dominic Carter's home and mobile numbers were at the top of the page. Below, a Mr and Mrs Marshall, who apparently bought the farm in 1972 and lived there for thirty-seven years. Their address was now a nursing home in Bowden near Marlborough. Shit. Hopefully, they were still compos mentis, or they had family and friends that worked or lived on the farm with them.

Next, she googled the architect's firm, Stribbling and Co. Located in Bath, their website was very high class, displaying panoramas of prefabricated, modern buildings. She needed to know if the well was on their radar. Afterall, it was their job to know that stuff.

Lucy checked the time, it was almost eight. Another job for tomorrow. She was just about to call it a night when her phone rang. Barrel's name flashed on the screen. Reluctantly, she answered and gave Barrel a rundown of the information she had so far, although she decided to hold back about the three possible matches until she had more information.

After confirming her itinerary for the next day or two a distorted tannoy announcement echoed down the line. She was confused for a moment, wasn't Barrel staying in Slough tonight. He quickly rang off as the bustle of voices grew louder.

Lucy settled back in her chair as she wrapped her head around their conversation. Barrel wasn't exactly a heart-to-heart kind of boss but something was going on with him, he sounded more tired and angry than usual. Maybe the court case was getting to him. She blew out a breath as she placed her phone back on her desk. It dawned on her then that she was on her very first cold case; she just hoped she was up to the challenge.

Johanna Hale walked through her front door into the dark house. With the lights off, she felt even guiltier about being late, again. She hoped the selection of cheese and olives she'd picked up on the way home would help to placate Steph for yet another late night. They were her favourites after all, a taste Steph had acquired on one of her many trips abroad. Maybe a late supper with a glass or two of wine would help build some bridges. Johanna's tardiness wasn't intentional, at least that's what she told herself as she tripped over a large box parked on the hallway floor.

"Shit!" She braced her hand on the wall to keep herself upright. "What's this in the hall?"

She shut the door and stepped around whatever it was. "Steph? she called out as she dropped her keys on the small wooden table. Switching on the lamp, she looked back at the lump she'd tripped over realising it was two suitcases, she immediately recognised them as Steph's. Shit! Johanna stood for a moment as she waited for an answer. She couldn't remember Steph saying anything about going away. A last-minute work thing maybe or visiting friends. She flicked through the recent conversations she'd had with Steph; nothing came to mind. Literally, nothing.

The house was still painfully quiet as she called out again. "Anybody home?" She picked up the small stack of mail from the table and blindly shuffled through it while she racked her brains trying to figure out what was going on. She tossed the envelopes on the table at the sound of muffled footsteps. She knew immediately that Steph was in the back room, the thick-pile carpet subduing her sharp footfalls.

Steph stepped out into the hallway, her high heels clicking as they made contact with the tiled floor. Handbag on her shoulder, coat draped over her arm, she looked prepared for a fast exit. Her familiar warm smile replaced by a look of detached indifference, the blood drained from Johanna's face. She had this coming and she knew it. Had she waited for her to get home to say goodbye?

"Are you going away?" Johanna asked, stating the obvious, but she wasn't quite sure how else to ask about the suitcases.

"Sort of. I'm leaving you." Her tone was even, practised.

Johanna felt her mouth dry up as she tried to speak. "What do you mean?" Except, it wasn't exactly out of the blue. They'd been on rocky ground for some time, had she pushed her too far. She reached out for Steph's arm, but Steph shrugged away before Johanna could make contact. Her hand clenched as it dropped by her side. Hurtful as it was, Johanna knew it was well deserved.

Tears welled in Steph's eyes. "I can't do this anymore. I can't put my life on hold till you have time for me."

Dropping her briefcase, Johanna stepped closer. "Steph, I-I ..." She didn't have any words; it had become one of those circular arguments they had every couple of months. Johanna would make promises of spending more time together, holidays, weekends off. The kind of promises a small business owner can't always keep, or rather she couldn't keep. She'd usually start off well, taking off a couple of weekends, then the workload would grow as new projects came in and she'd be back where she started.

It wasn't even as if Johanna's business was struggling, quite the opposite, and that was the problem. After graduating from art college, she began working in a small graphic design firm, at least it was small when she started there. Six years later, it had grown almost exponentially. So much so that she wanted to go out on her own. Luckily, she had several loyal clients that were happy to move with her. That was how she met Steph; she had been working for a property firm in need of a digital makeover. It had been good to start with, but Steph's nine-to-five hours had never quite gelled with her work schedule.

"I'm doing this for us, to build a future for us," Johanna replied frustration creeping into her tone. Christ, she'd come home with the intention of trying to patch things up not fuck them up even more.

Steph closed her eyes for a moment as she took a step back, away from Johanna. "The fact that you're not freaking out right now says a lot." Steph wrapped her arms around her own torso, her eyes focussed on the floor for a moment before meeting Johanna's. "You can be such a cold bitch sometimes, Johanna. I'd say Hale is a pretty perfect name for you right now."

Johanna barely registered her cutting words. "Steph, please, I know I've made mistakes. I can change. Please, don't do this. Just give me a chance to put things right."

"I'm not one of your unhappy clients you need to placate, Johanna. I'm your girlfriend. I moved in here to be with you, but you're never here. We barely see each other."

"I know, I'm sorry." Johanna scrambled for something to say. "I'll be better, I'll take time off. I –"

"Not this time," Steph cut her off as she looked back down at the floor.

"But …" Johanna tried to continue, although no words came. There was something different this time. Steph was different. "Steph," she sighed.

Steph finally looked up, meeting her eyes, before saying, "I've met somebody else."

Johanna physically crumpled at her words; a sudden coldness filled her chest as she struggled to focus on the room around her. "Wha …?" She wanted to ask who it was, but couldn't bear to hear the details. "Why are you still here then?" She struggled to hide the hurt from her voice.

"I need to get my passport and stuff out of the safe. I couldn't remember the combination."

The words were like icicles on the floor around them, how could she be this cold. Had she done this to Steph, made her hate her, hate what they had together.

Johanna said nothing as she moved past Steph, her legs trembled as she made her way to the small safe in the back room. She jabbed at the numbers and yanked the door open as soon as it released. "Help yourself," she said as she stepped away to give Steph space. Not wanting to witness another relationship failure, she skulked into the kitchen, opened the fridge and pulled out a half-full bottle of white wine.

Ignoring the glasses on the sideboard, she unscrewed the top and took a long swig to settle the noise in her head. What was wrong with her? Why couldn't she maintain a relationship? The sound of the front door clicking closed echoed in her ears as she took another drink.

CHAPTER 3

THE FOLLOWING day Lucy put in a call to the cereal company to try and get a more precise date of when the Frosties water game was available. After being fobbed off by various telephone operators, she managed to get through to the promotions department, who gave her a timeframe of between April and September 1987. "I don't suppose you kept the details of the people you sent these toys to, did you?" She picked up a pen in hopeful anticipation.

The deafening silence at the end of the phone said a lot.

"Hello?" Lucy said, hoping they hadn't been cut off. Their switch-board system left a lot to be desired.

"Sorry." The woman sounded a little taken back. "I-I'll have to check, but I think those records might have been destroyed when we moved to Manchester."

It was worth a try, imagine how long that bloody list would be. "Okay. Well, thanks for your help."

Lucy ended the call it was like she was wading through quicksand, she was desperate to get some solid footing. She checked through her current twenty-two matches. Unfortunately, she couldn't weed anyone out as they all disappeared after April of 1987.

Her next call was to the architect's firm to set up a meeting. The woman that answered gave a garbled introduction, and it took Lucy a second or two to realise she'd said 'Stribbling and Co.'. She introduced herself to the usual silence at the other end before she pressed on with finding out which of the architects worked on the Carter's project. A Mr Knight was away until Thursday, leaving her no option but to wait until Thursday morning.

Lucy ended the call and breathed a sigh of relief; only one more call to make before she could get out of the office. She hated trying to interview people over the phone. She could at least get a read on the person if they were in front of her.

The good Dr Reed had emailed her Dr Chadwick's contact details. She keyed them into her phone before placing the call to arrange a meeting with her later that day after her visit to the Carters.

Lucy turned in a circle, taking in the full, confusing scene around her, as she edged her way through the maze of corridors, trying to recall the directions Dr Chadwick had given her earlier over the phone. Why hadn't she written it down? How the students navigated endless identical floors and corridors baffled her. Maybe that was part of the university induction process. If you can find your way to the lectures, you can stay.

She let out a frustrated breath, the only thing she gained from her visit to the Carter's at Combe Farm was the name of the company that surveyed the land for Great Crested Newts, and how angry Mr Carter was about the whole situation. She hoped Dr Chadwick would be more forthcoming.

Finally, she spotted a sign for the science labs, indicating she was on the right track. She pushed through the doors and was immediately hit with a scent of something alcohol based, and not in a good way. Still feeling lost, she stopped the first person that looked old enough to be staff to ask for more precise directions to Dr Chadwick's office.

"Is she expecting you?" The man sounded sceptical, as if Dr Chadwick never had any visitors.

"Yes. I spoke to her earlier." The man's eyebrows raised at her reply.

"She's in her lab, I think," he said, before strolling off down the corridor to a door on their left. He opened it without knocking. Lucy followed behind. They entered a large airy room with an imposing wooden desk at one end in front of a wall filled entirely with brimming bookshelves. Several vacant workstations were scattered around the room, but no Dr Chadwick.

"Dr Chadwick, you have a visitor."

A sharp female voice came from somewhere in the room. "Thank you, David. DS Fuller I presume?"

"Yes," Lucy replied. She tried to follow where the voice had come from. Suddenly a figure appeared from behind the galvanised work-station nearest the desk moving towards the crammed shelving. She estimated the woman to be in her fifties, she looked every bit the university professor in her white lab coat, hands clutching a stack of books and papers to her chest. Her hair was held in a tight bun secured on the top of her head. Streaks of grey flecked the tight curl. She took a sideways look as if gauging Lucy's position in the lab, which gave Lucy a view of the doctor's spectacles with safety specs placed over the top. She proceeded to force the contents in her arms on the cramped shelving.

The door clapped shut behind Lucy, making her jump, as Dr Chadwick finally turned to face her guest.

"Like I said earlier, I can only give you basic information right now. I'll need more time to complete any kind of identification and write my report."

Dr Chadwick looked younger from the front; her thin face and high cheekbones matched her sleek figure.

"Whatever you can give me will help at this point." Lucy just hoped it would be more detailed than anything Reed had already told her. She was the anthropologist after all.

"What are those?" Dr Chadwick pointed in the direction of the paperwork Lucy still gripped to her side.

"Possible matches from missing persons reports. Dr Reed gave me a rough age and gender."

Dr Chadwick's eyes narrowed at the stack of papers.

"How many have you got?"

"Too many."

Her glare forcing Lucy for a clearer answer. "Twenty-two," Lucy relented, wondering if she was as intimidating to her students.

Dr Chadwick's shoulders rose as she sucked in a deep breath. "I might be able to weed some of those out if you have a little time to help."

Lucy balked at the thought of having to handle the bones she had seen the other day. "I-err-I'm not a forensics tec."

"I'm aware of that, DS Fuller. I just need you to write down the information as we work. My assistant is off sick today, so if you need the information as quick as I think you do, then ..." Her eyebrows appeared over the top of her safety specs as she stared at Lucy, letting the words hang in the air.

Lucy glanced down at the stack of papers in her arms. She thought of Barrel's words: *Get over it, Fuller.* "I'm sure I can manage that."

A faint smile appeared on Dr Chadwick's lips, followed by a curt nod. "Good. Follow me." She strode through an open doorway on the far side of the lab. "Oh, and ..." She hesitated in the doorway. "Don't show me any of those papers till we've finished our examination."

"Of course."

Lucy followed the doctor into the next room, in which long, thin windows lined the wall where it met the high ceiling, creating minimal light, dulling the off-white walls, ceiling and floor against the cool blue sky beyond. Dr Chadwick was removing her disposable gloves, only to replace them with a fresh pair from her pocket.

Her gaze fell on the clinical, metal table in the centre of the room. The surface was covered with a green sheet, but the contents below were obvious by their distinctive shapes.

"There's a clipboard on the side, pencils in the drawer if you need them."

Lucy placed her bundle of printouts to one side, on a fitted workstation stretching the length of the wall behind her and selected a clipboard with blank paper already attached.

"Could you switch on the lights?" Dr Chadwick asked.

"Err." Lucy scanned the blank walls until she spotted a switch next to the doorway. When she flicked it, she was forced to blink several times to acclimatise to the shock of the dazzling light as it bounced off all the white surfaces. Despite the stark, coldness of the room, she felt more at ease with Dr Chadwick in these few minutes than she ever did with Dr Creepy Reed. She searched for something else to say. "So, how long have you done this kind of work?"

Dr Chadwick turned to face her. "Longer than you've been a police officer I'm guessing."

Dr Chadwick turned her attention to a tray of bones she'd placed on the side. "The bones of a dog were also found in the well."

"Yes. Dr Reed thought the boy might have fallen in trying to get the dog out."

Dr Chadwick made no comment on her reply as she continued. "Medium sized, possibly a border collie by the size and shape of the skull."

"Would fit with the farm location," Lucy added as she made a mental note. Could the Marshalls have had a child and covered up the death?

"The age of a child can be determined by the number of bones. A baby has approximately three-hundred bones. Over time, they reduce to two hundred and six, due to ossification. Bones will develop and fuse at individual rates. So far, we have a total of two hundred and forty-one recovered from the scene."

Lucy moved a little closer, just as Dr Chadwick removed the sheet, and wished she hadn't. "What age does that give us?" she asked, pushing away the fact they were talking about a young life that had been ended far too soon. "Dr Reed gave me a ballpark age of eight to twelve years."

"As I say, bones fuse at different rates for different people," she replied, but she was distracted now, inspecting the ends of what looked like the leg bones. "The pattern of growth indicates the lower to middle end of Dr Reed's estimate."

"Eight to ten years old," Lucy said aloud, making a note on the clipboard, and felt her body relax a little. She was just about to thank the good doctor when she disappeared out of sight, re-appearing a few moments later with several x-rays in her hand. Lucy watched as she flipped on a wall-mounted light box to view the films. Dr Chadwick had obviously done some of the background work already.

"The fusion at the ends of the long bones confirms that." She removed the x-ray as she spoke, replacing it with a second, depicting a skull. "Dental eruption of first premolars also corroborates the age. The size of the teeth and impacted third molars also indicate the child is a Caucasian male."

Lucy shook her head in disbelief. "You can tell all that just by looking at the teeth?"

"Yes, DS Fuller."

Dr Chadwick's tone was mildly dismissive and Lucy instantly regretted her comment; it was her job after all. "Sorry, it's just surprising, that's all."

"Science is always surprising me." Dr Chadwick cracked a smile as she stepped back to the metal table holding the laid-out bones. "But, in this case –" she pointed to the skull with gloved finger – "the circular eye sockets with squared margins and a high, sharply angled nasal passage also indicate a Caucasian. Europeans tend to have long, narrow, flatter faces compared to people of Asian descent, who have more prominent cheekbones, circular orbits, and an inverted heart-shaped nasal aperture. If he were of African descent, he would have a wider nasal aperture, larger teeth with wider spacing."

Lucy just stared back in surprise; she'd come to the right place.

"The process of determining race from a skull is historically deemed inappropriate by some anthropologists, due to its origins in nineteenth century pseudoscience. Now, of course, it has a far more important use."

Lucy took a moment to soak up Dr Chadwick's words. "To return them to their families."

"Exactly. Let's look at the height estimation next," the doctor replied. Not even for a second had her focus left the bones.

"Right." Lucy added more notes before drawing a line across the page, separating the information.

"Males and females have slightly different body proportions: females have relatively longer legs and males relatively longer arms.

The fact that we have male Caucasian will determine the correct regression equation to use."

Lucy was starting to feel as if this were an Open University lecture, waiting patiently, pencil poised, as Dr Chadwick selected a tape measure from her trolley.

"I'll measure the long bones, starting with the femur."

"Right." Lucy noted down the bone name. "Fire away."

Dr Chadwick selected a large clamp-shaped tool from the trolley. Inserting the bone, she studied the end panel. "Length is thirty point five-one centimetres."

Lucy scribbled down the numbers, unsure of what to do next. She was just about to raise the question when Dr Chadwick spoke up.

"You need to multiply that number by two point three-eight. Then add sixty-one point four-one to the answer, and that will give you an approximate height. Give or take three point two-seven centimetres each way."

Lucy scribbled down the numbers then pulled out her phone and opened the calculator app to tap in the numbers. She watched as Dr Chadwick went on to check and measure several bones, after conducting some calculations under the instruction of the good doctor she was finally left with the height of her victim. Lucy read out the details for conformation, rounding up the calculations. "Caucasian male, aged approximately nine or ten years old, with a height of one hundred and thirty-four centimetres or fifty-two point seven-five inches."

Dr Chadwick returned her measuring clamp to the work trolley. "That should help you to make a start."

"It will. Thank you." Lucy made a copy of the details on a separate piece of paper. "Can you tell how long he was down there?"

"That is far more difficult to determine, I'm afraid. Once a body has skeletonised, it becomes exceedingly difficult to estimate a time or even year of death."

It was worth a try. "What about the damage to the bones? Does it indicate how he died?"

Dr Chadwick moved back to the examination table. "Damage to the ribs and left humerus are fresh; it occurred when the well lining was disturbed, from what I understand." She picked up the skull and added, "There is some damage to the skull on the parietal and temporal regions, but I'll need to do more work to establish exactly how or when that happened."

"Okay."

"Dr Reed informed me of the location in which the body was found. You're treating it as suspicious?"

"Yes." Lucy put the clipboard down on the side. "The well had been covered over, so ..." Lucy thought of the toy she had found in the boy's pocket. "He had an item in his pocket which might give us an idea of when he went missing."

Dr Chadwick raised her eyebrows. "Really? Artefacts can be beneficial when indicating the age of remains."

"I certainly hope so." Lucy returned to the workstation behind her, opened her file and sifted through the stack of missing persons reports. With this new information, she could exclude many of them for being too tall, too old or the wrong ethnicity.

By the end, Lucy was left with only a few to choose from. "What about these five? Are they possibilities?" She offered them to Dr Chadwick.

Dr Chadwick took off her latex gloves before taking the pages. She placed them all side by side on the workstation and scanned the information. "Heights and ages are a match, but the bones aren't old enough for this one. What about clothing? Anything distinctive?"

Lucy thought back to yesterday. "Not really. White trainers, jeans. Light blue t-shirt."

Dr Chadwick turned over one of the pages. "Not this one. He broke his leg two years before he went missing. There's no evidence of that on the bones we have."

That left them with three possibilities.

"This one's a good match; he's the right age and height, give or take the tolerances."

Lucy stepped closer to read the details. "Disappeared August 1988." It fitted their current timeline.

Dr Chadwick continued. "The case was reviewed in 1997. Familial DNA was taken as part of the National Database they were established by the Forensic Science Service. It should still be available."

"That's good, right?" Lucy asked.

"We'll need to take DNA from the bones or teeth to confirm. It gives us something to compare it with, though." Dr Chadwick slipped her hands in the pockets of her white coat. "I'll contact Dr Reed to request the dental records and DNA, if it's on file, for all three. Then we can illuminate him at the very least."

Lucy made a note of the MisPer case numbers and names. As soon as she had an ID, she could start to figure if he'd been in the well since the day he went missing or sometime after? And if it was after, where was he in the time between? She pulled her card from her jacket and placed it on the side. "Thank you, Dr Chadwick. I'll leave these with you." She pointed to the papers she had left behind before forcing her untidy file closed. "Don't suppose you know anything about wells, do you?" she asked, half-jokingly.

Dr Chadwick raised her eyebrows. "They are usually fed through groundwater slipping through cracks in the rocks and loose materials. It can take up to a hundred years for water to flow back to the surface. They dry up for numerous reasons, sometimes people drawing too much at a time. The water table might have lowered or new construction in the area may have disrupted the aquifers."

Lucy stood there in shock for the second time since meeting Dr Chadwick. Was there anything she didn't possess a basic understanding of? "Well, thank you again. It's been very informative."

Dr Chadwick cracked a brief smile. "I'll contact you when I have any results."

CHAPTER 4

LUCY MADE her way across the carpark to the reception of Greenview Nursing Home in Bowden, and the intense heat hit her as soon as she entered the building. No wonder nursing homes were so expensive. She moved towards the desk with a reception sign hanging above, behind which she found two chattering nurses. Unsure of which to address, she made a general announcement.

"Hi, I'm here to visit one of your residents, a Mr Thomas Marshall. I called earlier." This earlier phone call had informed her that Mrs Marshall had died two years ago, but Mr Marshall was still a resident.

One of the nurses turned to face her. "Are you family?"

"No." Lucy displayed her credentials. "I'm a police officer. I just need to ask him a few questions about his old farm."

The second nurse turned at her words. "Tommy? He's on rather good form today, so you should be okay for a short visit. I'll take you through."

Lucy glanced at the name on the nurse's lanyard. Nurse Thornton looked to be almost of an age to move into the nursing home herself.

"Thanks," she replied. "Does Tommy have any other family?"

"No, his wife died a while ago. No kids."

That answered one question. As the Marshalls probably lived at the farm when the body was put in the well, she had to consider him a suspect. But would you really hide a body on your own land? Maybe he thought he'd be long gone before it was discovered.

Nurse Thornton was light on her feet despite her appearance as they manoeuvred through several rooms lined with endless rows of armchairs before she stopped in front of a room off a corridor. The door was ajar with a small wipe board fixed to the outside. The abbreviated wording was unfamiliar to Lucy. She figured it referred to Mr Marshall's medication. Nurse Thornton knocked before pushing the door open and stepping inside.

"Good morning, Tommy. You've got a visitor," she told him, adding a surprised tone to her voice.

Tommy Marshall was a large man wedged into a rigid armchair near the window, listening to (or not) the radio playing in the background. He glanced up at them briefly before a cough made his hands shake. The room was bright and homely, with a hospital bed on the far side of the room. A wooden chair was pushed against the wall. Tommy must have some visitors, she figured.

Nurse Thornton turned to face her. "I'll be in the dayroom just down the corridor."

"Thank you." Lucy waited for her to leave before stepping further into the room and hovering near the wooden chair. "Hello, Mr Marshall, my name is Lucy. I work for the police."

Tommy Marshall was rugged looking. Clumps of coarse, white hair, that had been missed when he was shaved, sprouted from his weathered face. At least she hoped he wasn't still shaving himself considering the wobble in his hands. His furrowed skin was still rich in colour; working outside always seemed to age people quicker. Strong blue eyes lit up his face as he looked back at her. Despite his age, he still had a thick covering of unkempt white hair on his head.

A framed photograph of a woman was positioned on a set of drawers under the window. His wife, she figured.

"Mr Marshall, I need to ask you some questions about Combe Farm," Lucy told him as she perched on the edge of the wooden chair.

"Tommy," he mumbled before coughing again.

She smiled back at him. "Tommy, did you know about the well on your old farm?" Lucy spotted a large plastic jug of water on a table beside the bed, next to a plastic cup with a straw in. Figuring Tommy might need a bit of lubrication, she got to her feet. Filling the cup half-way, she picked it up and offered it to Tommy. He took a long draw on the straw before sitting back.

"Covered it over when I ran into it with the trailer trying to avoid the bloody dog," he grumbled as he pulled on his earlobe before succumbing to his cough again. "Smashed into the side of it. Useless anyway."

"What was?" Lucy prodded as she pulled the chair closer before sitting down.

"The well." He looked at the cup of water again, eyebrows raised.

Lucy smiled, offering him the cup again.

"It'd dried up after them industrial units was built across the way."

The buildings she'd spotted at the scene. She made a note to ask Knight about the industrial units when she met up with him later.

"Lost Billy down there. Jumping across the top when it was raining. Silly sod slipped and fell right in."

"Billy?" Lucy asked, her interest piqued. She couldn't recall if any of the missing boys were called Billy.

"My dog. Best bloody one I had too. Stone dead when I looked down there. Must have broken his neck." Tommy cleared his throat. "Flattened the bloody thing, covered it over the next day. Wife was so upset, wanted a new one straight away." He shook his head as he looked out the window.

That was one body accounted for at least. From the position of the bones Reed thought the dog had gone in first.

"Is that your wife?" Lucy asked, realising he was looking at the photograph. She stepped closer to get a better look. The woman in the photo, whom she estimated to be in her forties, was leaning on a fence with a dog at her side on its hind legs, poking its head through the fence. "She's beautiful," she said, before remembering the nurse had told her she was dead, although she couldn't help wondering if he kept the photo for the dog or his wife.

"Both dead," Tommy mumbled.

"I'm sorry. Billy was a Collie," Lucy said as she made a mental note.

Tommy nodded, his course hair brushing against the headrest of his chair.

"What did you cover the well over with?" Lucy asked.

"Had some wood, plywood stuff."

Not the metal sheet she'd seen at the scene. She was just about to ask another question when Tommy spoke.

"Worried I'd fall through it in the van. Had some thick metal in one of the barns, used it to cover a ditch on the drive. Too big though, had to get someone to cut it for me."

"I see." That made more sense.

"Do you remember when that was, what year?"

Tommy Marshall pulled at his ear again. His lips flinched as if he was about to speak. "Summer." He coughed again. "Start of the summer, before that kid went missing."

"Kid?" Lucy repeated. "Can you remember the name of the kid that went missing. Boy or girl?"

His face flinched again as he shook his head. "Boy."

Lucy tried to contain herself. "Did you know him? Was he from the area?"

He shook his head. "Not till he went mi –" His words were cut off by a cough.

Lucy remembered the cup in her hand and offered it to him in the hope of keeping him talking.

Tommy took a long drink, swallowing down the water in big gulps, then turned away from the protruding straw, indicating that he was done.

"You covered it over the same year the boy went missing?" she asked, seeking conformation.

Tommy nodded. "Didn't want to lose another bloody dog down there."

Lucy nodded.

"Came back from the wife's sister's wedding, all done." Tommy waved a wobbly hand in the air.

A perfect window of opportunity. "Were you away for a few days for the wedding?" Even a few hours would be enough.

"Overnight. The missus didn't like being away from the farm."

"Do you remember who cut that metal for you, Tommy?" They would've had uninterrupted access to the farm.

Tommy shook his head. "Just a chap with an oxy torch. Thick stuff. I couldn't do it."

Oxy torch, as in oxy-acetylene torch. "Did you pay him to do it?"

He shook his head. "Just asked around and he offered. That's how it was then."

Shit! If it had been a business, she might have at least got the name of the employee. Lucy nodded. She needed the date of the wedding. "When was your sister-in-law's wedding, do you remember the date?"

Tommy just looked back at her blinking for a long moment. "It was hot, late summer. Don't know when."

"What was her maiden name?" It would be quicker to trace later.

Tommy glanced back at his wife's photo. "Watson, Victoria Watson."

She scribbled down the name before asking her next question. "Do you remember much about the boy going missing, did they search your farm?"

Tommy's shoulders lifted in what she took as a shrug, "no."

His single word reply was hoarse. She considered offering him another drink but decided to press on. "Did you get many kids hanging around your farm?"

Tommy shrugged. "No. Too far out of town."

She watched Tommy waiting for a reaction to her next words. "The remains of a boy were found on your old farm, in the covered well." It took a moment; eyes widened, his chin flinched several times but no words came out. He looked away, out the window.

Footsteps in the hallway drew his attention away from the outside world.

Lucy offered a small smile, there was nothing more to be gained, "That will be it for now. Thank you for your help, Tommy." Getting to her feet, she offered him another drink. Tommy shook his head and she placed it on the side, within easy reach.

As she walked back to her car, she considered Tommy's words. It was difficult to see him as the killer, but thirty years ago he would have only been in his forties and more than physically capable of disposing of a body. He could have found the victim trespassing on his farm and accidentally killed him in the process of scaring him off.

She stood next to her car, waiting for it to unlock. She looked back at the building as she got in her car, confident Tommy wouldn't be going anywhere soon if anything else pointed to him.

Less than an hour later, Lucy was outside Stribbling and Co., parking her car. Their offices were suitably designer in style: part renovated old chapel, part new build, by the look of it.

Lucy walked through the elegant entrance. The receptionist desk was immediately in front of her, behind which a young woman was on the phone, forcing Lucy to glance around the large space as her eyes acclimatised to the dim light. The walls were covered with large, framed plans that had been backlit like x-rays. It reminded her of Dr Chadwick and her impressive intellect.

The clatter of a handset returning to its base brought Lucy back to the present, and she wandered over to the desk to announce her arrival and intent. The receptionist made a quick call before pointing to the small corridor on the left. "It's the second door on the right. He's expecting you."

"Thank you." Lucy nodded to the young woman and followed the direction. The second door held a large brass plaque, indicating the occupier. She knocked twice before entering.

"Yes." A firm voice rang in her ears as her hand still gripped the brass doorknob.

"Mr Knight?" she asked as the man behind the grand, wooden desk looked up. He frowned in her direction until he removed his thick glasses. "I'm DS Fuller, Thames Valley." It always sounded better than Woodley, less confusion. He remained seated as she moved closer to his desk offering her credentials. He replaced his glasses to inspect them before meeting her eye and waving a hand at one of the seats opposite his desk. "You've already spoken to the Carters from what I hear," he said as he released a sigh.

Knight looked to be a slender man with a potbelly that brushed against the edge of his desk as he sat, although it was hard to tell as he'd remained seated. His slicked back hair did nothing to soften his sharp angular features. Lucy took the offered chair, noticing it wasn't as comfortable as Knight's. Her initial impression was that she was wasting his precious time as he reluctantly moved aside the large plans spread across his desk.

"Yes, Mr Knight." She confirmed, sharper than she intended. "Just routine enquiries," she said, "I just have a few questions about the plans you drew up for them."

Knight's face formed a tight smile. "I thought you might. I spoke to Irving yesterday."

Mark Irving, the contractor, she presumed.

"He said the well wasn't located on any of his plans."

"Yes." Knight flattened his hands on his desk as he stretched out the word. "From what Irving said, the well is located a distance away from the current existing buildings on green belt land."

Lucy took out her notepad. "And it wasn't picked up on any of the surveys you do before planning a build?"

Knight glared at her for a moment. "Well, we did soil sampling, of course, to check for the foundations. We also did a land and topographical survey of the immediate area; and nothing was picked up."

"Is that usual?"

Knight raised his hands in a conceding motion. "There was no reason to think it was there. Dominic Carter said it wasn't mentioned on the estate agents' details when he purchased the property."

Someone knew it was there. She needed to find out who.

"The plans were updated a few times before the build started?"

"Umm. When we did the utilities and desktop surveys. New plans were issued when they changed the location of the building footprint to make it easier to connect up to existing services in the area."

"I see." Lucy made a note as Knight continued.

"To be fair, it wouldn't have been picked up on the buyer's survey either, unless they asked for a geophis' or something like that."

"A what?" Lucy asked, was he trying to blind her with science now. This guy was quickly pissing her off.

"A geophysical survey. It's a technique used to map out the subsurface of the land, picks up hidden structures below the surface."

Lucy had to wonder how many people go to the expense of getting the *Time Team* crew in before buying a house.

Knight sat back in his executive chair, his fingers forming a pyramid in front of him. "I've done a few checks on some of the older Ordinance Survey maps of the area. A spring was marked on some of them, but the British Geological Society had no record of it, and it's not on any of the recent survey maps. They probably thought it had dried up or been filled in."

"Have you ever heard of something like this happening before?" She had to ask, considering his field of expertise.

"Of course, but mainly on brown-belt sites; that's land that has previously been built on."

Lucy nodded, ignoring the condescending tone, as he continued.

"Hidden cellars and underground corridors are often a feature of places like that, especially on older sites that have been abandoned after being flattened for a number of years."

Fair enough. He had her there.

Knight was on a roll now. "I even called the Water Well Archive to check their records and see if they knew anything about it."

Lucy raised her eyebrows expectantly. "And?" she prompted, unaware that such a thing existed.

"Nothing. No record of it at all."

Okay, time for a different topic. "What can you tell me about the delays to the build?"

Knight took a deep breath. "Someone suddenly decided there were Great Crested Newts on the site. It was several hundred metres away from the pond, it wasn't going to stop the build, just delay it while they did the survey. We had to wait until March until they could start the survey, as it needed to be done during their breeding season. The Carters weren't pleased, but it was out of our hands."

Knight was a little too cocky considering he'd fucked up somewhere along the way. "Can I ask, what exactly is a mindfulness centre?"

The ends of Knight's mouth twitched upwards before he spoke. "Ah well, from what I understand, it was going to be some form of retreat with classes based around relaxation, meditation and health. But I'm no expert. It was Mrs Carter's personal project."

Something else to look up later, but if that were true, it was hardly something that would upset the locals.

"Are they continuing with it, the project?" she clarified.

"I just spoke to the planning office. They are sympathetic to the situation, and if we submit a revised site plan with the footprint away from the well location, they will fast track it through for us. So ..." He waved his hand.

Lucy checked her notes for anything else. Flicking through the pages, she saw a question mark next to the words *Industrial Estate*. "You don't happen to know when the industrial units near the site were built, do you?"

Knight looked genuinely surprised by her question. "Oh-err, no, but I'm sure I can find out for you."

"That would be great, thanks." Lucy pulled out her card and placed it on his desk.

"Can I ask why?"

"Just following up on something," she replied as vaguely as possible, then added, "Thank you for your time, Mr Knight," and got to her feet. "I'll call if I have any more questions."

———

Johanna arrived home to an empty house. She roamed from room to room, unsure of what to do with herself now she was there. The house looked the same, despite everything being different. Each room held memories of her life with Steph: weekend newspapers and travel magazines that she had read and discarded crammed under a side table; Lonely Planet Guide books and keepsakes scattered around on shelves. Even her choice of fruit in the fruit bowl. Steph had chosen to leave it all behind, taking only the essentials.

A thickness climbed up Johanna's throat as tears filled her eyes. She was responsible for this; she had let it happen; she had failed, neglecting Steph to the point she had pushed her into someone else's arms.

Johanna's head tipped forward, her chin tight to her chest. Closing her eyes, tears dropped onto the tops of her bare feet as her toes clung to the threads of the carpet below. Her hands went from tight fists to quickly crossing her body, gripping at her shirt for purchase as her body shook.

Catching her breath, she marched upstairs to the spare room in the hope of finding some unused storage boxes. She needed to cleanse her home, remove the shame she felt at not being able to fully commit to a woman that had loved her, at least for a time.

Two hours later, half-filled boxes and binbags were strewn over the floor of almost every room. Drawers and cupboards had been emptied, every surface scrutinised of its contents. Johanna tied up the last binbag and stood to survey the living room. It was almost bare, only the essentials remained that predated Steph's arrival, and it seemed so empty. Steph had somehow made it a home. The irony wasn't lost on her as she carried a bag into the sterile kitchen. She opened the fridge to glance at the stripped shelves; there was a reason the kitchen was pristine: cooking wasn't exactly second nature to her. Her eyes fell on the bottles of wine sitting in the door, but it was too early for that, shutting the door she walked away to finish what she'd started.

CHAPTER 5

WITH BARREL STILL IN COURT, Lucy sat at her desk, drinking her first cup of tea of the day. She clicked on her email, surprised to see Knight had already got back to her regarding the industrial units. He'd attached a link, saying it should give her the information she required. When Lucy clicked it, it took her a second to realise what she was looking at: an industry promotional paper titled 'Plastic World'. The main article covered the opening of a newly constructed industrial unit that housed a new production for Merlin Plastics. The other two units were being used by Lux Engineering and a trade paint supplier.

A thought struck her: Lux Engineering? Would they have oxy-acetylene torches to cut through Tommy's metal covering? She needed to know who occupied the units in August 1988.

According to Knight's information, the row of units were completed in July 1983, which meant if Tommy Marshall was telling the truth, it took almost five years for his well to dry up. She printed out the information for her file. She could at least start building up a timeline of the events leading up to the victim's disappearance now. She then put in a call to Glenfield Ecological. She wanted their opinion on the survey. Knight had already chipped in, but she needed conformation, especially on what or who triggered the survey itself.

After introducing herself, she managed to talk to one of the ecologists that had worked on the survey.

According to the ecologist the survey was legitimate with evidence the GCN's were indeed present on the site, but the surveyors were mainly concerned with the disturbance during the construction process and requested mitigation to be put in place. He did however have to field a few phone calls regarding the progress and outcome of his report.

"Phone calls from whom? Lucy asked.

"The first one was a man; said he was from the Kingsford Nature Trust. He just wanted to know how we were doing. Then a few days later, a woman called, wanted to know why we weren't stopping them from building. She sounded pretty drunk to be honest."

Lucy's interest piqued. "She didn't say who she was?"

"No."

"And she wanted the build stopped." Could a woman be involved in all this or was it just a local NIMBY.

"Pretty much."

"Was she young, old? Did you notice any accent when she spoke?"

"Err, I'm not sure. No obvious accent. A local, I think."

Lucy jotted down the information. "Do you remember when you received that call?"

"A few days before we finished the report. I was working late at the office. The call came through on my work's mobile."

She double checked that she had the ecologists mobile number just in case they needed to trace the call before hanging up.

Lucy sat at her desk, making notes as she tuned out the din in the office.

She was just about to look up the Kingsford Nature Trust when she noticed a new email notification. She clicked on the inbox to see an email from Dr Chadwick. The subject simply said *Information*. She smiled as she clicked on the message.

A number of similarities were found in one of the DNA sequencing results, which confirms that your victim is Daniel Dunderdale, as verified by profiles attached.

Shit! She had a name for her victim now. Daniel Dunderdale. She glanced further down the page. Dr Chadwick had gone on to explain how she had to use Mitochondrial DNA Testing due to some degradation in the father's samples held on file. The mother's sample had remained intact, which generated a direct link between mother and son.

She clicked on the first attachment. Two graphs filled the screen, both in landscape, one on top of the other. A blue line provided peaks along the base of the graphs; the numbers across the top and sides made little sense to her. One thing was clear: they weren't any kind of a match; the peaks were nowhere near the same.

Lucy opened the second document. Again, two graphs, except this time the peaks and troughs were an exact match. She clicked *print* before checking the final document, just for her own peace of mind.

With the buzz of excitement in her fingers at getting the first solid bit of information she immediately pulled up the initial Misper report for Daniel Dunderdale. She noted that Daniel had gone missing from his home on Compton Way in Kingsford during Saturday 20th August 1988, between the hours of 9.30 a.m. and 2.00 p.m.

With the conformation in her hand, she called Barrel, knowing his phone would be on silent, and cleared her throat, ready to leave a message.

"Fuller!" Barrel's voice echoed down the line.

Lucy blinked in surprise. "Boss, we've just had conformation from the forensic anthropologist. The body is confirmed as Daniel Dunderdale."

"Shit," was all Barrel could say for a moment. "Find the Dunderdales' current address. I'll call you back in ten minutes."

Lucy frowned as the line went dead. She didn't even get a chance to get a word out, although she should be acclimatised to Barrel's clipped nature by now. Driving; emails even conversations were conducted in an abrupt manner.

Five minutes later her phone rang again. "Boss."

"What have you got?"

She kept her words short. "The Dunderdale's live in Bracknell."

"Bracknell, okay that's only up the road from here. I'll visit them, you look into the Dunderdale case files, I'll get back to you after I've seen them."

"Err okay, I'll text you the address." At least she wouldn't have to suffer his terrible driving. A death knock, especially one this belated would never have been her choice of task.

"Hey!" a voice called, pulling her out of her thoughts. She looked up to see Tanner standing next to her desk. Despite his slender frame he seemed to block out most of the light from the window. His dark suit looked new; matched with a slimline tie, his cropped hair and well-proportioned features made him live up to the young police officer adage. One hand was deep in his trouser pocket while the other fiddled with the stapler he'd swiped from her desk.

"I heard you got a body." He blanched at his own words. "Caught one, I mean," he said, adjusting his feet.

"Yeah."

"Let me know if you need any help, with Barrel being tied up in court," Tanner continued.

Barrel must have talked to him; he knew she wouldn't ask for help. She never did.

"Thanks." She glanced back at her computer screen. "Actually, is there any chance you could pull some files from the archives for me?"

His face seemed to brighten at her request. "Which ones?"

"Everything we have on the MisPer file for Daniel Dunderdale–"

"Is that the body?" Tanner asked, cutting her off.

Lucy nodded. "Do you know the case?" Tanner was a local compared to her.

He shrugged. "No. Is that it?"

"Well, you could make a start on tracing his neighbours, so we can interview them again. Also, Tommy Marshall, the previous owner of Combe Farm. His wife has a sister; I need to know when and where she got married."

Tanner's eyebrows knotted in confusion.

"The Marshalls were away overnight; the farm was empty. According to Tommy Marshall, it's also when the well was covered over with the metal sheeting." Was she getting ahead of herself? Could it have been a terrible accident that had been covered up; she couldn't take that chance for now, she needed to be sure.

Tanner looked a little impressed by her explanation.

"Thanks," Lucy offered as she grabbed her mug, upping her pace to catch up with him. "Andy." She waited for him to acknowledge her before continuing. "Are we ... okay?" she asked quietly.

"We're fine." he replied with a grin.

Lucy studied the Dunderdale case file in detail. It was, as expected, still open. Not for much longer, she thought. At least his family could lay him to rest. And just maybe in the process Barrel would let her stretch her legs a little.

Daniel's father and brother were at a judo competition in Reading most of the day. His mother was home, but she hadn't seen him since around 9.30 a.m. She called the police, stating that she had looked in the immediate area and found no sign of him. She stated that he had left the house shortly after breakfast, when he went out to meet his friends on the street. He was wearing jeans, t-shirt and trainers. She noted nothing unusual about his demeanour, he often played on the street with friends. Later when he hadn't returned for lunch she had asked the friends, but they said they hadn't seen him all day. It wasn't like him to go off on his own.

A Detective Inspector Redland was the lead investigator in the case. He had initiated a helicopter search, and even used heat-seeking equipment borrowed from the military into the evening. An organised search of all nearby rivers and streams and a woodland proved fruitless. All residents on the street were questioned, garages and outbuildings searched. Nothing of interest was found.

Officers and tracker dogs conducted another detailed search one week later, but again nothing was found. A national poster campaign was set up, with a copy placed in every police station in the country, and Daniel's photo was published in local and national newspapers. Hundreds of calls were logged to a helpline with sightings of Daniel in various locations around the country and abroad. All leads were followed up, but still nothing solid was found regarding his disappearance or whereabouts.

One year later, there was still nothing to report, until Oxford-based David Levin was questioned regarding Daniel's disappearance. Lucy sat up a little straighter. Levin? She recognised the name but couldn't quite place it. She'd only lived in the area for two years; historical cases were still a bit of a mystery to her.

Lucy tapped on her keyboard, typing his name into the search screen. The first thing that came up was *Levin dies in prison*. He was stabbed to death by another inmate in 1996. Great! She wondered how many more dead ends she'd come up against thirty years after the case was opened.

According to the article, self-employed plasterer David Levin was a 'notorious child killer' from the Oxfordshire and Gloucestershire areas in the 1980s. Levin was found guilty of the abduction and murder of two ten-year-old boys from Farmington in Gloucestershire and sentenced to life in prison in 1989. He was suspected of murdering three more, but not enough evidence was found to support the claims. After the trial, several open cases were reviewed, including Daniel's, to see if there were any links. Levin was interviewed but refused to confirm his involvement in any other cases. Bastard! Lucy wanted to know what links were made between Levin and the Dunderdale case. Surely it was more than the simple fact that a boy had gone missing in the next county. She sent a message to Tanner asking him to pull the reports on the interviews with Levin.

She pulled up a map of the area where Daniel had gone missing. Zooming out, she plotted the location of Combe Farm. The distance was almost seven miles; too far to carry a body. Someone had a car, or maybe they lured him out there and killed him on the farm. A kid that age must have had a bike.

She returned her attention to Compton Way; it was a dead-end stretch of a long estate. There certainly wouldn't have been any passing traffic, only residents and visitors. Anyone else would have stood out like a fox in a hen house if they were hanging around.

According to the file, the Dunderdales lived at the top of the street, with a further seven or eight houses on either side. Not many, but both ends of the street were lined with a small woodland. A discreet way to enter or leave the street maybe. She wondered how easy it was going to be to trace all these residents after so many years.

Checking through again, she noticed the case was reviewed in 1997, but without a body or evidence to test with updated forensics, it was refiled, although DNA was taken from the parents and kept for comparison if anything turned up.

Two hours later Barrel was on the phone again. "Boss."

"Who was the lead on the Dunderdale case?"

Lucy tried not to smile at his approach. "A DI Redland."

"Shit. He was a DCI when he retired, I think."

Lucy found the note she'd made earlier on the SIO. "Retired in 2002. What do you know about him?"

"Bit of a salty bastard from what I've heard. Find his address, we'll pay him a visit. See what he remembers if anything."

"Yes, boss." A question had been niggling at Lucy since that first night back at the office when she was looking through MisPer cases. "Did you know it could be Daniel when the call came through about the body?"

Barrel was silent again for a moment. "I thought it could be a possibility, especially when Laxton said it was a skeleton."

She fiddled with her pen while she waited for more.

"I'd just joined the police in Winchester when he went missing, we thought we might be called in to help with the search."

Lucy was speechless for a moment, waiting him out had worked. Barrel played his cards remarkably close to his chest "But you weren't?"

"No."

It was just a single word answer, but she heard regret in his tone. She waited a few moments before continuing. "I've got all the files on the Dunderdale case."

"Good. We'll need to go through them, double check everything. According to the dad Barney Dunderdale's away for a few days, he's going to inform him."

"Okay." Tanner's making a start on tracing the other residents. I've also got him seeing what he can find on Levin," Lucy added and waited for Barrel's response.

"Levin. Why Levin?"

"They interviewed him about Dunderdale after he'd been convicted for the two boys in Oxford." Lucy waited for Barrel to add his opinion, but it never came. She tried another subject. "According to the ecologist who did the survey at Combe Farm, there was a bit of resistance to the project the Carters were building."

"Who from?"

"Not sure yet, could be the local nature group. They're the ones that kicked off the Great Crested Newt survey thing. The ecologist received a couple of calls, one telling him to stop the build."

"What was it going to be?"

"A mindfulness centre." She waited for the backlash.

"A what? A mindless centre?"

"A mindfulness centre," she repeated, checking her notes. "It's all about meditation and yoga apparently."

"Probably just tree huggers or something," Barrel barked as a horn blared in the background.

Distracting Barrel while he was driving probably wasn't the best idea. "Maybe," she finally said. They seemed to fall into an uncomfortable silence, she couldn't work out if it was the court case that was frustrating him or being landed with the Dunderdale case.

"What were the parents like?" She finally asked breaking the prickly calm.

"Broken, said he would never have just wondered off. Shy, sensitive boy. Not aware of any problems."

Pretty much what was in the file in front of her. "Right."

"He was always out on the street with his friends or with his brother."

"We need to speak to them next." She replied.

"Listen, Fuller," he began, "I wouldn't get too comfortable with this case. I don't think it will be with us long."

"What do you mean?" He'd just finished speaking to the bereaved parents of a dead boy, no doubt telling them that he would do everything in his power to find the person responsible. Now he was saying the opposite.

"I mean, I've already had a call from the Chief Constable. He's looking to close this case ASAP."

"Why?" They'd finally discovered the body of a missing child, were they really going to cover it all up.

"It's a thirty-year-old case with no forensics, half the eyewitnesses are either dead or won't remember anything. We need to focus on the crimes where we can make a difference."

Lucy sat back in her seat. Daniel deserved more than this, his parents too. She couldn't just leave it; she'd never be able to forgive herself. "So you're saying we shouldn't bother trying to find out who got away with murder, because it was thirty years ago."

"We don't even know it was murder, do we?"

She tried to keep her voice even. "Somebody didn't want him found, hiding him in a well for thirty years, it doesn't exactly scream innocence does it."

"But what can we prove now? *That's* what matters." A thumping sound echoed down the line.

She had to accept that Barrel was right at least about the witnesses; if they could find any, she doubted they would have anything new to add to their original statements, which would now have become fixed in their minds in the thirty years that had passed. She'd need to get them to see the events with fresh eyes, jiggle their perception, if she was going to get any new information. "Why does Kirby want to close the case so quickly?"

"*Deputy Chief Constable Kirby...*" Barrel growled, "wants to become more than a deputy one day."

Typical, since when did a promotion become more important than finding the truth.

CHAPTER 6

Lucy waited in the wings as the press conference concluded. She hated these things– reporters fishing for information, waiting for the opportunity to trip you up – but it was a part of the job that she couldn't escape. Although this time she'd managed to take a step back, out of camera shot. Prior to her move from Northamptonshire her mum had a habit of phoning her up to tell her she had seen her on TV and grill her for information on whatever case she was working on. Lucy stepped a little further back, she had a feeling this media event would reach a little further than regional news slots considering the national interest in the original case. Hopefully, her mum would have to occupy herself with her other current pastime of matchmaking Lucy with any suitable woman she came across.

With Barrel still required in court, the new Deputy Chief Constable was doing the honours along with Dr Chadwick. Thank God it hadn't fallen to her; stunned rabbit in the headlights came to mind, as Barrel had taken great joy in reminding her the last time she had to face the media.

Kirby tapped at the mic in front of him, getting the audience's attention. "Good afternoon, I am Deputy Chief Constable Kirby of

Thames Valley Police. I have a short statement to read before I can answer any questions."

Kirby looked in his element as he glanced up at his audience, compared to Dr Chadwick who nervously drank from a glass of water as she shuffled in her seat next to him.

"Thames Valley Police were called to a farm on the outskirts of Kingsford just before midday on Monday when recent construction work led to the tragic discovery of human remains. After intensive forensic investigation, I can confirm the remains are that of ten-year-old Daniel Dunderdale."

A murmur erupted in the room as the news sank in.

Lucy zoned out as Kirby laid out the details until several reporters finally broke the seal and began shouting out questions for Kirby to field.

"Do you still think Daniel was a victim of David Levin?" a voice from the back yelled.

It hadn't taken them long to make that link. Lucy scanned the audience to pinpoint the heckler. She didn't recognise him.

"I can't comment on that at the moment. DCI Barrel will be looking into that as part of the inquiry."

"How can you be sure it's Daniel after all this time?" another voice yelled.

Kirby looked straight at Dr Chadwick. "Dr Chadwick can answer that." Raising a hand, he urged her to reply as he passed down the microphone.

Dr Chadwick took a moment to take a second drink from the glass of water in front of her before beginning. "We have conducted a number of tests, including DNA and dental-record analysis, which confirmed that the remains are that of Daniel Dunderdale."

Kirby looked at her as if expecting more, but Chadwick sat back confident no more needed to be said. Raising his eyebrows he continued. "No more questions at this time. Thank you." Kirby promptly left the stage, leaving everyone else to trail behind.

Lucy was just about to follow the train of people leaving through a side door when Dr Chadwick waved her hand then pointed to the side of the staging she was on. She waited for her to catch up hoping she had more information to help her with the case. Her hair was set in it a familiar bun, her white lab coat had been switched for a black skirt suit today. "You survived the media gaze." Lucy said with a grin as she led the way to the rear of the room away from the bustle of the exiting reporters.

"Umm. It's certainly not my forte I'm afraid, bit out of practice now."

"Now? How many press conferences have you done?" She queried.

"Too many, Darfur, Uganda, Chechnya."

The words slipped from Dr Chadwick's mouth far too easily. Lucy took a sideways look at Chadwick as she smoothed the front of her skirt. It took a moment but she recalled Reed's comment about her working on historical mass graves, war crimes she figured. "That puts this case in the shade somewhat doesn't it?"

Dr Chadwick reached out touching her arm. "Not at all Detective. His family are still alive?"

"They are." Lucy confirmed.

"Then they deserve to know what happened."

There was no mention of finding the culprit, but that wasn't her job, hers was about giving closure to the family. Lucy nodded her agreement.

"With that in mind, I've been examining the injuries to Mr Dunderdale. Do you have a minute to discuss them?"

She noted Dr Chadwick's use of 'Mr'; it was sad that Daniel never got to be formally addressed in such a way.

"Of course," she said, "let's find somewhere to sit down." She led the way to a small side office, indicating for Dr Chadwick to take a seat as she closed the door.

Dr Chadwick jumped straight into it barely giving her chance to take a seat opposite.

"I've x-rayed all the bones, and although I can't speak for any flesh or superficial injuries that may have occurred, I can tell you that Daniel suffered substantial blunt-force trauma."

Lucy took out her notebook. "That's what killed him?"

"It's impossible to be certain, but he had two skull fractures, with further fractures to his clavicle and hip."

"And they're not from his fall into the well or the blocks falling on him?"

Dr Chadwick briefly shook her head. "From the photos Dr Reed has provided of the scene, he was found leaning back against the side of the well, knees up or to the side maybe. It's difficult to be certain, but the injuries are old with no signs of healing. Most importantly, they are all on his left side."

"All of them?" Lucy queried.

"Yes. The diameter of the well isn't large enough for him to have fallen flat on his left side. So, I would suggest he was injured or fell somewhere else and –"

Lucy cut her off, predicting the end of her sentence. "He was put in the well after."

"It looks like it. Obviously there has been some movement over the years, but from the position he was found in – legs bent, arms and torso slumped to the side of the well – he could have been lowered down into that position."

Poor kid was dumped and forgotten. "Could he have been conscious with those injuries and tried to get out?"

"The skull fractures would probably have left him unconscious or, at the very least, severely confused."

Not a definitive answer. Had she finally found a question Dr Chadwick couldn't answer? If he had been found earlier, they would have so much more, including the forensic evidence to nail the person responsible. "In your experience, how do you think he might have gotten these injuries?"

"It's hard to say for sure. May I?" Dr Chadwick pointed to her pad and pen.

Lucy offered it without a word, making sure she had a fresh page. She watched as Dr Chadwick started to sketch a stick figure.

"The injuries to his head, shoulder and hip are consistent with a fall onto a hard surface." She circled the three areas of injury. "But not from too great a height or there would be more substantial injuries."

"Not three separate blows then?" Lucy asked, looking up from the drawn image.

Dr Chadwick shook her head. "They all seem to be at the same angle, so I would say not."

Lucy looked down at the stick figure Dr Chadwick had drawn and was certain that the injuries sustained were inconsistent with those inflicted by David Levin. He tended to smother his victims, their damage barely visible, a minor relief to the parents till they started to think about what he physically did to them. Jesus, maybe it was Levin covering his tracks after things went tits up. Daniel could have fought back after being abducted, forcing his hand.

"And these injuries are definitely not from when he was discovered?" Lucy pressed.

"No. Strangely, the block that fell largely avoided him in favour of the dog."

"Poor old Billy," Lucy said without thinking. "The farmer's dog," she added, noticing Dr Chadwick's frown. Her eyebrows then rose again and she resumed her explanation:

"With regard to other damage to the remains, insect activity and oxygen were limited. Not much micro-organism activity; groundwater and moisture were present. If he'd been down there much longer, we might have missed our window for obtaining DNA. I've emailed you a copy of all the details."

Dr Chadwick got to her feet. "Call me if you have any questions."

As Lucy closed her notebook she realised Dr Chadwick had given her all this information without a reference note in sight, where as she needed notes and lists for virtually everything. Exactly how big was this woman's brain, she would certainly make the phone a friend list should she ever appear on 'Who Wants to be a Millionaire.' "Okay. Thank you, Dr Chadwick." Lucy stood to show the doctor out, she couldn't resist asking a few more questions. "So, are you retired from all the overseas work now?"

Dr Chadwick opened the door but turned to face her, framed in the doorway a faint smile on her face. "I decided I was getting a bit old for roughing it, wanted a bit more order in my life. When I was offered a teaching post I grabbed it with both hands."

Lucy nodded. "Passing on the knowledge." Not for the first time she thought it must be quite something to be one of Dr Chadwick's students.

Dr Chadwick pushed her hand in Lucy's direction. "Good luck, Detective."

"Lucy." She didn't often lose her formalities so quickly but this woman continued to intrigue and impress her. Taking the offered hand she shook it briefly.

"I have a nice with that name."

The skin around Dr Chadwick's eyes crinkled a little more than usual. "Excellent choice. You don't have any kids of your own?" The words came out without thinking.

"Philippa." She adjusted her feet for a second as if she was unsure of how to continue. "No. My husband died a couple of years after we were married."

"Oh, I'm sorry." *Shit, nice one Fuller. Is that why she worked abroad so much.*

Philippa Chadwick cleared her throat. "Call me if you have any questions."

"I will. Thank you."

Dr Chadwick gave her a broad smile before heading back towards the press room.

Steph's words had echoed in Johanna's ears for the third day in a row. *You can be a cold bitch. All you do is work.* She knew Steph was right about one thing: she'd worked solidly for almost ten years with barely a day off, let alone a holiday.

When they'd met five years ago, Johanna wasn't exactly looking for a relationship. She'd fallen into it in many ways; she could see that as plain as day now. What started out as a fling, grew into something else, something Johanna hadn't been expecting. It was unfortunate for Steph that it coincided with the launch of Johanna's company.

Sitting behind her large, empty desk, Johanna began to question her motives. Was she really doing it for both of them, to create the security that would sustain them later in life? If she was honest with herself, she knew that the desire she'd initially felt for Steph had waned all too quickly. Maybe she was a cold bitch, just as Steph had said. She'd pushed away someone that had loved and cared for her. Regardless of the reason, Johanna had been so focused on the future she'd lost track of the present, letting it happily run away from her.

Turning to look out of the windows, she blew out a long breath as her eyes fell on the disused railway sidings beyond. She desperately needed to feel a cool breeze on her face, and she realised, the stupidity of having windows that didn't open, in favour of passive air condition-ing. Occasionally, the rush of the breeze from an open window could make all the difference to easing her mind. Modern isn't always better.

Turning back to her desk the thought of attending another one of Travis's stand-up meetings filled her with dread. She much preferred to do meetings the old-fashioned way; although stand-ups, as she'd come to know them, thanks to her new management team, were all the rage. She wasn't a meerkat; chairs were invented for a reason. In her mind, if you didn't have time to sit down like human beings to talk about it, then it wasn't that important. Nevertheless, she had to hand it to them; Travis and his team were doing a great job. She would never have had the confidence or skillset to venture into game programming without them. With several projects on the go, business was looking particularly good, at least on paper. Investments in technology and 'talent', another of Travis's jargon words, were paying off. However, she would never admit it but some of the details discussed in these meetings went above her head; system programming had never been her thing. She had always been more comfortable on the creative side of the fence. She didn't have the 'bandwidth' for this meeting, as Travis would say.

Johanna picked up her desk phone to dial her assistant, as usual her call was picked up on the first ring. "Gail, could you pop in here for a minute."

"On my way, tea or coffee?"

"No thanks." Johanna smiled to herself as she ended the call. Gail was more of a mother to her that her own. She'd been her assistant since she started out on her own over ten years ago, in that time she kept her on the straight and narrow on more than one occasion.

Johanna believed in treating her staff with respect. Loyalty was a precious commodity.

The mature well-turned-out woman quietly entered her office, walking over to Johanna's desk she placed a bottle of water next to her keyboard. "Need to keep those fluids up."

Johanna smiled at her. "Thank you." She waited for Gail to take a seat opposite. "I haven't got any more appointments for the day do I?"

Gail glanced down at the iPad in her hand, despite her age she had easily taken to the introduction of modern gadgets over the years. Although Johanna knew she still made rigorous shorthand notes when she could. "Err...no, just the regular management meeting at three." Gail checked her watch before glancing back up at Johanna expectantly.

"Good. There were a couple of things blocked out but no details?" She said releasing a breath.

"Oh, yes there were some project reviews. But Travis has taken them."

Johanna noted the tone in Gail's words, she hadn't been keen on Travis since he'd arrived.

"Everything okay?" Gail asked a light frown on her brow.

"Fine, just need to take a few hours. I'll need to skip the meeting." She wasn't quite ready to reveal her failure to keep Steph in her life just yet.

"I'll let Travis know." Gail replied knowing not to push her for details.

"I can do that. Thanks Gail." She replied with what she hoped was a reassuring smile.

Gail hesitated for a moment before getting to her feet and leaving the office.

Johanna drafted a quick email, letting the team know she wouldn't be attending and to contact her on her mobile if there was anything pressing. Then, picking up her briefcase, she slipped her mobile phone inside before leaving her office offering a quick wave to Gail. As she approached the front of the building, she noticed several large blobs of rain landing diagonally across the glass façade. She hesitated as she pulled the small collapsible umbrella from the side of her briefcase.

The fresh, cool air was a relief as she slipped out the revolving, glass door. Pressing the button on the side of the handle, the umbrella sprang into life, shielding her from the worst of the rain, and she slowly strolled towards the carpark at the side of the building. The sound of the rustling trees in the distance filled her ears as she walked.

Johanna turned the corner to head towards her car, her mind still full of her personal drama, and came unexpectedly face to face with another woman. They attempted to dodge around each other fruitlessly for several embarrassing seconds until a resigned Johanna stood still, holding her ground. She gazed at the woman's face as it beamed with excitement; she seemed young, dressed professionally. Raindrops were visible on her dark grey suit. A business client maybe, as she looked like she was heading into the building that housed her offices. Surely she'd recognise her face if that was the case. It was an attractive face, oval, framed with dark blonde hair. The woman's hand attempted to tame her shoulder-length locks, tucking them back behind her ear as she tried to sidestep her.

Johanna realised she still hadn't uttered a word. "Sorry," she blurted out.

"My fault, I've got two left feet," the woman offered with a grin.

Her accent was familiar but not local. It was the kind of accent that stood out to her, considering her boardroom contained a variety of muddy Midland and Northern inflections. The woman grinned back at her expectantly, and Johanna felt compelled to look at the woman's feet just to check her statement. They looked normal enough, although her wide shoes could easily have contained a multitude of deformities.

"Probably why I usually insist on at least one stiff drink before I get on the dancefloor."

"Just one?" Johanna fired back, regaining a little of her composure. The rain continued to fall, and as if suddenly noticing, Johanna said, "Sorry, you're getting soaked." She was in two minds as to whether she should offer to shield the woman from the rain as she escorted her into the building.

The woman smiled as she motioned with her arms. "I'll go this way; you go that way."

"Great idea," she replied with a chuckle. It wasn't until she was several meters away that she realised that her simple interaction with someone new had lightened her otherwise dull mood if only for a moment or two.

Johanna turned on the TV as soon as she arrived home, anything to dispel the quiet of her empty house, damning updates about the economy filled the silence. Johanna was just about to pick up the remote to change the channel when the tickertape scrolling along the screen caught her attention:

Police are investigating after body discovered on farmland near Kingsford.

Kingsford, her home for the first eighteen years of her life. Johanna had bittersweet memories of that place. The idyllic, small town would have been the ideal place to grow up, except for the ugly scar that was imbedded across the middle of her childhood.

Her mind raced. Could it really be Dan Dunderdale, after all these years? A ten-year-old boy who'd lived on her street, a boy that she'd played swing ball with, caught bullheads in the local stream, who'd vanished during the summer of 1988.

His disappearance had marred them all, parents and children alike, and the fallout was widespread, like an atomic bomb, rippling through the town. No stone had been left unturned. Everybody was tainted in some way. As a child it didn't seem possible that Daniel wouldn't come back.

Finding the news channel, Johanna perched on the edge of the sofa, waiting for the news item to appear in more detail, while her brain transported her back to that time. Back then, it was so hard to believe anyone could just pick Dan off the street and whisk him away. He lived in the shadow of his big brother, Barney, only venturing out to sprag on someone. A tattletale, Dan was always the first to point the finger to keep himself out of trouble.

Johanna tore herself away from the television. It was loud enough; she would hear it in the kitchen if the story came on and dash back in. She opened the fridge, eyeing the contents on the door again.

She grabbed the half-empty bottle of Pinot; the cold glass nipped at her skin as she poured herself a hefty measure just as the news item she'd been waiting for came on. She stood in front of the TV, sipping her wine as a reporter repeated the headline from earlier while a press conference disassembled in the background. She scanned the small panel of people, but nobody looked familiar. She could barely remember what Dan's parents even looked like back then, let alone thirty years later.

In August 1988, when Daniel had gone missing, Johanna had been eleven years old. An age when the summers seemed infinite, and they played in the street till after dusk. It was a place where she had felt safe, had her first crush and felt her first loss.

Things are so different now; most youngsters have a mobile phone glued to their hands these days, hooked on social media.

The Hales had moved to Compton Way, Kingsford two years earlier. It was a steep, straight road at the tail end of a new estate, a sprawling development built over several years. Their house was semi-detached, three bedrooms, and Johanna couldn't wait to move in. She would have her own room, all to herself at last, after sharing with various unwanted and imposing items of furniture as they outgrew their last house. She had fond memories of working in the garage with her father, he would often give her a stack of timber off-cuts and a handful of nails to see what she could come up with. It was built into the downstairs, like most of the others on the street.

Their side of the street backed onto farmers' agricultural fields as far as the eye could see, with only a six-foot chain-link fence separating the fields from their garden. Her parents loved the quiet; their previous house was much nearer town, on a busy road. Their one and only cat had paid the price for living there before they'd moved.

Staring blankly at the screen, Johanna thought back to the day that marred her childhood, to Daniel Dunderdale.

CHAPTER 7

EXHAUSTED, Johanna finally dragged herself from her bed after turning off her snooze alarm for the fifth time. Her dreams had been consumed by the angry, terrified faces of her childhood friends from Compton Way, screaming and shouting, before fleeing a raging fire in the woods.

She rubbed her hands over her face to try and wake herself up, dropping her legs over the side of the bed she used the momentum to sit upright grabbing at the yoga pants and a t-shirt on the nearby chair. As she descended the stairs her legs were like lead weights, forcing her to grip the handrail a little tighter. The cold tiles were pleasant under her feet as she entered the kitchen, but the bright morning made an invisible vice tighten around her head.

She had never been big on breakfast, and today was no exception, so she pulled a bottle of water out of the fridge, downed a couple of painkillers and closed her eyes, waiting for the throbbing to abate. She desperately needed something to distract her mind and reached for the radio, gripping the worktop to steady herself.

"Police have announced that the remains discovered on a farm are that of missing schoolboy Daniel Dunderdale. Daniel went missing from his home in August 1988."

Johanna clasped the worktop a little tighter. Shit! She'd already known deep down as soon as the discovery was announced. Still the confirmation weighed heavily on her chest; a sour taste developed in her mouth, forcing her to take another drink to wash it away.

As the radio report continued, she strained her mind to think of the people in her life back then, to picture the faces from the past, but the passing years had made the exact details of that time hazy and confusing. She suddenly needed to look at their faces one more time, if nothing else, it would banish the horror-filled faces from her dreams. She vacated the kitchen in favour of her office, grateful for the gloom of the unopened curtains.

Sitting behind her desk, she rummaged around in her bottom drawer until she found the bright red hard drive her bother, Simon, had given her. He had digitised all her old photos for her birthday a couple of years ago. Since he had become a father, he'd become the more sentimental of the two of them.

She had been a keen shutter-bug as a child; with several 110 and 35mm auto-focus cameras to her name. Being the one behind the camera was a sure-fire way of avoiding being in front of it. She still hated having her photo taken now, looking at the dissecting blank lens as if it stole part of her soul each time it flickered.

Johanna turned on her computer, and as the screen flashed into life, she could just make out the large oblong shape on the wall behind her in the reflection. She turned to see the familiar painting that had been demoted to her office at Steph's request, as she found it unsettling. The abstract had been a great find, an early Noa Stevens. They rarely came on the market, and Johanna had snapped it up. She was a keen follower of Stevens' work and had recently visited a new exhibition, knowing full well all the works would be out of her price range now. With no pause for thought, she got to her feet, plucked the painting from the wall and carefully took it back downstairs to be re-installed to its rightful place. She removed the dull, off-the-peg skyline photo, turning it to face the wall as she placed it on the floor. The screw sticking out of the wall didn't look strong enough for a permanent fixing, but she couldn't wait and offered up the large canvas, slipping it over the screw. It hung at a slight angle, but it would do for now. She stood back with a look of satisfaction before returning to her office with a little more spring in her step.

Retaking her seat, Johanna clicked on the hard drive, feeling a little guilty; it was the first time she had even plugged the drive in to look at the contents, preferring to leave it all in the past. As the contents appeared on her screen, she was surprised to see that Simon had organised the photos into folders. He must have spent hours sorting them into various holidays and outings. She scanned the titles, stopping at a folder simply labelled *Compton Way*, then clicked on the folder, starting a slideshow. An image of their house on Compton Way flashed on the screen; her grandmother was standing on the path outside the front door, flanked by herself and Simon. It must have been a special occasion; she'd been forced to wear a dress. Her white ankle socks were stiffly pulled up to within an inch of their life, her white and red dress floating around her knees.

She leaned in for a closer look as the photos were displayed one after the other, and it wasn't long before Dan appeared on the screen. He was playing Swing ball with Simon. He looked so young, they all did. Then there was Little Mark, with his scarred upper lip from the cleft pallet operation he'd had as a baby. It left him with an unfortunate sneer on occasion, making people look twice, which just made it worse. *How could I have edited out that information? What else have I forgotten?*

Before she could look at any more, a knock echoed down the hallway. Johanna considered ignoring it – she wasn't expecting anyone; she wasn't even meant to be here – but a second, more insistent knock put paid to that thought. She made her way down the hallway, the solid wood door gave her no indication of who was on the other side.

Johanna opened the front door, surprised to see a woman dressed in a slightly crumpled suit. Her face held a familiar, open smile that she could have sworn she'd seen before. She frowned in confusion. How did she know her? Was she a client that somehow needed to see her at home? Hadn't she heard of phoning or emailing?

"Hello. Can I help you?" she reluctantly asked.

"Johanna Hale?"

Johanna nodded. Her mind fizzed at the tone of the woman's question. *What the hell is this all about?*

The woman offered up a black wallet containing her credentials. "I'm DS Fuller. Can I come in for a moment?"

Johanna barely glanced at the documentation. "Police!" Her thoughts immediately leapt to her family. "What's happened? Is everyone …?" She couldn't finish her sentence.

"Miss Hale, as far as I know everyone's fine. I'm here to talk to you about Daniel Dunderdale."

"Dan!" A trace amount of relief followed by guilt filtered through Johanna. When exactly was the last time she had spoken to her parents, or her brother for that matter? Nevertheless, she should have been expecting this, considering the news of his recent discovery. "Of course, come in." She stepped aside, allowing the detective to enter.

"Thank you," DS Fuller offered.

"Tea? I was just about to make some," Johanna lied. *Why am I lying to a police officer?*

"That would be great, thank you."

There was that smile again. Johanna quickly looked away and moved down the hall, stopping by the sitting room doorway. Turning, she glanced back at the police officer. "Make yourself at home. I'll just be a minute," she told her, moving to the kitchen she closed her eyes and blew out a breath as she dropped two teabags into the teapot and filled it from the instant hot water tap. Assembling the teapot and other accoutrements on a wooden tray, she then made her way back to the sitting room.

DS Fuller was standing in the middle of the room, her head tilted to one side as she studied the Noa Stevens painting. Hearing Johanna approach, she began flicking through her notebook. Johanna smiled. It had only been back up a couple of hours, and it was already piquing someone's interest.

"You have a lovely home, Miss Hale."

"Thank you. That painting's by one of my favourite artists." Johanna nodded towards the painting as she took a seat in the armchair next to the sofa. The tray wobbled slightly as she placed it on the coffee table. She was ridiculously jumpy and grateful for the interlude of conversation. *Why am I so bloody nervous? I've run my own business for years, scored major contracts, from hardnosed clients, hired and fired people, but apparently, I can't talk to one police officer in my own home.*

"I sometimes wish *I'd* gone in a different direction at art school," Johanna continued babbling, regardless of DS Fuller's lack of reply.

"It's never too late. My mum only took up willow weaving a few years ago and now she teaches beginner courses."

"Really." Maybe there was hope for her yet.

DS Fuller moved across the room, perching on the edge of the sofa next to the armchair. Her face then changed to something more serious. "Anyway I won't keep you long, I'm sure you've seen the news."

Johanna nodded as she blindly attempted to stir the tea without crushing the teabags.

"You're reopening the case?" Johanna asked, stating the obvious.

"It was never closed," DS Fuller replied with a tight smile, then flicked through her notepad again before saying, "I understand from the old case files you were on holiday at the time Daniel went missing."

"Uh, yes. Simon and I were on holiday for a few days with our grandparents in Southend. It was sort of an annual trip. We got back on the Saturday. Grandad called my mother to let her know he was bringing us back, and she thought it would be better if we stayed there for the night with them. He took us back home on the Sunday."

"He brought you back the day after, on the twenty-first of August."

"Yes. My mother was worried we'd get upset, I think. We ended going back to stay with our grandparents on and off till it was time to go back to school, when the worst of the searching was over."

Fuller nodded. "I know it's a long time ago, but do you remember anyone odd hanging about around that time on your street or in the area, before you went away?"

Johanna sat back in her seat. Detective Fuller was an attractive woman; her dark blonde hair was tied up in a short ponytail, which sat just above her jacket collar.

DS Fuller continued, "Maybe someone that didn't fit?"

It was several days before Johanna's parents would let the police question her back then. Her age had been a good buffer, just like Simon. Not that she knew much about what happened anyway.

Johanna sighed; these were the same questions as thirty years ago. "No. I'm sorry." Johanna thought for a moment. "We, at least I, thought we were a tightknit community. I mean, I was only a kid back then, but even now I find it hard to believe anyone in the street was responsible or involved," she said and dropped the teaspoon on the tray, making a clatter. "Sorry." Her hand moved to silence the spoon. "I've never spoken to the police before, apart from ...You're making me nervous. I've already lied to you."

Fuller held her gaze, just letting the words hang in the air, as if waiting for her to continue.

"I mean about making the tea. I've still got half a mug of tea upstairs. Not about anything else."

"I see." Fuller half smiled at her before directing her gaze around the room. "Have you just moved in?"

Johanna was confused as she followed DS Fuller's gaze around the room, realising it was devoid of any knick-knacks. Her harsh clear-out had left it looking fashionably sparse. In her daze since Steph's departure, Johanna hadn't realised just how much Steph had made her house into a home. "No. My ex-girlfriend recently moved out."

"Oh. I'm sorry." Fuller sounded genuinely apologetic. *Sensitivity training.*

"My own fault. Far too in love with my business. I neglected her."

"In my experience, it's rarely just one person's fault." DS Fuller stretched out an arm to place her mug back on the tray. "People are never just the worst thing they do or say; they're much more than that."

Johanna was a little surprised by the woman's words and relieved, considering Steph had called her cold-hearted. "Well, it looks like I'm destined to be a crazy cat woman who probably gets eaten by her cats as soon as she drops dead."

"Not good. I've seen the aftermath of that scenario. I'm not convinced they waited till he was fully dead either."

"Oh, great."

DS Fuller must have seen the disgusted look on her face and began laughing. No doubt, this was police humour, designed to fortify against a more emotional response. Johanna continued her reverie, enjoying the sound of Fuller's laughter.

"What kind of lesbian am I anyway with a cat allergy?" she added and looked on in awe, feeling parts of her body spring to life as DS Fuller laughed even harder, with fantastic hilarity lines framing her squinted eyes, shaped like tiny smiles, reminiscent of a cartoon character from TV. The sound of her laughter was equally captivating, buoyant and melodic, and filled the room freely until she reached up to clutch the bottom of her nose, muffling the sound. Her face was bright with energy as she finally met Johanna's eyes. Looking away after a moment, she then made a show of checking her watch. But Johanna wasn't quite ready for the detective to leave. Feeling a bit more at ease, she began to talk.

"Compton Way was such a great place to grow up, or at least I thought it was until … Our house backed onto farmers' fields with those massive straw bale rolls. I used to love it when they burned off the fields at the end of August."

"It always reminded me that the summer holidays were about to end and I had to go back to school," Fuller said with a sigh.

So, Detective Fuller was a country girl, to some extent.

"True," Johanna nodded. "I always remember my mother trying to clean all the ash off the window sills at the back of our house.

"You'd say it was a good street to live on?" Fuller asked.

"Oh yeah, there was a woodland at the top of the road. We used to play in there all the time, building dens, climbing the pine trees. Then we had our own little private play area next to that, and at the opposite end there was a small stream." She purposely left out the abandoned industrial buildings that were there too. "That's what makes it so unbelievable that someone could just grab him off the street without anyone seeing it."

Detective Fuller's lips formed a straight line. "And how long had you lived there before Daniel Dunderdale went missing?"

"Err, a couple of years. I was nine when we moved in."

Fuller took out her notebook again. "How many other kids lived on the street?"

"It took a while for the street to fill up, but there were seven of us after a couple of years: three girls and four boys. There were other kids on the surrounding streets, but we were a clique of similar ages, so we hung around together. A bit of a gang of misfits I guess, in some ways."

"And they all lived there at the time Daniel went missing?" Detective Fuller asked.

Johanna nodded. "Yeah, it wasn't till after that people started moving away."

Detective Fuller settled back in her seat. "Can you tell me about them?"

Pleased as she was that Detective Fuller was staying, Johanna wondered what she was getting into, but then she'd opened the door to this.

"Okay," she said and tapped a finger on the side of her mug. "So, at the top of the road were Daniel and Barney Dunderdale. The Dunderdale's moved away a year after Dan disappeared." Johanna figured they couldn't stand the thought of not knowing if someone they were acquainted with had taken their son.

"What was Daniel like?" Detective Fuller asked.

"Well, he was quite small and shy, I guess, compared to Barney. Lived in his shadow a bit. I probably shouldn't say, but …"

Detective Fuller raised her eyebrows. "But?"

"He was a bit of a squealer," Johanna said quietly, as if others might hear and take offence.

"Really?"

"Bit of a soggy KitKat when someone put him under pressure." Johanna fidgeted in her seat as she considered how much to tell the detective.

"Okay." Fuller pursed her lips. "Did it cause problems within the group?"

"No, not really. We just didn't tell him anything we didn't want our parents to know." A faint smile appeared on Detective Fuller's lips. Johanna continued. "Barney was a couple of years older and probably the bravest." A keen fire starter, many of which got out of hand in the woodland, requiring decisive action to prevent unwanted parental attention.

There was no response from Detective Fuller, so she pressed on. Looking at the photographs earlier had certainly refreshed her memory. "Then, two doors down, was Little Mark Evans, named due to the fact there was a bigger, older Mark living further down the street. Deaf kid, I can't remember his surname, although he never played with us very often as he lived at a residential school most of the time."

Johanna waited for Fuller to stop writing before going on. "Then there was Amy Bell who lived next door to us. She was my best friend for a while, till they moved away for her dad's work." Amy was a year older, tall, blonde, and beautiful. The fact that she lived next door was a bonus for Johanna. They both occupied the front bedrooms of their respective homes with only the party wall dividing them. They often hung out of their windows to call and chat to each other. Had they been able to run the type of kite system used in jail, they would surely have utilised it. Johnna's would have contained subtle love hearts in the hope that Amy would see her as more than just her sidekick. But she saw no point in offering that piece of information to Detective Fuller.

"Then opposite us was posh Sarah Moody. She went to a private school, only appearing at weekends and school holidays. She was two years older than me and liked to remind me as often as possible, especially when she wanted everyone to do what she wanted."

Johanna caught the grin that appeared on Detective Fuller's face. The Moody's snobbish family dynamic was appropriately disrupted by their dog, a liver and white Springer Spaniel called Scamp. Endlessly hungry, it raided the fridge and freezer on a regular basis when left alone. Johanna could recall going around to call for Sarah one summer only to find her digging up a half-frozen turkey in her back garden. He was also an avid fence jumper, leaving Sarah's mother to do the walk of shame to collect him. Karma, if ever there was any.

"Sarah's mum was a real snob, you remember that comedy 'Keeping up appearances', it could have been modelled on her." It was odd considering her father was a RAC man with one of those tiny

Morris Minivans. Her own father had little faith in his abilities. Looking back, he was just dismissive of less practically minded people, much as he still is today.

Her father, David Hale had little time for whimsical fancy. She found out in later years he'd had the opportunity to go to art school but had to turn it down in favour of employment. It explained a lot of her childhood, his desire for Johanna and Simon to carve out sensible careers for themselves.

"I guess, as a child, you never really take much notice of what your friends' parents do for a living," she continued. She just knew to avoid them when they were home, unless it was to fix something.

Detective Fuller's pen was poised. "Then there was you and your brother?"

Johanna felt her face go a little warm. She'd already excluded herself and her brother from the list. "Oh sorry, yes. My brother is three years younger. My parents tried to get me to include Simon in all our games and antics." Which meant, of course, he had to be sworn to secrecy about anything he saw. "He used to get whiney at times when we made him fetch and carry for us, but on the whole, he was a pretty reliable little brother."

"Well, thanks for that and the tea. I really should get going." Detective Fuller got to her feet.

"Sorry, I'm probably boring you to death." Johanna stood to show her out. It had been a long time since she had chatted like that with anyone, and now she was worried about the impression she'd given Detective Fuller, considering everything she just said. "I guess you'll be talking to everyone from back then?" she asked.

DS Fuller turned to look at her but didn't answer.

Johanna felt compelled to continue. "We moved to a different street a couple of years later. I didn't really keep in touch with anyone after that." Realising she was rambling, she clamped her mouth shut as she led the way to the front door. As she turned around, she realised why the woman was familiar. "You came to my work yesterday?"

DS Fuller smiled. "I did."

Johanna opened the front door. "I'm sorry, I didn't realise you were coming to see me." Detective Fuller passed by but remained on the doorstep.

"My fault. I should have checked out who I was coming to see. I won't forget next time."

Next time? What does that mean? Johanna was left with that question as she watched DS Fuller walk away.

CHAPTER 8

Easter in the Hale household was usually a quiet affair, pepped up by a visit from Johanna's grandparents for lunch, followed by a bit of TV with her grandmother while her father and grandfather played dominoes at the dining table. This year was no exception, but

as she sat on the sofa next to her grandmother, grinding a sugary egg with her back teeth, making sure she pulverised every piece before swallowing it, her ears pricked. A football was being kicked about on the street; she couldn't see who it was, but if she had to guess, she'd say it was Barney and Dan. Her feet itched to get out there with them. Maybe Amy was with them, Johanna had barely seen her all week. Surely she had to come out for air sometime.

"Can I go out for a bit, Mum," she asked.

"No. You've got visitors." Gillian's reply was stern.

Johanna frowned as she pushed out her bottom lip; she'd been stuck indoors all day.

"Let her go. It's fine." Her grandmothers wrinkled face flinched to generate a quick wink in Johanna's direction.

"Thanks, Gran, and thanks for the egg." Johanna stood to press her lips to her grandmother's cheek. Her grandmother's hands were chilled as they grasped hers for a second before letting go.

"You're welcome, sweetheart."

Johanna trotted through the dining room, avoiding her father's gaze as she headed for the kitchen. She wasn't about to be stopped now. She fought to get her trainers on before her mother could say another word. And then it came …

"Take your brother with you," her mother called just as Johanna's hand landed on the door handle. So close.

Simon skidded into the kitchen, a wide grin on his face. Johanna sighed as she folded her arms. "Si, get your shoes on."

"I'm doing it," he moaned as he shoved a handful of eggs into his jeans pocket.

He wasn't doing it, he was thinking about stuffing his face as usual. "Come on. I'm going." Johanna turned around and slowly opened the back door.

"Wait!" Simon whined, but she had every intention of leaving him behind and slipped out before he even had one shoe on. Leaving the door open behind her, she made her way across the back of the house and down the alleyway separating their house from next door's, but footsteps were soon echoing behind her. She followed the pathway to the drive, making her way around her grandfather's Ford Marina, and scanned the street in the hope that Amy was out. Her face dropped when she saw the boys huddled at the bottom of the path to the woods. The football was no longer being hoofed up and down the street. She glanced back to Amy's house but saw no movement.

Amy's excuse was always the same: homework. Being two years older than Johanna, Amy was at Kingsford's Secondary School. Johanna had that to look forward to and wasn't sure how she would cope with all the extra homework. Thankfully, with her birthday only last month, she had another year to work herself up to it.

With Simon in tow, Johanna made her way up to the boys. Dan, with his back to her, and Little Mark, gripping the football between his feet, were both staring at Barney, who was dropping something onto the grass. She couldn't tell what it was. As Johanna moved closer, she could see it was shiny, a knife maybe. It was chunky with a black handle, a big blade protruding from the top. Barney was just dropping it blade first onto the ground, and it cut through like butter.

"What's that?" she asked as she stopped next to Dan.

"I found it in my grandad's shed," Barney said smugly as he dropped it again.

Which meant his grandad didn't know he had it.

"Can I see?"

Barney pulled it from the ground and held it a bit longer before wiping off the mud on his jeans, closing the blade and offering it to her.

Heavy in her hands, it was unlike any penknife she'd seen before. She loved it, she wanted it. Wedged into one side was a thick spike, which she couldn't even force open. Ignoring the snigger from Dan as she tried, she had better luck with the other side; two blades were tucked inside the handle. The first was the wide blade that Barney had been using. She was surprised by how sharp it was when she ran it across her finger, and she heard her brother suck a breath through his teeth as she did it. She glared at him to keep him quiet. The other blade was a funny hook shape.

"What's it for?" she asked, turning to Barney.

"I don't know, but it's mine now." He took it from her using the larger of the opened blades to trim off a loose thread dangling from a patch on his jeans then closed them both. It snapped shut with a satisfying click.

Johanna clenched her teeth. She wanted it despite the heavy weight and difficulty she had opening it, but all she could do for now was watch as he threw it from one hand to the other. She knew he'd be bored of it within a week though, and he wouldn't be able to take it home in case his parents found it. He'd have to keep it in their communal hiding place with all the other treasures they'd acquired, which meant she'd be able to get her hands on it. She smiled at that thought as Simon pushed something into the palm of her now-empty left hand. She turned it over to find a blue, speckled egg wedged between her fingers. It was his way of trying to make her feel better. She thanked him with a small grin before slipping it into her mouth.

"Want one?" Simon asked Little Mark as he shoved one into his own mouth, making a large growth in his cheek. He pulled another one from his pocket, tossing it in Little Mark's direction.

The fumbled catch forced a sudden movement, which meant the football that had been trapped between Little Mark's feet slipped free. His frayed P.E. shorts rustled as he made a move after it.

"Div," Barney mumbled as they all watched Little Mark's valiant attempt to catch up with the speeding football, which rolled further down the hill.

"Oopsie." Dan mumbled sarcastically, chuckling as he turned to watch Little Mark.

Johanna was convinced he wouldn't make it and turned back to keep track of the knife still in Barney's hand.

"Ahh! Come and see this!" Little Mark hollered from down the hill.

"Why?" Johanna shouted back, convinced there wouldn't be anything more interesting than Barney's new knife.

"'Nake!"

Even with Little Mark's barely audible, muffled 'S', they all knew what he meant. And that was all it took for each of them to bomb it down the hill at full speed. The velocity of the steep hill made it difficult for them to stop accurately, and Simon and Dan had to skid to a stop, where they found Little Mark at the edge of the Moodys' lawn, staring at something on the grass. He never took his eyes off his target, even when Simon crashed into him.

Although he'd had surgery years ago for his cleft palate, Little Mark still avoided certain words; 'S's were a challenge when he was excited, like now. Johanna felt sorry for him. Whenever his mother was around, she always made a point of correcting his speech mistakes, something Amy had also taken to doing in the last couple of months.

Johanna scanned the patchy grass as she came to a stop. The mottled, grey-brown creature's dark, beady eyes seemed to implore them as it curled around itself on the edge of the lawn. It looked more than a little sad and sluggish, but Simon squealed as it slowly edged closer to his foot.

Johanna slipped her arm around his shoulders as he stepped closer to her. She didn't like the thought of him being scared, especially if he reported back to her parents.

"I think you'll find that's a *snake* Mark." Dan said without looking up.

"It needs the sun to warm up," Barney mumbled.

Johanna wasn't quite sure if the information was meant for everyone, but she had to admit she was a little impressed by his confidence. The sun had barely shown itself all day. Looking up, she could see only a few patches of blue sky.

"What is it?"

They all turned at the familiar shouting voice. Amy was standing at her open window with a book in her hand, a finger holding her place as she leant out the window.

"Nake!" Little Mark bellowed, oblivious to his missing S, his gaze firmly back on the slowly writhing beast.

"What?" Amy asked again. Without the evidence in front of her, she couldn't correct Little Mark.

"It's just a slow worm," Barney snapped, directing his gaze at Amy. "I've seen one before," he continued at a more acceptable volume.

"Slow worm," Johanna repeated. Sounded about right.

"Kill it!" Amy shouted back from her perch.

Johanna baulked. Why would they kill it? It wasn't doing them any harm. It just wanted to get away. But she still said nothing to defend the creature.

"No!" Barney barked, and his arms flew up defensively to stop anyone getting any closer. Thankfully, he had his sensible head on, despite having the tool to do the job in his hand. "Someone get a bucket," he continued. "I'll move it down the bottom." He then nudged his brother into action when no-one else moved.

Johanna glanced down to the bottom of the road, wondering where exactly Barney was planning to put the giant worm. The forgotten football had already come to a stop next to the bottom kerb. She looked back to see her brother and Little Mark utterly mesmerised by the creature. She, on the other hand, was perfectly happy to keep her distance. The thought of that slippery thing coming near her made her shiver as she unconsciously stepped a little further away.

Dan pulled a face as he turned to trot off back up the hill.

"Bring that little spade," Barney shouted back to him as he stopped near their open garage, reappearing a few moments later with a black bucket in his hand. A rattle accompanied him as he halted next to Barney.

Despite Johanna's initial fear of the worm, she still felt sorry for it, surrounded by five giants staring down at it. But Barney was gentle as he got to work with his tools. Placing the bucket on its side, he used the small plastic spade to coax the worm into the bucket. With it mostly inside, he quickly tipped it upright, preventing escape. Johanna sighed with relief now the oversized worm was out of sight.

Simon released a shaky laugh as he stepped forward, taking the plastic spade from Barney. "Where did you see one before?" he asked as they all followed Barney down the hill while he carefully cradled the bucket.

Johanna felt a wobble in her legs as she moved and silently reprimanded herself. She was meant to be the big sister here, but Simon was putting her to shame.

Barney turned to Simon and replied, "Near the woods, at the top."

Simon immediately looked back at Johanna, asking the silent question. "Let's go and look after," he voiced when she didn't respond.

Johanna said nothing as they moved in single file, stepping over the strand of barbed wire that separated the end of their estate from the scrubland and industrial estate beyond, careful to keep to the thin pathway between the overgrown weedy bushes, all too conscious of the creepy crawlies that could be lurking nearby. She held her position at the edge of the patch of scrubland near the stream as Simon pushed past her to see what Barney was going to do. There was no sympathetic release of the captive, like she'd seen on nature programs on TV; Barney simply turned the bucket upside down and walked away.

Simon stood to watch the worm for a few seconds before announcing, "It's gone under the bush."

"Let's go," Johanna said, more to her brother, but they all complied with her request.

"Look, the doors open!" Dan whisper shouted.

"What door?" Barney back peddled almost bumping in to Simon in his haste.

Johanna turned to see Dan pointing around the corner to the front of the building. She stepped back next to Barney, glancing along the face of the long industrial building. A fire door hung open, a *'Push Bar to Open'* sign emblazoned the inside of the door facing them. Johanna scanned the area in front of the building there were no cars in the parking area, if there was anyone inside they hadn't driven there. She knew from walking past the building for the last couple of years that it was split into three separate sections. The first two were occupied but the last one had been empty for as long as she could remember.

"Wait here." Barney ordered dropping the bucket at his feet.

She watched as Barney edged along the front of the building. The empty fields opposite and the protection of the open door meant he was unlikely to be spotted. It still didn't dispel the bubbling panic that rose in Johanna's stomach. Barney flattened himself against the wall for a moment before stepping inside. He was out of sight for less than thirty seconds but it felt like a lifetime.

There was a collective sigh of relief when Barney reappeared. He pulled the door closed and fiddled with the catch before returning to the safety of the corner. The door was left slightly ajar.

"The locks been smashed off-." Barney said as he made a grab for his bucket.

"What's inside?" Dan asked cutting Barney off.

"Not much, there's loads of plastic bottles everywhere."

Johanna could see the spark of excitement in Barney's eye's at what he'd seen and done. He loved being first at doing everything.

The sound of a van arriving at one of the other businesses signalled it was time to go, they all edged around the corner out of sight.

"Come on. Barney said and once again led the way back to the street. "We'll come back another time."

They were all remarkably quiet considering what had just happened. She had to admit it was an exciting prospect; exploring an empty building, but would they actually go inside, she doubted it.

Little Mark stopped to retrieve his football as they emerged at the bottom of the road.

"What do they eat?" Simon asked.

"Who?" Johanna replied. *What the hell was he talking about now?*

"*Slow worms*?" He yelled. "People? I bet they eat people." Simon was buzzing now. "It was probably after Moody's dog."

"Si –" Johanna was just about to tell him to quit when Barney cut her off.

"No, they eat insects and slugs. They're basically lizards without legs. They can even leave their tail behind if they need to escape."

"Wow!"

Johanna caught Barney's eye. "How do you know all that stuff?"

"Read it in a book."

Johanna smiled. She was more than a little impressed. Glancing back up the street, she was surprised to see Amy next to her gate.

"Where is it?" the older girl demanded.

"It's gone," two of them replied in unison.

"Boring," Amy huffed.

Dan ran off up the hill towards Amy, was he going to blab about the door to the factory. As they got closer she could hear him asking her about the book she was reading; that was Johanna's job, she was her friend. Dan couldn't take his eyes off her. The fact that Amy was even gratifying him, answering his questions as she smiled back at him brought an instant scowl to Johanna's face. Amy was rarely like that with her; preferring to remind Johanna that she was too young to understand her school work, yet here she was with Dan who was a year younger than she was.

"We're going to look for more," Simon said, swinging the spade around.

Johanna wanted to take the spade from her brother and bury it in Dan's head.

"I've got homework to do," Amy said, stepping back inside her gateway.

"Still?" Johanna frowned. Although she didn't press the situation, the thought of watching Dan moon over her anymore made her feel more than a little sick inside.

"Yes!" She turned to glare at Johanna. A split second later she spun to look at the rest of them. "See Yah." Her tone light once more, and Amy was gone, disappearing through her front door.

Barney kept hold of the bucket as they walked past the small field towards the woodland.

"You'll need a fork stick for snakes," Barney said to everyone as they entered an opening between the trees.

"Right," Simon said as he began searching the woodland floor.

Johanna had no intention of snake hunting. She was going to climb her favourite tree and watch it all unfold below. Once in position, she sat on the branch, swinging her legs as she leant against the trunk. She needed a minute to think, how had she not noticed that before, Dan liked Amy. A smile stretched across her lips as she heard Simon's laughter below. But then a thudding sound broke through the laughter. She tried to locate what was making the noise but couldn't see through the branches from her elevated position.

Jumping down, she went in search of the noise, hoping her brother wasn't battering something to death. She stepped through the brush, still overly conscious of creatures as the sound continued up ahead. A few moments later, she found Barney next to a pine tree with his knife clenched in his hand, the spike poking out between his knuckles. He was using the tree as a punchbag.

"What are you doing?" Johanna snapped and moved closer, inspecting the tree trunk. Puncture wounds plagued the soft, layered bark, with sap dripping from the holes. She pressed her fingers to one of the lesions, and the strong scent of the sap filled her nostrils as it stuck to the pads of her fingers. "You're hurting the tree," she mumbled, almost to herself. The thick sap made it difficult to separate her fingers.

"What!" Barney glared at her, his brow heavy. "No I'm not."

The silence stretched between them as laughter sounded in the background. The call of a familiar voice in the distance stopped her from saying anything more, not that she even knew what to say, and as more footfalls headed their way, Johanna held her finger to her lips to shush everyone. It was her mother, and her voice was clearer now as she called her name, followed closely by Simon's. Johanna looked out from between the branches of a holly bush; her mother was getting closer now. The cream cardigan she always wore was wrapped tightly around her, beneath folded arms, as she walked up the path to the woods.

"She's in here," Dan said, stepping out from behind a tree, his fork stick pointing her out.

Johanna glared at the back of Dan's head, wanting to instantly explode his head with her thoughts.

"Is she?" her mother said with a grin. "Well, she'd better come out and say goodbye to her grandparents before they go."

Johanna reluctantly trudged forward. "Come on," she grumbled, nodding for Simon to do the same, as she walked out from the sheltering trees.

CHAPTER 9

"MORNING, BOSS," Lucy offered as she got in Barrel's car. She braced her arm against the door as she reached for her seatbelt, knowing he wouldn't wait till she was secure. Settling back in the passenger's seat, she pulled out her notebook to get Barrel up to speed.

"Forensics got back to me this morning with a report on the plastic that was placed over the body."

"Anything useful?"

"The blue plastic was consistent with a commercially available rubble bag."

"Not a feedbag from the farm, then," Barrel added.

"No. They found traces of blood on the inside of the bag, which is a match to the victim. There were also partial fingerprints, small fingerprints in the blood, which are possibly also the victim's. They were found on the inside, some on the outer edge at the top, but nothing on the outside in terms of fingerprints of our perpetrator. Not much of anything, just debris from the well."

"The assailant put him in the bag to transport him to the well," Barrel stated. "All the fingerprints are from the same person?"

"Possibly. Due to the timeframe and deterioration they can't be positive." She waited a moment before continuing. They did match one of the partials to the prints found on the plastic game in Daniel's jeans pocket." Not for the first time, she realised how easily Barrel distanced himself from the victim. All she could think about was the young, injured boy tumbling around in a bag before being dumped in a well.

"He must have been alive when they put him in that bag," she mumbled, feeling a lump rise in her throat.

"Even your new friend Dr What's-her-name couldn't tell you that. Don't get emotional on me, Fuller. Stay focussed." Barrel's tone was sharp.

Lucy took a breath. "It also means our suspect could have driven the victim to the dump site."

"Agreed," Barrel replied.

Lucy returned her notebook to her pocket. She hoped this would be her one and only case involving a young child, but instinct told her a different story.

"Now, from what I hear, Redland had a stroke a while back, so don't stare if he starts to dribble," Barrel said as he slowed to a crawl in front of a row of bungalows. "He was a bit of an asshole, but on the whole a good copper."

"That's it," Lucy said as she pointed to the number 12 daubed on the front of a wheelie bin in a driveway. Barrel stopped abruptly, making her body jerk forward. She was sure she could file for whiplash injuries if she let Barrel drive much longer.

Lucy followed Barrel to the peeling front door of the simple, tiny bungalow, fully intending to let him take the lead. She'd already formed an opinion of the crusty, old-school copper; he probably still called female police officers 'Doris' like they did in the seventies.

The front door swung open a split second after Barrel had knocked. Redland must have spotted them coming up the driveway. The outline of a stocky figure appeared in the dim hallway.

"Ex-DCI Redland?" Barrel asked.

The man stepped out of the shadows, she got her first good look at Eric Redland. He hadn't aged well, rough and unkempt like a badly dressed scarecrow, his checked shirt was tight across his plump belly and upper arms, as if he'd gained weight quickly. Still he made no reply, his head nodded as if waiting for more information.

Barrel offered his credentials. "I'm DCI Barrel, and this is DS Fuller. We'd like to ask you about one of your old cases."

"Come in, come in," Eric Redland offered with a wave of a hand, his demeanour changing a wide smile covering his face as he stepped back from the door.

Lucy shut the front door before following Barrel down the dim hallway into an equally gloomy sitting room. As her eyes adjusted, she remembered Barrel's words about Redland having a stroke. No doubt he'd been laid up for a while. His head was round and balding, a heavy five-o'clock shadow covered his chin. No shave this morning; he obviously wasn't expecting visitors.

A faint aroma of stale cigarettes drifted up her nose as she noticed the yellowing ceiling; an ex-smoker forced to give up due to ill health, she suspected.

The room was dull and old fashioned, not so much untidy but missing a woman's touch, if she had to guess. A large, flatscreen TV sat on an old metal stand with wheels, making a noise behind Lucy. She turned as a series of antiques flashed across the screen, but the voice-over was quickly muted. Looking back across the room, Lucy saw Redland stuff the remote control back into the pocket of his jogging bottoms. Whoever was responsible for making that item of everyday wear had a lot to answer for.

She felt Barrel glaring at her as she noticed Redland's wonky eye, but she struggled to look away, unsure if Redland was looking at her or not.

"So, who do we have here?" Redland asked, looking straight at her.

Barrel nudged her shoulder, and she pulled out her warrant card ID.

Eric Redland stooped to look at it in detail. "DS Lucy Fuller. Lucy-Lucy?" His tone was slow and steady. "Umm, patron saint of the blind. Sounds about right; the blind leading the blind." He chuckled to himself, his lazy eye flickering as he did so.

Lucy snatched away her ID and tucked it in her pocket. If she didn't know any better, she could easily have mistaken the ex-detective in front of her for the child killer she'd been reading about. She shivered, despite the warmth, as she moved further into the room to stand in front of the window, away from Redland.

Redland took a seat in a well-worn armchair in the corner of the room, with the best view of the TV. "So, to what do I owe this dubious pleasure?"

Lucy glanced out the window behind her, realising Redland had a perfect view of the street from his armchair. No wonder he was at the door so quickly.

"A body of a young boy has been found hidden in a well just outside Kingsford. It's been identified as Daniel Dunderdale." Barrel let the words sink in.

Lucy looked for a reaction on Redland's face. Nothing.

"The case is still officially open; you being the original SIO, we just wanted your take on it." Barrel was playing nice.

Redland nodded. "We searched day and night for that boy, for weeks. He was nowhere to be found."

Lucy recalled the details she'd read about the investigation; he'd thrown everything he had at it, at least to start with.

"Was Combe Farm searched during the investigation?" Lucy asked, ignoring Barrel's frown.

"What?" Redland turned to glare at her with one eye. The other was half closed.

"Do you still think David Levin was responsible for the Dunderdale boy?" Barrel asked, taking over.

Redland's lips puckered up as he dragged his eye back over to Barrel. "We found evidence of Levin being in Kingsford. He knew the area."

Area? As in knew about the well at Combe Farm or he knew where Kingsford was?

"Around the time of Daniel's disappearance?" Barrel asked.

Redland took a deep breath before starting. "One of the industrial units at the bottom of the housing estate kept getting burgled, so the owner put up a camera, caught an image of Levin's van a few months after. It's all in the files." His tone was practiced, as if he had said it all before.

Lucy's ears pricked up. Industrial units. As in the ones on Cherry Lane that stopped the well from working.

"Bit early for CCTV in eighty-eight, wasn't it?" Barrel asked.

Redland smiled wide, exposing his yellowed teeth. "Just started to be introduced. The owner had a brother-in-law, worked in computers, wanted to help him out, stop him losing all his profits."

Convenient was all Lucy could think. She wanted to know if the case still haunted Redland. Or maybe he was so sure that Levin was responsible that he could just walk away and forget about it. Had Levin, of all people, turned out to be his saviour in this case? She needed to find that footage.

"Nothing on the camera before that?" Barrel asked.

"It was put up a month after the boy went missing."

"And the van was identified as Levin's?" Barrel clarified.

"The number plate was obscured, but it was him, I know it," Redland grumbled.

"Which one of the industrial units had the camera?" Lucy asked. She knew there were three to choose from, according to the industry paper Knight had sent her.

Redland looked at her, minus the glare this time. "The engineering place. Kept getting all their scrap nicked."

Lucy flicked through her notes. "Lux Engineering?" she asked.

"I don't remember the name." Redland shrugged. "So, Saint Lucy, who do you think did it?" he challenged.

She didn't like the way he lingered over her name. Focusing on his working eye, she offered her opinion. "A local maybe, to hide Daniel in that well for so long."

Redland grunted. "Lucky break, that's all."

"Anyone local catch your eye as a possible suspect back then?" Barrel asked.

Redland chuckled, his eye flickering again. "It was put down to everything from chain letters to alien abduction at one point. Even had a medium chiming in, saying a woman had taken him."

"Did Levin ever work with a woman to abduct any of his victims?"

"Don't know. Wasn't my case, as I'm sure you know."

Redland obviously wasn't going to give them anything else. Barrel must have thought the same. He stepped forward, stretching out a hand to Redland. "I appreciate you giving us your time today, Eric. Thank you."

Redland didn't look too keen on the use of his Christian name as he reluctantly shook Barrel's hand.

"We'll see our own way out."

Lucy followed Barrel, happy to leave Redland behind.

Walking back down the driveway, she could feel Redland's eyes on her.

"Jesus, did you see his toenails? He could climb the flock wallpaper with them," Barrel laughed. At least he waited till they were in the car.

Lucy wasn't about to admit she'd missed the unsightly toenails. "Flock wallpaper? What's that?"

Barrel gave her a disapproving look as he started his car. "He'll need a bloody angle grinder to trim them talons."

Barrel pulled away, just as her seatbelt clicked into place. She looked out the side window, and the residential streets went by in a blur. "He didn't even ask about where the body was found," Lucy said as she gripped the door rest. "Not one question, even when I told him about the farm."

"He's not interested. Already closed the case in his mind."

She had to ask, if only to see if Barrel had also done the same, "Do you really buy into Redland's story that Levin was responsible for Daniel's death?"

"Maybe." She could only see his profile, so it was difficult to read his expression.

"Even if it doesn't fit with his other crimes, and there's no record of his green van on the street?"

Barrel pulled to an urgent stop at a junction. "Come off it Fuller, he could have been parked up on the industrial estate Redland mentioned, a little works van. Maybe no-one noticed it." He gripped the steering wheel as he revved the car engine. "Why are you pushing this?"

Why aren't you? Was the first question that came to mind but she decided to bite her tongue. "What about that CCTV? Levin wasn't a thief, was he? Why would he draw attention to himself by getting picked up for theft?" It made no sense to her at all. Surely a guy like that wanted to fly under the radar as much as possible.

"Okay, fine!" He pulled away from the junction with force. "Find that footage if it's still watchable. And look into Levin's alibi for when Dunderdale went missing. He must have had one."

Satisfied, she allowed a small grin to pull at the edges of her lips "I'll find out," Lucy said with purpose. Or Tanner will, more like. She'd already put together a list of jobs for him. He'd managed to trace a few of the old residents from Compton Way, including Johanna Hale, who'd certainly been a pleasant surprise. Her background information on the residents and area could prove interesting, at least that's what she was telling herself. Her earlier visit to her brother, Simon had been far less useful.

"How's Tanner getting on?"

Lucy frowned a little at the question. "Good. He's found a few of the residents. I'm in the process of interviewing and eliminating them."

"Buried the hatchet then," Barrel confirmed with a quick glance in her direction.

What, Jesus, was there anyone that didn't know? "Yes, boss."

"Okay, send him out to interview if you need to. The sooner we close this case the better."

What's the rush? Was he still catching heat from above? Is that why they'd given her the case in Barrel's absence, hoping she'd screw it up? He'd barely loosened the leash he kept her on. She couldn't let it go unsolved again; it was her case to close one way or another.

"I don't buy it," she blurted, the silence driving her crazy. "Levin left his victims where they would be found, not hidden for thirty years. He wanted them to be found."

"Jesus, Fuller, I leave you alone for a few days and you turn into Inspector bloody Morse."

"I just think it's someone local, that's all." Someone who knew about the well at Combe Farm at least.

"Not likely to be local anymore, though, are they. Possibly not even alive."

Lucy had to concede to that fact, but it wouldn't stop her from tracking them all down.

CHAPTER 10

As Lucy parked up outside Woodley Station, she spotted Andy Tanner arriving with a female, uniformed PC. She smiled, grateful that he'd moved on. She quickly got out of her car, locked it and headed towards the two figures.

"Andy." She hated asking for help, but she had little choice with so much paperwork to trawl through. She waited for him to turn towards her, then said, "I've got another job for you today."

His companion nodded to her before they continuing into the station.

"Okay. I managed to trace a few more of the residents yesterday."

"Good. I need you to TIE some more of them." She started with the good news as they continued to make their way into the building.

"Trace, interview and eliminate. I can do that, no problem."

Lucy frowned at his need to explain, then realised his companion was still in earshot. She continued, skirting over it, not wanting to make a fool out of Tanner.

"According to the old SIO on the Dunderdale case, there's CCTV footage from an industrial estate near where Daniel went missing which shows Levin's van in the area a month later."

"CCTV, from back then?" Tanner sounded incredulous.

Lucy acknowledged the sergeant on reception before swiping her card to enter the station offices. Tanner followed. "I know it's bound to be in shit condition, especially after all this time. We might be able to clean it up a little better than back then. Also, there might be some stills from the footage in one of the case files. I want them too."

"Right. Not much then, just the odd miracle."

Lucy sighed. "I know it's a big ask, but I think it'll be key in dismissing this Levin bullshit once and for all."

Tanner slowed his pace near the bottom of the stairwell. "You don't think he was involved?"

Lucy turned, realising Tanner wasn't following anymore. She figured he was on his way to the canteen. "No, I don't, which is why we need to crack on with tracing the rest of the previous residents from Compton Way."

Tanner blew out a breath. "Found a few death certificates already."

It didn't surprise her considering the timeframe. "Okay, but there were quite a few kids living on that street around Daniel's age. From what I understand, they all played together, so they might have some useful information." Johanna Hale and the Dunderdales had given her some insight on the dynamics of the group, but she needed more.

"Okay. I'll get on it."

"Thanks, Andy," she said before turning to climb the stairs. She entered the office, noticing the large wipe board Tanner had set up with a map of Compton Way. Each house was labelled with the names of the residents in August 1988 and their current address. As she stepped closer, she realised that dates of death were indeed scrawled next to some of them. The Hale family's neighbours on one side were now deceased, along with another couple near the bottom of the road.

Lucy pulled the file she'd been collating from her drawer. Walking back to the board, she picked up a marker pen to make notes on the things they still needed to investigate.

She wanted to put the various events in order with a timeline. Using the bottom section of the board, she drew a long line from one end to the other. Her first note on the far left was to detail the completion of the industrial units in July 1983. There was something about that place that kept cropping up. Levin's van caught on CCTV, not to mention the person who cut the metal to cover the well, could have been from Lux Engineering.

The next note on the timeline was for the Marshalls' well drying up. She didn't have a date for this but knew it was before it was covered up. A few inches along the timeline, she marked a line for August 20th 1988, the day Daniel went missing.

Lucy knew from Redland that CCTV had been installed at the industrial estate in September of the same year, supposedly with Levin's van being captured in October. Levin himself had been caught and charged in December and interviewed in April the following year about Daniel's disappearance. No joy from Levin about Daniel. Seven years later, Levin is killed in prison by another inmate. Daniel's case was then reviewed a year later, and DNA was taken from the parents. Then the Marshalls sold the farm in 2009 to the Carters.

Calls made to the council about GCNs on site, survey done, calls to the ecologist during the survey. The last note to add was the discovery of Daniel's body in October 2019. She stood back to admire her work as she capped her pen.

Lucy was just about to look up the local nature group to get the details of members or contacts when a voice behind her made her jump.

"I see you've found the board," Tanner said from the doorway.

"Yeah. Thanks for setting it up."

"No problem. Before I start digging in the archives, I thought you should know Marshall's niece got back to me yesterday from New Zealand."

"About the wedding?" Lucy asked.

"Yeah," Tanner said as he rummaged around in the paperwork on his desk. "So, it was the sister's second marriage after divorcing in 1981. Married a Paul Black on August twentieth, 1988 in Stratford."

"Okay." Lucy uncapped her marker pen.

"Black's daughter is from a previous marriage; she was fourteen at the time and remembers the Marshalls staying over in the hotel on the night of the wedding. It was a bit of a standing joke that they never left the farm. She sent over a photo of them at the wedding."

"Excellent." It confirmed Tommy's story, but not necessarily his innocence. He could have come back home, discovered Daniel on the farm, had an altercation and dumped him in the well. She added a note next to Daniel's disappearance that the Marshalls were at a wedding in Stratford and returned the next day.

"Thanks, Andy." She hated to say it, but Andy Tanner was proving his worth on this case. "Do you want to divide up the residents? You take the left side of the road and I'll cover the right, as I've already made a start."

"Uh yeah. But I thought I was strictly paperwork."

"Well." Lucy perched on the end of her desk. "Barrel wants to get a shift on with this one. So, the sooner we get a full picture of the situation, the better." Or the sooner they can bury it, she thought, if Barrel's words were anything to go by. She'd need more leverage if she was going to keep the case open. "You can even take your girlfriend if you like."

Andy glared at her. "Don't you bloody start."

Lucy parked up outside Barney Dunderdale's home, she hoped her visit would be more fruitful than her conversation with Stuart Francis from the Kingsford Nature Group. Francis was unable to offer any insight as to who if anyone from the group would have made the calls to the ecologist. Unfortunately the nature group is not a formal one, with people turning up to volunteer on the day. All she could do was request a list of people that had turned up in the last three months.

She knocked on Barney Dunderdale's ultra-modern, hardwood, fashionably wide front door. The SUV in the driveway gave her hope she'd caught someone in, although it took a while for anyone to get to the door. The façade of his nineteen thirties house had also been extensively modernised making it inconsistent with the other houses on the street.

"Mr Barney Dunderdale?" Lucy directed her question to the man as he opened the door, offering her credentials. He was a thickly built man, dark hair and stubble framing his square face "I'm DS Fuller." Before she could continue her introduction, he cut her off.

Dunderdales lip curled. "I wondered how long it would take for you to get around to me." He walked away from the front door, back into the depths of his home. The frustrated tone of his reply was unmistakeable. Regardless, she followed him inside, closing the door behind her. "You've spoken to your parents?" she asked, finding him in the kitchen at the back of the house. The large space was a work in progress, the extension on one side was empty with only bare plaster on the walls. He scowled at her as she stood in what remained of the small kitchen.

Dunderdale finally stepped back leaning against the sink unit. "Saw it on the bloody news."

Shit. "I'm sorry. We tried to contact you. Your father said you were away. He said he would inform you."

"You need to make this quick. I don't want you here when my wife gets back. She's … fragile," he finally said, as if searching for the right descriptor.

What was it with people wanting everything quick and tied up lately? Lucy hid her annoyance, nodding. "Of course, this won't take long."

Barney Dunderdale picked up his mug and stared at her. He certainly wasn't shy in his hostility towards the police.

"Last time they spent more time searching our house and interviewing my parents than actually looking for Dan."

Open-door searches were standard practice and often invasive for family members that have already conducted their own search. What they generally want is action, boots-on-the-ground searching.

"I'm sorry you feel you were let down by the police, Mr Dunderdale," she conceded. "Things have changed a lot since then. We have new methods and protocols."

Dunderdale said nothing, just stared back at her.

"We're re-interviewing the residents from Compton Way. You were out most of the day with your father at a –"

"Judo competition. We got back home around four." Dunderdale put his mug down heavily on the side then edged it slowly to the front of the worktop, leaving the handle hanging over the edge. Was he toying with the idea of it falling off? It made Lucy feel uneasy. Her eyes locked on the mug, willing it to stay upright as Barney continued.

"The police were already there searching the place. Mum was ..." He shook his head, unable or unwilling to meet her gaze, but there was barely a hint of emotion in his words. He seemed oddly cold considering the scene he was trying to paint for her. Had the loss of Daniel done that to him? From the kid's shoes and coats she'd seen on her way in, he was a family man now. Maybe he was scared it would happen again.

"You still think that paedo took him?" he asked, with a grimace, as if he'd stood on a Lego brick with bare feet. He was going right for the jugular.

"David Levin," she clarified, careful not to answer his question.

"No way he would have gone off with him. That copper was useless, didn't have a fucking clue."

She resisted the urge to agree with Dunderdale, despite wanting to. In fact, before she could say anything else, the front door opened behind her, followed by a hail of footsteps and voices. Lucy closed her notebook, taking her cue to leave, although she hadn't really asked any questions yet.

Dunderdale stepped past her into the hallway. Taking the opportunity, she pushed the mug to the back of the worktop. Hushed voices echoed down beyond the kitchen, telling whoever had entered that he was dealing with something and needed to be left alone for a while. A door closed somewhere before he returned to the kitchen. So much for not having time for her.

"That farm where you found him, on the outskirts isn't it?" Dunderdale asked as he moved across the kitchen to lean back against the worktop next to the sink.

"Yes, about seven miles from where you lived."

"He would never have gone that far from home; we didn't even know about that place. We went out and about on our bikes sometimes but never that far away."

"Was his bike missing?" She hadn't been able to find any record of it in the files so far.

Dunderdale frowned. "No. It was still in the garage next to mine."

Another mystery solved. "You were close with your brother, spent a lot of time together." It was more of a statement than a question.

"Yeah, I guess. There were a few of us that hung out."

That confirmed Johanna Hale's account of her time on Compton Way. "Were you aware of anything bothering Daniel in the weeks leading up to his disappearance?"

"No, not really." Dunderdale looked at the floor. "He was meant to come with us to the competition, but he changed his mind on the Saturday morning. He gave me some sob story about belly ache. I didn't really believe him."

"He usually went with you?" Lucy queried; this was not in the files.

"He went the previous time, but I don't know; he was probably bored or something." Dunderdale's focus returned to the floor. "I don't know," he shook his head for a moment "he could be really moody sometimes when he put his mind to it. Mum always let *him* get away with it."

Difficult to compete with a dead brother. *Did Daniel have something else planned for that day?* "And that was the last time you saw him?" It was a shitty question, but she needed to ask it, if only to register his reaction to the question. She made a note to call to PC Jackson, the FLO assigned to the Dunderdale's. She needed to know if Daniel had been ill or feigning illness before he went missing.

Dunderdale nodded.

Lucy pressed on. "You don't remember anyone hanging around during the summer holidays that didn't fit in?"

Dunderdale shrugged. "No."

Lucy remembered Barrel's idea about the industrial estate as the place Daniel could have met his abductor. "What about the industrial estate at the bottom; did you spend much time down there?"

Dunderdale sighed. "It was the summer holidays; we were everywhere."

Lucy tried again. "But you don't remember anyone hanging around down there?"

"No." Dunderdale folded his arms. "I think that's enough now, don't you?"

"Of course, Mr Dunderdale. Thank you for your time." Lucy put her notebook back in her pocket. "I'm very sorry for your loss."

She turned, leading the way down the hallway to the front door and stepped outside. The door was closed sharply behind her, but she didn't take it personally. She glanced back at the house as she walked down the drive, a blonde woman stood at the window clutching a young child to her chest watching her leave.

Johanna Hale blew out a breath as she dialled her parents' number; it had been two days since the press conference. By now, her mother would have the whole story, including the inside leg measurement of every possible suspect. Her father had already left a message on her answer machine, tipping her guilt over the edge.

"Hello."

To her surprise, it was her father that picked up the phone.

"Hey, Dad, how are you?"

"Good, good. How're you doing? I take it you've heard about the Dunderdale boy."

"I have. Saw it on the news. Already had the police round asking questions." An image of DS Fuller flashed through her mind.

"Really? Oh, I've got to go. I've got a curry on the stove. Your mother's here. I'll put her on."

Her mother rarely let him loose in the kitchen. She must have been in a weakened state of some kind.

There was a crackle down the phone as it was passed around, and then her mother's voice echoed down the phone. "Hello?"

"Hi, Mum, how are you?"

"Johanna? I thought it was your brother calling about the grand-children. So, how are you?"

"I'm ... good," she decided there was no need to mention her recent relationship failure just yet. "I was thinking of coming for a visit tomorrow, maybe stay around for a few days." Not that it mattered to them. She always stayed at the hotel in town. The spare room in their house was the size of a cupboard and fully stuffed with her mother's hobby crap. She considered herself too old to sleep on the sofa, especially as she planned to stay a while. It would however give her the opportunity to dig through whatever remnants they still had from her childhood, she was sure they still had several boxes packed up in storage somewhere. She'd already arranged with work to take the time off but would, of course, be on the end of a phone or computer if needed.

"Oh, yes, that sounds great. Your father would love that."

Dad would love that! Jesus! Johanna ignored the barb. This was the other reason she didn't visit much. She wasn't sure if anyone else saw it, but it was painfully obvious to her; she'd never had the courage to ask her mother just why she insisted on keeping her at arm's length all the time.

"You've heard about Daniel. I've asked the vicar if he'll do a service on Sunday for him. You'll have to come to that."

"Uh, sure." Johanna hadn't set foot in a church since her school carol services, apart from her brother's wedding – she'd never felt a pull towards religion of any kind – but since her parents had moved back to Kingsford, her mother had become obsessed with the church, filling up her time organising fundraisers and community groups.

"When will you be here?"

"Oh, err, in the afternoon, I guess. I'll check in with work before heading over," Johanna lied, delaying the inevitable.

CHAPTER 11

LUCY PULLED over to the side of the road, accepting the call on her mobile as she turned off the engine. The family liaison officer PC Jackson was calling, she'd left a message earlier for him to call with an update. "Fuller."

"Sarge, you wanted an update."

"What have you got." She asked hopefully.

"Not that much to report. I did speak to Janet about Daniel's so-called illness."

"Okay."

"She says he was quiet for a couple of days before he went missing-."

She jumped in before Jackson had a chance to finish. "Do they know why?"

"At the time they thought it was just back to school blues, I don't know about now she was a bit cagey. I asked about the judo competition too?"

"And?"

"She said Barney could be a bit over zealous at times but there was never any malice in what he did. Daniel always preferred to stay in the background."

"Okay. Thanks, keep a record and let me know if anything else comes up."

"Yes, Sarge."

Lucy glanced back at the Hale house. She recalled the conversation she'd had with Johanna Hale a couple of days ago about her parents returning to the area after many years in ... where was it? She couldn't remember. If she was being honest with herself, there was only one thing on her mind, and that was seeing Johanna Hale again. She had been able to think of little else since they'd met, even though she spent just as much brain time scolding herself for it; witnesses and suspects were strictly off limits, no matter how unlikely they were to be involved in the case or how attractive they were. Considering Johanna's age at the time of the incident and her apparent solid alibi, it was unlikely that she was involved in Daniel's disappearance.

Lucy rested her head back in her seat as she rolled her eyes clearing her throat she focused on the Hales' home once more; it was a modest house, located a few minutes away from Compton Way in an affluent part of Kingsford. Lucy had to admit she was a little curious to meet the parents of Johanna Hale. She already knew from interviewing Simon Hale that he had a lot more contact with their parents than Johanna did, was he the favourite like Daniel Dunderdale? Is that why she preferred to stay at the hotel in town if she stayed over. On first impressions, Johanna appeared to be a level-headed woman but parents were enough to push the buttons of even the calmest of people. Still she couldn't imagine the same situation in her own family, considering her own mother's desire to live her life vicariously through her job as a police officer.

Lucy tried to clear her mind once again as she walked towards the house and knocked on the front door. A woman answered a few moments later. Her shoulder-length, greying hair was curled and coiffured into a delicate style, and Lucy could see a mild resemblance to her daughter, although the woman in front of her was slightly shorter than Johanna.

"Mrs Gillian Hale?" Lucy confirmed, offering her credentials. "I'm DS Fuller. Can I ask you a few questions about Daniel Dunderdale?"

"Uh, yes. Please come in," Gillian Hale said as she stood to one side to let her through.

Lucy smiled to try and reassure the woman, but she was as flustered as her daughter. Must run in the family.

"You're looking into it again, then?" Gillian said as she led the way through to the back of the house.

"Yes. The case has remained open the entire time, though."

They emerged in a bright kitchen overlooking a large, meticulously kept garden. Gillian took a seat at a small wooden table covered with piles of folded clothing and housewares. "Not that chap then, the one that died in prison?"

Lucy avoided the question. "We're just re-examining the case." She figured Gillian Hale was in the process of her weekly iron when she noticed the ironing board on the other side of the room. She pulled out her notebook but waited for Gillian to offer her a seat opposite before sitting down. Settling on the wooden chair, Lucy asked her first question.

"You were at home the day Daniel went missing?"

Gillian busied herself re-arranging a stack of ironing in front of her, offering a brief smile when her actions gave them a better view of each other.

Lucy was tempted to give her a hand as she waited for an answer while Gillian meticulously placed each item in a new pile, checking the folds and corners of each.

"Yes, I was decorating most of the day. Much easier when the kids are away on holiday. Fewer fingerprints to tidy up."

Lucy noticed the wobble in the woman's hands as she fiddled with the edge of a towel.

"I know it was a long time ago, Mrs Hale, but is there anything more you can tell me about the day Daniel Dunderdale went missing?"

Gillian Hale's previous statement in 1988 had been brief. She claimed to have come down with a migraine after painting interior and exterior woodwork all morning. Not all day, just the morning, Lucy recalled.

"Oh no, I don't think so. I-I don't remember much about it, to tell you the truth, until Janet ..." Gillian hesitated for a moment. "Daniel's mother came around asking if I'd seen him. I'd been having a lie down, headache. Fumes from the paint, I think."

"I see." Lucy had been expecting that answer. No-one she'd interviewed so far had exactly dazzled her with new information. She hoped Tanner was having better luck. She needed to ask different questions, make people think, jog memories. "And roughly what time would that have been?"

Gillian pulled her hands below the table. "Around lunchtime, maybe a little later."

"What was your impression of Daniel?" Lucy wanted another parent's view.

Gillian looked a little flustered by her question. "Well, he was, I don't know, quiet, I guess, compared to some of the others."

"Daniel played with your two children," Lucy stated, purposely not mentioning Johanna or Simon by name. She didn't want her to think she was digging into her family in particular.

Gillian nodded. "They were always out in the street or in the woods doing something."

Lucy allowed a small smile to cross her lips as she recalled Johanna's words about the gang of misfits. "Do you recall anything odd or out of place in the days leading up to the day Daniel went missing, or maybe after that Saturday? Anyone acting odd or out of character?"

"No." Gillian gently shook her head. "I don't think so. I mean a few people moved away obviously, but, no, nothing stands out."

"Okay." Lucy placed her card on the table. Then, convinced it would be lost in the neatly stacked ironing, she picked it up again and offered it across to Gillian Hale. "If you think of anything that might be relevant or remember anything, please don't hesitate to contact me."

"Okay." Gillian studied the card for a moment before getting up and attaching it to her noticeboard on the far wall.

Lucy double checked through her notes then asked, "Is your husband home, Mrs Hale?"

"Oh, yes. He's just in the garden. Do you want to talk to him, too?"

"If he's not too busy," she said, offering a smile. Taking the neat garden into account, one of them had to be green fingered.

"I'll just call him for you." Gillian briskly left the room via the back door.

"Thank you," Lucy called after her. She remained in the kitchen, her eyes scanning the room. Four small, framed embroidery samplers lined the main wall, delicately stitched with a biblical verse. The closest one to her displayed a short verse from Genesis framed by numerous varieties of herbs, each one distinctive and precisely detailed. Her focus then moved to the noticeboard on the far side of the room, with numerous fliers for services and events sticking out of it. The Hales were certainly in touch with their town. Lucy got to her feet to take a closer look. The board itself looked homemade, with criss-crossing elastic creating diamonds, securing the leaflets and business cards in place, including her own. There were several circulars for church events at St Peter's in Kingsford and poking out from behind a piece of blue paper calling for items for a bring-and-buy sale was a notice for the Kingsford Nature Group.

Lucy put her questions to David Hale but again there was nothing new to report. His visits to the Nature group were infrequent due to his commitments elsewhere.

As Johanna parked up next to her parent's driveway, there was an unfamiliar car parked outside her parents' house. She had already made a reservation at The Fox, a hotel on the main road out of town. This place had never been her home; she had never really felt welcome here. Her parents had only moved back to Kingsford three years ago, largely due to her brother still living in the area and having three children with his wife. Grandchildren: another black mark against her name in their eyes. It didn't matter to them that Steph had no interest in having children with her. A fact she was now grateful for considering how it had turned out now.

Her brother, Simon, had been an unlikely candidate for marriage, at least that's what he told them all frequently as a teenager, yet he was the first to tie the knot and settle down. She saw him only a couple of times a year now, along with her parents. They had grown apart quite quickly when they both left home, focussing on their own lives, establishing themselves in the world: Johanna in graphic design and Simon in construction; not the hands-on work their father did, but white-collar management.

Johanna plucked the flowers from the passenger footwell before she stepped out of her car. Walking towards the front door, she remembered she didn't even have a key. She would have to knock to gain entry. Except, on this occasion, she didn't have to. It opened as she approached the short flight of steps that led to the door. Her parents had never rushed out to greet her before. Maybe the news of Dan had made them more curious as to their visitors. Johanna held the flowers aloft ready to greet her mother.

"DS Fuller!" Johanna said, trying to hide her surprise as she eyed the woman over the top of the flowers. All she could think about was how much she'd babbled on during their last meeting, and the embarrassment crept up her throat, paralysing her tongue.

"Miss Hale." The way she said her formal name made Johanna shiver. "For me?" she said with a nod towards the flowers, a grin plastered across her face. Her eyes were more blue than grey today, Johanna noted silently.

"Johanna?" She heard the surprise in her mother's voice. "This is a surprise. Are you on your own?"

Johanna looked over to see her mother hovering in the doorway. Obviously not a 'lovely surprise', which was her usual phrase. Surely her mother had been expecting her after their conversation yesterday.

Johanna looked back at DS Fuller, ignoring her mother's question. "Any news on the case?" she asked hopefully.

"Still gathering information," Fuller said, shutting down her line of questioning. "Just visiting?"

Why did she want to know? Was she a suspect? Or did she feel it too?

"Err, yeah, for a few days." Johanna fumbled over her words. "Maybe longer." In truth, she hadn't made any concrete plans. For once, she was playing it by ear.

Detective Fuller's eyes seemed to sparkle at her reply. "Maybe I'll see you around," she said. Her voice was low, preventing anyone else from hearing.

Johanna half smiled at that thought, her stomach fizzing as she watched DS Fuller swagger away to her car, and then she was gone, leaving Johanna alone with her mother. She took a second to clear her mind before approaching her.

"Hi, Mum," she said, but her voice didn't quite sound itself yet. "How are you?" She handed her the flowers. "Where's Dad?"

"These are lovely ... He's in the garden. No, err, no-one with you?"

"Nope, just me." Johanna moved past her, allowing her mother to shut the door. She had never liked Steph. She hadn't said it outright, but she had dropped enough hints over the last few years.

Her mother continued to coo over the flowers – did nobody else ever buy her flowers? – and Johanna felt a pang of guilt for her continued absence as she entered the kitchen avoiding the ironing board and laundry basket on the side.

"Was she asking questions about Dan?" Johanna asked, even though she already knew the answer.

"So sad, but at least he can be laid to rest now." Her mother's voice held a sombre tone.

A *mother's response*, Johanna thought. Not that she would know. "It's like they think one of us did it," she replied as her mother filled a vase for the flowers.

"Look at the mess your father's made, as if I don't have enough to do."

Johanna glanced around, looking for the object of her mother's annoyance in the spotless kitchen. Finally, she saw the trail of mud on the floor leading to the back door.

"I'll make some tea. Your father will want cake, of course ... I made a fruit cake the other day if you want a slice."

Johanna decided not to repeat her ignored statement. "No, thank you." She didn't like fruit cake, never had. At Christmas time, she would peel off the marzipan and icing, leaving the fruit sponge behind. "What are these?" She asked fiddling with the corner of a neat pile of what looked like ledgers poking out from under the stack of washing.

Her mother glanced up from cutting the cake. "Oh, just a bit of paperwork I wanted to finish for next week."

"Paperwork for who? Have you gone back to work?" Her mother had been retired for the last three years or so, if they had money worries why hadn't they said anything.

"Reed and Whittaker." Her mother appeared over her shoulder swiping the books away from her prying eyes, clutching them to her chest.

Reed and Whittaker. Johanna's mind was blank she hardly kept up with local businesses. Finally her mother gave in to her questioning look as the kettle clicked off.

"The solicitors on the high street. I just do a bit of accounting and filing, it's just a few hours a week.

"If you need money I can help-."

"It's not always about money." Her mother snapped as she placed the books on the worktop.

"I'll take Dad his tea," she said, hoping to escape anymore of her mother's wrath.

She found her father at the bottom of the garden, finishing off a dwarf wall that enclosed a small flowerbed, mirroring a second one on the opposite side of the lawn, a new edition since her last visit. He was using cement and a piece of upside-down guttering to mould a finishing course to the top of the brickwork.

"I thought I heard voices again," David Hale said as he turned, wiping his hands on his overalls.

"Topping out?" Johanna said, unsure of her wording. She'd seen a few episodes of *Grand Designs* but wasn't sure she'd used the correct phrasing.

He smiled back at her. "Sort of." He sounded pleased as he looked over his ingenuity. "Thanks. Police were here earlier," he announced as he took the tea from her.

"I know. I saw them leave," Johanna said, knowing full well it was an individual not an entire force. In this case, it was an individual she was developing an interest in. She drifted off into thoughts of DS Fuller, and her penetrating, blue-grey eyes that seemed to change colour each time they met. A shiver ran through her body at the thought of getting to know her.

"Is that cake for me?" Her father's voce broke through her thoughts. "I'm sure she's trying to fatten me up for something. You're cold. Go back inside. I'll be in after I've tidied up."

She smiled as she handed him the plate. "Mum just told me about her job."

"Oh." Her father said between bites.

"If it's about money, I can help." She didn't fear her father's reply.

Her father's frown quickly turned into a smile. "It's not, but thanks for the offer. More about boredom I think."

Really. "I thought the church and environmental thing was meant to solve that."

"Well, strike me down but I don't think the church was enough for your mother." Her father looked to the heavens for a long moment before glancing back at her. "Phew."

Johanna chuckled. "You shouldn't push your luck, one day you might not be so lucky."

"You mean if your mother overheard me."

His whispered words brought an instant smile to her face. "Exactly." She turned on her heel and returned to the kitchen, where she found her mother, still ironing. Gillian Hale was a firm believer in ironing every item, even socks and bras. Johanna glanced down at the floor, noticing it was spotless once again.

"Will you stay for dinner?" Her mother asked as she forced the iron into all the nooks and crannies of a black sports sock. Her father's, she imagined. He'd never been particularly sporty, but like most people, it didn't prevent him from wearing the clothing.

"Of course," she replied.

"You're staying for the service, at the church on Sunday?"

"Are they having a funeral already?" Johanna queried, confused.

"No, no, it's just a service. I asked the vicar to do it as a mark of respect for the family, give the whole town the opportunity to pay their respects. It really shook the place up when it happened, you know."

Her mother almost sounded offended at her response, as if everyone had suffered equally, but they hadn't, had they.

"I know." Johanna leaned against the kitchen cabinets. "Of course, I'll be there."

"Good. Simon can't make it, so it's good that you'll be there."

Great. There's nothing like feeling valued. How was it that Simon was always allowed to get out of things but she wasn't? Grandchildren seemed to go a long way in placating Gillian Hale.

"How's Stephanie?" her mother asked, as she paired up socks into a neat pile.

There it was, the innocent enquiry. Johanna didn't answer straight away, unsure what to share and what to keep to herself, and then she heard herself blurting, "We broke up!"

Her mother looked up, meeting her gaze, and said, "Oh Johanna, I'm sorry," but she didn't look sorry. "Maybe it's for the best," she added and turned to face her daughter, placing her hands flat on the ironing board. And then, with a breezy smile, she said, "Lamb curry alright, tonight?"

"Sounds good," Johanna confirmed. And that was it; cosy talk over. She needed to change the subject before she could say something she might regret, she settled on one of her reasons for the visit. "Do you still have any of my old stuff from before?" Johanna didn't quite know how else to phrase it. She wasn't even sure what she was expecting to find: more old photos maybe of the friends she had back then. She knew some of the stuff had been packed up when they left Compton Way, when it fell out of favour or just didn't fit anymore.

"Before?" Gillian repeated, with a frown, as she picked up the iron again. "When you were at home, you mean?"

"Yeah, when we were kids," she said, referring to Simon too.

"The movers put most of the stuff we didn't need in the storage attic above the garage. There are probably some crates in there. Ask your father; he'd know better than I would."

Sounds about right: resigned to the garage.

"Crates?" Johanna questioned as she washed out her mug.

"You know, those wooden box things your father insists on using."

Johanna nodded. Tea chests. Ever the practical man, she bet some of them dated back to their first house.

Slipping out the front door, Johanna walked around to the sizable and very well-organised double garage. She had no intention of asking her father for his assistance; she didn't want anyone looking over her shoulder. She knew the garage was already open, she had noticed it on her arrival, and slipped in unnoticed. As her mother had told her, the pitched roof provided sizable storage space, and a ladder fixed to one side afforded her access to the space above where she spotted a group of tea chests, each with newspaper taped over them to preserve their contents. Simon's name had been scrawled in black marker pen diagonally across the side of one of them. Turning the others, she saw her own name on two.

The brown tape had lost some of its stickiness over the years; yet undisturbed, it probably would have stayed in place for several more years. She ran her hand along the surface of the newspaper until she found the end of the tape, scratching at it with her fingernail she slowly peeled it away trying not to tear the paper too much. Inside was precious cargo, memories that could never be replaced. Removing the newspaper, the chest was crammed with colourful boxes of different sizes, most of which she recognised as familiar childhood games. The Spirograph looked worn, the sides of the box repaired with tape on more than one occasion, and an elastic band held the lid in place. She'd lost interest after one of the main cogs went missing. It became a bit of a lame duck after that; just taking up space in her wardrobe. She never did find out what happened to it. Simon was her first guess but he denied all knowledge at the time. It held fond memories of the times she'd spent with her neighbour Amy Bell, she put it to one side, already planning to take a couple of things with her. As she shuffled through more of the games, a black plastic storage box was revealed below. She recognised it immediately. Pulling it out of the chest, she pressed the release button and lifted the handle to reveal the row of cassette tapes hidden inside. Johanna wasn't surprised to see it was full, mostly a selection of compilation tapes she recognised from the nineties. At one end, three recordable tapes caught her eye, their white spines standing out in the gloom. She looked more closely at their handwritten spines, unable to recognise the partly faded handwriting. She knew it wasn't hers. Pulling all three out, she smiled at the faded felt-tip decorations of flowers that made up one cover, a brown rabbit peeking around one edge on another, a particular trait of Amy's doodling. She tipped it towards the light at the end of the garage, allowing her to make out the pink lettering, *August 88*, the same month Dan disappeared. Johanna knew from memory it would be a snapshot into their lives. They often talked over the selection of their songs, while recording, with no thought that it would be preserved on tape in the process. The third tape had only colourful stripes on the cover, making it easier to select in a hurry, from what she could remember.

Johanna desperately wanted to hear what was on the tapes. Back then, she and Amy had made endless mixtapes cooped up in Amy's bedroom. Amy's dad let them use their double tape player. The Hale household didn't have one: a bit too modern for David Hale. Johanna really needed one now. A quick rummage through the rest of the box didn't produce one, which was ridiculous considering how many they had gone through as a household over the years. Instead, she found a small photo album, with each page holding two photos back-to-back. A quick scan brought back fuzzy seaside images taken with her 110 camera; she guessed these were the photos Simon had digitised for her. Closing it, she put it aside for further inspection later and returned to her search, rummaged through the closest box with Simon's name on it, and eventually found an old, bright yellow Walkman, minus the earphones. She vaguely remembered him having it as a teenager. Heart pounding, she set it on top of the photo album and began throwing everything back in the chests. She then placed the newspaper carefully on top, confident her father would be along soon to seal in the past. Arms full, she descended the ladder to the garage below.

Her father was a methodical man when it came to storage, everything had its place, and she found the right drawer on the second attempt, containing every shaped battery under the sun. Selecting two AAs from an open packet, she slipped off the battery cover, pushed the batteries home and resealed it. But before she could do anything with it, her mother's shrill voice made her jump out of her skin.

"Dinners ready!"

"Okay!" Johanna quickly shouted back, hoping her rapid response would prevent her mother from coming to find her. She slotted the August mixtape into place ready for later, quickly picked up the Spiro-graph box and photo albums and took them to her car, placing them in the footwell, before going back into the house.

CHAPTER 12

JOHANNA HALE, May 1988

The momentum of the slope pushed Johanna down the hill, through the woodland, skipping over surfacing roots and lumps of dead wood that littered the ground as she moved. Footsteps thumped all around her as the limbs of her friends blurred in her peripheral vision. Amy's blonde hair floated in the air ahead of her, the light beyond the woods illuminating each golden strand, and Johanna was blinded for a moment.

"Don't follow me stupid, he's after you." Amy shouted behind her.

She trained her eyes back on the floor to secure her footing. She knew she'd thrown the last stone, and she knew the man has seen her do it. She was desperate to get away, even though it hadn't had any effect on their combined actions. The pots had all been smashed by that time, at least one by her, she was sure of it. But the man had spotted her as he came around the side of his house. She hadn't seen him to start with, her focus trained on her task, but he'd seen her alright.

"Come back here you little…!"

His angry words still echoed in her ears.

They fled like ants escaping a fire as they left the shelter of the woodland, scattering in all directions, some taking a sharp right away from their homes in favour of going deeper into the estate, while Johanna slid down the nearest slope on the left. Once at the bottom, she ducked inside the first dark space in the hope the man wouldn't spot where she'd gone. Barney and Dan's garage door was open, offering her the perfect opportunity. She quietly stepped over garden equipment and toys, trying not to touch anything as she edged further back into the darkness. She tried to catch her breath, ducking down as the mumbling of voices came closer. How had the old man got there so quickly, and who was he talking to? She wanted to look, but a cold fear gripped at her insides as footsteps approached outside the garage. Getting on her hands and knees, she peeked around the side of the lawnmower. Legs were all she could see: one big pair wearing trousers and one small pair wearing shorts. She pulled back immediately, tucking herself behind the edge of a discarded kitchen unit.

"She's in here!" a voice shouted.

Johanna's eyes widened. Was that Dan's scared voice? She waited a moment, hoping they were talking about another girl, or maybe someone would step in and save her. But they didn't. Eventually, she risked peeking over the top of the unit and saw Dan in the driveway, and he was pointing right at her. She blinked, unable to speak. A large shadow appeared at the mouth of the garage. She had nowhere to go.

"Come on, out you come!" The man's voice was firm almost aggressive.

Johanna reluctantly stood in the confined space. Her skin was hot and her legs shook as she stood there. Where was a parent when you needed one? All she could do was hope that someone, anyone, would step in and shoo this man away. She vowed to never throw another stone ever again if he went away right now.

His eyes were fixed on her as she climbed over Dan's bike. Unfocused, she caught her foot on a stray pedal and nearly fell over then reached out her hand to the wall to steady herself, the rough, grey surface pressed against her palm. Sweat trickled down her back as she made her way out of the garage into the daylight.

The man was tall, older than her father, with wispy eyebrows peeking over the top of his thick glasses. His large eyes glared down at her.

"Where do you live?" he asked, his voice still firm.

Johanna caught Dan's eye. He looked as wide eyed as she felt. He'd done this. He'd dropped her in it, was he was so scared of being caught himself he'd made sure he wouldn't be? Her hands shook as she froze to the spot. She couldn't believe he'd blabbed. Unable to speak, she numbly pointed in the direction of her house. Her mother was going to kill her.

"Come on, then," the man replied in a frustrated tone as he began walking.

He swung his arms in time with his gangly legs, each step made her feel sick with worry as they got closer to her driveway. Johanna trailed behind, raking through her mind for what to say to explain the situation to her parents. They would be so disappointed in her. She was the older sibling; she wasn't meant to get caught.

As Johanna closed in on her house, she could see movement in the open garage. She prayed for her father's steadying presence, knowing her mother would be far less understanding.

The man nodded for her to take the lead. She slipped down the side of the path, trying to avoid touching her father's car. A scraping sound in the garage urged her on as she quickened her pace, hoping to leave the man behind. She blinked with relief at the sight of her father, his back to the door as she entered the garage, the florescent light above yellowing the contents, including her father.

He turned at her footsteps and said, "Hello. What have you been doing up there? I thought you were playing swing ball with Amy."

He must have heard them flee the woods. Struck dumb, Johanna rushed to him, almost tucking herself behind the shield of her father. She didn't reply.

He looked down at her, brow furrowed, until he noticed the shadow at the opening of the garage behind them. He glanced up at the man, frowning at his presence.

"I didn't do it, Dad," she pleaded, tightening her grip around him.

Her father looked down at her face in the shadow, but his frown was still visible. "Didn't do what?"

"I'm sorry, Dad." The sting of tears filled her eyes.

"Why don't you go inside and let me talk to this man."

Johanna reluctantly let go of her father, but she had to make her way towards the man to get away from him. She moved to the very edge of the garage entrance to avoid him as she ran around to the back of the house.

The door to her bedroom slammed against the wardrobe as her mother stormed into her bedroom. "Did you break that man's pots?" She yelled as soon as she laid eyes on her.

Tears immediately bulged in her eyes as Johanna's frame drooped, she sat crossed legged on the floor, her back against her bed. Her mother had barely looked up as she ran through the kitchen to hide in her room five minutes earlier. Was it too much to hope for that her father would keep this little indiscretion to himself. She sank down lower onto the floor, she wanted the thick pile carpet to swallow her whole. Her gaze travelled to the underside of her bed; she should climb under, anything to escape her mother's disappointment.

"I-I..." She glanced at her mother. What could she say, she didn't want to implicate the others. She decided that saying nothing was her best option. She looked away escaping her mother's venomous scowl.

"Well, you're bloody paying for them, I can tell you that for nothing."

"What!" She snapped her head back up. Her mother's hands gripped at her hips as she stared down at her daring her to respond. How could she possibly explain the unfairness of this whole situation.

"Out of your own pocket money." Her mother continued.

"But mum-."

"I don't want to hear it Johanna. What the hell do you think you're doing smashing someone else's plant pots. And don't even think about playing out with your friends for at least two weeks."

Two weeks. Johanna's mouth gaped, but with the summer just around the corner she dare not argue the point. Heavy footsteps came up the stairs, she desperately needed someone on her side to strike a balance here.

Her father ambled along the landing towards her room. He bobbed up and down behind her mother's rigid frame.

"Thank you very much for thoroughly embarrassing us, no doubt everyone on the street will know now." Her mother finally took a breath. "Your father's going to take you to the garden centre to buy them, then you can take them round and apologise to Mr Mercer."

"We'll go tomorrow." Her father said, his voice noticeably calmer.

"Christ Johanna!" Her mother threw her hands into the air. "You're meant to be setting an example to your brother."

Johanna looked up to see her father hovering in the doorway for a moment as her mother stomped back down the stairs.

He came in and sat on the edge of her bed, resting a hand on her back. He gave it a gentle rub before squeezing her shoulder briefly. "I'm guessing you weren't the only one throwing stones."

Johanna focused on the long threads of the carpet, pulling at them as she shook her head in reply. What had that man told her father, that she was the only one stupid enough to get caught. This was all that creep Dan's fault.

"Don't worry, I'll talk to her."

Her father's words interrupted her thoughts, the tears began to flow freely now.

He got to his feet stepping towards the doorway turning as he reached the door. "Next time, just don't get caught." He winked as he turned to leave.

Johanna carried the heavy stack of new pots in her hands as she walked towards the front door at the end of the path. She snuck a look at her father, waiting in the car behind her, and saw his nod towards the man's house. The pots vibrated as they rubbed against each other, setting her on edge. It felt as if they were going to break apart in her hands.

She inwardly groaned at the thought of being cooped up every evening and weekend for the next two weeks. At least she had the summer to look forward to.

Johanna stared at the bare patch of ground that had previously been occupied by the plant pots: pots they had all smashed, not just her. She was annoyed at the injustice at being the only one caught all over again.

Two steps led up to the front door. With her hands full, she had to hug the large pots to her chest to free up a hand and stretch to press the doorbell. The sing-song tune played as she waited. She'd been dreading this moment for days, ever since her mother had doled out the punishment. Painful as it was parting with half of the money in her money box, that wasn't the worst part. By far the worst was having to face the man again and apologising to his face. Her mother had even made her buy a card and write it down too, for good measure.

She felt the fear rise inside of her as she saw movement through the patterned glass at the side of the door. She clung to the thought that it would all be over soon. But it wasn't going to be soon enough for her.

The front door swung open with a flourish. It took the man a moment to look down from his elevated position and find her. His checked shirt was partly untucked from his trousers, a layer of stubble across his face.

"Hello, again." His voice still held the firmness of a teacher. "Johanna, isn't it?" he said with a slight frown.

She nodded, standing there dumbstruck. She couldn't remember his name. Her father had just told her, but it was gone as a fresh wave of panic swept over her.

"I'm-sorry-I-broke-your-pots." She fought to get the words out without blubbing, making them come out in a blur. "I got you these." She looked down at the pots, determined she wouldn't let him see her crying.

"I see that," the man replied, a small smile on his face. "Are they heavy? Shall I take them from you?"

"Yes." Johanna stretched out her wobbly arms, offering the pots to him. The card was sticking out between two of the pot trapped between the rims. Her arms felt heavy, despite not carrying the pots anymore.

He placed them on the floor inside his house. Standing upright, he looked back at her. "Now, you won't be throwing stones again will you, young lady?"

"No." She shook her head with gritted teeth at the man's tone.

"It's a very costly business, isn't it."

Johanna nodded her head, more concerned with her curbed freedom than the money.

"I managed to rescue most of the plants, so tomorrow I'll plant them back up ready for the summer."

Johanna rubbed the dust from her hands onto her jeans.

"My wife always likes a bit of colour around the front of the house."

Johanna just stood there, unsure of what to say. She'd delivered her apology, now she had nothing left to offer. Suddenly, something came to her.

"My dad does all the gardening at our house too."

The man smiled at her reply. "Does he indeed?"

She nodded with nothing more to say.

"Well, thank you, Johanna." He looked up, waving his hand in the air at someone.

She turned around to see it was her father, still sat in his car.

"Your dad's waiting for you." He slid the pots away from the doorway with his foot. "Now, be good." He wagged his bony finger at her before gripping the edge of the door.

"Bye," Johanna said, turning around before the front door was shut. She rushed back down the path towards her father's waiting car, relieved that he was there, even though she knew he wouldn't let her off the hook.

"All done?" he asked as she opened the passenger door.

Johanna nodded and climbed in, her focus on her hands clasped in her lap.

"Good." Her father's hand lightly gripped her shoulder. "I'm proud of you. You did the right thing."

Johanna couldn't meet his gaze, determined to get her own back on Dan for dobbing her in. She was convinced if they'd all stuck together, she would have been spared this shameful episode.

Her father started the car and drove off in the direction of home; no doubt satisfied he had done his duty but all she could think about was revenge. Fingers gripped at each other as they rested secreted between her thighs, her toes doubled over with rage in her shoes as she tried to release the tension in her body.

It seemed to take only a few minutes for them to end up at the top of the hill on Compton Way. Someone was playing football on the street, Simon waved to her father with his free hand while the other gripped the football as he ran to jump on the pavement. Johanna looked to see who he was playing with, she gaped with anger as she spotted Dan stood further down the road. How could Simon betray her like that.

Dan moved to step on the pavement as her father drove past him, she glared at him burning holes into his scull as their eyes met, she felt a bubble of victory inside as Dan quickly looked away.

They came to a stop in the driveway, Johanna instinctively looked up at Amy's bedroom window as she took off her seatbelt. Was that why Dan had shopped her to keep Amy out of trouble? She slowly exited the car savouring the fresh air, knowing full well she wasn't allowed to play outside with her current curfew thanks to Dan. She moved towards the front of the car then realised she'd have to walk around the back of the vehicle as her father had parked so close to the garage again. Retracing her steps around the car, a familiar football came to stop at her feet, glaring at Dan then her brother she booted it as hard as she could down the hill knowing he would have to fetch it. Ignoring her brothers pleas she walked into her house. She needed to think of a way to really make Dan pay, she wanted him to suffer.

CHAPTER 13

JOHANNA GOT into her car and pushed her key into the ignition. She leaned across, opening the glove box, and quickly dug around for some earphones. Grateful when her fingers hooked onto a pair from her old mobile, she plugged them in, realising that she was probably breaking every common-sense rule by listening to earphones while driving, but she didn't care. She pushed the play button and jumped as Bros's 'I Owe You Nothing' blared in her ears.

"Fuck!" she shouted as she pressed the rewind button, just managing to stay in control of the car as she wrestled with the ancient technology. As she negotiated the familiar roads of her childhood home, the dusky light was waning as she neared The Fox hotel.

The tape clicked off as she pulled into the hotel carpark. She just hoped it hadn't drained the batteries too much.

Pressing the play button, a fuzziness resounded, the kind that vinyl aficionados lament over compared to the cleaner compact disc. Background mumbling and bashing about then gave way to the more recognisable squeaking of female voices, laughing, followed by a clattering and the first song: Bananarama's 'I want you back', a favourite of Johanna's at the time. It brought back fond memories of her and Amy jumping around on Amy's bed together.

In need of fresh air, Johanna got out of the car as the song ended abruptly. There was someone else there, in the background. A young boy's angry voice blared in her ears. It was over in a second. Was it Dan? It sounded like him. Why was he there? He sounded frantic. This was *their* thing, she and Amy. They'd shut themselves away for hours just the two of them. Johanna rewound it a short distance to try and make out what he was saying, but the words were muffled. He sounded upset more than angry. On second hearing, it sounded like it had been recorded over, cutting off the end of the song. It was just a snippet, a few seconds of Dan's voice somehow preserved on tape for thirty years.

More music immediately boomed in Johanna's ears as she wandered across the carpark towards the main entrance, facing out onto the main road. She vaguely recognised the song but not the artist, but the sounds barely registered; her mind was still reeling over hearing Dan's voice. Why was it on the tape at all? Was Amy secretly making tapes with him? He'd had a crush on Amy back then. Johanna didn't want to accept it any more now than she did all those years ago; Amy was *her* friend. She felt betrayed as she pictured them alone in Amy's bedroom where she'd spent so many hours making lists of their favourite songs to tape from the top forty charts every Sunday night.

Johanna felt her foot slip off the kerb, but it didn't register. She was so wrapped up in the sound of UB40's version of 'Breakfast in Bed'. Her eyes drifted closed for a second as she tried to recall the times Amy and Dan had been together. Was there a connection between them? Then the music changed again, briefly replaced by her own childlike voice in the background, followed by another song.

Johanna then heard someone call her name in the background, a female voice, older, her mother? It was muffled over the sound of Debbie Gibson's bouncy voice. Johanna's full name was used, which usually meant her mother wanted her to do something or she'd been caught doing something bad. Had her mother really come to fetch her from Amy's house? But it wasn't her mother ... it wasn't even on the tape ... It was ...

And then, before she had any idea what was happening, a loud rumble shook her whole body and she was slammed to the floor, with something landing on top of her, pushing the breath from her lungs as a thunderous horn filled her ears. She thought the blackness would swallow her whole, but just as quickly as it had invaded her senses, the noise dissipated, the weight on her slowly moved, and she realised it was another body. Her clenched eyes flickered open to see a shadowy profile looming over her, and panic climbed up her chest once more. She was about to cry out and struggled for freedom when a familiar voice broke through her terror.

"Johanna! Johanna! Are you okay?" DS Fuller quickly got to her feet and crouched next to her. Johanna could feel her eyes scanning her crumpled figure.

"I-I don't know-I think so," she mouthed, but she was struggling to catch her breath. The cold pavement pressing against her back sent a chill through her body. "What happened?" she asked as she cautiously sat up. "I'm sorry, I … I wasn't–." She did a mental inventory of her body, nothing seemed badly hurt except maybe her pride. "I'm okay."

"You were very nearly roadkill." Fuller's voice had a serious edge as she cut her off.

"What!" Her voice was barely recognisable. Had she really wandered into the road so recklessly? How could she be so distracted? The tape? She scanned the ground around her. The streetlight in the distance did little to illuminate the immediate area, which probably explained why the driver hadn't seen her, although she had been distracted and hadn't heard a horn blaring. And now, the paleness from the shock quickly reversed as embarrassment set into her face and neck. Did it really have to be Detective Fuller coming to her rescue?

"What are you looking for?" Fuller asked. Anger had turned to concern now.

"My Walkman," Johanna said, not wanting to elaborate.

"Walkman?" Fuller sounded incredulous. "I haven't seen one of those in a while, here." She edged behind her, reaching for something before presenting the yellow box she had found on the ground. "It's a bit scratched, I'm afraid."

"It's fine," Johanna said, taking it from her and wrapping the dangling headphones around the cassette player.

"What were you listening to?" Fuller's voice had returned to its usual timbre.

"An old mixtape." Johanna cringed, realising how stupid it sounded.

"Ooookay." Fuller elongated the word as her eyebrows flew up, which only made it worse. Johanna had planned to impress this woman at least a little on their next meeting after her previous babble-fest. Now, here she was, scrabbling around on the ground after stepping in front of a lorry. But Fuller obviously wasn't thrown by it, as she added, "I think a near-death experience deserves a drink, don't you?" and grinned widely.

"Definitely," Johanna replied, still shaky. She felt weak as Fuller gently pulled her to her feet. Dusting off the back of her jeans, she led the way into the bar entrance of The Fox. From the outside it had changed little since her last visit, still dark and a little dingy. She'd stayed here several times since her parents' return to the town, The Fox had been the largest hotel in the area for as long as she could remember, employing a glut of people, including her brother at one point when he was a student during summer holidays. Its location on the edge of town, along the main road that cut through the edge of Kingsford on the way to Bath, made it perfect for visitors to the area. A five-minute walk across the small humpback bridge over the canal would take them right into the centre of town. Inside, weirdly, the interior didn't feel dated; the dark, aged wood and faded walls seemed to have swung right back into timeless fashion.

Approaching the bar, Johanna caught the eye of the young barman.

"What can I get you?" she offered, "as you just risked your life to save mine."

"A hefty gin and tonic, I think," Fuller replied.

"Good choice." Johanna ordered two doubles, hoping it would calm the throbbing in her chest. Handing over the cash, she picked up both drinks and led the way to a table with comfy chairs. All that was missing was a warm open fire. She placed the Walkman on the table as she took a gulp from her drink to settle her nerves.

"Thanks." Fuller gestured with her glass as she sipped her own drink.

"You're welcome. Was that you calling my name?" Johanna asked, recalling the female voice. She had used her Christian name, which was informal for a detective if she was planning on interviewing her again.

Fuller carefully placed her drink down on the table before looking up at her. "You were wandering into the road ... I was trying to get your attention."

"I'm sorry ... Thank you ... I can't keep calling you DS Fuller after you just saved my life. What's your first name?"

Fuller studied her for a moment as if weighing up the possibilities. "Lucy."

Lucy Fuller. "Well, thank you, Lucy Fuller." Johanna raised her glass, clinking it gently with Lucy's. The yellow lighting in the bar seemed to bring out a slight green tint to the detective's eyes tonight.

"You're welcome." Lucy offered a wide smile. "Lucky I was passing."

"It certainly was." The slight crinkle around Lucy's eyes made Johanna's heart beat a little faster. "So ..." She played for time as she loosened her scarf, trying to regain a little of her composure. "How's the case going?" Johanna immediately held up her free hand. "Sorry, you probably can't tell me anything about it."

"Nope, sorry." Lucy smiled. "Have you acquired any cats yet?"

"Not as yet, but my mission has only just begun."

"So, what was on your mixtape?" Lucy asked before taking another sip of her drink.

"Ahh, well. I think you might be a bit too young to appreciate it," Johanna teased.

"Try me."

Johanna racked her brain, trying to think of the coolest song from her mixtape years. "INXS, 'Never Tear Us Apart'." A lie, and in truth, it wouldn't have been her choice anyway, more Amy's. She always had more sophisticated taste compared to Johanna. Amy had a thing for "bad boys", as she called them. It was guaranteed at least one of their songs would be on that tape.

"Not bad." Lucy looked a little impressed. "I thought you were going to say Debbie Gibson or something."

Johanna hoped the colour hadn't filled her cheeks once more. Debbie Gibson had been one of her first celebrity crushes. She took a drink from her glass, hoping to mitigate the need for a response.

Lucy's eyes widened in surprise. "Oh my God, you liked her." Lucy sounded like a schoolgirl acknowledging an infatuation.

"How do you even know who that is?" Johanna managed to get the words out, despite her acute embarrassment.

"I'm thirty-six, not six." Lucy grinned despite the harder tone that had crept into her words. "I had a cousin that was crazy about her when he was a kid, had her picture all over his bedroom walls." Her tone had softened once more. "I always thought it was a bit weird undressing in front of all those eyes looking back at him every night."

Johanna chuckled at her words. Lucy Fuller was fast becoming the most interesting person in this town. In fact, the most interesting person she'd met for some time.

"Amy and I used to make mixtapes in her bedroom, recording songs from the radio and other tapes."

"You were close, with Amy?" Lucy clarified.

What was she fishing for? Was this her interview technique? Save their life, put them at ease, then ask the real questions? "I thought she was my best friend at one point, but then she moved away." Johanna skirted over the hurt she'd felt all those years ago. It was long forgotten, or at least it had been.

"You didn't keep in touch?"

Johanna sighed. "She said she'd write to me, but she never did. I never heard anything from her again."

"How long did you live in Compton Way?"

Surely, she'd already found out this information. Johanna frowned slightly before answering, as if she was thinking back. "Oh, about five years in total. We moved to Harbour Close after that. Bit more up market: the next rung up the ladder, as they say."

"And before?"

What was this all about? "Before Compton, we lived in Prospect Place, just off Picture Hill."

"Picture Hill?" Lucy questioned, as she reached below the table to scratch her leg.

"I don't think that's its official name, but years ago there used to be a cinema at the top of the road, so it was forever called Picture Hill, according to my dad, that is."

Johanna took another swallow from her drink, noticing that Lucy had barely touched hers. Still on duty, she figured. Was she ever off-duty?

"I even remember going to look at our house on Compton Way before we moved in. It was a brand-new street. There wasn't even tarmac on the road or grass in the gardens, just kerb stones marking out boundaries."

"How old were you?" Lucy queried.

"About eight I think." Her mind flashed back to the street. "To be honest, I always thought it was a bit weird that someone just drove past and grabbed Dan from there."

"What do you mean?" Lucy asked as she reached below the table again.

"Well." The last thing she wanted was to patronise Lucy, but she was on a roll now. Damn her interview tactics. "I'm sure you've been there. Compton Way's at the far end of the estate, a dead end. It's not somewhere you just drive past. That's why we were all allowed to play out on the road so much; there was hardly any traffic."

Lucy propped her elbow on the table, resting her chin in her hand. "Okay." Using her other hand, she turned her glass around on the table.

"And anyone hanging about would have stood out; we would have all seen them," Johanna continued.

"But you were away at the time," Lucy replied.

"I know but …"

"What are you saying?" Lucy looked up, meeting her eyes.

"I don't know. Someone came through the woods maybe," she speculated as she realised that dismissing one possibility brought other scenarios into focus.

Lucy leant forward. "The woods at the top? Did that happen often?"

"Not that I can think of. There's another housing estate on the other side, but Dan did live right at the top of the street next to them." Her mind flashed back to the old man and the plant-pot incident.

"Or someone who lived on your street took him," Lucy offered, her face serious, clinical in her reply.

"Umm, there is that, of course," Johanna answered, but she was now distracted enough by Lucy's fidgeting to lean to one side and look at what was niggling her; she caught a flash of red as Lucy tried to push down her trouser leg. "You're bleeding." Johanna announced as if she was unaware.

"It's nothing." Lucy's tone was dismissive, self-conscious.

"Come with me," Johanna said calmly and tugged on Lucy's arm, leading the way to the toilets off the far corner of the room. The bright light was shocking as they entered the white-tiled room. Johanna pulled her over to the far wall, where there was a line of small, pink basins. She quickly washed her hands, catching Lucy's concerned look in the grubby mirror before wetting a clump of fresh tissue.

"Can you put your leg up here?" Johanna asked and tapped the edge of the sink with her empty hand.

"Honestly, its nothing. I can deal with it later."

Johanna ignored her statement, tapping the front of the sink again.

Reluctantly, Lucy complied. Resting her foot on the sink, she pulled up her trouser leg, revealing a grazed, bloody knee.

Johanna swallowed back her guilt as she spotted the gaping hole in Lucy's trousers, followed by Lucy's pale, toned leg. She'd been too shocked to even ask if her rescuer had been injured in the process. The wound was a blot on an otherwise perfect landscape; ragged edges brimmed with blood where the skin had been torn away.

"I'm sorry, I didn't realise—"

"It's fine, really," Lucy cut her off. "All in a day's work."

Johanna looked up to find Lucy was biting her lower lip as she watched her lame attempt at first aid. "Regular occurrence is it?" she asked as she held the back of Lucy's leg and dabbed at the wound. The warm skin was soft against her palm.

"No, thank God, or I'd run out of knees pretty quickly."

The guilt settled on Johanna's shoulders once more as she

continued to clean the wound. She needed to at least offer to compensate her for her losses.

"Ow!" Lucy flinched.

"Sorry." As Johanna continued wiping away the semi-congealed blood, she remembered the adage that you can tell a lot about a person from their footwear. Looking down, Lucy's reminded her of pixie boots, although they were more rounded in the toe. They were unfussy and practical. They suited Lucy Fuller perfectly.

Moving along the row of sinks, Johanna dropped the wet, bloodied tissue in the bin and looked up to see Lucy studying her in the mirror. "You'll need to put some antiseptic on it," she said and pulled out some fresh tissue from the dispenser to wipe away the moisture she'd created.

"I'll do it later. Thanks," Lucy smiled and dropped her foot back to the floor, re-adjusting her stance.

"I'm sorry about your trousers," Johanna added. "I'd be happy to buy you a replacement pair. It was my fault after all."

"Oh, don't worry about it. I've got plenty more." Lucy sucked in her bottom lip as her hand almost reached out between them. "You have some dirt on your face," she said, her voice just above a whisper as she pulled down the cuff of her jacket to brush it against the side of Johanna's cheek.

Johanna leaned into her touch before she could stop herself, as the cuff turned into a warm hand. She closed her eyes at the intimacy of the touch and imagined Lucy's soft lips pressed against hers. She parted her lips at that thought, releasing a small breath, and reached out her hand to touch the side of Lucy's body as her eyes flickered open. God, what the hell was wrong with her? She barely knew this woman. Now she was fantasizing about kissing her.

"I should ... get going," Lucy finally said, pulling back, breaking any contact between them.

Johanna's hand went to her mouth, as if to erase the last few seconds of desire she had felt for the woman in front of her. But there was something in Lucy's glowing blue eyes that indicated it wasn't all one sided.

The click-clacking of high heels heading in their direction seemed to bring Lucy to her senses as she turned to leave.

Johanna didn't get a chance to speak as the bathroom door slowly swung closed behind the retreating figure.

CHAPTER 14

JOHANNA STROLLED into the restaurant for breakfast with no real plans for the day beyond catching up on the work emails she'd ignored for the last few days, although there had been no phone calls, so she was sure there were no major issues to worry about. She eyed the colourful, healthy buffet, preferred by the business clientele at The Fox Hotel to the alternative full English, but her mind was largely occupied by the strange events with DS Fuller the previous evening. She still couldn't fully explain her actions. She was attracted to Lucy Fuller, of course, but she'd never been quite so forward with anyone quite like that before. She barely knew her after all.

She helped herself to a banana from the heaving bowl of fruit and made her way to the small bank of toasters, realising just how hungry she was. She wasn't usually much of a breakfast person – when she was at work, she was often too busy to bother with it – but since taking a back seat the last few days, she'd grown increasingly peckish in the mornings.

As she dropped in a slice of seeded bread, she scooped up some chilled butter packets and gripped them tightly, hoping to soften them a little as she waited for her toast to re-appear. She turned to scan the room, she was alone apart from an elderly couple on the far side near the windows. She nodded a brief good morning to the man, who smiled before returning to his breakfast. She glanced back at the toaster, hoping it wasn't burning, and her mind drifted back to the look on DS Fuller's face just before she made her brisk escape, but looking back on it now, she was convinced the attraction was mutual. The look in Lucy's blue eyes was unmistakable, at least she hoped it was.

The popping up of her toast made her jump. Taking a breath, she grabbed it, and the radiating heat forced her to drop it on a plate before heading for a table. Once seated, she buttered her toast, slicing her banana to sit on top. Footsteps headed her way as more diners entered the breakfast room. An involuntary grin took over her face as Lucy Fuller headed in her direction. Johanna hadn't been expecting to see her quite so soon.

"Hi." Lucy looked a little sheepish as she hovered by her table.

"Good morning, Detective Fuller." Johanna was careful to use her surname. "How's the knee?" She figured friendly with a splash of nonchalance was the best approach as the line between them had become slightly blurred.

"It's good, thank you."

"Would you like some breakfast?" She offered as she cut her own toast into two triangles while trying to keep the banana slices in place.

"No, thank you. I err, I wondered if you had any free time today, or tomorrow maybe?"

Johanna looked up. Lucy held her gaze for a moment before she looked around at some new arrivals to the buffet. She was nervous. Johanna's chest fluttered at the thought that she made Lucy Fuller nervous. That had to mean something, right?

"Why? Are you going to haul me in for questioning but want to see if I'm free first?"

Lucy took a seat in the chair opposite, returning Johanna's gaze, a smile tugging at the corner of her lips. "Not quite. I was thinking about what you said last night."

As Lucy's words filtered through to her brain, Johanna placed her butter knife on the table, giving Lucy her full attention. She arched an eyebrow as she reviewed their varied discussion topics from last night.

From what Johanna could remember, their conversations had been innocent enough. It was more Johanna's thoughts that had been suggestive.

"About living on Compton Way," Lucy continued, clearing her throat. "I thought we could have a walk around and you could show me all the places you hung out with the other kids on your street."

"Oh." Johanna smiled with relief; at least she hadn't scared Lucy off, and she'd get to spend more time with her. "I'd be happy to do that, if you think it would help."

"Thank you." Lucy got to her feet. "I can pick you up. When's good for you?"

Aware that there was a church service for Dan tomorrow, Johanna knew today would be the better option. And having listened to the weather forecast as she snoozed in bed, she knew the rain that was currently falling was due to clear this afternoon. "I've got a bit of office work to do this morning, but I can be free after lunch about two-ish?"

"I'll see you then." Lucy leant forward, taking one of the triangles of toast from Johanna's plate. "Thanks for breakfast," she offered a wide smile as she took a large bite before turning and walking away.

Johanna just sat there too stunned to say or do anything. Was Lucy Fuller this forward with all her suspects?

They'd both been quiet on the short journey from The Fox after exchanging a few pleasantries about the weather clearing up. Johanna figured DS Fuller was in work mode, she stared out of the windscreen as Lucy pulled over to the side of the road at the top of Compton Way hill, just short of the final bend. She heard the engine die as Lucy sat back in her seat. She'd left Kingsford at eighteen, desperate to get out in the world and escape this claustrophobic town. Now she was back and unable to leave until she had the answers she needed.

From their stationary position, Johanna could see almost halfway down the road. She scanned the front of the houses on the opposite side, including the house her family had occupied. It held a special place in her memories, it always would despite the incident with

Daniel Dunderdale. She'd been part of something here, something that had not continued after they moved away. She'd never been particularly good at making friends; it seemed to get harder the older she got, but here they all lived on the same street. They were equals; well, mostly. She glanced at the window that had once been her bedroom, the front garden her father had enclosed at the request of her mother to prevent the Moodys' dog from using it as a toilet. A small porch had now been built onto the front of what had been Amy's house next door. Her gaze shifted further up the road; someone had planted a hedge along the garden boundary of Little Mark's house. Despite the subtle differences, it looked almost exactly as she remembered it.

"So, where do you want to start?" Lucy asked, breaking her reverie.

"Umm, how about up there." Johanna pointed to the rough area of higher ground just beyond where they were parked. You couldn't tell from their current position, but the small patch of grassland that edged the woods beyond was about the size of two tennis courts. Johanna figured it was mitigation land, made at the request of the planners to tick a box for the residents, providing a play area for kids. It was an oasis for her and her friends back then.

It was elevated enough that parents couldn't see what they were doing if they looked from their front garden. It didn't get much better than that, at least in her eyes.

Johanna released her seatbelt, grateful the rain had stopped. Getting out of the car, she waited for Lucy to join her before crossing the road. The edges of the grassed area were heavily overgrown, with white and pink flowering weeds fighting for the last of the autumn sun.

Johanna pulled her coat tighter around her as the breeze picked up, she could feel the stiff photo in her pocket. She slipped her hand inside freeing it.

"I brought this along. I don't know if it'll be any use, but I thought it might give you an idea of what we were all like back then," she said, holding it out for the detective.

Lucy took the photo, stopping as she reached the pavement to study the image. A small lopsided grin appeared on her lips. "You were all so small. Who's that?"

Johanna glanced over to see who Lucy was pointing at. "Oh that's Little Mark Evans. He had a cleft palate when he was born. He had to have quite a few operations when he was little." Mark's hand was raised to obscure the lower half of his face as if he was wiping his nose at the exact moment the photo was being taken. Johanna felt a shadow of regret for the way they all treated him back then. "He hated having his photo taken. He hung out with my brother a lot; less chance of being bullied, I think."

Lucy nodded. "Where were you?"

"Behind the camera. I was a bit of a shutter bug back then; had one of those auto-focus cameras."

Lucy gave her a brief smile before pocketing the photograph "Thank you. I'll take a copy and get it back to you."

"No need, I have plenty more."

They walked towards a steep path that led up onto the flattened plateau. The path was scattered with brown pine needles from the trees at the top. A few feet up the path, Johanna's eyes fell on a round, hinged drain cover. Only this wasn't a drain; the large lettering was worn but still evident on the surface. *TW*, Thames Water. It covered some form of stopcock, from what she could remember. Inside, there was a space around six inches deep, perfect for hiding things. It bought back such fond memories of those days. She used her boot to point out the metal cover.

"We used this as a hiding place: things we didn't want to take home, things we didn't want our parents to see."

Lucy turned to look at her, a serious look on her face. "Like what?"

"Knives, matches, caps. Like the reels of red gun caps. They were great to set fire to." Johanna remembered vividly plunging her hand in the dark space for goodies, despite the constant fear of being bitten by something nasty.

Lucy took out her phone, taking a quick photo of the drain, and looked back at Johanna with raised eyebrows. "I'm guessing you spent a lot of time up here."

"Yeah." Johanna continued up the path towards the trees, avoiding Lucy's gaze. She felt silly, uncomfortable even, revealing all her childhood secrets, especially to Lucy Fuller of all people.

"We spent a lot of time in the woods too," Johanna continued. "We were all trainee fire starters and den builders."

Lucy sniggered at her words. "Why do I feel like I missed out when you talk about your childhood?"

"I don't know. Where did you grow up?" It was Johanna's turn to ask some questions.

"On the outskirts of a city. It wasn't that dissimilar from somewhere like this." Lucy moved her head, indicating the area around them. "Minus the farmers' fields of course."

"Which city?" Johanna pressed. She noted that Lucy had failed to mention any friends. She didn't have the heart to pursue that line of inquiry.

"Chelmsford."

"Oh, where's that? My knowledge of UK geography is pretty terrible, I'm afraid."

"It's just north-east of London. Although I was born in Reading, we moved away before I started school."

"Really? You came back to your home turf then." They'd grown up within thirty miles of each other, minus the five-year age difference of course.

"Something like that."

The path below their feet became obliterated by pine needles, and Johanna stopped to look at the field to their left. It looked much smaller. The grass had been left to grow. No longer the place for swingball marathons for hours on end. It was more like patchy scrubland now, abandoned by the local kids in favour of other distractions.

"That's a pretty sad sight."

"Not how you remember it?"

"Not at all." There was no sign of life or use of any kind. She turned to scan the street below. If any kids had been here in recent years, they left no sign. It was a Saturday afternoon, but the street was like a graveyard. No bikes left in front yards, no footballs wedged under cars or rolled to a stop at the bottom of the hill. "Are there no kids on this street anymore?"

"Err, I think so. Why?"

"Looks a bit dead, that's all."

"It's a rainy afternoon. Everyone's inside glued to their TVs I guess."

But it was hard for Johanna to dismiss it quite so easily.

Lucy pointed towards the trees. "Is this how you got in the woods?"

Johanna spun to face the woods. "Yeah." The path had narrowed. Self-seeded pine trees and bramble bushes had taken over.

"Where does it lead?" Lucy questioned.

"There are or were a few paths. We used to be able to get all the way along to the far side of this estate and through to the estate above." The thick scent of damp soil filled her lungs.

"I see." Lucy pulled out her phone again, taking another picture. Johanna waited until she had finished before stepping forward, slipping in-between the shrunken gap. The dull light forced her to focus on her footing as she made her way up through the steep bank of trees. More pine needles littered the sandy soil floor. She knew it was sandy from digging holes for firepits, not to mention the odd trap they'd set. Or rather Barney would set. God knows what they would have done had they'd caught anything or anyone. Her mind flashed back to the pigeon in the factory, the horror on their faces at what he had done.

"It's pretty dense in here. I'm betting people couldn't see you from the street." Lucy appeared next to her.

Johanna shook the thoughts from her head. "No. I don't think so, not back then." She turned to face the road below. Thick ivy growing up the slender pine trunks obscured the view beyond the tree line. "There used to be a fence between Dan's garden and the trees." Johanna moved off in the direction of what was the Dunderdale house. The fence had been replaced by a six-foot, panelled barrier. "The fence was much smaller back then, only post and rail. Barney and Dan used to step through or over it all the time."

Lucy nodded. "Thirty years is a long time. What about the other gardens along there?" She pointed to the houses that backed onto the woodland near where they had parked, beyond the curve of the hill.

"Oh, yeah, most of them had big fences. Some had gates to get into the woods, but most had just a fence of some kind." Johanna felt her heartbeat begin to race as she realised what she was saying. She'd just widened the possibilities of what had happened to Dan. Could someone have taken him from the estate? A chilly breeze made her hunch her shoulders as she pushed her hands deeper into her pockets.

"Okay, where's next?" Lucy asked, turning to face her.

Johanna considered her for a moment. Was Lucy playing it down or had she been useful? "There's a little place down the bottom," she said, "if it's still there."

"Lead the way."

As she led the way back down to the street, all Johanna could think about were the times she'd raced down this same path at full pelt, momentum pushing her all the way.

She stepped onto the pavement at the bottom of the hill, grateful for the surer footing, and they continued to make their way down the road that Johanna had ridden her bike and played frisbee on a thousand times. She was lost in memories for a few moments until Lucy spoke again.

"How long after Daniel went missing did people start leaving the area?"

"Oh." Johanna had to think for a moment, thrown by the question. "Err, the Dunderdales left after about eight months maybe, and then Amy and her dad left a few months later."

Lucy nodded. "Did Amy say why they were leaving?"

Didn't they talk about this last night? Was Lucy testing her? "Yeah, she said it was to do with her dad's job. He'd been transferred or something. Why?"

"They left owing two months' rent."

Seriously. "Rent?" She had no idea.

Lucy frowned. "You thought they owned the place?"

"I guess. I don't know what I thought at the time. At that age you think everyone's the same as you. It makes sense though. A friend of my dad's moved in just after." Home ownership wasn't exactly a topic she would have discussed with Amy.

As they neared the bottom of the road, a thin line of trees edged their path. "There used to be a small gap here somewhere," Johanna said, spotting it just as the words left her mouth. "Here, this looks like it." She smiled to herself. It was good to know the current residents still trod the same path as she had years ago. This shortcut had obviously stood the test of time.

"Where does it lead?" Lucy questioned.

"It's a cut through to the marsh." She decided to omit the fact that they used to break into the deserted factory just beyond the treeline. "There's a river just through here. We used to catch bullheads in there with our hands." It was a cruel sport in many ways, keeping them in water-filled ice cream containers until they pegged out a few days later.

"Bullheads?"

Johanna smiled at the woman looking back at her. "They're little fish. Bit ugly looking, I guess. Little fat things. The water was so shallow and clear you could lift up big stones and find them."

Johanna stepped over the low-slung, thin wire that barred their way. It did little to prevent anyone from using the path. "Come on, I'll show you." She stood on the other side of the wire to encourage Lucy to join her.

Lucy reluctantly stepped over the wire.

"Just follow the path," Johanna instructed as she indicated for Lucy to make her way ahead of her along the narrow route. Bushes protruded on their path on the left and a steep drop fell away to the right, where the old plastics factory stood on lower ground. Walking in single file, her focus fell on the back of Lucy's tight figure as she edged along the path. Lucy tucked her hair behind her left ear, drawing Johanna's attention to the back of her neck and the fine, wispy hairs that grazed the collar of her jacket.

"Shouldn't you be in front?"

"You're doing fine." Johanna wasn't about to change her position.

"So, where are we going again?" Lucy asked.

"You sound nervous." Johanna grinned at her own words as she ducked to look past Lucy's figure to get her bearings. "It's just up ahead, where the clearing is. Wow, it's just the same." Johanna looked ahead to the edge of the farmers' fields. An old post and rail fence lined the far side of the narrow river. The small, concrete-cast bridge was still in place, providing access to the fields beyond. "We used to spend quite a bit of time down here."

"Where's the nearest farm?" Lucy enquired as she took out her phone again.

Johanna raked through her memories, but nothing came to mind. "Not sure," she said and pointed to the rough edge of the field ahead, blocked by a fence. "There used to be a path here that led up the edge of the farmers' fields at the back of the houses on this side. We could walk up the entire length of the street without being seen if we were careful."

Lucy took a couple of pictures. "Really?"

It hadn't escaped Johanna's notice how pleased Lucy looked about the information as she took more photos.

"What's around there?" Lucy pointed further around the edge of the factory building.

"There's a little path that follows the river past the industrial building. At the end, you can take a right at the fork and walk down to the marsh."

Lucy walked ahead, looking around the corner, snapping another picture of the view she found.

Johanna glanced up at the face of the nearest building, no longer a deserted bottle factory, it was now a car body repair shop. Lumps of dented and abandoned bodywork were stacked next to an overflowing skip near a large metal garage door. There was no company sign, it looked more than a little sketchy to her. The last time she'd been inside that building she'd been full of adventure and excitement, Barney had put a swift end to that. Closing her eyes she could still see the blood splatter on the concrete floor.

"Okay?"

Lucy's half question brought her back to the present. "Yep."

With nothing more to look at in the neighbourhood, they took a slow walk back to the top of the road. When they reached the car, Lucy unlocked it, and Johanna took one final look at her old house before getting in the passenger seat. She waited till they'd moved off before speaking.

"So, am I still a suspect?" She didn't wait for Lucy to answer. "Surely I'm more of a consultant now, after today."

"You're definitely suspect."

Johanna's ears pricked up. "*A suspect or just suspect?*"

"You heard that then?"

"I'm a shrewd business woman. I have to keep track of all the finer details."

"Won't your business be missing you?"

"No," Johanna sighed. She'd had little contact from work, making her feel a little surplus to requirements. "Apparently, I employed some really good managers. It's pretty annoying actually."

Lucy sniggered.

"I don't know what you're laughing at. It just gives me more time to stick around and annoy you."

"Luckily, I have a high tolerance for annoying witnesses."

"Oh, so I'm a witness now?" Johanna said, triumph in her tone at finally getting an answer from Detective Fuller.

"I'll let you know." Lucy replied as she pulled into the carpark of The Fox. Smiling, she turned in her seat to face Johanna then said, more seriously, "Thanks for all your help today."

"No problem, happy to help," Joanna smiled and felt surprisingly good about herself as she got out of Lucy's car.

"By the way."

Johanna turned back at Lucy's words. "Yeah?"

"You should try Nutella with your banana in the mornings. I think you'd like it."

Johanna caught the smirk on Lucy's face. "Thanks for the tip," she beamed. "I'll give it a try." She closed the passenger door and watched Lucy Fuller drive away.

CHAPTER 15

JOHANNA APPRAISED her black suit in the mirror before slipping into her shoes. Her one concession in being a grownup was wearing high heels; not dresses, just high heels. She'd hated being forced to wear pretty dresses as a child; it felt so unnatural to her at the time, even if she didn't know why. Her brother's outfits were always far more appealing and practical in her eyes. Dresses were so unsuitable for climbing trees – this she knew for a fact – much to her annoyance, and her parents' when a certain party dress got ripped. Coming out to her parents at seventeen had somehow alleviated their desire to see her in skirts and dresses, despite their stunted understanding at the time.

High heels, on the other hand, had been part of her work attire for years now. She liked the added height they gave her, and lording it over shorter, annoying male colleagues gave her just the advantage she needed on occasion.

She pulled on her long, black, woollen coat and grey silk scarf, finishing her outfit, and felt entirely overdressed, but it was too late to change now. She checked her watch; her reluctance had made her late, again. As she added the finishing touches, her mind bristled with the thought of spending her Sunday morning in a church. She didn't have a religious bone in her body.

Leaving the hotel, her shoes skittered along the pavement as she made her way through the town to the small church in the croft. She slowed down as she passed the paper shop she'd frequented religiously as a kid with her friends, as it was the best place in town to relieve their hankering for penny sweets. Amy was crazy for sherbet fountains, although Johanna always preferred cola bottles and chocolate bananas.

Johanna pushed on, slipping down an alleyway between two shops, she entered the croft, the posh part of Kingsford, housing the tennis club and bowls green on one side. She passed them with barely a glance, having never indulged in either during her youth. The other side accommodated the village green, a row of pollarded lime trees edged the green and her path to the church at the end. The other three sides of the green were edged by a mixture of mews cottages and larger town houses. Johanna couldn't recall knowing anyone that lived in these properties. As a family, they didn't exactly mix in the upper echelons of Kingsford society.

As she headed towards the church, the number of parked cars began to increase. Was this par for the course on a Sunday or largely due to the dedication of the service to Daniel Dunderdale? As she entered the church gates, stragglers huddled outside the church entrance, one man turned to face her, waving her in. It wasn't till she got closer that she recognised him as her parents' neighbour. Did he even know Daniel, or was he just someone her mother had roped in? She offered a curt nod as she passed through the entrance.

It took a couple of seconds for her eyes to adjust to the gloom, the cool air hit her lungs at the same time as the organ music in the background. Johanna glanced around both sides of the church, wondering if tradition dictated where she should sit, like at a wedding. Thankfully; she soon spotted her mother on the far left and headed in that direction, her heels made an ugly echo as she walked making her self-conscious.

St Peter's Church, where she had endured numerous school carol services and even a Christingle service as a child, seemed unchanged. Either that or her memories of the place had faded over her years of absence.

Some people were still in the aisle. As she made her way around them, a familiar boot peeked into the walkway. Johanna turned her head until DS Fuller's figure came into view. Her face held a solemn expression until their eyes met in the gloom. A small smile flashed on Fuller's lips, but it was gone as quickly as it came. Johanna replied with a discreet nod of the head as she continued across the church.

Her mother offered her a look of annoyance before moving along and offering her the space at the end of the pew, no doubt ticked off by her lateness. Glancing around, two rows ahead, sitting on the front pew, was a large, dark-haired man next to a smaller blonde woman, both with young children climbing over them. Barney? She hadn't seen him for almost thirty years, tilting her body to one side she tried to get a better view, another glare from her mother halted her actions. She turned her attention to an older couple to one side of the pair in the front row, she recognised Dan's parents from the local newspapers, confirming it for her.

The organ music ended abruptly allowing the deafening sound of whispers to fill the void, it was like being in the cinema when the lights go down.

The vicar, a mature man slowly made his way to a small podium on the far side of the isle. He took a moment adjusting some papers in front of him. "Over the last week I've had the pleasure of spending time with Daniel's family and getting to know their son." He looked up meeting the faces of Dan's parents. "He was a bright loving boy who always had a smile on his face."

The service was deliberately focused on Daniel's young life and the potential he had before it was cut short. The vicar mentioned his parents and how they were now able to say goodbye to Daniel.

With the service finally over, Johanna stood with intent; she at least wanted to pay her respects to the family. Compton Way seemed like a lifetime ago, but days like today brought it back into sharp focus.

Barney lingered with his family for a moment before slowly heading down the aisle to the entrance, but a hand on her arm prevented her movement to follow him.

"Are you coming for lunch after?"

She turned to see her mother holding on as she waited for her reply.

"Of course," she replied, and the older woman relaxed her grip, obviously satisfied. "I just want to catch Barney before he leaves."

Johanna tried to move quickly through the people fleeing the church towards her target outside. She waited patiently until he'd finished talking to an elderly woman then called out to him, making him turn around.

"Hey." He looked nonplussed for a moment before managing a thin smile. "Johanna? Is that you? Wow! It's great to see you. I wasn't sure anyone would come."

Johanna looked around them. They were just about to be swallowed up by the last of the attendees vacating the church. "I wanted to pay my respects." She hadn't set eyes on Barney since she'd watched his car drive away when the family moved from Kingsford. It's not like they professed a desire to stay in touch; not after what he'd done, but they had at least parted as friends.

"I think your parents might have had something to do with that, putting out their feelers." Barney held out his hands, wriggling his fingers. He had grown into a tall, strong man. It shouldn't have been a surprise, considering his stature as a kid. She saw that familiar grin as he slipped off his suit jacket. His white shirt was spotless, and a sharp contrast to the interior of the church. Johanna wished she'd brought her sunglasses; the sun had finally appeared, despite the cloudy start.

"Well, that doesn't surprise me; they seem to have fingers in lots of pies," Johanna answered and adjusted her jacket, regretting her funeral attire, despite the occasion. "I'm sorry we're not meeting under better circumstances."

Barney took a breath, and his big shoulders slowly jerked at the movement. "It's, err, a relief in many ways. It's not like we expected him to walk back through the door." He sniffed loudly. "At the same time, it brings it all back, you know."

Johanna saw the glassy covering on Barney's eyes as he looked back at her and said, "I do." Although, of course, she didn't; her younger brother was alive and well. Still, there was something about the expression on Barney's face that seemed forced, as if he was playing the part of the grieving brother. Johanna put it down to the stress of the occasion. He was, after all, a father himself now, if the young child earlier was anything to go by.

"Did you see that police woman inside?"

Johanna heard the disgust in Barney's question.

"Just doing their job, I guess," she told him. Was she really standing up for Detective Fuller now?

"If they'd done their job right thirty years ago, then they wouldn't have to do it again now."

Barney's thunderous tone took her by surprise, forcing her hand. "I'm not sure you can blame Detective Fuller for that."

"They're all the bloody same."

As Barney folded the jacket over his arm, Johanna noticed a teddy bear squashed into his left trouser pocket, the head poking out awkwardly. She had no idea Barney had settled down, but why shouldn't he have? Not everyone was destined to be a lonely cat person.

"So, what are you up to these days?" Barney asked, as he covered the stuffed toy with his jacket, "still beating your brother at swing ball?"

"Uh." Johanna was taken aback for a second. "No, not for a while." She decided to go with the abridged version. "Went off to art college, became a graphic designer. I have my own game-designing business in Bath now."

"That's great, all that spirographing really paid off. You've done well for yourself." His interest was waning as he looked at the chatting people surrounding them.

Was it great? "And you?" she asked, looking towards the woman Barney had been sitting with in the church. "Looks like you've been pretty busy yourself."

"Yeah, yeah, I have two lovely boys, married now too."

"Amazing." Johanna had never thought of measuring herself by personal relationships and achievements; she'd always seen it in professional terms, employment and promotion. The thought of doing it now made her queasy inside, no wife, no children and a hand full of disappointed lovers in her past. Would she ever have a personal life that was equally as successful as her professional one.

Their conversation was cut short by the appearance of Barney's wife.

"Barn, darling, have you got Mr Snuggles? I can't seem to find him anywhere."

The woman was red faced and flustered; the small boy in her arms was equally distressed. Tears rolled down the cheeks of another young boy clutching her left hand.

"Uh no. Let me check in the church," he said, then added to Johanna, "I'll just be a minute," and edged towards the struggling woman, patting the small boy on the head as he moved past them, before disappearing into the black hole of the church doorway.

Johanna stood awkwardly with the group of distressed individuals. Why hadn't Barney introduced her before he left, unsure of what to do, she introduced herself.

"Hello, I'm Johanna. I grew up on the same street as Barney and Daniel."

"Oh, yes, hello. I'm Samantha, Barney's wife, and this is Harry." She indicated to the boy holding her hand. "And Rubin, who is currently very unhappy."

"Oh well, I'm sure your daddy will find Mr … err …"

"Snuggles." Samantha provided.

"Yes, exactly." Her feeble attempt at placating the boy was an obvious failure. Still, she continued, "And how old are you, Harry?" Johanna had spent only the briefest time with her brother's children. They felt like an enigma to her. She had no idea how to interact with them. A fact that was becoming glaringly obvious to everyone.

The boy just stared at her, tears still rolling down his cheeks.

"He's almost four and overtired, I think," Samantha offered.

"Wow, are you going to be big and strong like your daddy?"

Nothing. Johanna had to look away from Harry's blank face. She caught Samantha's apologetic smile as the heat of embarrassment crept up her neck. Johanna breathed a sigh of relief as Barney appeared over Samantha's shoulder.

"Found it! It was under the seat." Barney handed a bear to the toddler in Samantha's arms. "Here you go, little man." The relief was swift on Ruben's face, his brow unfurrowing in an instant.

Johanna frowned at the cuddly toy being hugged by Ruben; it was the same bear that had been poking out of Barney's pocket earlier. Had he really forgotten he had it, then tried to cover it up? Why would he do that?

"I see you've met my wife." Barney's smile seemed genuine for the first time although the grip on his wife's arm seemed a little possessive.

"Where are you staying?" Johanna asked, she knew full well that Barney's parents didn't live in the vicinity, at least according to her mother.

"At The Fox. Mum and Dad are driving back today, but we're going to stay for a few days, see if the police come up with anything."

Their decision to stay around was surely a long shot after all these years, but Johanna knew she would have done the same thing had it been her brother.

"Me too. Maybe we could meet up for a drink later?"

"Sounds good."

Over the shoulder of Barney she could see her father being cornered by the vicar, no doubt he was trying to get him more involved in the church like her mother. "I better go and rescue my dad, see you later."

Lucy arrived back at the station to find Tanner waiting for her.

"What's up?" she asked as she walked into the office. Tanner was grinning from ear to ear as he sat at his desk. She thought for a moment that he knew about her interest in a certain witness. She'd never hear the end of that. How would she even begin to explain to Constable Tanner that she was feeling compromised each time she met Johanna Hale? Seeing her at the church had only confirmed that fact. Yet she couldn't seem to stop herself. If Barrel ever got to hear about it, he would kick her arse every step of the way out of the station.

"Got the old CCTV footage of Levin's van at the Cherry Lane

Industrial Estate back from forensics and it looks like they've cleaned it up a bit."

"Really?" Lucy replied with relief. "Let's have a look, then." She dropped her jacket on her chair as she made her way to Tanner's desk.

Tanner's hands hovered above the keyboard. "Apparently, there were two cameras at the site not just one."

"Redland." Lucy mumbled. Why hide evidence? Unless it didn't fit with *his* story of what happened. "He shaped the evidence to what he wanted."

"Looks like it." Tanner tapped on his keyboard to cue up the footage.

"What does the other camera show?" Lucy asked, irritation growing in her tone.

"Patience. I've put it all in order."

The black and white video flickered to start with. Poor storage, she figured, considering how old it was. The camera view was high up, parking slots were marked on the ground to the left-hand side, next to the industrial unit building, she figured, from walking around the site with Johanna. It was dark, the only lighting coming from some exterior lights by the look of it. The view looked quite central, above the entrance to the small estate. The camera couldn't have been attached to the existing buildings.

"How did they get this view above the entrance?"

"According to the file, there was a lightweight gantry frame near the entrance. Camera one was attached to it, along with some floodlights."

Focussing on the screen, a few moments later, Lucy watched as a vehicle passed through the entrance, a small van of some kind. As Redland had said, the number plate was indeed covered with something. The fact that the footage was black and white made it difficult to be sure what colour the van was. It could have been dark green, like Levin's. Equally, it could have been a similar, dark colour.

"Now for the next camera," Tanner said.

The time code ticked away in the bottom right-hand corner: October 16th 1988, 2:13 a.m. A few seconds after the first camera. This time, the view was looking out from the building. A van passed through the frame, consistent with the earlier footage.

"What's missing?" Tanner asked, tapping a key to pause the video.

"Huh?" Lucy frowned. There was nothing to miss, just a plain old van. Shit, plain van. "There's nothing on the van. Levin's van advertised his plastering company."

"Bingo!" Tanner smiled. "It was painted on too, not like the ones today which are magnetic and can be easily taken off."

"Shit! And it's the same on the way out?" She needed to be sure when she told Barrel.

"Yep!" Tanner sped through the footage. "They head back out seventeen minutes later."

Lucy glanced at the time stamp in the corner as the plain-sided van passed in front of the camera, then out the entrance. Again, the front number plate was covered.

"Bastard!" Redland was so keen to close the case, he didn't care how he did it or who he pinned it on. "We need to print out some stills of the van. What about the make is it a match to the one registered to Levin."

"Same make, but they can't be sure it's the same model. According to forensics, the plate is unreadable. Could be tape over it. Also ..." Tanner clicked onto his email. "They couldn't be definitive on the colour of the van due to the age of the footage, lighting conditions and reflective luminosity of solid colours or inferred wavelengths." Tanner frowned as he looked up at her. "Basically, if it was an old photo with a negative, they might be able to tell us more."

"Shit!" Lucy wiped her hands over her face. She couldn't believe Redland had screwed up the case.

"You were right," Tanner said. "I looked into Levin's alibi for the day Daniel went missing."

She prepared herself for the worst. "And?"

"He had a plastering job lined up, but the woman cancelled on him, so he stayed home all day, received a phone call just after seven p.m., which he didn't answer. Doesn't answer the phone after seven apparently, a habit he picked up from his parents. He said he watched TV all evening, listed all the programs, etc."

"Any neighbours confirm that?" Lucy asked, hoping someone saw his van parked up.

"Lived in the middle of nowhere, no neighbours in earshot."

In other words, no solid alibi, and the perfect patsy. Lucy rubbed her forehead. Barrel was going to go mental. "I better call the boss."

"Good luck," Tanner said with a smile.

She rested a hand on his shoulder for a moment. "Good work. Now we just need to locate those missing residents ASAP."

"I'll need to eat before I do any of that." Tanner got to his feet. "Do you want anything?" he asked, turning towards her as he slipped an arm into his jacket.

"Err." Lucy was still considering her phone call to Barrel. "Whatever you're having is good," she mumbled, her eyes fixed on Tanner's computer screen.

"Won't be long."

"Okay."

Lucy walked back to her own desk. Sitting heavily in the chair, she let out a long breath. They had just removed Levin from the suspects list, but without Levin to fall back on, what did they really have so far? Nothing. Was she making an awful mistake here, she rubbed at her tired eyes. So far she had a cooked-up theory that was built on unreliable evidence and a gut feeling that someone local was responsible. If not Levin, it could still have been a stranger abduction, they just hadn't found any evidence to support that so far. The only way to find out was to eliminate the residents.

She opened her email and scanned the list of local conservation volunteers that Stuart Francis had finally sent through. David Hale was the only name she recognised. She sent it to the printer to add to her growing file. It was hard to know what would be important in cases that were far from cut and dried. She picked up the photo Johanna Hale had given her the previous day: six figures varying in size and stature, like a small mountain range with a solid blue sky set behind them. She couldn't say for sure, but it looked like it had been taken at the top of the hill on the estate. Could one of these kids really be responsible? Maybe more than one? It happened.

The biggest of them by far was Barney Dunderdale at the centre of the group, his face slightly hidden by his cap. He leaned an elbow on his younger brother's shoulder to his left. Daniel looked incredibly young and small, his delicate features avoiding the scrutiny of the camera as he looked off to his right at something.

Amy Bell stood on the other side of Barney. She was almost the same height as him, but her thin clothing revealed a much smaller frame. Lucy couldn't help but notice that Amy appeared to be a well-developed individual. No doubt, she caught the eye of many, even at that young age, especially when put next to Sarah Moody, the only other girl in the photo who looked every bit her young thirteen years, despite her best efforts.

Glancing back at Daniel, she tried to follow his line of sight. Was that what he was looking at? Amy? A crush, or maybe something else?

Amy Bell and her father, Paul, had so far proved elusive. She'd put out some feelers with the MOD, considering Paul Bell's line of employment at the airbase, but had yet to hear back. The fact that they left the area so abruptly certainly rang a few alarm bells for her.

Mark Evans stood next to Amy. She felt for him, growing up with a disfigurement. The teasing must have been relentless. Had someone pushed him too far? she wondered, but it was a question she would need to phrase delicately as he was next on her list. She'd been hoping he might appear at the church service, but his absence signalled a long drive for her tomorrow.

Taking a deep breath, she pulled out her phone to call Barrel.

"Boss." She greeted as soon as the call was accepted.

"What have you got Fuller?"

She took a breath as she looked around the empty office. "We've got the old CCTV footage back from forensics. Looks like it wasn't Levin's van, there's no signage on it and thy can't even be sure it's the same colour."

"They can't or you can't?" Barrel grumbled.

She'd been expecting some blowback considering their conversation the other day. "They can't?" She replied as muffled noises and talking came down the line.

"Bollocks! What does that bloody leave us with? Have you rounded up all the old residents yet?" Barrel's voice held a now familiar annoyance.

"Almost." She scratched around for some good news the "I'm going to London tomorrow to track down Bell and Evans." She hoped she hadn't overstretched herself as her appointment with the MOD archives hadn't been confirmed yet.

"Get it done. And send me a copy of the footage, I want to see it."

She flinched at his tone, it was hardly her fault. "Yes boss."

"And let me know what you find in London." He hung up without another word.

CHAPTER 16

FULL OF HER mother's substantial roast dinner, Johanna pulled into the carpark of The Fox, intending to go straight to her room for a lie down, but taking a shortcut through the bar, she came face to face with Barney Dunderdale, a pint of lager in one hand and a chaser of what looked like whiskey in the other.

"Hey, I thought you were never going to get here," he bellowed, an edge of annoyance in his voice, as if she were late for an appointment. She could only recall a general offer to meet up for a drink, but by the look in Barney's eyes, this wasn't his first.

"Sorry, I, err." Johanna fumbled for an adequate reply. They were hardly close anymore. "Got caught up at my parents," she offered with a grin.

They stood there in an awkward silence, broken only by Barney's gulp as he downed his short. She couldn't see a way out of this situation that would end well. "I best get a drink then."

"Where do you want to sit?" Barney asked, as he placed his empty glass on the nearest table.

"You choose." Johanna loosened her scarf, wondering how she could cut this short. The idea of spending time with an intoxicated Barney did not fill her with joy. There was something about him that made her feel uneasy. Instead of her usual gin and tonic, she opted for a plain tonic water with a slice of lemon, hoping it would fool him, then took a seat at the small table Barney had chosen. Draping her coat and scarf on the chair back, she carefully placed her fake gin and tonic on a round beer mat. She noticed Barney had failed to do the same as she pushed a replacement whisky towards him. A slight puddle had already formed around the bottom of his pint glass.

She wasn't quite sure where to start the conversation. She figured his wife should be solid ground. "Is Samantha joining us?"

"No. She's upstairs with the kids." He took a long drink of his pint before wiping his mouth on the back of his hand. "I needed to get out for a bit, so I came down to wait for you."

Johanna immediately felt stupid for asking. Where would they get a babysitter away from home. "Oh, of course."

"She's not great with new people anyway," he offered.

She's not or Barney *says* she's not? Johanna couldn't help wondering whose opinion he was spouting. She couldn't stand the thought of a partner talking for her in such a way.

"She seems lovely. You're a lucky man." She felt the need to build Samantha up, despite only meeting her for a few minutes.

"I am," Barney nodded. "She's had a rough time since Ruben was born, postnatal depression. She gets pretty frazzled sometimes. I have to sort her out."

Sort her out! Johanna thought back to the incident at the church. Even more reason not to stress her out with a missing teddy. Or leaving her alone with two kids in a hotel room maybe. "I'm sorry."

Johanna waited a few beats before steering the conversation in a different direction. "Where are you living now?"

"Near Guildford." Barney downed his short. "It's not as picturesque as Bath."

Johanna flinched at his bitterness. Guilt climbed up her throat, even though she had nothing to do with his living circumstances. Gone was the brave happy go lucky boy she'd once known; she'd always felt safe in his company as a young girl, till she'd seen his volatile side that day in the factory. She took a gulp of her drink to take the edge off his comment and then placed her glass down carefully as an elderly man with a chocolate Labrador came through the bar.

"Do you remember the Moody dog?" she asked, trying to lighten the mood.

"That dog could jump every bloody fence in the street, even with the fat gut he carried around with him."

Johanna laughed, despite the venom in Barney's tone. The Moody dog, aka Scamp, was just that, a total trouble maker. Made even more amusing by the fact that he belonged to the pseudo-poshest people on the street, something Scamp failed to realise during his regular escapes, or even better when he broke into the Moodys' freezer and ate several frozen pheasants.

"He certainly liked his food," Johanna smiled. "I can still picture Moody Dad trying to catch him on one of his break outs."

"Moody Dad and Moody Mum, God, they were a pair." Barney's face sparked a genuine laugh for the first time.

"Do you think Sarah's still got her posh accent?"

"Definitely! Moody Mum wouldn't have it any other way." Barney drained his pint glass. "Another?" he asked without even placing his glass down.

"Thanks." She didn't really want another, but it was obvious that Barney needed to talk.

"Gin and tonic?" he queried as he got to his feet.

Johanna simply nodded. A part of her wondered if Barney drank like this all the time, or if it was the occasion that had brought about the need. There were no obvious signs, apart from a slight pudgy appearance.

On his return, Barney almost tripped as he approached their table. Johanna held onto the table top to steady it.

"Do you remember Sarah's birthday party?" he asked as he sat down heavily in his chair.

Johanna chuckled as she recalled the clashing of the posh kids from Sarah's private school and the rest of the reprobates from Compton Way, including herself. "Little Mark dressed up as Scamp the dog," she offered with a laugh.

"God, that was weird," Barney sniggered. "He was a weird kid."

Johanna frowned. That was exactly the kind of talk that made Mark a target for bullies. It made him introverted in many ways, and he avoided verbal communication as a result, hence the choice of dog costume at the fancy-dress birthday party. Of course it wasn't helped by the fact that Amy used to love making a point of correcting him when the rest of us just ignored or accepted it.

She didn't fully understand the dynamics of it all back then, but children can be vicious when it comes to inconsistencies. They were all cruel to Mark in their own ways. Johanna may not have inflicted the blows, but she was just as guilty for not standing up to Amy each time she ridiculed him. Barney, on the other hand, simply refused to pair up with him when there was any kind of sporting contest. His martial arts training seemed to harden him to any kind of weakness, and Little Mark was the feeble one in his eyes, a sharp contrast to his own broad stature.

"Your parents look well. They moved back then?"

Barney's half question pulled her from the past. "Oh, yeah. They moved back a few years ago to be near my brother and his family." She realised the weirdness of her statement, as Barney knew who Simon was.

"What about you? Married?" Barney questioned.

Johanna knew she had a choice here: be upfront or hide exactly who she was. She didn't exactly hide in her professional life, but she didn't flaunt it either. "No. I haven't found the right woman yet."

"Really?" Barney flicked his eyebrows up with interest.

She drank a healthy gulp of the real gin and tonic for good measure. "How are your parents doing?" It was a swift change of subject, but she needed it.

Barney blew out a breath. The stench of stale beer turned Johanna's stomach, forcing her to sit back a little. She'd never been a fan of lager, preferring wine or spirits.

"Relieved." Barney drank a couple of inches from his pint, wiping off the foam with the back of his hand.

"And you?" Johanna wanted to tread lightly, but there was no easy way to ask.

"The same, I guess." Barney erratically rubbed his upper thighs with both hands. "It's just –" he took a breath – "everything is always about Daniel. Even now it's 'Daniel would be doing this or that'. It's never about me." His words came out at gunshot speed. How long had he been holding this in? Was this survivor's guilt for moving on? Johanna was just about to try and placate him when he continued.

"I mean, I'm right there in front of them and all they can talk about is Dan." His eyes remained fixed on the table between them and Johanna was lost for a reply. Instead, she reached out for Barney's shoulder and gripped it loosely enough for him to shrug out of it if he wanted too. He didn't. He simply covered his eyes and his shoulders jerked as he sobbed.

"They've got grandchildren now, and it's still not enough. Mum wanted us to name Harry after him. How could I do that? Every time I called him for his tea, I'd be thinking about what happened to my brother that day." Barney rushed to wipe at his eyes, removing all evidence of his breakdown.

The door to the bar opened sharply as Barney grabbed for his drink and downed the last of it. Johanna was surprised and relieved to see DS Fuller enter the bar. She'd seen her at the church earlier and the previous day, but it still wasn't enough somehow. DS Fuller barely acknowledged them as she made her way to the bar, was she on duty. Johanna surreptitiously watched her over her glass as she approached the barman, no warrant card, instead she just ordered a drink. A warm feeling fizzed in her core as she ogled Lucy casually pulling a tenner from her pocket.

Johanna turned to see Barney's glass hovering in the air as he eyeballed Fuller too, although his expression was far from happy. He placed his glass down, missing the beer mat again, and the glass clattered on the table, drawing the attention of Fuller.

"I should go up," he grumbled. "It's starting to stink in here." His voice rose considerably drawing the attention of the few customers present, including Lucy.

Johanna glanced across to Lucy catching her blank expression.

Barney stood to leave. "It was good to see you, Johanna," he added, and made it sound like he was never going to see her again.

"You too," Johanna replied and watched as Barney disappeared through the bar to the stairs. Turning back, she could see Fuller had turned her back to the bar, as if waiting for her attention. A moment after, their eyes locked, and Fuller nodded towards the beer pumps. Johanna shook her head, indicating the two drinks in front of her.

After she had been served, Fuller headed over to her table, a small glass of red wine in her hand. Lucy didn't appear to be on duty, was she looking for Johanna?

"Mr Dunderdale looked a little distraught. Is he okay?"

"He's a little overwhelmed and intoxicated, I think."

"I see. Can I join you?"

"Of course." Johanna indicated to the seat Barney had vacated. "Detective Sergeant Fuller, how can I help you?" She saw the flash of a grin on DS Fuller's lips at her use of her full name, even though she'd gone to the effort to discover her first name.

"Just doing the rounds, making sure no-one's playing chicken with the traffic."

Johanna pursed her lips. At least she'd made an impression. "Good to know you're keeping an eye on things," she said and took a sip from her drink while she thought of a suitable change of subject. She wanted to know more about this woman; but where to start, there was one obvious question of course. "So, what made you become a police officer?"

If Lucy was surprised by the question, it didn't show.

"Persistent nosiness I think, much to my boss's annoyance."

Johanna laughed. "I'd ask how the case was going, but I'm guessing you won't tell me anything as I'm clearly still a suspect."

Lucy grinned back at her, then looked down at her drink for a moment. "We're still trying to track down the old residents that were interviewed thirty years ago, to be honest?"

That explained the look of exhaustion on DS Fuller's face. "Jim and Jesse Hooper?" she frowned. "They were pretty elderly. I'm guessing they've passed away by now."

"Your old neighbours." Lucy looked up to the ceiling for a second. "They did, I'm afraid. Sorry." Lucy adjusted her glass on the beer mat.

Johanna blinked away her surprise and took another sip from her drink while she thought of a way to steer the conversation in a new direction once again. "Good to see you at the service earlier."

"Just paying my respects."

Johanna nodded. She'd seen enough crime dramas on TV to know police officers go to check out the family and friends of the deceased, looking for anyone or anything out of place. Deep down, she wondered if she was still a suspect, regardless of her alibi.

Then Lucy surprised her by volunteering, "I'm not sure your friend Barney likes me very much."

"I wouldn't take it personally. He's just upset. It's brought a lot of stuff to the surface."

"Oh yeah?" Lucy's eyebrows raised.

"Survivors guilt, I think," Johanna guesstimated, hoping Lucy wouldn't press her on it.

Lucy nodded. "So, what made you go into graphic design?"

Johanna smiled. Was DS Fuller trying to get to know her? "Well, I've always had an interest in art, right from school. It was all I did when I first started out in the business, but now it's about the only thing I don't do. I'm mainly management now really, especially after we diversified into gaming and programming."

"Diversification? I thought that was for farmers."

"Unfortunately, you have to move with the times. I'd still prefer to be at the coalface but ..." She let the statement hang between them. She hoped taking a break from her business would allow her to recharge and get a bit of perspective. "Maybe I'll look at diversifying into something else."

"It's a competitive market." Lucy replied.

She grinned, aware that Lucy wouldn't have to deal with these kinds of problems in her job, she just had to stay ahead of the criminals. "It is, even my mother has gone back to work apparently."

"Oh?"

"Filing for a solicitors on the high street." Why was she talking about her mother.

They were quiet for a few moments, Johanna fiddled with her glass, turning it around on the beer mat. She looked up meeting Lucy's deep blue eyes; there was a connection between them she was sure of it, why else was she here. The ends of Lucy's lips stretched up creating a warm smile, Johanna reacted immediately mirroring her expression as her pulse quickened. The appearance of Lucy's tongue as it separated her lips took it to another level, she was mesmerised as she watched the tip if Lucy's tongue skim across her bottom lip.

Heat rose to Johanna's cheeks as she took a steadying breath. She drained the last of her drink. She was desperate to see where this was leading. A thought occurred to her that maybe she needed to help it along, the alcohol had given her the courage she needed. "It's been a long day. I should turn in." Although she made no move to leave.

"I should get going, too."

"You're not thinking of driving I hope, Detective Sergeant Fuller."

"I'll get a taxi."

"You could." Johanna considered her words for just a moment. "Or, and I'm going to be a little forward here because I like you and I've had at least one stiff drink." She let the words sink in for a moment before continuing. The smile was back on Lucy's lips. "You could stay here, with me," she offered, hoping she'd read the situation correctly. It really wasn't her forte.

"I'm not sure that it would be appropriate for a police officer to be fraternizing with a suspect."

Lucy still hadn't moved, surely she was on the right lines. "Do you normally drink with suspects?" Johanna asked, as this was the second time they'd met in the bar.

Lucy's eyebrows raised a little; other than that she declined to answer, which gave her a little more optimism. Getting to her feet, Johanna studied Lucy for a moment. She was wide eyed and unsure as she gripped her empty glass. Johanna picked up her coat and stepped around their small table, lightly gripping Lucy's shoulder as she passed by. "I'm staying in room two-o-seven, if you change your mind," she told her and left without looking back. Walking into the corridor there was a quiver or arousal in her body, she'd just propositioned a police officer. She pressed the button for the lift, hoping Lucy wouldn't be far behind.

Lucy looked across at the empty chair Johanna had just vacated. She could still feel the touch of her hand on her shoulder. It was a breach of trust, she knew that. She was in a position of responsibility in relation to members of the public. It was gross misconduct to abuse that position, to pursue a sexual relationship with a member of the public. But Johanna's offer had given her food for thought. She scolded herself. The fact that the attraction was mutual made no difference. She'd come here to unwind a little; coupled with the hope of seeing Johanna again, and now she had. Although she hadn't been expecting events to escalate quite so quickly, nevertheless the invitation was hard to dismiss. She knew there was a spark between them. Now she was just torturing them both. She needed to leave, to remove the temptation. But as she got to her feet to leave, she saw the tail end of a grey, silky scarf on the chair opposite. Johanna's, she presumed. Was this a sign? She'd already saved Johanna from being squished like a bug; now she had to save her bloody scarf too. She reached out to pick it up. It was soft as it slipped between her fingers, and a familiar scent filled her nostrils as she examined it, finding a subtle zig-zag stitching across the width of the material.

The door opened on her first knock. Johanna appeared, reached for her hand, and she was quickly pulled inside. She was done for. She knew it the moment she met Johanna's eyes. The door swung closed with a click.

Lucy held the scarf aloft. "Is this yours? You left it in the bar." Her voice was small in the spacious suite. Were all the rooms this big? She glanced back to Johanna, registering the look of achievement on her face. Lucy regretted her decision again as a tingle covered every inch of her body.

Subtle music drifted across the room. She wasn't sure if it was real or in her head. She was just about to ask when Johanna answered her initial query.

"Thank you." Johanna took the offering and tossed it towards the chair tucked under the petite desk.

"Listen, I don't normally ..." Lucy stuttered. "I've never done this before ..." She was desperate to clear the air. Hurting Johanna was not what she wanted. Witnesses and suspects can be fickle, and the last thing she needed was Johanna kicking up a stink. "I mean with a suspect or witness." The fluster in her voice annoyed her. This woman had gotten under her skin. Besides, they hadn't done anything yet, and she wasn't about to, whatever it was.

Johanna's eyes softened as she stepped back towards her. "Good." She took another step closer as the music came to life, filling the space between them. The deep reverberations vibrated through Lucy's body as Johanna stepped in front of her.

"What's this music?" she asked. Thankfully, her voice had regained some of its strength.

"It's Grant Green, bit of mellow jazz. My dad got me into it. He used to play it all the time at home." Johanna slipped her arms around Lucy's waist, pulling their bodies together. A small gasp escaped Lucy's lips as a puff of air hit her neck when they gently collided.

Johanna was a couple of inches taller, giving Lucy a perfect view of her lips. The discrepancy must have spurred her into action as Johanna slipped her shoes off. A musky, flowery scent invaded her senses as Johanna began to sway Lucy's hips in time with her own movements to the music. But it was ungainly movement to say the least. Lucy didn't dance, not even at weddings.

"Dancing is not a good idea, for me anyway," she said and pulled back, meeting Johanna's darkened eyes.

"Really? You've had at least one drink."

Lucy's gaze fell to Johanna's parted lips, and she delighted in the effect this woman had on her, her was breathing heavy, she wanted her so much, and before she could stop herself, her hand moved to Johanna's cheek. Once she crossed the line she knew there was no going it back, still she couldn't stop herself. They were only an inch or two apart now, but it was still too far for Lucy.

Johanna stepped forward, the brush of her bare feet against the carpet just noticeable over the music as she moved into Lucy's personal space. But Lucy pulled her hand away and took a step back, keeping the same invisible barrier between them. They were dancing all over again, except this time they were in sync.

A smile curled at the edge of Johanna's lips as she took a second step forward. She was enjoying the game.

Lucy replied, taking a second step back, but she felt something touch her heel as she came to a stop.

Johanna looked away at something over Lucy's shoulder. She had a feeling it was a wall or at least a piece of furniture. The room was big, but not that big.

"I should warn you, you're trapped," she said, edging forward.

Lucy took a moment to enjoy the nearness of Johanna's body next to her own and made no effort to escape this time, even though she wasn't exactly pinned. It seemed inevitable now as Johanna's tongue appeared, sweeping across her bottom lip.

Lucy was transfixed as she reached up, tucking stray hairs behind Johanna's ear, her hand lingering before gently urging Johanna forward. But the panic was rising now that she was finally faced with the possibility of being intimate with Johanna Hale. Blood rushed in her ears as the headiness of Johanna's scent filled her head, and she staggered forward, bringing their lips together. The kiss was soft and the warmth from Johanna's lips forced a whimper from her throat. Her fingers digging into covered flesh, needing more contact as she leaned into her.

Johanna parted her lips as her arm wrapped around Lucy's hip. The heat from Johanna's mouth was making Lucy dizzy as her tongue slowly passed the threshold of her own lips into Johanna's mouth. Lucy could feel herself disappearing into this incredible ecstasy, losing control moment by moment, and she knew that she couldn't allow that to happen. She had to end this while she still could, before she was completely overwhelmed by this incredible feeling.

"I can't do this," she managed to say, pulling away and dropping her head back against the wall. "You're a witness on a case." Her voice was horse, her words aimed at the ceiling.

"Hardly, I wasn't even there when it happened," Johanna tried to reassure her. There was a pleading tone to her voice.

Lucy tilted her head forward to look at her. "That's not the point, and you know it," she said and closed her eyes to block out Johanna's attack on her senses. She regretted opening them again as the disappointment in Johanna's eyes cut into her.

"You're right. I'm sorry," she told her and released the hold on Lucy's body, reluctantly stepping back out of her space. "I shouldn't have put you in this position."

The loss of Johanna's touch was palpable. "I'm sorry," she tried and glared at the carpet as she searched for the right words. Nothing came, so she said, "I should go." Her attempt to move towards the door was cut short by Johanna's hand on her arm.

"We can at least be friends can't we?" Johanna's hand slipped lower cupping Lucy's her thumb softy rubbing the back of Lucy's.

The tender touch ignited a familiar throb in her core, she glanced up meeting Johanna's eyes one more time. She saw no regret for their actions. "We can do that."

Lucy gripped Johanna's hand briefly before she walked out of the room, softly closing the door behind her.

CHAPTER 17

LUCY SLUMPED BACK in her seat. With Tanner occupied, TIEing the last few residents on the side of the street she'd allocated him, she had no-one to vent to. Her struggle to locate the Bells was becoming epic. Her initial enquiry was with the Ministry of Defence, as Paul Bell had worked as a specialist technician, or mechanic in layman's terms, on a UK airbase, but she had been passed from pillar to post. She'd told Barrel she was making progress but it looked far from that right now.

The airbase itself had closed over twenty years ago when the Americans had returned to their homeland. This was the initial problem, as employment records had been moved several times in the intervening years. She'd even gone through the original interview record from the Dunderdale case and found Paul Bell's employee number noted down on a piece of paper. Although, by the looks of things, it hadn't been followed up, thanks to Redland's tunnel vision. She had, however, sent the details through to the MOD over a week ago.

Now, finally, a little daylight was beginning to break. The reason Bell had been so difficult to find was due to the fact he'd changed his bloody name. Bellamy became Bell when they moved to Compton Way in early 86'. The question was why? Was it a simple administration error created by HR when he transferred to the airbase from

Northampton? Or something more questionable? She'd need to visit the National Archives based in Kew for more information. according to an email she'd just received. At least she could combine it with a visit to interview Mark Evans in London at the same time.

Lucy studied the name as she'd written it down: Bellamy. Bell-Amy. Was it really a coincidence that the letters that had been removed from his surname also made up his daughter's Christian name? An honest clerical error maybe. She could see how that might have happened when the information had been inputted. But it was a bit too convenient for her liking. And it was the only decent lead they had right now. After all, she'd managed to dismiss Levin's involvement in Daniel's disappearance and death, but she needed an alternative if Barrel was to take her seriously. She considered calling him to keep him in the loop but decided to wait until she had more information from London.

She needed it, today of all days. A chance to get her mind off Johanna Hale, at least for a few hours. She hadn't been able to think of anything else since leaving her in the hotel room. She knew she was in the wrong, she should never have gone there, but she had no control around that woman. Johanna wasn't exactly a suspect, but still it was morally wrong and she knew it. If word got out, it would damage the public's trust in the police and her as an officer. She couldn't let the Dunderdale's down.

Before leaving, she reacquainted herself with the statements Mark Evans and Paul Bell had made regarding their movements on the day Daniel went missing. Paul Bell had left his house just before nine in the morning to take his car into the local garage on the Bath Road; issue with the exhaust, apparently. The garage had confirmed that, and the car had remained at the garage until the Monday morning when it was picked up. Bell had then gone shopping in the town and walked home, arriving there at around eleven-thirty. This was confirmed by receipts and his daughter, Amy Bell, who was home all day as she was suffering with her first menstrual cramps.

At first glance, this did, of course, throw a spanner in the works if there was cause to connect Bell with the murder regarding her theory of moving the body to the well with a motor vehicle. But Daniel was quite small in stature; a fully grown man like Paul Bell could easily have carried him. He could have clambered over the back fence, escaped the street unseen. Then all he had to do was carry Daniel across the fields to Combe Farm. It was a decent walk, but it was possible.

Eleven-year-old Mark Evans, on the other hand, was inside most of the day with his family. With Simon Hale away on holiday, Mark stayed home watching TV and helping his dad in the garden. None of the Evans family had any idea Daniel was missing till Janet Dunderdale came looking for him.

An hour and a half later, Lucy walked through the stunning, manicured settings that housed the Archives in Kew. It was a world away from the traffic she'd battled to get there. She just hoped her earlier call to let them know she would be coming was going to be enough for them to release the information she needed.

Entering the main reception area, she was surprised by the size of the open, cylindrical space as she moved towards the young woman sitting beneath a *Welcome* sign behind a reception desk. The woman moved her head to look up at her visitor but it took her a moment to tear her eyes away from the screen in front of her.

Lucy offered her credentials as she introduced herself, receiving a wide-eyed look in response. She made a point of dropping Susan Green's name, as she was the person she'd spoken to earlier, hoping it would speed up the process. She still had to meet up with Mark Evans before she could leave London. The receptionist pointed her to a seat while she made a phone call.

Ten minutes later, another woman, in her forties, appeared next to the receptionist before coming over to introduce herself.

"I'm Susan Green." A large pair of glasses framed the woman's eyebrows as she pushed them up her nose. Her long hair was held in a thick plait hanging over the front of her left shoulder.

"Hi. DS Fuller, we spoke earlier."

"Follow me, I've dug out some of the information you requested," she said, appearing so efficient that Lucy was hopeful that she would beat the rush-hour traffic back home, but doubts crept in as they navigated the massive site at a snail's pace, with it taking them an age just to reach the archive rooms.

"We're just in here," Green offered adjusting her large glasses again.

Lucy noticed the coded numbers on the doors as they entered, followed by the endless rows of shelved box files.

Green tossed her plait over her shoulder as she tucked herself away behind a desk with two screens in front of her and said, "Okay, so I've found Paul Bellamy's service record. Date of birth: third of March nineteen fifty-seven."

That tallied with her notes. "Great." This was sounding promising already, but it took another hour for her to get any real answers, despite Susan Green's so-called head start, and unfortunately the news wasn't good.

"So from your records, these records," Lucy said, waving the meagre papers in front of her. "Paul Bellamy did not have a daughter or any other children, wife or civil partner at all."

"That's correct," the woman replied.

Lucy tried to get her head around the new information. To everyone else concerned in Compton Way, Amy Bell was Paul Bell's daughter.

"He began working for the MOD in Wellingborough near Northampton in February nineteen eighty until July eighty-seven when he was transferred to Oldbury in Berkshire."

That fitted with what she knew about the Bells. "Do you know if he requested the transfer?"

Green adjusted her glasses as she clicked through several screens. "Yes, he put in the request in May of that year."

"And he worked there till sometime in eighty-nine, is that right?" she asked as she made notes.

Green went back to the earlier screen. "Err … yes, April eighty-nine he transferred to Cosford in Shropshire. It looks like he made that request too."

Lucy was starting to get a picture of the Bell's transient life.

"His death in service benefits were paid out to his parents," the woman added as she scanned her computer screen. "Well, his mother, to be precise."

"He's dead?" Lucy snapped. Christ, this case was maddening. She was just about to ask for a current address as she figured he would be receiving his pension around now.

"Yes." The woman was becoming a little curt with her now. "He died in ninety-five."

"Do you have the details for his mother or other family members?" She figured his mother would be dead by now, but someone might know about Paul's living arrangements. There was still a daughter or at least someone's daughter that needed to be found.

"I can give you his last address, and his mother's, but it was over twenty years ago, so ..." Green let the depressing statement hang in the air.

"Thanks," Lucy said and forced a smile. "Could you print out a copy of his work records for me?"

"Of course. I think we have copies of his transfer letters on file too."

"That would be great, thank you."

The woman printed out the details she had for Bellamy's next of kin, probably in the hope it would make Lucy go away.

Mark Evans was based in Paddington for the Crossrail project, which meant a trip across the river into Central London. According to her sat-nav, it was just over seven miles and would take only thirty-three minutes, but she very much doubted that fact.

After a frustrating hour in traffic, she finally found a parking space on a surrounding street. The site entrance was equally hard to find. She showed her ID to several nameless site security workers before she was eventually given a Hi-Viz jacket and hard hat and granted entrance to the security cabin. The security guard got straight on his walkie-talkie to get her an escort across the site. A few minutes later, a young guy dressed from head to toe in Hi-Viz yellow and orange appeared in the doorway with a can of unbranded soft drink in his hand.

The security guard nodded to the man. "Mark Evans, expected."

Lucy smiled, partly in greeting to the young man but mainly at the fact that she suspected the security guard and Barrel would get on like a house on fire with their love of everything abrupt and clipped.

"Okay. This way, stay very close to me."

Jesus, were they going into a lion's cage or something? "Right."

They gave various mammoth machines operated by their puny humans a wide birth before coming to a standstill next to a large scissor-lift platform, which held two people, their arms expressive as they surveyed the area around them. The site was so noisy she was surprised they could hear anything either of them were saying.

Lucy edged closer to the cordoned, gaping hole in the ground in front of her, feeling like she was on the set of a disaster movie. How the hell did Evans visualise and manage a site like this?

"Mark!" the young man bellowed next to her. She flinched at the noise, despite the background din around her.

The scissor lift descended with grace. Lucy pulled out her ID again, offering it to the man that stepped off the platform towards her. "Mark Evans?" she asked hopefully and took his nod as confirmation. "DS Fuller."

He pointed towards a set of stacked site huts nearby. She nodded, not bothering to try and compete with the noise.

Entering the hut, the stench of greasy bacon and heat wafted over them.

"Sorry, it's a bit ripe in here."

Lucy glanced around the cabin. It was being used as a canteen, with chairs and tables scattered around the space. Evans moved towards the window, opening a small fanlight, letting in a percentage of the outside noise. Unfortunately, the angle of the window was restricted by the external mesh in place, protecting the windows from flying debris. It was a toss-up as to which was worse: the noise or the smell.

Lucy took a seat while Evans removed his hat and jacket, placing them on one of the tables. Mark Evans had certainly changed in the intervening years; a thin line of a scar was just visible on his upper lip. Apart from that he looked nothing like the scrawny kid, ashamed of his own appearance, she'd seen in the photo Johanna had given her. *Shit.* She'd been doing well to push Johanna from her mind; now she was right back where she started. She pulled out her notebook and said, "Looks like you've got your work cut out here."

Evans smiled as he perched on the edge of the nearest table. "Looks worse than it is."

She ignored the power game of his superior position. She wasn't putting on the thumb screws here. "So, I just need to ask you a few questions about Daniel Dunderdale."

"I can't believe you found him after all this time."

Lucy nodded as she recalled the finds they'd made during the earlier Crossrail digs. "I'm guessing it's an unfortunate perk in your line of work, isn't it."

Evans raised his eyebrows. "I guess, thankfully the Crossrail remains were just an ancient burial ground. Still delayed us by months."

Lucy flicked through her notes, focusing on her task. "On the day Daniel went missing, you were home all day?"

"Yeah, I was helping my dad in the garden. He was clearing out his shed, and then I watched TV most of the day. Saturday mornings used to be surprisingly good TV back then."

Lucy smiled. She'd never been that big on TV. "You didn't go out in the street at all that day? Didn't see any of your friends?"

"No, we went out to the garage a couple of times to put stuff in there, but I didn't see Dan, or anyone. Simon and Johanna were away on holiday, and Barney was out too, so there would only have been me, Sarah and … and Dan around."

He'd totally missed out Amy Bell. She wasn't sure if he'd done it on purpose or if she just didn't register with him after the way she'd treated him. Lucy put that thought on the back burner and asked, "When was the last time you saw Daniel?"

"Err …" Evans frowned. "The Wednesday, we were playing football on the green at the top. Barney, his brother, was a bit of a bruiser. Liked to throw Dan around a bit practising his judo."

Lucy nodded. She could believe that after meeting him. "He was doing that when you were playing football?"

Evans nodded. "I think judo translates to 'gentle way', but there wasn't much gentle about Barney when he was in competition mode. Dan walked off. Went home, I think."

Barney hadn't told her that snippet of information. Was it just run-of-the-mill sibling squabbles or something more? Did it continue after Barney went home? Would their parents cover it all up to save the child they had left? From what she knew of the Dunderdales, she found that hard to believe. "Who else was playing football that day?"

"Just me, Barney and Dan."

"Okay." Lucy decided to probe the Amy Bell angle, considering the new information she had. "And what about Amy Bell? Did you see much of her that week before Dan went missing?"

Evans took a breath. "She was, well, I guess you'd call her a mean girl now. Towards me anyway. We didn't get on. I had a few speech problems back then." Evans cleared his throat. "She was more Johanna's friend really."

Evans' walkie-talkie sprang to life with distorted voices.

"Sorry." Evans reached for his jacket, turning down the volume.

"So," Lucy continued. "You didn't see Dan at all after the Wednesday?"

"Err ... no, well, not to talk to. Barney came out a couple of times, but not Dan. I saw him at his window. His bedroom faced the front. I waved, but he didn't come down."

Lucy frowned. "Why was that, do you think?"

"Don't know. He could be a funny bugger sometimes. He'd dob anyone in to save his own skin."

Lucy nodded. She'd heard that before. "When did you see him at his window?"

"Oh, the Thursday or the Friday. Not sure which. Sorry."

"And Amy?" She asked again aware he hadn't answered her original question.

"No, don't think so."

Lucy made a quick note. "Do you know if anything was bothering Daniel before he went missing?"

"No, he was fine on the Wednesday till he went off."

So something happened between the Wednesday and the Saturday, but he barely left the house. "Were you aware of anyone hanging around on your street or nearby, maybe on the industrial estate at the bottom of the street?"

"No. The only people that came down our end were other residents really."

"And the industrial estate?" Lucy pressed.

Evans' face shrugged. "It was pretty derelict when we went down there. I don't remember anyone hanging around."

"Anything else stand out to you as odd back then?" Lucy was willing him to say something about Amy Bell and her dad, or non-dad as she now knew.

"Sorry." Evans shook his head.

Shit! "Okay." Lucy closed her notebook. "Thank you for your time, Mr Evans."

"No problem," he said and grabbed his hat and jacket, quickly slipping them on. "I'll take you back to the security office."

"Thanks." The full force of the din washed over her again as Evans opened the cabin door, it was hard to think as she made her way back across the work site.

Returning to her car, Lucy pulled out her notebook. She had the name and number of the school Amy Bell had attended in Kingsford. Dialling the number, she prepared herself for another battle for information. The woman that answered was softly spoken, making Lucy relax a little.

"Hello. This is DS Fuller from Woodley Police Station. I'm trying to find some details of a pupil that attended your school some time ago."

"Right." The woman on the other end paused for a moment. "Do you have a name?"

"Amy Bell. She was a pupil between nineteen eighty-seven to eighty-nine."

"Eighty-seven to eighty-nine!" The shock was evident in the woman's tone.

"I know it's a while ago, but she was a transfer from another school and –"

The woman cut her off. "Those records will be in our paper archives."

"I thought that might be the case. Is there any chance that I could come and take a look at her records tomorrow?"

"I'll have to check with the headmaster."

"Okay." She'd expected that. "Just out of interest, what information would have been required back then for a school transfer?"

"Usual stuff, I believe: birth certificate, last school's records and proof of residency."

Lucy quickly made a note. "And would she have needed to provide all those details before she could attend the school?"

"Normally, yes. Obviously, I can't speculate as to this specific case as I wasn't here back then. I don't think any of our current staff were, to be fair."

"Okay. Thank you for your help." Lucy gave the woman her contact information and made an appointment time for the following day.

Her next call was to Tanner. "Hi, Andy, where are you?" Lucy hoped he was back at the office. She needed him to do some digging for her.

"Just on my way back to Woodley, that older lad Mark Wallace checks out, he was on a residential trip in Wales. Sarah Moody was a washout, couldn't remember anything new. She barely even remembered her original statement."

"Not surprising." From what she'd learned so far, people moved on, and thirty years was ample time for people to do that. She hadn't told him about the possibility of expanding their search for other residents with access to the woodland; she wanted to wait till they'd both managed to track down their current quota before adding to it.

"How about you? Any luck with Bellamy's MOD records?"

Lucy let out a long breath. "Sort of. I'll fill you in later. When you get back to the office, could you find out what you can on Paul Bellamy's death? He died in ninety-five."

"Another one bites the dust," Tanner replied. "When in ninety-five?"

"Err." Lucy checked through the paperwork Green had printed out for her. "September. I want to know how he died and if it was suspicious in any way." According to the records, his mother received his death in service payment.

"Okay. I'll see what I can find."

"Great." Lucy tided her paperwork, dropping it on the passenger seat. "I'm leaving now. We'll catch up when I get back."

CHAPTER 18

Barney Dunderdale, July 1988

Barney walked down the driveway, tossing the football between his hands. Dan trailed behind. He could hear him wrestling with the Wagon Wheel he'd grabbed on their way out. Passing Mark's house, he thought he spotted him in the front window, but whoever it was, quickly ducked away. He knew as soon as he started kicking the ball around in the street the others would turn up. If not, he'd go anyway, dragging Dan along with him.

He liked to think their gang was tight, despite his brother's need to blab and drop people right in it. He could only imagine the embarrassment Johanna had suffered with the plant pots and that creepy old man. He hadn't had a chance to talk to Johanna yet, she was joined at the hip with Amy most of the time, but he'd seen the looks she'd directed at Dan. Annoying as he was, Dan was still his brother.

When the school holidays began last week, they were all on a natural high, especially when they broke into the old plastic factory next to the stream. Not that it was locked someone had already seen to that taking what they wanted and leaving the door wide open as they left. He'd been cautious leaving the door propped shut for a couple of weeks hoping no one would notice, and they hadn't. They were minus

Sarah then, as her posh school hadn't broken up for the holidays. That was probably a good thing, considering where they ended up. Johanna and Simon had family around so they couldn't join in, but today they could, maybe it would make up for what Dan had done.

He'd been first to go inside. All the machinery had been removed with only wires left trailing along the floor, leaving a massive open space, surrounded by mezzanine offices. They'd spent all afternoon pulling out all the strip lights and launching them onto the concrete floor below, each of them eager to see the next puff of powder when it disintegrated into nothing. He had a new plan now, something better than that.

One by one, they slowly started to appear, first Johanna with her Frisbee, as it was the only thing Amy would play apart from swing ball. Amy came out next, book in hand, as usual. After a short conversation with Johanna, she draped the book over her gate to keep her page while she played Frisbee. Simon tagged along with his bike, but he quickly dropped it on the pavement in favour of playing football with Dan.

There was no car in the Moodys' driveway, so they were probably out, which was a relief; he wasn't in the mood for a snobby lecture. Little Mark was the last to surface. Barney said nothing about seeing him lurking earlier; he knew Mark would wait and see if Simon was around before coming out.

Barney grabbed the football as it skittered along the ground towards him and called out, "This is boring. Let's go back to the bottle place. I've got an idea."

"What!" Dan's eyes were wide with fear.

The others said nothing, but he thought he saw a glimmer of something on Amy's face.

"Come on, I'll show you when we get there," he called, and ball in hand, Johanna appeared in his peripheral vision. "You'll like this place, you can smash up everything."

"Yeah." There was a spark of excitement in her face. She threw the Frisbee in the direction of her front lawn, it clipped the top of their fence before flopping over inside.

Dan stood on the other side of the road talking to Amy, he could see Johanna glaring at them. He knew he needed to clear the air between her and Dan, he had a responsibility for his brother and what he did to others. "Look, I know Dan dropped you in the shit with the old guy and the pots."

Johanna let out a long sigh as she began to walk down the hill. "I had to replace all of them."

He walked with her. "I'm sorry. He can be a real nob sometimes."

"How do you deal with him?"

Barney shrugged. "He's my brother. The same way you let Simon off the hook all the time." He turned and waited at the bottom of the road. As he dropped the ball at the kerb, he looked back to see they were all following.

The barbed wire squeaked as he stepped on it to get over the low fence. He walked on down the short path to the stream, hearing the same squeak as each one of them trailed behind him in a line. The back of the abandoned factory was half-hidden by the overgrown bushes and trees surrounding it.

Barney peeked around the corner of the building, the car park was empty of vehicles only a skip and a few pallets occupied the space. Holding up his hand he turned to Dan and the rest of them. "Wait here, I'll check it out first." Johanna nodded, he saw the mixture of fear and excitement in her eyes before ducking around the front of the building. The skip hid him from any onlookers as he edged towards the fire door they'd used before, he noticed two vans parked at the far end of the long building but nothing more. The broken off padlock was still there, just as they'd left it the other week. He grabbed it and slipped it off, dropping it in his pocket before opening the clasp and pulling the door open.

Inside, the air was cool, and he took a moment to scan the tall space. Darkened windows on the mezzanine floor above were empty, the glass already smashed with the help of his black widow catapult. Several timber pallets were stacked just to his right, as he moved further inside a crunching sound echoed from under his feet. Glancing down he saw the remains of a smashed strip light scattered around his trainers, a grin stretched his lips as he recalled their antics a few weeks ago. Piles of different-coloured plastic bottles still littered the floor as if they had just come off the production lines. Nothing had changed since they were there the last time, he mentally puffed out his chest knowing it was his idea to come back. He poked his head out the open door, "Dan!" His face quickly appeared next to the brickwork, and he nodded for them to follow.

With everyone inside he secured the fire door and got to work, searching for the big coil of ripped-out cable from their last visit. He ran up the mezzanine steps on the left to the row of offices finding it in the middle office. He grabbed it from the floor, turning he noticed a picture on the back of the office door. The flash of flesh registered in his brain halting his movement. He stood still for a second; there were no footsteps nearby, by the sound of it everyone was occupied downstairs. He pushed the door closed to get a better look, it was a calendar. The blonde naked woman was draped over the bonnet of a red sports car, her legs open. He'd never seen a naked woman before, it stirred a feeling in his core. A squeal from below brought him to his senses.

How had he missed that before. Pulling it from the door; he ripped the image of the woman from the calendar section, folding it roughly he stuffed it into the front pocket of his jeans. He was sure his friends at school would want to see it after the holidays.

He returned to the floor below just in time to see Simon attempt to throw a lump of wood at a series of plastic bottle lined up like skittles, he missed. Mark was next, he at least managed to knock a few down with his feeble attempt. Glancing across the room he could see Amy and Johanna were huddled in a corner messing with some strips of wire; they were talking about something, he couldn't hear what over the nose of the skittles contest. The sour look on Amy's face told him it wasn't good, Johanna looked at the floor as she slowly moved away from Amy.

Barney looked up at the large metal trusses above his head, they looked more than strong enough to hold their weight. He then pulled out his knife to trim off the stray ends of the wires to make it easier to tie off and searched the floor, looking for just the right bit, something he could tie the cable to and throw over the beam above.

It took him a few minutes to find what he was looking for. Grabbing the pipe from the floor, he quickly tied the cable to it, keeping the beam in sight he launched the short metal pipe at it. It hit but didn't go over. He stood back as it clattered to the floor. The sound was lost in the noise they were all making. He picked it up, trying again. This time, it sailed over, trailing the cable behind it, and he had to jump to grab it. Pulling it down, he tied a simple loop knot in the end then threaded the other end through the loop pulling it tight to the beam above. He'd seen his dad tie the same knot at home to bind stuff together.

"What's Barney doing?"

He turned at the question unsure if it was Simon or Mark's voice.

"It's a swing!" Amy squealed from across the open space.

"Get all the plastic bottles, bring them all over here," he yelled, intent on getting his plan into action now the cat was out of the bag. "Make a pile, like a pit."

"Yeah. Come on," Simon yelled.

"What are we doing?" Dan asked again.

"You'll see," Was all he'd tell him. He cut off any stray wires so they wouldn't dig into his hands. the skittles game had been replaced with the sound of bottles scratching across the floor as they were moved. Laughter made him turn around; Amy had found an old broom to make the job easier while the others kicked at the bottles.

He needed to test it first. If it held his weight, the rest would be fine. Gripping the cable, he held his breath as he raised his feet from the ground. It held, but it was above shoulder height on him making it a little high up for some of the others to use. Looking around, he saw a wooden box nearby and dragged it closer. He used the cable to steady himself as he climbed on. By now, the plastic bottles were piled up, ready to go.

"Out the way!" he yelled and launched himself in the direction of the bottle pit. Dan pushed Little Mark out of the way making him stumble. Whoops from the others followed him the entire way. Releasing his hands, he prepared for the pain, but he simply sank into the thick pile of plastic.

Barney jumped up. Looking back, he was surprised to see Dan had already grabbed the cable ready to have the next go. Jumping up, he seemed to travel in slow motion towards the pit, except he didn't let go; he held on, body tense, gripping the cable.

"Let go!" Barney yelled. A sliver of fear shot through him, what if Dan got hurt? How would he explain it to their father?

"I can't," he screamed back as he swung away from the bottles.

Finally, on his third approach, he let go, laughing wildly as he sprang up in the sea of plastic.

Barney released a sigh of relief.

Johanna then took her turn, barely waiting for Dan to crawl out of the pile of bottles before she landed near him, sending bottles flying everywhere. Barney picked up a piece of wood to gather the bottles back into a thick pile.

Just then, a noise caught Barney's attention. With the racket they were making, he thought maybe someone had heard them and a wave of panic swept through him. The sweat quickly cooled down his back as his hands shook.

"Quiet!" he called out in a half whisper. He knew he was drawing attention to them, but he didn't know how else to get them all to shut up. "Someone's here!" he yelled. The piece of wood was still in his hand as his feet became magnetised to the floor.

Someone behind him gasped. They were all trapped, there was no other way out. This would all be his fault, it was his idea. Would Dan dob him in as easily as he had Johanna? He turned to see the fear etched on their faces as they looked towards him and the door they'd all entered by.

"Who is it?" Someone whispered. His eyes were fixed on the far side of the room. It sounded again, a flutter of movement to the left of the door. It was inside whatever it was; hidden by the pile of pallets, but what or who was it? He started to edge towards it.

"Barn don't?" Dan called from across the room. He could hear the fear in his brother's voice.

He held up his free hand as a gesture. "It's fine, stay there." He swallowed back his fear knowing his father would never forgive him if he got caught, or rather if Dan did. As he moved closer, something fluttered near the floor, then a flicker of movement through the gaps in the pallets.

The wobble that threatened his rigid frame subsided a little and he peeked around the side of the pallets. It really was just a bird. A bloody pigeon, but this one was trapped, its tiny black eyes blinking at him. Barney saw the fear, the terror he'd felt only moments ago.

"It's just a bird!" he yelled, turning to see Amy on his shoulder, almost bumping into him. He hadn't noticed her get so close.

He looked back at the bird. Its leg was caught on a piece of stray wire, preventing it from taking off. The noise in the room grew again as someone else took a turn on the swing.

"Stupid bird," Amy mumbled. Her tone was dismissive, although her focus never wavered.

The wire had an unkind curve on it, and as the bird pulled away, it tightened, trapping it even more. If he could get close enough, he could easily release it. He watched the bird as it dithered on the concrete floor, their presence alone making it panic. His stomach churned at the noise it made as it skittered around in a ragged circle. He waited for his moment to step in and be the hero and handed Amy the lump of wood to hold as he moved closer. He didn't really want to touch it – his dad hated them, called them winged rats – but he couldn't just watch it suffer in front of him. It could easily find its way out of the building if given the chance; it got in after all.

He crouched down smaller, hoping to reduce the fear he saw in the pigeon's tiny eyes.

"What are you doing? It's dirty. Don't touch it," Amy snarled. Disgust was evident in her tone.

Barney looked up; Amy's gaze was focused hard at the bird.

"We can't just leave it," he told her and edged a little closer. He was sure he could save it.

He looked up in confusion as Amy's foot crept further along the wire, she closed in on the creature as it squirmed across the floor. Was she trying to help him, he was the hero, he'd saved the slow worm when she wanted to kill it. The bird's panic heightened as it's circle of movement became reduced by her actions. Barney's mind was in a fog as the squeal of the bird escalated. He couldn't make out what was going on. "Amy!" He tried to get her attention. She glanced down at him, her lips were twisted in a scowl. He opened his mouth to speak, but his trembling lips prevented anything coming out. The noise of the bird fogged his mind. He was the oldest, he was the strong one, but at this moment he was chilled with fear. She was only a couple of feet away from the bird now, the noise was excruciating. His thick muscles tightened as his heart raced. The moment dragged. What was she waiting for? She was in touching distance as the bird flailed.

He blindly stretched out an arm for the length of wood, freeing Amy's hands for the task ahead. His fingers brushed against the side of the wood and he tried to wrap his hand around the timber section, but it was swiftly pulled out of reach. He turned to search for it, confused, but before he could react, the timber was thrust down onto the bird's head. It wasn't the simple tamping action his father had used to compact the concrete path the other day. The force of the wood against the floor crushed the life out of the pigeon. A second blow was administered as he was numbly rooted to the floor. The thud of Amy's actions were easily lost in the din of the cavernous room, the happy voices of the others masking the sounds.

He snatched a look at Amy, unsure what to think, and bile rose in his throat at the grin on her face. Her eyes bore into the crushed head and body of the bird. A wing still flickered with life, but he knew there was no hope.

Blinking into action, he grabbed the wood from Amy's clutches afraid she would continue her actions.

"No! Don't! Give it!" Amy yelled, her eyes wild as she glared at him. Her words echoed in the large warehouse and seemed to create a vacuum in the room as it fell silent, except for the faint flutter from the flailing bird.

The fear of defeat washed over him as a lopsided grin pulled at one side of Amy's mouth before she quickly returned her attention to the fidgeting pigeon.

"What are you doing?" Johanna yelled as she walked towards them. Her stride faltered as she got closer.

Barney looked at the ground, unable to cope with the disgust on Johanna's face. Simon's mouth was a gaping hole in his head as he stared at the scene in front of them.

"Did you ...? Why, Barn?" Johanna demanded, sounding lost as she looked at him.

"I-I-didn't!" was all he managed to get out before he was cut off.

"Barney?" Dan called from across the room. "What's –?"

Johanna cut him off. "Come on! We're going!" She grabbed Simon's hand before marching off towards the exit.

"God, she's such a drama queen." Amy huffed.

His eyes landed on a spot of blood on Amy's pink trainer as she stood there glaring back at him, but the wood was in his hand. He threw it on the floor. A smear of blood appeared as it skidded across the hard surface.

Barney looked from Johanna's retreating figure back to Amy. Her smug grin sickening his stomach before approaching footsteps drew his attention. Dan was rushing towards him, but he couldn't let him reach them. His legs sprang into action, moving to meet him. He needed to cut him off before he saw it too. "No Dan, don't." But it was too late.

"Wh-what's happened? Dan was out of breath as he spoke, The grin falling from his face as his eyes fixed on the crushed carcass next to the pallet.

"It's nothing, just a dead bird." He tried to brush it off.

"Your brother put it out of its misery." Amy said with a smirk as she walked away.

The shock on Dan's face made the bile surface again. His brother had always looked up to him, but now he wasn't so sure. He placed a hand on Dan's shoulder turning him towards the door. "Let's go home."

CHAPTER 19

LUCY WAS groggy as she woke to the sound of her phone. The room was dark, but at this time of year, it didn't mean anything, and it took her a moment to realise she'd crashed out on the sofa after her long day. She turned over, squinting at the TV. The news was blaring on. She made a grab for her phone on the table. Seeing the station's name on the screen, she groaned inwardly, although, in truth, there was only one reason for her phone to be ringing at what felt like the middle of the night.

"Fuller," she answered as she reached for the remote to mute the TV.

"We've got a body. Old guy, could be a burglary gone wrong."

The desk sergeant's words echoed in her ear. "Shit!" She had enough on with the Dunderdale case, but they didn't have the luxury of taking one case at a time. "What's the address?" Lucy wiped at her eyes, trying to wake herself up.

"Grove Lane. It's just off the main road between Oldbury and Kingsford."

"I'm leaving now," she said and got to her feet, slipping on her boots. The one good thing about falling asleep fully dressed is that you're ready to go straight back out again.

"DCI Barrel is on route. Laxton was first on the scene. He'll meet you there."

"Okay," she replied and glanced back at the TV, spotting the time in the bottom right-hand corner. Jesus, it was almost two thirty in the morning. "Thanks," she replied out of habit rather than courtesy, considering the time. Laxton again! West Heath Station was obviously still stretched.

With this development, Lucy could feel the Dunderdale case slipping further and further away. She was getting nowhere fast. After finding out Bell or Bellamy was dead, she'd been hopeful when she visited the school. Unfortunately, the only details they had for Amy Bell regarding the transfer were the MOD letter informing them of Paul Bell's transfer to the local airbase, which apparently, back then, was a green light into any school. No birth certificate or previous school records, so again the trail of Amy Bell had gone cold.

Lucy slowed as she pulled onto Grove Lane. It consisted of two rows of detached bungalows, one on each side of the road. The two police cars parked outside the fifth one on the left indicated which she was looking for. Several other cars were parked further on; including a crime scene technician's van, but no sign of Barrel's Volvo. Lucy parked on the opposite side of the road, hoping she wouldn't be here long enough to be an obstruction to the residents.

She extracted herself from her car and began preparing to enter the crime scene.

"DS Fuller, you must be on someone's shit list."

Lucy looked up to see Laxton appear from the front of the bungalow, his Hi-Viz vest standing out in the darkness. His torch was aimed at the floor around his feet as if he was scanning for something. "Must be," she replied, although surely he was in the same boat. She decided not to labour over the point as Laxton had a quick tongue, and she wasn't up to a war of words right now. She zipped up her Tyvek suit and headed in his direction.

"What have we got?" Laxton's bright face told her he was far more used to nights than she was.

"David Booker, aged seventy-one, lived alone. Neighbour reported a disturbance just after one a.m." Laxton pointed to the bungalow on the left of the Booker residence. "We got here around one-thirty, knocked but got no response. Went around the back, found the door open, glass in the door broken. We entered the property, finding Booker on the floor in the hallway. He was unresponsive. My partner tried to revive him. I called an ambulance, but they couldn't do anything more when they arrived."

"Burglary?" Lucy asked as she stepped towards the bungalow.

"Looks like it. Hard to say if anything is missing. They've turned it upside down. I think he was still warm when we got here. Thought we could bring him back, but ..." Laxton trailed off.

Lucy stopped, turning to Laxton. "You did your best. Can't save everyone." He nodded but didn't meet her gaze.

"Hope you haven't had any supper. His head's a mess."

"Noted." Lucy took a deep breath. Gore really wasn't her thing. Finding the bastard that did it, *that* was her thing. "What alerted the neighbours?"

Laxton flipped through his notebook. "John and Heather Cole heard raised voices around twelve forty-five. It went on for some twenty minutes or so. They knew he lived alone, so they were worried. Mr Cole called the police. Mrs Cole looked out the back window and saw three or four youths running away about fifteen minutes before we got here."

"Any lights on when you got here?" Lucy asked.

"No, nothing. Front door was locked, all windows closed. Only the back door open."

"They didn't hear the glass being smashed?" she asked, wondering if that was what initially alerted them. "Neighbours," she clarified.

Laxton looked confused for a second. "Nope, didn't mention it."

"Okay. Thanks. Are they still up?" She couldn't see if their lights were still on, not that anyone in the street would be sound asleep now they'd arrived. She wanted to get their first account as soon as possible.

"Yeah. I've stuck a WPC with them."

Irritation at Laxton's phrasing threatened to overflow, but she bit her tongue. He'd had a rough night after all. "You mean a constable that happens to be a woman is currently keeping them company."

"Yeah. Sorry."

She nodded her acceptance of his apology. "Barrel's on his way. You might want to keep an eye out for him." This was the second time she was first on the scene, was he starting to finally trust her.

"Right." Laxton backed away as he pointed to the ground. "Follow the slabs."

Left alone, Lucy made her way to the front of the bungalow, which was partly illuminated by a street light situated on the opposite side of the road. She then ducked under crime-scene tape that had been stretched between an old wooden post edging the far side of the driveway, across the outside of the front hedge, and tied off at the brick pillar that lined the path to the front door. She walked up the drive, following the slabs past the attached garage around the far side of the property to the back of the bungalow. A tent and lights had been erected around what she figured was the back door. The kitchen light was now on, the light shining through onto the patchy lawn in the back garden. She glanced towards the end of the garden; the outline of a high fence was just visible on three sides. The runners had only one exit.

The shadows inside the tent indicated that there was movement beyond. Taking out her notebook, she took a deep breath. With a gloved hand, she separated the plastic, stepping inside where she found a tec, doubled over, dusting the back door while another picked up the glass from the kitchen floor. Realising they had company, they turned to face her before standing aside for her to enter the scene. Lucy carefully navigated the metal plates they had placed on the floor; numerous bloody footprints were visible in the kitchen going to and from the hallway. More than one offender, by the different shoeprints they had left behind. She hoped the tecs would be able to narrow down the brands.

A thick doormat sat at the entrance to the back door; could be why the neighbours hadn't heard the glass breaking: soft landing. Maybe a rock or something from the garden had been used to gain access. She made a note to ask later as she took in the scene around her.

The kitchen was in mild disarray. It was hard to say if the mess was out of the ordinary or not; it wasn't exactly what she would call ransacked. The long hallway beyond had five doorways leading onto it: two each on the left and right and the front door at the end. As she moved inside she hovered in the kitchen avoiding the inevitable that lay beyond. She felt the gloominess that she always associated with bungalows, lots of hallways leading to pokey rooms.

Lucy groaned inwardly when she saw Dr Reed's hulking figure bending over the body that was prone on the hallway floor, his assistant crouched next to him, clipboard in hand. Taking a deep breath, she stepped closer, mentally preparing herself, just as Reed moved back, giving her a clearer view. The first thing she saw was the bloody lump that had once been the man's head. Blinking, her gaze quickly travelled further down the body. There was no obvious blood on his hands, no defensive wounds. Had he been taken by surprise? He was still fully dressed. No PJs or whatever he slept in. Grey trousers, white shirt, vest and woolly jumper by the look of it. Dr Reed or the paramedics must have undressed him a little to get access. The bungalow was warm too warm, her skin prickled inside her protective suit. She glanced back at the victim was it too warm considering the weather had become milder in the last day or two, and the numerous layers he wore.

"From the look of the scene around the body, I'd say the attack started and finished here," Reed said.

Lucy finally looked up, finding her voice. "Right." She glanced around. Several markers had been stuck to the wall and floor, indicating directionality of blood splatter.

"Any idea of the weapon?"

"Not yet. It was something heavy and quite a frenzied attack by the look of it. The first blows to his head knocked him to the floor, followed by multiple blows when he was down." Reed said as he pushed his glasses up his nose.

"So, the killer should have blood on them?" Lucy asked.

"Yes. I would say so. The heating was on high, so time of death is a little tricky to narrow down at the moment. Back door was open, but he was fully clothed and found near a radiator. His age will also be a factor. I'll need to do a few calculations with the ambient temperature to be able to give you a more accurate time of death."

Lucy made a note to ask the tecs to dust the heating controls. "Okay," she said, and a silly question occurred to her; the Dunderdale case was having an effect on her already. "Are we sure it's the homeowner?"

Reed frowned at her. "Pockets are empty except for a handkerchief. Apparently he lived alone?"

Lucy nodded, trying not to look at what was left of the man's face. It would have been a perfect opportunity for misdirection.

"We'll print him to make sure they match prints in the house. Might help to confirm ID considering his current state. I'm not sure dental will help. We'll bag the toothbrush too." Reed said and nodded to his assistant.

"Thanks," Lucy replied.

"There's no sign of rigor mortis yet, but there are signs of lividity in the body. It's not very pronounced, so it could be up to three hours, but not much more. That's your lot right now. I'll need to get him back to tell you more."

"Okay, thank you, Dr Reed. Let me know about the autopsy." Lucy turned to make her way back down the hall.

"How did you get on with Dr Chadwick?"

"Oh." Lucy was flummoxed by the swift change of subject for a moment. "Very well she's ... err, very informative."

Reed chuckled. "Yes, she is that. Worked all over the world on mass grave sites and what not."

Lucy nodded to Dr Reed recalling her conversation with Philippa Chadwick before stepping into the nearest room. It was Booker's bedroom, she figured, by the unfussy bedding. There were signs it had been tossed, a small electric heater near the bed had been kicked over, thankfully it wasn't on. Due to the sparse contents, the burglars must have gotten bored quickly.

She heard Barrel's voice in another room. Stepping out into the hallway, she tried to spot him in the sea of white bodies. He beat her to it.

"Fuller!"

She turned to see Barrel in the room opposite. "Boss."

"What do we think?" he asked, watching Reed begin to prepare the body for removal from the scene.

"David Booker, seventy-one, lived alone. Reed can't give us an accurate time of death yet. No lights on when Laxton and Springer arrived at one thirty. Also, the heating was on full too." Lucy stepped into the next room to get out of the way of the tecs. She turned, realising she'd ended up in the front room. It had been rifled through more thoroughly than the rest of the rooms she'd seen. Sofa cushions thrown around the room and drawers pulled out and emptied on the floor, another electric heater sat in front of a blocked off fireplace. Even the TV had been pushed over; vandalism but not burglary.

Barrel shrugged. "Old people, I thought they were scrimpers."

"Exactly. It's weird he was fully dressed, woolly jumper and all. That's why we can't get an accurate TOD." It didn't feel right to her. "Looks frenzied, not someone just hitting him to get away," she continued.

"No, they smashed his head in alright."

Lucy cringed as she nodded back to the kitchen floor. "Looks like a number of individuals were here during or after the murder."

"This is the fourth burglary in the area over the last two months, but the only one with a fatality," Barrel continued.

"Targeting elderly people?" she questioned. His time in court had obviously given him time to read up on current statistics.

"Yeah. Sick bastards. Never much taken from the scenes, though."

"Any suspects so far?" she asked, hopefully.

Barrel shook his head. "Go and talk to the Coles, get a bit of background on our man."

Lucy nodded.

"And get Tanner to look for any CCTV in the area. See if we can get a picture of the lads she saw running away."

She being Mrs Cole, she figured. "Yes, boss." Tanner would be so pleased.

Lucy left via the back door. Pushing through the white tent, she was grateful for the cool October air hitting her lungs. Unzipping her suit, she pulled it down, not caring about the fine rain that had begun to fall. She then retraced her steps to the front of the house and stopped to give the front door the once over. It was your standard, solid, wooden front door knocker, fixed at eye level but no letterbox. She looked to the side of the door. Two panes of patterned glass were separated with a timber rail containing a letterbox. Moving away, she saw Laxton lurking near the police cordon.

"Did you knock or use the doorbell?" she asked him as she removed her arms from her Tyvek suit.

"Err … knocked. Well, Brad did. I looked through the window there." He pointed to the bay window to the left of the front door. "But I didn't see anything. Curtains were closed."

Lucy glanced back at the bungalow. The other front window had a large shrub planted in front of it, making Laxton's choice for him. PC Brad Springer; she hadn't seen him yet.

"And the letterbox? Did you look through it?"

"I didn't. Not sure about Springer."

"Where is he?" She looked around, hoping to locate him.

"Wasn't feeling well. He's gone back to the station."

Lucy nodded. Bloodied bodies had that effect on people, including her. It didn't matter anyway; she wanted it dusted for prints.

"Okay, find out for me. And get the tecs to dust the doorbell and letterbox for prints." If the offenders wanted to make sure the house was empty before breaking in, they were more likely to have used the doorbell rather than alert the neighbours with knocking, maybe even peeked through the letterbox.

"Okay," Laxton replied as he looked back at the bungalow.

Lucy stripped off the rest of her suit, tossing it into the boot of her car before heading towards the neighbours bungalow. It looked well-maintained even in the glow of the street lamp. The clusters of shrubs and flowers in the front garden must have produced a riot of colour in the daylight. She used her knuckles to knock on the white plastic front door.

A familiar face answered. It was Tanner's new lady friend.

"Hi."

Lucy squinted at her ID. She wasn't in uniform; she must have been called in too. "PC Goff."

"Sarge." Goff opened the door, letting her into the hallway.

"Lucy Fuller," she offered.

"I know," she replied and held her hand out to Lucy. "Rachel."

Lucy took the offered hand. "How are they? I just need to have a word with them."

"Not too bad. Bit shocked still, I think."

Understandable. It's not every night you wake up to your neighbour being beaten to a pulp.

"I'll make some tea," Goff offered as she pointed to the first room on the left.

"Thanks."

Lucy pulled out her identification as she entered the room and turned towards the two figures sitting in separate armchairs.

"Hello, I'm DS Fuller. I know it's late, but would it be okay if I asked you both a few questions?" The room was quite different to Booker's, not just the tidiness but the flowery nature of every surface. Heather Cole had a heavy hand when it came to decorating.

"It's not like we're going to be able to sleep now anyway," Mr Cole replied as he shuffled around in his armchair.

The pen in his hand and folded paper on the arm of his chair indicated he hadn't exactly been racked with fear. Mrs Cole, on the other hand, looked far more frayed.

"Thank you."

Lucy settled on the edge of a small two-seater sofa. Fatigue was beginning to settle in after the rush of the scene.

"How well did you know Mr Booker?" she asked as she opened her notebook, pen poised.

"Is he dead?" Mrs Cole replied.

"Course he is. You just saw him being put in the ambulance all covered up, didn't you?"

Lucy focused on Mrs Cole, ignoring her husband's brash reply, and said, "I'm afraid so." She paused for a moment to let the news sink in. "Did you know him well?"

"No. Well, not really. Just to chat to occasionally, over the fence or in the street."

"Any family that you know of?"

"We didn't really know him well enough to know." Mrs Cole looked at her husband.

"He never mentioned anyone?" Lucy pressed.

Mrs Cole's hands were clenched. "No."

"Has he lived there long, do you know?" She could find out later, but she wanted their view.

"Longer than us and we've been here ..."

"Twelve years," Mr Cole interjected, the annoyance clear on his face. She was getting nowhere.

"Did you ever go inside his house?" She addressed both of them.

Mr Cole sat up straighter. "What exactly are you accusing us of here?"

"Nothing, nothing at all, Mr Cole. We're just trying to establish if anything is missing that's all. We need all the help we can get right now."

"We wouldn't know." Mr Cole's frown cleared.

"You didn't like him?" Lucy asked, tired of skirting around the subject.

"No, not really, always thought there was something weird about him. He threw stones at cats and birds when they were in his garden. It was like he didn't like anything living in there, no flowers, grass, nothing."

"He was a bit tight with his money that's all." Mrs Cole added.

"Tight! That's one way of putting it.."

Mr Cole was on a roll now.

"Every time I saw him he had about five layers on, too tight to put the bloody heating on."

Lucy's ears pricked up. "I'm sorry."

"I went round there once to give him a parcel that had been delivered here when he was out, great big thing," Mr Cole waved his hands around in the air. "Don't know what it was, I had to take it inside. It was warmer outside than it was in his place, tight sod."

Lucy let out a breath as she made notes, it certainly wasn't for a lack of heaters. They still needed to formally identify Booker. She thought she knew the answer but asked the question anyway. "Would you be willing to formally identify him?"

"We don't have to, do we?" Mrs Cole asked, looking at her husband.

"No, we can get his GP to do it," Lucy conceded. "When was the last time you saw him?"

"I saw or rather heard him in the garden earlier today, yesterday," Mr Cole corrected. "He was humming like he always did."

PC Goff then came into the room, tea tray in hand. She nodded to Lucy before placing it on the table between the armchairs. Instead of leaving, Goff stood by the doorway. Lucy would have preferred her to leave, but she wasn't about to say anything.

"Would you say he was a night owl?" she asked.

"Not that I noticed."

"And you told the officer you heard raised voices around twelve forty-five."

"Yes. Our bedroom's at the back of the house; overlooks the garden."

Lucy nodded. "Mrs Cole, how many people do you think you saw running away from the house?"

"I'm not sure. Three or four?"

"Could I take a look, just so I can get a clearer picture of what you saw?" It was the perfect opportunity to separate the witnesses.

"Of course." Mrs Cole got to her feet.

Lucy nodded to Mr Cole before following his wife into the dim hallway, her mind mentally picturing David Booker lying on the floor. She stepped around his phantom body as she moved down the hallway to the Cole's bedroom, which was lit by a bedside lamp. The fingers of flowery design stretched their way into this room too. A lace mat was draped over the dressing table, the flowery design was repeated in the bedspread and wallpaper.

"What time did you turn in?" Lucy asked as she took it all in.

"I turned the light out about eleven-thirty. John had already dropped off."

"Did they wake you up?" She knew from experience how confusing it was when you were rudely woken.

Mrs Cole nodded.

"How many voices do you think there were?"

"Hard to say. They were all talking at once."

"Was the shouting inside or outside?"

"Both, I think."

Disagreement over the incident maybe. "And when you got up to take a look, what did you see?"

"Nothing at first. Just noise. Talking, people crashing around." Mrs Cole pointed to the wooden chair that had been pulled away from the dressing table. "I stood on the chair to get a better look."

Lucy could see the heat rise in Mrs Cole's cheeks at her admission. She decided to skirt over it. She'd called it in after all. "There were no lights on in Mr Booker's house?"

"No. Then, about five minutes later, I looked again and saw them all running away."

Lucy stepped towards the chair. "May I?"

Mrs Cole nodded. Lucy slipped off her shoes and stood on the chair. The view across the fence to Booker's back garden was virtually unrestricted, and she could see the shadows moving in the white tent. The darkness would have been Mrs Cole's only obstacle with no lights on.

Their respective back gardens couldn't have been more different. The Coles had thoroughly gone to town with pergolas, solar lighting and all sorts.

"Retired?" Lucy asked.

Mrs Cole looked confused for a second before answering. "Yes, we both are."

"And which direction did they go?" She wanted to be able to give Tanner something to go on with CCTV.

Mrs Cole stepped closer to the window. "They went around the far side. Oh, then another one came out a minute or so later. He hesitated for a moment then followed after them."

"So, is that three or four, do you think?" Lucy repeated.

"Four, I think. Yes, definitely four of them. Three and then one." Mrs Cole turned to face her, a look of triumph on her face. "It's funny what you remember, isn't it."

Mrs Cole seemed a little more relaxed without her husband in the room.

"It is," Lucy smiled. "I don't suppose you recognised any of them, did you?"

"Sorry," she replied, shaking her head.

Lucy returned to the sitting room, waiting for Mrs Cole to retake her seat. "Thank you for your time. We'll need to you both to make a witness statement." She pulled a card from her pocket and placed it on the sideboard. "I'll leave my card in case you think of anything else."

Mr Cole replied with a grunt, while his wife nodded her reply.

"PC Goff will give you the details." She nodded to Rachel before returning to the Booker house to fill in Barrel on the Coles.

CHAPTER 20

THE CROFT HALL was still packed an hour after the short church service had ended. A service that was attended by the immediate family only, on their request. It all seemed a bit rushed to Johanna: first the service on Sunday, now this pseudo funeral the following Saturday. Dan's body had only been discovered two weeks ago, but after waiting so long for closure, she figured they couldn't wait any longer. Dan's parents had decided to skip the wake, although Barney and his family were in attendance. Maybe his parents had the same feeling she did, that someone in the town was responsible for Dan's death. And standing around eating sausage rolls and carrot sticks with those people certainly wasn't going to make that feeling go away.

Her mother had seemed a little snubbed at first when she'd told Johanna; she said she understood, but Johanna had heard the edge of disappointment in her tone. Yet she'd still managed to outdo herself in organising a team of people to prepare a banquet for the occasion.

Johanna occupied a space near the buffet tables, scanning the crowd for familiar faces. The Croft Hall, with its ancient, exposed timber trusses holding up the roof, were still only painted on one side, the place hadn't changed much since she attended the first few Girl Guide meetings. It was her mother's idea; a way of making new friends after they left Compton Way. It only took a couple of weeks for her to realise it wasn't for her, too girly-girly.

She took a sip from her wine, struggling to find a recognisable face in the room. Twenty years was a long time for people to age and change shape. By contrast, her parents seemed to know everyone in the room; they were social butterflies, or at least her mother was. Her father had made his excuses and left as soon as politely possible, preferring to spend the evening on his own. Johanna was just about to find her mother and do the same when the profile of a woman hovering at the adjacent buffet table caught her eye. She was pulling the clingfilm from a tray of sandwiches and used her free hand to tuck her hair behind her ear. Except her hair was short; there was nothing to move. She looked closely at the woman; she was of a similar age, slightly shorter than herself, her cropped, dark hair stark against her pale skin. She was just about to walk over and introduce herself in the hope that she would remember her when the woman turned towards her. Johanna immediately looked away, avoiding her searching eye. The other side of the woman's face was horribly scarred and inflamed. Moments later, Johanna placed her drink on the table and risked another look at the woman, who was now rearranging the sausage rolls. Her scars still appeared inflamed. She looked like two different people fused together. Her eyes locked with Johanna's and there was something there, recognition maybe. Johanna offered a weak smile, still unsure if she even knew the woman.

Then Gillian Hale appeared via a side door with another platter. Johanna sidled up to her and asked, "Who's that?" nodding towards the woman at the buffet table. Her mother barely glanced over at the woman.

"Oh, she's just a volunteer. Mia, I think. She's new in town."

Johanna frowned. "Did I go to school with her or something?"

"I doubt it. She only moved here recently. She's from up north somewhere, I think."

"Oh." Johanna was a little disappointed. She dearly wanted to find someone she had common ground with.

"Hey, Johanna?" a questioning voice called as a presence appeared by her side. She turned to see a vaguely familiar face.

"Mark, Mark Evans?"

"In the flesh."

His wide smile was faultless.

"Wow, you look great."

The shy boy with a lisp was gone. Only a shadow of a scar remained on his upper lip.

"Thank God, someone I actually bloody know." She threw her arms around his shoulders, almost spilling the orange juice-filled glass in his hand.

Mark laughed as he shoved his free hand into his trouser pocket. "I saw you looking a bit forlorn over here. Thought I'd better rescue you."

"Thank God someone did." She picked up her wine again, taking a sip. "Have you seen Barney yet? His folks aren't here."

"Yeah. I was just talking to him." Mark adjusted his feet. "He seems good, considering."

Johanna nodded.

"The MET should look into hiring your mum, the way she tracked me down."

Johanna frowned, although why was she surprised at all?

"I've only been back in London a few months, but she still managed to find me."

Mark had grown into a confident, outgoing man.

"Where were you before?"

"Oh, I'm an engineer. I was working in the UAE for years then in the States. Now I'm back in London working on the Crossrail project."

"You certainly get about a bit. That's amazing."

Mark was reserved about his achievements, which made her like him even more.

"Your mum said you'd done pretty well, setting up your own business."

"She did?" Johanna was genuinely shocked; her mother barely acknowledged the fact that she was a success in any way.

They spent the next twenty minutes sharing the milestones in their lives, or at least the bits they wanted to tell, during which she learned that Mark was on his second marriage after the first one quickly fell through. He was also a father now and quite happy to settle in one place for a while to bring up his family.

"Are you staying nearby?" she asked when she saw him check his watch for the second time.

"No. I'm just passing through, on my way to a conference in Brighton. I wanted to show my face, pay my respects." He checked his watch again. "I should get going really. It was really great seeing you again."

"Yeah, well, if you're ever passing through Bath, let me know. I might even stretch to dinner."

"I'll do that." He stepped forward, giving her a hug. "Take care."

"You too." Johanna watched as Mark disappeared into the crowd of people that were heading her way. The buffet table had become a popular place to be. Moving away from the bustle of paper plates being handed out, she became cornered by Barney's wife, Samantha. Her face held a rigid smile as if her taught ponytail had frozen her features, her black dress hung loose around her slim figure. Johanna noticed the tremor in Samantha's hand as she held an empty plate.

"Your mum's done a great job with the food," she offered.

"She has." It took a moment for Johanna to realise Samantha was child-free for a change. Maybe they were with their father. She racked her brain for something to say. "Barney said you're living in Guilford now."

"Yes, well just on the outskirts, in a village called Shalford. Barney said the fresh air would be good for me."

Barney said. Johanna made no comment. She wondered what it would be like to be a fly on the wall in the Dunderdale house. Barney had been her ally, always the voice of reason in the gang. The decision maker. She wondered if he ever talked to Samantha about Daniel.

"Do you have any children, Johanna?"

"No, I don't. Haven't found the right person yet, I guess." Would she ever, the way she was going? In truth it hadn't really been an option with Steph but she hoped it might happen in the future.

"You need a Barney," Samantha announced.

Barney was the last thing she needed, for obvious reasons. Regardless of that, she couldn't imagine someone having control over her life like Barney seemed to have over Samantha. But the insanely happy smile on Samantha's face told a different story. "I don't know about that."

"Trust me." Samantha reached out to touch her arm with her fingertips. "He's such a good father, and provider. I'm so lucky. We're all so lucky."

Johanna nodded, Jesus, she was sick of listening to her sycophantic drivel. From the little time she'd spent with Barney in recent days, let alone all those years ago, he seemed far from the perfect man or father.

"Yeah, we all wanted to be like Barney till he killed that pigeon." The words were out before she could stop them. They'd been bubbling under the surface for days, now they were finally out.

"What?" Samantha glared at her, mouth agape.

"Oh, he didn't tell you?" Johanna took a sip from her drink, but the wine had barely gone down her throat before a shocking slap threw her off balance, forcing her to clutch at the edge of the table, dislodging a plate in the process. The blood rushed in her ears as the din of conversation in the room immediately hushed and everyone turned to look at the commotion playing out. Regaining her balance; Johanna looked up to see the shock on Samantha's face, her eyes gaped in fear along with her mouth. The hand that had slapped Johanna now moved to cover Samantha's own mouth, tears slipped down her cheeks as she turned on her heel quickly disappearing out of sight. A second later, her mother appeared to steer Johanna out of the room. They entered the small side room from which her mother had appeared earlier.

"Sit down," the older woman snapped and the grip on her arm finally relented, allowing her to settle in the only chair in the room. The grey, plastic seat looked more suitable for a child and creaked under her weight.

"Why are you angry with me? I'm the victim here," Johanna whined as she glanced around the small room. It was a tiny kitchen of sorts, the dim light bulb giving it a dingy feel. A single base unit with a sink set in it sat against one wall while a wooden table lined another wall. Empty platter plates, along with a kettle, cups and other tea-making accoutrements littered the top. The small window behind was a black hole. When had it got so dark? How long had she been there?

Her mother stood at the sink and released a heavy sigh as she turned on the tap too hard, forcing her to step back a little.

Johanna tilted her head to see what she was doing. She hoped her mother wasn't planning to place some dirty wash cloth on her face. She risked touching her cheek and felt the heat radiating from her skin before she even got close. It felt bruised already, as her fingertips grazed the hot surface.

"What did you say to Samantha?" Gillian still stood with her back towards her.

"Nothing," Johanna lied. Is that why Barney treated her like that, controlling her.

"You must have said something for her to do that."

Johanna watched as her mother wrung a cloth out with a little too much force. "It's a wake, for Christ's sake, Johanna."

"Why are you taking her side? Shouldn't you be out there giving her a piece of your mind for slapping your daughter?" Johanna got to her feet and moved to the door. Her mother was still avoiding her gaze.

"Where are you going?" Gillian shouted as she passed through the doorway.

"Home!" She snapped, although she didn't mean home. She meant the hotel, as it had become her makeshift home.

She continued through the hall, avoiding all the glaring eyes as she headed for the front of the building, grabbed her coat, slipped it on and stomped towards the exit. Outside, the cool night air was soothing to her face as she strutted off in the direction of the hotel, cursing her mother as she walked. Why couldn't she be supportive just this once?

"Johanna! Wait, please!"

She turned at the pleading voice to see Barney. Grey smoke surrounded him, blurring his image for a moment. She hadn't realised he smoked. The last thing she needed was another row. She continued walking, the sound of rushed footsteps echoing behind her.

"Are you okay?" He looked like the boy she once knew, when he let his tough guy façade drop, when he was truly scared.

"I'm fine," she told him, but her skin throbbed. She wished she'd taken the cold towel her mother was preparing.

"I'm sorry. She's not well," Barney said, as he fiddled with his packet of cigarettes.

She frowned. Was this another story about his wife? But then she suddenly felt worried about Samantha and what Barney might have done to her. "Where is she?"

Barney pointed to one of the benches on the small green next to them. A rigid figure sat illuminated by a street light. Had he put her in isolation on the naughty step like his kids?

"She had a couple of drinks to calm her nerves. She doesn't usually drink. She can't on the medication she's on but –"

Johanna cut him off. "It's okay, Barney. You don't have to explain." She couldn't stand to hear another sob story from Barney's life. She just wanted to go home.

He was quiet for a moment as he pulled out a fresh cigarette. "She told me what you said."

Johanna was unsure what to say to that and managed an unconvincing, "Sorry," then turned and began to walk away. "Get her a bloody coat, Barney," she called back, "it's freezing."

"It wasn't me, you know."

Johanna stopped in her tracks.

"It wasn't me that killed that pigeon. Amy did it."

"What?" Johanna turned to face him. How could that be true? She was there; she'd seen it happen.

"I was trying to stop her –" he waved his hand in front of him – "get the piece of wood from her, but she was crazy, just kept hitting it."

Johanna frowned, recalling the bloodied bird on the floor. "But she was telling *you* to stop."

"Because I was trying to take the wood from her. She wouldn't let me."

"Jesus, Barney!" Johanna looked away as she tried to recall Amy's words that day, *"No. Stop-it! Give-it!"* was all she heard as Barney and Amy both wrestled with the wood. Barney had the piece of wood in his hands when she got there. Could it really have been Amy? She shook her head.

"She made it look like it was me, made me take the blame." Barney lit his cigarette, taking a long drag. "She said her father would kill her if he found out the truth."

"I'm sorry, Barney." For the first time in days, she felt genuinely sorry for him.

"Dan thought I'd done it too?" Barney mumbled, looking at the floor as he blew out smoke. "I tried to explain to him but…" He trailed off taking another drag of his cigarette.

Barney turned quickly to face her, making her flinch a little.

"He probably thought I was a bird killer when he died?"

More navel gazing. "Get your wife a coat Barney before she freezes to the bench," she told him, and turning on her heel, she walked away.

Johanna turned on the shower, kicked off her shoes and moved towards the mirror, inspecting her face while she waited for the water to warm up. The ancient plumbing was not kind. Neither was Samantha Dunderdale. The small cut on her cheek was beginning to swell. Had she turned her ring around purposely to mark Johanna's face?

She looked down, noticing the red stain on her trousers: red wine from the incident. Slipping them off, she left them in a pile on the floor, removed her shirt and hung it on the back of the door. There were so many questions rushing through her mind. Top of the list was why Barney would take the blame for killing that bird all those years ago. Her hands moved behind her, removing her bra. Then a knock at the door made her jump as she added it to the pile on the floor.

Johanna softly walked to the door, she didn't need any more drama, Barney had said more than enough for one night. A smile crossed her lips as she saw a distorted image through the spy hole. Johanna scampered back to the bathroom, turned off the shower, grabbed her dressing gown. She slipped it on and tied it loosely before opening the door.

CHAPTER 21

LUCY PICKED THROUGH THE PRELIMINARY FORENSICS' findings from the Booker house. So far, the only prints found in the house matched those from the body found. So whoever was in there had had the sense to wear gloves. They were still waiting for DNA to come back from the toothbrush to see if it was also a match, but right now it looked like David Booker was the body found at the scene. Finally, she got to the part she was looking for: heating controls. It was on a timer apparently. It should have clicked off at eight-thirty after being on for an hour, but instead, someone had switched it to constant. Unfortunately, like everything else in that house, there was only one set of prints on there: David Booker's. She'd get Tanner to contact Booker's heating supplier or find any heating bills that should give them an idea of his heating usage, was switching it to constant a regular occurrence, especially with those electric heaters.

Shoeprints were identified as being from four different types of shoe, which fitted with Mrs Cole's statement. The shoeprints were all from trainers; they just needed something to compare them with now.

"Fuller!"

Lucy looked up to see Barrel's head poking out of his office.

"Reed's ready for us. Call the GP. Get him to meet us there."

"Yes, boss," Lucy replied and flicked through her notes for the surgery's phone number.

Lucy waited outside the mortuary and pathology labs for Dr Sharma to appear. She turned up the collar of her jacket as an icy breeze blew across the entrance. The two connected buildings were in an annexe of Reading Hospital, far away from the living and difficult to find for a first-time visitor. She couldn't help thinking Dr Chadwick had a much better office environment: less gore.

An Asian man in his thirties rounded the corner, heading towards the entrance.

"Dr Sharma?"

"Yes."

"I'm DS Fuller. We spoke on the phone." Sharma was sharply dressed in a navy-blue suit and light-blue shirt. His long, pointy shoes tapped on the ground as he moved towards her.

"Oh, hello." Dr Sharma offered his hand.

It was soft and warm, despite the chill in the air.

"We're ready for you inside." Lucy led the way. "Have you done this before?"

"Well, I've seen a few in my time, but I've never actually had to identify anyone before."

Lucy smiled. "No problem, it's just a simple form after we've viewed the body," she reassured him then nodded to the receptionist, who reluctantly buzzed them through, and quickly navigated the corridors to the observation window. Dr Sharma was wide eyed as he looked through at Dr Reed, holding a clipboard in his hand next to the covered body. Noticing their presence on the other side of the glass, Reed placed his clipboard down before folding back the sheet, stopping at the base of the man's throat.

The body on the slab beyond somehow looked both better and worse at the same time. The blood had been washed away, but it had revealed the extent of the man's injuries.

"Yes, that's him," Dr Sharma confirmed. His voice had deepened.

That was quick. How the hell could he tell, considering the state he was in? Lucy rephrased before asking her question. "Sorry to ask this, but how can you tell so quickly?"

Dr Sharma looked at her, a slight grin pulled at the ends of his mouth. "He has a nick to his ear, just here." He raised his hand, pointing to the back edge of his left ear.

"Oh." Lucy looked through the window, spotting the slight V shape in the back of Booker's ear. Not surprisingly, she hadn't noticed it at the scene. "I see."

"He had an accident at work apparently; industrial manufacturing is a dangerous business."

Lucy made a note to look into Booker's employment, if Tanner hadn't already done it. "Was he a frequent visitor to the surgery?"

"Not really, usual stuff. Came in a couple of weeks ago for his annual flu jab."

"Okay. Thank you for your time, Dr Sharma," Lucy said and led the way out to the main corridor. "I just need you to sign a form to confirm the identification, if that's okay."

"Of course."

With Dr Sharma squared away and identification confirmed, she went back in search of Barrel. She found him back in the room with Dr Reed.

"GP confirmed it," she said as she entered the room. She always felt a bit weird talking about someone that was stretched out on the mortuary slab, especially when they were still uncovered.

"DS Fuller." Dr Reed nodded in her direction. "I was just telling DCI Barrel I've managed to narrow down the time of death to between ten-thirty pm Thursday night and twelve-thirty am on Friday morning."

"Shit!" Barrel barked as he glared at the floor. "No later? How sure are you, I mean?" He shrugged his shoulders keeping his hands buried deep in his trouser front pockets as he looked up frowning at Bookers body.

Part of Lucy was pleased that someone else was at the end of Barrel's current annoyance, but he wasn't usually this abrasive and certainly not with Dr Reed.

"I'm As sure as I can be." Reed replied with equal volume, "considering the issues with the ambient temperature."

"So they put the bloody central heating on to throw you off then," Barrel stated, as if it was a fact.

"The kids?" Lucy asked. It sounded ridiculous. Barrel was clutching at straws. Surely he could see that. What had she missed while she was with Dr Sharma, the timeline still fit so why the grilling of Dr Reed. What was getting Barrel's back up.

Dr Reed's mouth held a firm line. She'd never seen Barrel question his professionalism before. "Are you saying you want a second opinion DCI Barrel?"

Lucy looked away, considering the facts. It was right on the edge of their timeframe with the suspects that had been seen at the house. "It could still be them. It's not impossible." The witness could have been mistaken with the times; five or ten minutes either way was an easy mistake, but another thought was nagging at her. "Or somebody else killed him before the kids broke in," she blurted. The words were out of her mouth before she could stop them.

Barrel directed his glare at her. "No. Thank you Dr Reed that won't be necessary." His furrowed brow hovered above red rimmed eyes.

Well done Fuller; you've just put yourself right at the top of his shit list, again.

"As I was saying," Dr Reed continued, "the stomach contents might confirm that if you can find out when he last ate. Some of the contents were semi-digested, which indicates that he ate between two and six hours before he died."

Lucy focused on her notebook, considering what the Cole's had said about Booker's lifestyle and lack of friends, she couldn't see that happening anytime soon. "Any defensive injuries?" Lucy asked, more out of habit considering what she'd clocked at the scene.

"No, nothing. Caught by surprise I'd say. The first blow was to the back of his head." Reed lifted a hand to indicate the area at the back of his own head. "It knocked him to the ground, then when he was on the floor, he was beaten with the same object. Overkill. The damage would have been done from the second or third –"

"How many times was he hit?" Lucy cut him off, unable to look at the man's misshapen head any longer.

"Including the one that put him on the floor, I'd say about ten times." He replied slipping off his glasses.

She hadn't realised how small Reed's eyes were without his glasses on.

"What about the weapon?" Barrel prodded.

"The object is approximately eleven by seven centimetres, oblong in shape, with defined corners. Can't give you the length, but its slightly larger than a standard UK brick."

"But not a brick," Lucy clarified.

"No. Nothing in the wounds to indicate that, no brick dust splinters, nothing at all, in fact. I'd say it's something that can be swung, with force."

"What if they put it in a bag?" Barrel asked, pushing again.

"As I say, Chief Inspector, the shape is slightly larger."

Reed's frustration was beginning to show. Lucy tried to step in. "But heavy like a brick? Any ideas?"

"Heavier maybe, depending on the person wielding it," he answered, and his glare softened a little as he looked down at the uncovered body between them. "Find me something and I'll compare it with the wounds." He then reached forward to cover up Booker's body. "He had some arthritis in his knees and hands, but apart from that he was in good health."

"Thanks," Lucy added with a tight smile, her mind already on what they would find in Booker's garden. It hadn't escaped her notice that Barrel had said nothing about her theory that someone else other than the kids were responsible for Booker's death. She decided to bide her time let the dust settle before pushing it any further, he wasn't exactly approachable right now.

"I'll send you through my report."

"Thank you, Doctor," Barrel said and turned to leave the room.

Lucy stared at the computer screen as the CCTV footage played. Tanner had sent her the best images he'd found of the four youths he'd discovered running to and from the Grove Lane area. Although there was nothing from Grove Lane itself; there was footage from the surrounding streets near the estate. It had to be them. She hoped Tanner could produce the same magic with Bookers gas supplier at some point.

She squinted at the screen. The image wasn't perfect, but she hoped their clothing could be used to confirm identity once they had some suspects. One of them wore a distinctive hoodie with stripes down the arms and something printed on the back. Not to mention there should be blood on their shoes and clothing if they hadn't already got rid of them. But as she took a closer look, one thing stood out in each of the images; there was nothing in any of their hands. No weapon to be seen. Regardless, she downloaded a copy to her iPad. Maybe Mrs Cole would recognise them from the night of the incident. She also organised a search of the gardens and their route through the estate.

"Boss," she said as soon as Barrel came into the room. His gaze was firmly on the Dunderdale case board on the far side of the room. "Tea?" she asked, hoping to talk through some of the developments on the Dunderdale and Booker cases. He'd been out of the office since the autopsy visit that morning. Rank prevented her from asking where he'd been; they didn't have that kind of relationship yet.

"Can't stay, got a meeting with the ACC." His tone was firm, aggravated even.

The Acting Chief Constable? What did he want now? He'd already done his bit at the Dunderdale press conference. She pressed on, trying to sound upbeat, despite the ache in her head that had condensed over the last couple of days. Dividing her time between cases wasn't easy.

"Tanner and I have managed to trace most of the original residents of Compton Way; we've only got a couple left to TIE," she reported as she walked closer. Barrel's rigid frame bothered her, arms crossed as he glowered at the map on the board.

"Then what?" he grumbled.

Lucy frowned for a moment. He was the official SIO. That decision was surely down to him. "Boss?" He didn't even acknowledge her question. She decided to continue. "Did you watch the CCTV footage from the industrial estate?" She didn't wait for him to reply. "It wasn't Levin's van."

"It just means he wasn't a thief, not that he wasn't responsible for the Dunderdale murder."

She used two fingers to massage her left temple. He was right, of course, but Redland's case against Levin had been shredded by the evidence that he'd conveniently withheld. She needed to offer an alternative, but who? "It has to be someone local," she said. "There's something off about the Bells for a start. He changed his name when he moved to Compton Way. Why would someone do that if they weren't hiding something? And his daughter wasn't his daughter, so there's that too."

Barrel made no reply.

"Bell's death could be suspicious too," she added, recalling the details Tanner had found out. Bellamy had been found at the bottom of his stairs with a broken neck. The pathologist had found high levels of alcohol in his system. He was a hard drinker, according to his liver. A neighbour found him two days after he'd died.

"He broke his neck falling down the stairs, drunk as a lord. Hardly suspicious."

Lucy shook her head. "The neighbours heard arguing on the night he died."

"Did they? From their statements, it's not clear, is it. One of them said it could have been a loud TV."

Lucy relented as she leant against the nearest desk. With several of the residents as dead as Levin, maybe she *was* on a hiding to nothing. Was this a child abduction driven by the perverse appetite of the killer. If not, then who would possibly want Daniel Dunderdale dead? What had he done to deserve that?

"Somebody didn't want that well discovered," she continued.

"What?" Barrel frowned as he finally turned to face her. He looked tired, dark smudges underlined his eyes.

"Two people called the ecologist doing the survey wanting the build stopped."

"We've been over this. Maybe they just didn't want a mindless centre there. It doesn't necessarily prove anything."

"Mindfulness," Lucy corrected. "It's hardly a drugs den is it." She bit her tongue. She was beginning to lose her temper.

"We've still got nothing," he stated.

We've got nothing. He'd been apathetic from the start. "What?" she seethed.

"I told you not to get the bit between your teeth. This is a dead case."

Lucy couldn't believe what she was hearing. "A ten-year-old boy is *dead.*"

"I know that, but the person responsible is probably dead too. If it wasn't Levin, maybe it was Bell, both of whom are dead."

Probably. Levin again? "What! Levin didn't do it. Nobody saw his van; it wasn't even his MO."

"If no-one saw the van thirty years ago, they're not going to suddenly remember it now, are they. As for Bell, for all we know, it could have been his daughter from a previous relationship that he didn't know about for years, and maybe he hadn't got around to updating his MOD records. Or maybe it was just a clerical error. Computers weren't exactly everyone's friend back then."

Lucy refused to concede those facts. Barrel wasn't listening to her. "But how would Levin know about the well? He wasn't local. He wanted his other victims found." She waved her arm to express her point. "He purposely left them out in the open."

"I don't know. Maybe something went wrong; he knew there was evidence on the body, so he hid it."

Evidence? What evidence? They'd found nothing to link anyone so far, not even on the plastic. Lucy shook with frustration as she walked away from him. Levin wasn't exactly a student of forensics. Besides, if he was, he could have burned the body or dumped it in the river if he had something to hide. Why risk it being found at some point if it held the evidence that would convict him? Why was Barrel so convinced it was Levin? Surely, Redland wasn't still pulling the strings on this case.

She focused on Bellamy again, grabbing the MOD letter from a file. "They let Amy Bell straight into the secondary school on the strength of this MOD letter of transfer," she snapped, waving it in the air. "They did no further background checks on her previous school. Bellamy could have had access to the stationery and faked this letter to suit."

"Lucy."

She heard the incredulity in his voice as she turned to face him; he rarely used her Christian name. His face was ruby red. She'd had enough; there was something more going on here. "Look I know it's none of my business but-."

"You're right it's not." He quickly cut her off staring her down. "This case will destroy you if you keep on pushing."

Was he threatening her? She narrowed her eyes at him. "What are you saying?"

"I'm saying drop it, now. That's an order. I want to be able to make an arrest for Booker's murder in the next few days, understood?"

His eyes never left hers, still she refused to reply. He was being irrational.

Barrel grabbed his jacket, headed straight out the room without waiting for an answer. Lucy stomped over to her desk, slumping back in her chair. She couldn't let it go, not yet. In her frustration, she grabbed a pen from her desk snapping it in half at the thought of being forced to drop the case. Opening her hand, she saw the smudge of black ink as it stained her skin.

Condensation from the pint glass in Lucy's hand trickled from her little finger to the floor as she knocked on the door. She knew she shouldn't be here, but she couldn't keep away. She'd found yet another excuse for returning, despite how the last visit ended. She'd overheard PC Goff talking to Tanner about a fracas at the wake on her way to the vending machine in the canteen, but all Lucy could think about was Johanna's safety. She needed to know that Johanna was okay before she could drown her sorrows after her argument with Barrel.

"Hey," The brief look of surprise on Johanna's face was replaced with a wide smile as she opened the door wider. She looked relaxed; stunning even despite her altercation.

Lucy had tried to keep away, she'd done her best for the last five days but standing at Johanna's door she was too tired to fight it anymore. She wanted her, even if it was only for tonight.

The tie from her navy-blue dressing gown swung as she stood back. The left side of her face already looked inflamed.

"I heard about your little incident. Are you okay?" She didn't know how else to start the conversation.

"Bad, or should I say embarrassing news always travels fast," Johanna told her as her hand moved to the side of her face. Her eyes widened a little as she touched her skin. "I'm fine."

"I brought you some ice." Lucy held up her peace offering in the shape of a pint glass. The ice cubes sounded like marbles as they knocked against each other inside.

"Thanks." Johanna took the glass. Stepping aside, she tilted her head as if encouraging her to come inside.

Lucy scanned the corridor before stepping inside and closing the door behind her.

Johanna had moved across the room to lean against the small work desk, a dim lamp on which provided the only light in the room.

"Who told you?" she asked. Her dressing gown had split open, exposing her lean legs.

Johanna seemed oblivious, Lucy dragged her eyes away as blood pulsed rushing to her core. She'd ran out of this room only days earlier after their last entanglement, now she didn't want to leave.

"There was an officer at the wake," she replied and moved closer to Johanna. Needing to occupy her hands with something, she took the pint glass from Johanna and backed away towards the bathroom. Inside, the light was already on, the mirror a little fogged with steam. Clothes were piled up on the floor. Johanna must have been about to take a shower. The curve of a bra cup caught her eye. The thought of that piece of clothing clinging to parts of Johanna's body brought heat to her cheeks. A red stain covered the rumpled grey trousers below. Goff had said something about drinks going flying.

Lucy pulled a hand towel from the rail, emptied half the ice into the centre, then twisted the towel, securing it inside. The smudge of black ink on the sides of her fingers caught her eye. *Bloody pen!* Setting the towel down, she rolled up her shirt sleeves, washing her hands with the soap pump provided.

"Here, try this," she said when she returned to the bedroom and handed Johanna the towel, noticing the darkened red graze along her cheekbone. Had the Dunderdale woman drawn blood?

"Thanks." Johanna smiled, then flinched as she adjusted the towel before gingerly placing it over her cheek, wincing as it touched her skin.

Lucy's mind raced. What had made Samantha Dunderdale slap her so viciously? She stepped closer and asked, "Can I take a look?" She waited for Johanna's subtle nod before pulling the ice pack away. Gently cupping the unspoiled side of Johanna's face, she tilted her bruise towards the glow of the desk light. Two small red cuts followed the line of her cheek. The skin was inflamed, but it didn't look too serious. "It looks like you've escaped a black eye."

"I guess I should be thankful for small mercies," she said and as she tried for a smile, they locked eyes. Lucy felt the weight of her gaze but was unable to look away.

"Was she wearing a ring?" she asked and barely recognised her own voice as she reluctantly looked away from Johanna's darkened eyes, but her fingers remained, hovering above the graze, heat radiated from Johanna's inflamed skin.

Johanna nodded. "I think so. There was something sharp."

Heat climbed up Lucy's neck. She wasn't sure if it was from the lamp or Johanna's proximity. "I could arrest her for assault, if you like," she smiled and her thumb stroked the side of Johanna's face before she could stop herself.

"You'd do that?" Johanna's brow furrowed and her lips twitched into a smile.

"I'd do it for you."

She dipped her head closer, desperate to kiss the pain away, and Johanna's eyes flickered shut. Lucy closed the remaining distance, pressing her lips to Johanna's soft cheek, placing several kisses along her soft, warm skin before pulling away. Hovering so close, she was scared to pull away in case it ended too soon. But there was no danger of that as their bodies pressed together and Lucy trailed her nose down the side of Johanna's. An Eskimo kiss came to mind, bringing a smile to her lips as she took in Johanna's delicate scent. Her chest struggled to keep up with her breathing as she edged closer to those full lips. This woman was assaulting her senses again. But hadn't she instigated it this time? Still, she couldn't pull away and their lips met once again, soft, tentative kisses.

"Lucy."

The word came out in a warm breath. Was it a warning? Lucy's mind couldn't compute the information as Johanna parted her thighs, allowing her to get closer. She slipped her left thigh in between. If she didn't stop soon, there would be no going back at all. Her mind blurred once again with what she wanted and what her moral duties were. Then she felt Johanna's hands on her hips, jerking her closer. A gasp escaped her as Johanna edged forward, claiming her lips, her tongue demanding as it entered her mouth. All the while, Johanna's hand circled the back of Lucy's neck, deepening the kiss, fingers trailing through her hair, drawing her closer. For once, there was only one thought in her head.

Lucy drew her hand down Johanna's neck, and her fingers slipped under the edge of the bath robe, cupping Johanna's bare shoulder. Spreading her fingers, they moved lower, her palm grazing a firm nipple, forcing a groan from Johanna. Their lips parted as Lucy cupped her full breast. The weight hung in her hand as her thumb rubbed across the nipple.

The boom of Lucy's ringtone halted any further progress, her fingers stilled as she withdrew from Johanna's warm lips. Darkened eyes flickered open and focused on hers as her phone rang again.

"Do you need to get that?" Johanna whispered.

"I do," she mouthed, her voice low. As she slowly withdrew her hands and stepped back, pulling out her phone she saw Tanner's name on the screen. *Shit! Caught red-handed.* "Sorry, I need to," she held up her ringing phone, "Can I call you tomorrow?" was all Lucy could muster as she straightened her clothing.

Johanna got to her feet, pulling her dressing gown around her body. "You'd better."

Lucy gave her a lopsided grin as she closed the door behind her.

CHAPTER 22

LUCY STOOD IN HER KITCHEN, drinking tea. Last night had been eventful in more ways than one. First Barrel's order/plea to leave the Dunderdale case alone. Then Johanna ... And she'd made the first move this time. Had that been the plan when she picked up the ice from the bar? Would it have happened if she wasn't so wound up over Barrel's words? Who knows, but either way, she'd barely got a wink of sleep. And it wasn't Barrel's plea that had kept her awake; it was Johanna's touch, her soft lips as they brushed against her own, the thought of what could have happened in that room had Tanner not called to make sure she was okay. That station had more leaks than a sieve, no doubt PC Goff had heard their heated words and called him. She closed her eyes, sighing as she placed her mug in the sink. She needed to get on, set things right. The one positive thing about not working on the Dunderdale case was Johanna Hale no longer being off limits.

She checked her messages as she brushed her teeth. One text from Barrel.

Take the day off. Meet at the station tomorrow AM. His texts were as blunt as his driving.

She checked the time; it had arrived twenty-three minutes ago when she was in the shower. He was trying to distance her from the case, ween her off it, but she had no intention of letting him do that. She'd work the case in her own time if she had to, the killer was someone in that town; she was sure of it.

Johanna had purposely avoided breakfast, not wanting to bump into Barney and his family; she couldn't face a rehash of yesterday's slap. Instead, she sat at the small desk in her room and tried to work, but it probably wasn't the best place to try and concentrate, considering what had transpired there last night. Had she encouraged Lucy? To begin with maybe. Nurturing a mutual attraction she'd felt when they'd met at the hotel bar, spending time walking around the old estate, had only encouraged her pursuit. Not seeing herself as a suspect, she hadn't realised it would be such a problem if they became close. But last night, she hadn't been expecting her at all, turning up with a glass of ice to soothe her face. And Lucy seemed so different last night. A little more forward, open to the idea that something could happen between them. Unfortunately, she didn't get the chance to raise this question before Lucy had been called away.

Her phone vibrated across the desk; Lucy, she said she'd call. Johanna sighed as her parents' home phone number flashed on the screen. She let it go to voicemail; her mother had scolded her enough for now. She toyed with the empty wrapper from the breakfast biscuits she'd found in her bag earlier, carefully tying it into a tight knot before tossing it in the bin below. She smiled to herself at the thought of Lucy's offer to arrest Samantha Dunderdale, her being taken away in a police car. Barney would never forgive her. Still, she was tempted to say yes as she gingerly touched the side of her face.

Finally giving up on her work, she closed her laptop. She needed some fresh air, a bit of perspective on last night. She dressed appropriately in her walking boots and waterproof jacket before leaving the hotel. The earlier drizzle had stopped, but the day was still dull and threatening more rain. She strolled through Kingsford, and like most small towns, a slow Sunday bustle ensued. Approaching the canal, she decided to walk along the tow path towards the marsh. At the end, the large wooden gate in front of her was the only barrier preventing the grazing cows beyond from running amuck through Kingsford.

Johanna pulled her hand from her pocket to release the metal locking mechanism. Stepping through, she let the spring-loaded gate close behind her. Her phone buzzed as she entered the first field of the marsh. Not her mother again; she was about to let it go to voicemail again when the number on the screen changed her mind.

"Hello, Detective," she greeted openly, unsure what to expect by means of reply.

"Where are you? I'm at your hotel, but you're not here." Her voice was warm with a hint of humour.

"I went out for a walk. Thought I could do with a bit of fresh air."

"Could I ..." There was a slight hesitation before she continued. "... come and meet you?"

"Sure." Johanna felt her face stretch into a smile. "I'm on the marsh. Do you know where that is?"

"Err. No. What road is it on?"

Johanna stopped walking, realising she had no idea. "Umm." She pictured the journey she'd made on foot so many times in the past. "Go past the industrial estate we walked by the other day, past the turning to Stype Hill and take the first turning on the right. It's a dead-end road. The marsh is at the end."

"I'll find it."

"I'll meet you by the gate at the end," Johanna told her and hung up. Slipping the phone back in her pocket, she continued towards the large wooden gate that opened out onto the marsh from the road that she'd just directed Lucy to find. Unable to go any further without her, Johanna leant back against the gate, looking across the fields to the Friesian cows grazing in the distance. The green space was cut in half by a canal, edged by a railway line on one side, a main road in the distance on the other. Yet it still felt like it was a world away from civilisation. It still held the feeling of calm she enjoyed from her childhood.

She spun around to look along the road in search of Lucy. There were a few cars parked on the left-hand side of the road. Residents, she figured, from the new houses that had been built opposite. The sound of a car drew her attention, she saw Lucy's car pull up behind a white SUV. Lucy greeted her with a wave as she exited her car and swiftly moved to the boot to retrieve something before walking down to meet her.

Johanna heard the clump of wellies before she could see them clearly. "Do you wear those boots to crime scenes?" she asked as she opened the gate for Lucy to enter the marsh. Lucy's formal suit jacket had been replaced by a heavier black peacoat; a rich blue shirt peeked out along the neckline, matching the blue of her eyes.

"Uh." Lucy stood in the gateway, looking down at her feet. "Yeah, if it's muddy."

"Gross." Johanna turned around to walk away.

"You didn't seem bothered when you were mopping the blood off my knee the other day."

"That's different, it was your perfectly formed knee," Johanna quickly replied without turning around. She was relieved at the ease of their conversation. Slowing her pace, she waited for Lucy to catch up, then led them down towards the canal, past the first swing bridge, the clumping of Lucy's boots following them.

"How's your face?" Lucy enquired.

Johanna resisted the urge to touch it, preferring to keep her hand in the warmth of her pocket. "I'll live."

"I saw her this morning."

Johanna looked across at Lucy, confused for a moment.

"Samantha Dunderdale," Lucy confirmed. "When I went to your hotel earlier. She looked a little nervous when she saw me."

Johanna chuckled. She could almost picture the fear on Samantha's face, much as she'd seen the day before when she realised what she had done after slapping her.

They walked in silence for a few moments as they approached a lock. "We used to spend a lot of time down here as kids, playing golf with my dad, paddling in the little rivers with –"

"Golf?" Lucy's face held a hint of a grin.

"I know, I should have known back then," Johanna smiled and looked up, realising how far they had walked. "My grandparents used to live down here when they were young. My father and his brothers were brought up here." She pointed to the cottage next to the canal lock. "In that white house over there."

"Were they lock keepers?"

"No, the cottage next door was the lock keeper's. My grandparents had a smallholding, chickens and stuff, around the back." Johanna remembered her father's fond stories of growing up with his brothers. "You seem to have strong links to the area. Why did you move away?"

"I-I don't know, I guess I just wanted something bigger. Do my own thing. Kingsford is a small town, especially back then." Everybody knew her father and his family. She was scared about who she was, who she wanted to be. "Growing up gay in a small town was never going to be easy, so I fled as soon as I could."

"Is that why you don't stay with your parents when you visit?"

Johanna raised her eyebrows at the question. "We don't always see eye to eye on things. We sort of drifted apart when I moved to Bath. I'm trying to repair some of that now." Although she'd made little progress on that front so far.

They continued across a wooden bridge, walking along the edge of a narrow river.

"So what did you say to make Samantha Dunderdale slap you so hard?"

"I'm not sure really." It was a lie. She looked up to see Lucy staring at her, head tilted, waiting for more information.

"I might have mentioned something that happened when we were kids, and she disagreed with me." A half-truth was better than none.

"Something like what?" Lucy pressed.

"Oh, it was nothing, really." Yet, it still didn't make sense to Johanna. "We were in an abandoned building and –"

"We?" Lucy queried.

"Err, me, Simon, Amy, Dan and Barney. Urban exploring, I guess you'd call it now, but it was plain old trespassing back then."

"Okay. Where was this?"

"The industrial estate I showed you the other day at the bottom of our road, the end part used to make plastic bottles. We made a big swing that landed in the leftover piles." She slowed her thoughts, trying to get them in order. "A couple of pigeons had gotten in through a broken window."

Lucy just nodded, waiting for more.

"One of the pigeons was trying to get out. Maybe it couldn't fly or something." Johanna felt tongue-tied for a moment as she tried to recall the moment she heard Amy and Barney shouting in the corner of the factory. "I was helping Simon. He was trying to use the swing. When I looked up, Amy and Barney were huddled around something on the floor. I went over to see what they were doing. The bird was dead; there was blood on the floor where it had writhed around before it died." Johanna closed her eyes for a moment, but it just made the image worse as it floated through her head.

"Shit," Lucy mumbled under her breath.

"I thought Barney had done it. He was holding the piece of wood. Amy was shouting at him to stop."

"He didn't do it?" Lucy frowned.

Johanna shook her head, letting out a long breath. "I don't know for sure. It was such a long time ago." Maybe Amy held the answers. "Yesterday, Barney's wife wouldn't stop going on about how great Barney was as a father and husband, it was pretty sickening, and I said, 'We all wanted to be like Barney till he killed that bird.'"

"And she flipped!"

"Umm." Their footfalls were heavy on the wooden swing bridge as they headed back to the gate. "She'd been drinking, so ..." Johanna trailed off. She knew she'd picked the fight; she saw no need to pursue it.

"So what? It doesn't mean she can go around slapping people."

"I know," Johanna conceded. She'd pushed Samantha too far was all. "She's got a nervous thing, apparently."

"Apparently?" Lucy repeated.

"Barney said she's got a condition. She had a couple of drinks to settle her nerves."

"I get the feeling Mr Dunderdale is a little tightly wound," Lucy replied.

Johanna sniggered. "I think you might have the measure of him,

Detective. He seems to like women that are a bit helpless. It's probably why he was immune to Amy's charms."

"Unlike the rest of you, you mean."

Johanna frowned. Was that a spark of jealousy? She ignored it. "She was a real live wire, totally different to the demure Samantha."

"You make her out to be a real Lolita character."

"Do I? I guess she was, in a way." She thought of Dan, his voice on the mixtape. "Have you had any luck tracing her yet?"

"No. She's like a ghost."

They walked on in silence for a few moments, and Johanna considered Lucy's words. *Lolita*. Just like all those years ago, when Dan went missing, Amy was still the main talking point. "It changed things for a while, after the bird I mean," she clarified. "I think we all saw Barney a bit different from then on. I felt terrible. I'd taken Simon there. We left straight away. I had to make him promise not to say anything to our parents."

"What does Barney say about the bird incident?"

Incident. But that's what it was in many ways. "He said Amy did it, he was trying to get the wood from her. That's why she was telling him to stop. He said she made him promise to take the blame, said her dad would kill her if he found out."

"What about Dan? Where was he?"

"Err ... I'm not sure. I don't think he saw what happened, if that's what you mean." She had a feeling the cogs were ticking around in Lucy's mind.

Johanna stopped as they approached the main gate where she had met Lucy earlier. "So is that why you wanted to see me, grill me a bit more?" She immediately wanted to take back her words, as she had offered all the information willingly.

"No. Not exactly." Lucy's expression quickly changed from amusement to something a little more serious, earnest even. "I wondered if you would like to have lunch with me."

Lucy moved closer, within touching distance.

"I mean, I wanted to see if you were free, today." Lucy continued to edge towards her. There was only a couple of inches between them now.

"Today? You're not working?"

"No. I seem to have the day off."

"I see." There was something in Lucy's choice of words, but she didn't question it, too excited by the fact that Lucy wanted to spend her time off with her. The breeze picked up, blowing her hair across her face, breaking up the image of Lucy stood in front of her. She was about to tame it herself when Lucy reached up to do it for her, tucking the wayward locks behind her ear.

Johanna sucked in a breath as Lucy's hand continued to trail down to cup her jaw, before leaning towards her in one swift action, brushing their lips together. Johanna's eyes flickered closed in surprise. It took a moment for her to react, leaning forward a second too late to extend the gesture.

A lopsided grin appeared on Lucy's lips as she opened her eyes.

"I'd love to," Johanna whispered.

"Great. I'll drive." Lucy turned on her heel, headed for the gate and held it open for Johanna, before returning to her car, unlocking the boot and pulling off her wellingtons.

Johanna looked down at her own footwear. They weren't muddy, but they were wet from the rain-soaked grass. "Shall I take these off?"

"No, its fine."

Johanna glanced down at the interior of Lucy's boot. A plastic box at the far end held Lucy's now-familiar ankle boots. Several bags and boxes were artfully arranged around it, one of which, she noticed, contained shopping. Fresh bread and potatoes were visible through the open top. Was she planning on cooking for her?

"Do you have somewhere in mind for lunch?" she probed as innocently as possible.

Lucy didn't look up as she slipped on her right boot. "I do."

"Okay," was all she managed, her body now giddy with excitement.

Once in the car, Lucy pulled into the steep gravel road that led into the small housing estate overlooking the marsh to turn around. From what Johanna could see, they were modern shoebox houses. A woman stood in the front window of the closest one drinking from a mug her face was partly in shadow.

Johanna waited until they were moving along the road before showing her hand. "So are you a good cook?"

Lucy turned to look at her, a smile on her face that reached her eyes. It reminded her of the time Lucy had come to her house. "Terrible."

"Oh. Is it too late to get a rain check?"

"Yep."

Johanna waited a few beats before asking her next question. "Where do you live?"

"Oldbury."

"I went to college there after leaving school." She'd barely set foot in the place since. Despite Johanna's excitement at spending time with Lucy, one question kept rolling around in her head. What had changed between last night in her hotel room and this morning? She had just kissed her in public, several people could have seen them, not just the grazing cows. Eventually, after turning it over in her head again and again, she said, "So am I no longer a suspect or something?"

"I'll let you know." Lucy flashed her a look before returning her focus to the road ahead. Her hand settled on Johanna's thigh. "You're one of the few people that couldn't have done it." Lucy attempted a small smile. "I'm sorry. This is all –"

"Is it illegal or something, unethical?"

"Something like that," Lucy replied, "although my boss has asked me to drop the case so …"

"What!" Johanna sat up a little straighter. "He can't ask you to do that. We don't know who did it yet."

Lucy frowned at her for a moment. "I know."

"What are you going to do?"

"Keep digging, I guess."

"Good, and if you've got some free time on your hands, you can help me with something," she said, half smiling.

Lucy turned towards her, eyebrows raised. "What's up?"

She felt a bit silly asking now. Letting out a breath, she continued, "I saw someone at the wake yesterday. I'm quite sure I knew her, but I can't figure out who she is."

"Why didn't you just talk to her?"

Good question. "I was going to. I mean, I thought I recognised her, but then she turned towards me and she's got these massive scars on one side of her face, like she's been burned or something. And I lost my bottle."

"Okay. I'm not sure what you want me to do. Doesn't your mum know who she is?"

"I did ask. She said her name was Mia and that she'd only moved here last year." She was starting to feel stupid for bringing it up.

"Where did she move from?"

"Up north, according to my mother." Johanna fidgeted in her seat. "You know what, forget about it. I'm sure I'll figure it out. Barney might know who she is."

"Really, you want to go there?"

She caught the smirk on Lucy's face. "Umm, maybe not."

CHAPTER 23

Daniel Dunderdale, 17th August 1988

Dan cupped his hand over his watch, shielding it from the sun. It was after five o'clock, time to go home. Tea would be on the table soon. His mother would be yelling for him or worse, she'd send Barney to find him. He'd purposely been avoiding Barney since he'd decided to use him as a training aid for his judo competition at the weekend. This time he'd slipped out through the back fence. He loved his brother, but he could be such a bully sometimes.

He had already decided to tell them that he wasn't feeling well; spending the day at the judo competition was the last thing he wanted to do, waiting around all day to see his brother mangle some unfortunate boy, grappling with him on the floor until he submitted. He'd been there, done that, too many times to mention. He suffered enough at the hands of his brother; he didn't need to see others suffer too. Why did their dad never see it? He only ever saw Barney's strength. Never him, never how much he hated being his brother's walking punchbag.

Last time he'd hoped to see Barney get his comeuppance, but he'd had to watch as Barney cut his final opponent down to size. With another victory under his belt, Barney had been unbearable. He lorded it over him for weeks, repeating the moves he'd made to get one over on his opposition.

He gave himself another minute, stretching out his arms behind him, supporting his upper body as he swung his legs off the end of the concrete bridge. All he could hear was the bubbling stream below. He hardly ever came down here alone, but with the recent heat of the last few days, it had seemed the best place to go. The fast-running stream was always cold, despite the hot sun.

The bullheads had been too fast for him today, despite his best efforts. He dragged his trainers towards him and pulled out his socks to dry off the last few drops of stream water from his feet. The damp socks felt comforting against his cool skin. Just as he was slipping on his trainers, he spotted one darting upstream under the cover of the bridge. Typical.

Dan climbed over the fence, entering the edge of the farmer's field and felt the pull of a bramble bush on his t-shirt. Jerking his body away, he heard the sharp tear as the thorns scraped on the material. Released, he fell forward, just managing to stay on his feet. He could almost hear his brother's laughter in his head as he stumbled. Annoyed, he stepped into deep zig-zag troughs left by tractor tyres during previous wet weather. His small shoes fit perfectly along the line of each zig and zag; it was satisfying to be the right size for a change. He felt so small compared to his brother.

The thick bushes beyond the garden boundary fences provided just enough cover for him to pass unnoticed. Moving up the edge of the field towards home, he scanned the gardens as he passed. A couple of people still sat on their sun loungers, but most had gone inside. The chatter of people and TVs followed him as he made progress. His mother would be angry if he didn't appear soon. He didn't want to get Barney into trouble; he'd only pass it on later.

He picked up the pace till he passed Johanna's garden; they'd planted some small trees across the back, and it was always so neat: the bushes trimmed, a selection of flowers on show. Her parents were green fingered, like his mother.

The house was quiet with Johanna and Simon away. Their mum was visible through the kitchen window, from where he could also hear the sound of clattering plates. Maybe he'd get to spend more time with Amy with Johanna out of the way. He could fill the gap, at least for a while.

The back door was wide open, giving him a view into the kitchen, as it did with most houses on the street, he spotted their dad as he walked past the opening, glass in hand.

He stealthily moved on, trying not to make a sound, past the fence that separated Johanna's garden from Amy's, and the difference was obvious. Amy's garden was vastly different, simpler. No bushes or flowers, just grass. Long grass. A greenhouse had been attached to the back of the house to make a conservatory.

He had to move till he was almost directly in front of the conservatory to see in, as the sides and roof had shades. He could see that the back door of the house was open, but the sliding conservatory door was shut, and he could only imagine how hot it must have been inside.

His gaze immediately found Amy, sitting cross-legged on the kitchen unit that lined the brick wall. Her long hair draped over her face as she read the book that was open in her lap. He couldn't see what it was from this distance, a novel by the size of it. Always reading, he smiled; she was so grown up.

Amy wore only a vest top and skirt, her pointy, pale shoulders standing out against the red brickwork, her skirt neatly draped over her thighs. His eyes travelled down her slender legs to her toes, which twitched as her eyes scanned the pages in front of her. Movement in the kitchen behind her then caught his eye, and her dad's profile appeared in the dark hole the back door usually occupied. He wore only a towel tucked into his waist. The bright blue, flowery pattern stood out against his pale skin. This was his chance to finally see the leg her father limped on constantly. Polio, his mum had told him. He'd been inoculated against it years ago with a sugar cube. But still, Dan was fascinated to see what the leg looked like. He often imagined a wooden leg, like a pirate by the way he walked on it. Although her dad always wore shoes, so he couldn't have an actual peg leg. He never wore shorts, though, no matter how hot it was, not that he'd seen anyway. His own father couldn't wait to get into his shorts when he got home from work in the summer.

Her dad remained in profile as he leaned against the door frame, and Dan heard mumbled words. Amy made no reply, just stared at her book. Her dad shrugged away, back inside the dimly lit kitchen. Dan squinted, trying to get a look at his left leg as he limped away, scrunching up his mouth; it was too dark for him to see clearly. It wasn't wooden, but it did look different compared to his other leg.

He returned moments later, a can of beer in his hand. Dan glared at the man's leg as he stood in the doorway surveying his plain garden. Instinctively, Dan felt the need to duck down, a little worried he would be spotted. He could now see that his left leg looked a lot thinner, smaller than the other one, but his knee looked normal as it disappeared under the towel. Other than that, it looked ordinary . He was a little disappointed, expecting it to be more gross.

A thistle grazed his leg as he prepared to move and continue up the hill to his home, but events unfolding in front of him stopped him from going anywhere. He watched as Amy's dad took a long drink from his beer before turning to face his book-worm daughter. Placing the can on the side next to her, his hand cupped her closest knee. It remained there for a moment, then it travelled to the edge of her skirt, his thick fingers slipping under the hem, disappearing out of sight.

Dan held his breath, his eyes transfixed by the events in the conservatory, but Amy was indifferent to her father's actions, her eyes never leaving the pages of her book. He said something to her again, but she made no reply. Her shoulders simply shrugged as he continued to move his hand under her skirt. Undeterred, he pulled at her, bringing her to the side of the unit next to him, and still she made no effort to pull away as her legs dangled over the edge. All she did was calmly place her book down as she rested her hands behind her, much as he had earlier on the bridge.

Dan dragged his eyes away. *What was going on here?* He felt compelled to look again.

Her father leant forward, placing his hands flat on the unit either side of Amy's legs, their faces just inches apart. They were talking, but he couldn't hear what they were saying. Then her father moved closer still, pressing his lips to her cheek then her lips. It wasn't just a peck, the kind Dan gave his parents before he went to bed, it was much more.

Dan swallowed hard. This was wrong, all wrong. He wanted to cry out, say something to stop him, but no words came out. His fingers gripped the wire fence separating him from the scene. He looked away as they continued kissing. He had to tell someone, save her.

He glanced up again. Amy was on her feet now, her father pulling her inside. He watched as they disappeared into the darkness, then staggered to his feet, falling backwards over a clump of soil as he tried to run away. When he made it to his feet again, he sprinted till he reached his garden fence. Grabbing hold of the wooden post, he stopped to catch his breath. What was he going to say? What could he say without people knowing he was spying, watching them? He needed to think. He had to do something, find a way to save her.

CHAPTER 24

Lucy led the way into her flat, kicking off her boots before entering the open-plan kitchen diner/lounge. She had liked the open space from the moment she first saw it, light and airy with a modern touch to the fittings. She placed her shopping on the island and glanced around, checking for mess as she removed her jacket. Satisfied there wasn't anything to be concerned about, she began unpacking the shopping. She hadn't exactly had a plan when she walked the aisles of the supermarket earlier.

Johanna moved around behind her. She turned to see her guest washing her hands.

"Nice place. Have you lived here long?"

"Nearly two years. I was transferred from Hitchin when I was promoted to DS." Lucy couldn't help but compare her flat to Johanna's spacious home. It came up short.

"Hitchin, where's that?"

"Hertfordshire, just north of London."

Lucy studied the ingredients in front of her, as Johanna's warm arms wrapped around her from behind, and relaxed her body, leaning into Johanna's firm frame, any further doubt evaporating. She'd been attracted to her from the very start. She had no idea where it would go, but she wasn't about to let a strong mutual attraction pass her by.

"So; why am I here, why now?"

Johanna's whispered words filtered through her mind. She deserved an explanation after all her erratic behaviour. She turned in Johanna's arms to face her.

"Because you're off the case?" Johanna continued.

Lucy tried to put her words in order. Johanna's eyes were wide with expectation. "Maybe, partly if I'm being honest. But it's more than that, when I heard about you being hurt I had to see you." She glanced at the blemish on Johanna's cheek." I haven't been able to stop thinking about you since that first time in your room." She saw the warmth in Johanna's eyes. "I tried to keep my distance but..."Johanna leant forward bringing their lips together, the heat from Johanna's parted lips was intoxicating, warmth flooded her system. A groan escaped her throat as the tip of Johanna's tongue entered her parted lips. It was over far too soon as Johann pulled back.

"Dare I ask what we're having?" Johanna asked, her face producing a wide smile as she scanned the shopping over her shoulder.

"Well," she conceded catching her breath, "I was trying to recreate a recipe my mum makes. It's like a warm winter salad type thing."

"Sounds good. Can I help? I could be your sous chef."

She felt the breath of Johanna's words crawling up her neck, bringing goosebumps with them as Johanna leaned a little closer. "Umm. I should really check your credentials. You can never be too careful these days."

"I thought you did that last night."

Lucy grinned. "I did, didn't I, but it never hurts to double check." Resting her hands back on the worktop to steady herself. Johanna's proximity made her heart race, and her breath fought to catch up as Johanna stepped towards her, their lower bodies brushing together.

Johanna leaned closer and mouthed, "Although, full disclosure, I do burn toast with an alarming regularity." The low, raspy edge to her words sent a shiver all the way down to Lucy's toes, and she struggled to find a reply, her voice hoarse in her throat.

"I see. Well, honesty is the best policy, and with that in mind, I'm not sure either of us is up to this particular task."

With her boots removed, Johanna was almost at eye level. Lucy pushed her body away from the counter towards her and felt her breath on her face and neck as they remained only inches apart, occupying the same space, interlocking but separate. Lucy's gaze then dropped from Johanna's eyes to her slightly parted, full lips. She tilted her head slightly, avoiding those full lips as she edged closer, grazing Johanna's cheek with her lips. The smooth skin had a faint scent under her inspection.

"I've wanted you since that night outside the hotel," she whispered as her lips gently located the pulse point on Johanna's neck.

Johanna's breathing increased at the contact. "When you saved me." The words came out in a gasp, sounding more like a statement than a question.

Johanna's hands were still attached to Lucy's waist as she gently placed her own either side of Johanna's face. She then leant forward, bringing their lips together. The kiss was soft at first, until Johanna's hand cupped the back of her neck. She toyed with her hair for a moment before releasing it from the band. It draped around her neck until Johanna's hand clawed through it, pressing their lips firmly together.

"Nowhere to run now," Johanna whispered as she pulled back.

There was concern in Johanna's eyes as she looked back at her. "I don't want to run anymore," she replied and used her strength to reverse their positions, pressing Johanna against the counter. The firm body was welcome against her own. She covered Johanna's lips with hers, concealing a gasp. Wanting more, she slipped her thigh between Johanna's, rolling her hips to press against her as she edged forward, seeking more contact, trailing kisses down Johanna's throat as she felt her shirt being tugged.

"This colour is good on you, brings out your eyes."

By the time the words registered in Lucy's brain, she looked down to see her shirt was fully undone. The surprise must have registered on her face. Johanna was smiling when she glanced up.

"Take me to bed." Johanna's words were barely above a whisper.

Lucy smiled as she moved to smother Johanna's parted lips with her own, pushing her tongue inside as a groan escaped Johanna's throat. Taking Johanna's hand from her waist, she led the way to her bedroom.

Johanna turned over as Lucy re-entered the bedroom. She watched as Lucy drank from a bottle of water and walked towards the bed and smiled broadly as Lucy settled on the edge, offering her another bottle. The grey t-shirt Lucy had pulled on rode up her thigh as she sat. Johanna adjusted a pillow as she propped herself up against the headboard, letting the duvet slip down her body. It was a little late to worry about her dignity now.

"Thanks," Johanna said, taking the bottle. She hadn't realised how thirsty she was until she had it in her hands. Unscrewing the top, she took a long drink.

Then Lucy was on her feet again, pulling her phone from her discarded trousers on the floor. Johanna noted that she made no effort to check it. She simply walked back, settling on the bed.

"Is there a phone charger on the floor down there?" Lucy asked, nodding in the direction of her side of the bed.

Johanna peered over the side of the bed, but the floorboards were bare. "Nope," she answered, and a thought struck her. "Am I on your side of the bed?"

Lucy stretched over her lap, dangling her arms over the edge of the bed, searching for the charger, she presumed. "I don't really have a side of the bed." Her words were muffled by her position.

The t-shirt continued to ride up Lucy's back, exposing her smooth, rounded buttocks as she stretched out for the elusive charger. Johanna swallowed hard at the woman writhing around on her lap. Placing her water on the side, she slipped a hand between Lucy's parted thighs. Liquid heat immediately covered the tips of her fingers and the thighs seemed to part a little further, encouraging her exploration.

Now empty-handed, Lucy reappeared, making brief eye contact with her as she sat more upright.

"I see. One of those hard-boiled non-relationship types," Johanna said, referring to her non-side of the bed comment.

Lucy adjusted her position to settle on her lap, slipping a thigh either side of Johanna's hips as she pulled her t-shirt off, letting it drop to the floor. "Why? Are you offering?"

Johanna smiled at the challenge. "Maybe," she mouthed and leant forward, capturing one of Lucy's nipples between her lips. She felt the pressure of Lucy leaning into her, the warmth of her body pressing against her face. The bud between her lips was firm, and she grazed her teeth along the top before slowly releasing it with a small pop. She pulled back to see Lucy had braced herself, with one hand pressed against the headboard. Lucy ducked her head, bringing their lips together.

Johanna's hand immediately went to the other breast, gently massaging it, her thumb quickly finding the hardened nipple. Lucy's body was still new territory to her, but she already knew how much Lucy liked attention lavished on her breasts.

Johanna put her other hand to work reaching between Lucy's parted thighs. She slowly made her way along the soft skin to continue her earlier exploration, and the small patch of blonde hair brushed against her palm. As she felt Lucy press against her hand, seeking more contact, a small noise escaped her throat, adding to her request.

Desire almost consuming her, she pushed her fingers through silky folds, finding the pool of heat at the centre of Lucy, all the time focusing on Lucy's dark eyes. She was ready for her, coating a finger, she pressed it deep inside, relishing the heat as Lucy gasped. Her finger followed the gentle curve of Lucy's inner walls as she explored her depths.

"So good," Johanna whispered as she removed her finger to the final knuckle before slowly pushing it back in to its full depth again. This time when she removed it she added a second finger as Lucy gasped once more. Johanna began a slow and steady pace, thrusting her fingers inside as Lucy rocked her hips against her. She captured Lucy's lips as she pressed against her, increasing her thrusts in time with Lucy's pace. Johanna adjusted her palm to press against Lucy's clit with each thrust, the gentle intimate moans grew in cadence as she took Lucy to the edge. She pulled away from Johanna's lips, glancing down at her with dark hooded eyes, her breath hoarse as she tried to suck in air through parted lips. It was a look of pure ecstasy, and one she wouldn't forget.

Lucy pushed her hips forward, thrusting Johanna's fingers deeper, and released a muffled cry against her neck. The shudder that emanated from Lucy's body was intoxicating as powerful muscles pushed against Johanna's fingers. Relishing the sensation, with her fingers still inside, Johanna wrapped her free hand around Lucy's frame, drawing her closer and pressing her lips against her bare shoulder as Lucy's breathing slowed to its usual tempo.

Face glowing, Lucy sat back a little, allowing Johanna to recover her fingers.

Johanna took a breath grinning at the hue of Lucy's cheeks. "That was..." She searched for the right words to describe the incredible scene she's been a part of but nothing seemed to do it justice. It had never been like that with Steph, ever.

"It was." Lucy confirmed her confident demeanour returning.

She reached up cupping the side of Lucy's face, she wanted to keep hold of this, whatever this was.

Lucy edged further back on her knees before placing a searing kiss on Johanna's lips. Her tongue was insistent as it sought entrance to Johanna's mouth before making her way down Johanna's body, finally settling between her parted thighs. She lifted Johanna's knees, pulling her down the bed, bringing her to the surface of the mattress then climbed back up her body, once again settling between her parted thighs, pressing herself against Johanna's sensitive skin as she devoured her lips.

Johanna could only hold on under the weight of Lucy as their tongues battled and Lucy's hand trailed down the outside of her thigh, her palm then moving to the inside, pushing gently at her soft flesh. Johanna complied, bringing her leg up before letting it fall flat against the mattress. She earned a groan of approval for her actions as Lucy moved her hand between her thighs. She could tell she was wet, Lucy's fingers easily skating through her hot centre, approaching her opening, slowly circling, as if waiting for permission.

She wanted it, wanted Lucy inside her.

Nudging her hips forward, Johanna gave her the approval she sought. Heat radiated from her core as Lucy pushed inside, forcing a gasp from her throat. Lucy adjusted her position, using her hip to increase the focus of her thrusts, her thumb moving to circle her clit, sending wonderful shockwaves through her body as her fingers continued their actions. Lucy pulled back to look at her; she was panting as hard as Johanna was from her actions.

Lucy kissed the side of her neck as she slowly eased down her body, focusing on her breasts. She pressed her head back against the mattress as Lucy sucked a nipple into her mouth, her continued thrusting sending Johanna closer to the edge with each drive.

Johanna raised her hips to meet Lucy's actions, feeling the pull of her orgasm as tension built in her core. Lucy's thumb continued its movements, sending tingling heat radiating through her body as she toppled over the edge, jolting into submission.

Lucy's hand stilled but remained in place as Johanna's body pulsated. Spent, she melted into the mattress. Lucy's lips continued to caress her body as she slowly came to the surface, stroking the back of Lucy's neck as she nuzzled next to her skin.

"I'm glad you came to find me," she said.

Lucy twisted her head to make eye contact, her lazy smile radiant, her cheeks still a little flushed from their exertions. "I was running out of ideas of how I could seduce you."

Johanna turned on her side to face Lucy. Her hand continued to draw slow circles on Lucy's stomach. "Seduce me!" she snapped.

Lucy's low chuckle made the bed tremble as she said, "You're kidding right!"

"What do you mean?"

"Do you think I just happened to be outside the hotel when you were in the road that night?" she said and smiled at the nonplussed expression plastered across Johanna's face. "I was coming to find you," she added with a grin.

"What for?" Johanna asked, trying to tone down her suspicions. She didn't want to think she'd put her trust in someone only to have them pull the rug from under her yet again.

"I wanted to see you, talk to you."

Johanna felt her shoulders physically drop in relief, grinning at the quick exit Lucy had made that night in the toilets. Then she found herself asking, "Do you still think one of us did it? Killed Dan?"

Lucy seemed unshaken by the question. "It's most likely statistically and from the evidence we have so far."

Evidence? What did they have? There was still nothing of interest in the paper or on the news. "I see. Anyone in particular?"

"Everyone's a suspect."

"Even now?" Johanna asked, wondering if this was really the first time Lucy had slept with a suspect. Was this a tactic she had used before to draw information from witnesses and suspects. "So when you came to my hotel room?" she asked, returning to the original subject. She wanted to know just how much Lucy had planned.

"That was a bit more off the cuff."

"I see, well, it was definitely … informative," Johanna replied with a grin.

"Informative! Really? What exactly did it tell you?"

"Enough." Johanna's grin widened.

Lucy leaned closer, capturing her lips in a soft caress. "And that about that?"

"Umm. I think it means you've recovered your stamina."

Lucy edged closer, adjusting her body to fit precisely on top of Johanna's. "Did you mean to leave your scarf behind that night?"

"No," Johanna smiled. "But I wish I had. It was a touch of genius, wasn't it?"

Lucy chuckled. And now it was her turn to ask a risqué question. "So, who do *you* think did it?"

Her question seemed innocent enough, considering the situation, but Johanna couldn't resist it. "Are you pumping me for information?"

Lucy raised her eyebrows. "Maybe."

Johanna sighed. "I don't know. It's so long ago. I didn't exactly have my finger on the pulse back then." She knew from experience that things were rarely what they seemed at that age. "It's hard to imagine any of us doing it. We were just kids."

"Maybe there was more than one person involved."

Johanna scanned Lucy's face for a moment, trying to figure out what she was telling her.

"Another person? An adult, parent?"

"We don't know yet." Lucy's voice had changed tone, softened.

"I spent a lot of time with those people, learnt to ride a bike, had my first crush." Johanna was rambling now, but the thought of a parent being involved sent a chill through her body.

"First crush!" Lucy repositioned her body, resting her arm under her head. "Spill."

"Amy Bell," she said quietly.

"Your next-door neighbour?"

Johanna nodded, feeling the heat spread to her cheeks. "We shared a love of swing ball and Spirograph."

"Sounds serious. Should I be jealous?" Lucy's thumb moved like a windscreen wiper caressing the skin on Johanna's stomach.

Johanna turned to face Lucy before shaking her head. "No." Amy was so different to everyone else back then. She looked back up at the ceiling, recalling her time with Amy. "She was a year older. I tried to be *so* cool around her, but I failed miserably every time."

Lucy dipped her head, kissing her shoulder. "If it helps, you're much better at flirting now."

Johanna smiled at the compliment then said, "So, do you think you might actually feed me at some point today?"

"Oh, so you do actually want feeding," Lucy answered and blew out a breath. "Umm, I guess I did invite you for lunch."

"You did." Johanna replied with a smile.

"Wan's Palace is usually my go-to place, as they have the best dumplings in the world."

Chinese? Acceptable, Johanna thought. "Okay, sounds good."

Lucy rolled back on the bed. "What day is it today?"

Johanna had to think for a second. The days had certainly blurred since she'd left the stability of her work routine. "Sunday."

"Shit! It's not open. We'll have to make do with pizza."

CHAPTER 25

DANIEL DUNDERDALE, August 20th 1988

Three days had passed and three nights with very little sleep. Dan rolled over in bed. He'd been awake for hours. He could hear his brother crashing about in the kitchen, pumped up as usual. He knew they'd be leaving soon and he'd have to let them know he wasn't coming, but he was dreading it. If he left it till the last minute, he thought, they wouldn't have time to try and change his mind. Not that he'd be missed – it was Barney's day after all – but his mum would pester him, and his dad would try and talk him in to going; he just needed to stick with his story, though, till they got bored asking, because his mind was made up – he had to do something. He couldn't unsee what he'd seen; he couldn't forget it either. He knew he couldn't tell anyone; his parents would never believe him, neither would Barney. It fell to him and him alone; he had to do something. He had to save her. It was time for him to be the hero for once. A quiver of panic bubbled in his stomach, maybe he really would be sick.

"Dan, you up yet?"

He flinched as his dad's words crept under his closed bedroom door.

Dan watched from his bedroom window as his dad reversed down the driveway, Barney sat in the passenger seat glaring back at him. His mum had threatened him with a trip to the doctors if he kept moping around; he'd barely left the house in the last few days, worried he'd have to see Amy or her dad. She had already taken his temperature twice and found nothing wrong. She was worried, but he still couldn't bring himself to tell her. Instead, he simply stuck to his story, saying he had stomach ache.

His lip curled as he thought back to that day, how Amy just gave in to her dad like she had no choice. It made him sick; her dad was a bully too. It was wrong. He needed to make her see that she had a choice. Every time he closed his eyes, he saw the flowery towel her dad wore. It must be so different for Amy with only her dad to look out for, he mused. If her mum were there, this would never have happened; he was sure of it.

Dan continued to stare out of his bedroom window, this time across at Amy's house, waiting for her dad to leave. The sickness rose again in his stomach at the thought of what he had to do. He went shopping every Saturday like clockwork. Amy joked about it, saying it was her music time, no fear of getting yelled at to turn it down. Dan had kept an eye on her dad since that day, and he seemed to come and go at all times, so this was his first clear chance to talk to Amy. But although he'd had time to think over the last few days, he still struggled to come up with the right answer to the problem. This wasn't like school or maths, where there was only one answer. His hands were sweaty as they gripped the window sill Amy could be difficult; he'd seen it before, the way she could turn on people if they said the wrong thing. Mark had been her target ever since she moved here. He didn't want to be another victim of her wrath. He took a second to steady his breathing. If he could convince her to go to the police station, they'd have to do something, he was sure of it.

He checked his watch before quickly changing out of his pyjamas. There was a gentle thud as he pulled on his jeans, he scanned the carpet around him, the face of Tony Tiger grinned back at him. He bent to pick it up from the floor slipping it into his pocket. Her dad would be leaving soon. He would tell his mum that he wanted to get some fresh air and go around there. All he had to do was tell Amy what he'd seen, and he was sure he could get her to leave, to make her safe.

CHAPTER 26

Lucy parked up in the station carpark, after spending the entire drive trying to wipe the smile off her face. Spending time with Johanna had been incredible. They just clicked, there was no denying that, but there was still a sliver of doubt that she'd made a mistake. She truly hoped not, and leaving her scantily dressed as she drank tea in her kitchen was far from easy. Although Johanna was the reason she was back here so bright and early; Johanna, like Daniel's parents, deserved to know what happened.

She pulled her keys out of the ignition and sat back in her seat, running through what she was going to say to barrel in her mind. She needed to focus. The Dunderdale case was far from at an end, and she needed him to see her side. He was asking the impossible for her to just drop it, and she'd work on it in her own time if she had to.

The office was quiet when she walked in. Barrel was nowhere to be seen. She checked the clock; it was just after eight. He was normally in, swigging his second cup of tea by now.

Tanner's eyes were on her. She caught his expectant look and, beating him to the punch, said, "Is he in yet?"

"Not seen him. I'm guessing you're keeping your distance after the other night."

"Umm." She sat at her desk. Was Barrel avoiding her now? "Did we get anything on the search for the murder weapon?" she asked, changing the subject.

"Nothing in his garden or the neighbours. They searched the route the lads took, didn't find anything." Tanner sat back in his chair. "Managed to get through to the gas supplier though, Booker's annual usage was pretty constant not much fluctuation."

"High, average?" She asked feeling a tinge of frustration.

"Low apparently. They took regular meter readings for a few years to make sure he wasn't scamming them."

Jesus. How do people even do that these days.

"I did a bit of a background check on Booker." Tanner continued.

"Yeah, anything?" Lucy hoped there was at least one reason David Booker had been bludgeoned to death.

"No, but he was questioned over a domestic abuse allegation. It was made by a Ruth Adams."

"When was this?"

"Late seventies."

Lucy frowned. Booker was in his thirties back then. "Pull the case file, see if anything stands out." Lucy got to her feet. "I'm going to take your CCTV footage to the Coles, see if they recognise anyone from that night."

"Okay."

If Barrel was avoiding her, then her best tactic at this point was to make progress. After all, he'd said he wanted to make an arrest this week.

Heather Cole answered the door. There was a hint of something in her eyes when they landed on Lucy, worry maybe? Not unusual when the police are at your door, whatever it was evaporated in an instant. Mrs Cole dug her free hand into the pocket of her blue cardigan while the other gripped the edge of the door.

"Morning, Mrs Cole, can I come in for a few minutes?"

"Of course." She stepped back, opening the door fully.

The house was quiet as she followed Mrs Cole into the kitchen. She was relieved, to be honest, considering the looks Mr Cole had been giving his wife the other morning. But, unfortunately, she would need to show him the video stills, too. The pale-yellow kitchen was made up of two parts, units on one side and an oval, wooden table and chairs on the other. The warming smell of coffee and toast made her stomach groan. With Johanna staying over, she'd missed breakfast.

"Is your husband around, Mrs Cole?"

"Oh yes, he's just taking a lie down."

Code for still in bed, she figured.

"Okay, so we manged to find some CCTV of a group of people that might be involved in the incident next door. Would you mind looking at it to see if they look familiar?"

"I didn't recognise them."

Lucy was surprised by the slight jump of panic in the woman's voice. "No, no," Lucy rephrased. "I just want you to see if you think they might be the people you saw coming out of the back of the house."

"Oh, yes, of course."

Lucy pulled back the cover of her iPad, queuing up the footage. She gave it to Mrs Cole before pressing the play button in the middle of the screen and standing to the side, watching the footage play out, hoping it would be clear enough for Mrs Cole to be able to identify the individuals.

"I'm not sure. It was very dark."

Shit! Lucy's shoulders dropped. She knew Barrel would want them identified anyway, if only to eliminate them, but looking for actual suspects sounded like a much better use of her time.

John Cole entered the kitchen. If he was surprised to see her there, it didn't show.

"Mr Cole." She nodded. "We managed to find CCTV footage of some potential suspects."

He said nothing as he moved towards his wife, looking at the iPad over her shoulder.

"That's them," he said before walking to the dining table on the far side of the room.

Lucy frowned. From what they'd said the other day, it was only Mrs Cole that had physically seen the lads running away. She was just about to question it when Mrs Cole spoke up.

"Yes, you're right; that's them."

"You're sure?" Lucy confirmed. She wanted to be able to make a start on trying to ID them, but something was off here.

Mrs Cole nodded, unable to meet her eyes. "Yes, I recognise the top that one's wearing with the stripes down the arm."

"Thank you." She looked at Mr Cole, but he had already turned his attention to the newspaper spread out on the table. "You've been a great help. I'll send a PC over to take your statement, if that's okay, save you going to the station."

Mr Cole looked up before glaring at his wife. Lucy wasn't sure if she'd overstayed her welcome or something else was going on between them. She wasn't about to be the catalyst for a domestic.

"Thank you for your time. I'll leave you my card in case you think of anything else."

Lucy checked her phone as she got back to her car. She was hoping for something from Barrel so she could find an in to start a discussion about the Dunderdale case. Nothing.

With a positive ID but no names for any of the youths, she wanted to canvas the other residents to make sure. Two hours later, she still had nothing. Leaving the estate, she tried the nearest shops, figuring they could have shopped for food, drink or cigarettes at some point if they were local. Again, she came up short. No-one recognised them at all, or at least were unwilling to admit it.

She put a call into West Heath Police Station to see if Laxton and Springer were on duty. They were still on nights and due in at six. She left a message saying she'd stop by and catch them before they went out on patrol.

She mulled over the details of the case, if they weren't from the immediate area, how did they get here? If it was a burglary, why was nothing taken? Had he interrupted them, recognised one of them and they had to silence him? Having seen the aftermath, it seemed too frenzied for that. It felt personal, targeted. And she just couldn't work out why, as Booker wasn't exactly a social butterfly. She kept coming back to the heating; surely it had purposely been put on to try and throw them off, to muddy the time of death. Hardly the actions of a group of teenage burglars.

She needed to talk to Tanner, find out where he first picked them up on CCTV and what Cole's did for employment before retiring. The answers had to be out there.

Johanna walked into her room. She'd taken a leisurely trip back to the hotel in Kingsford, deciding to catch the train rather than get a taxi. Sitting on the bed, she slipped off her shoes and took out her phone. Realising it was out of battery she blew out a breath as she got to her feet. Her body ached. How Lucy had gone into work so early she'd never know. She plugged her phone into the charger trailing across the desk and was surprised when her phone sprang to life with a call straight away.

Her assistant Gail's details flashed onto the screen. Gail seemed equally surprised that she'd answered this time after calling for the last couple of hours.

"Sorry, what was that?" Johanna asked.

"I'm just making sure you got the message about the meeting tomorrow. Travis wants to run some stuff by you about a new client," she offered with enthusiasm.

"Okay." First she'd heard of it. She turned quickly grabbing her computer to check her emails, but in doing so, she knocked the Spirograph box she'd retrieved from her parents to the floor. Her eyes crawled over the scattered items as she listened to the voice of her assistant echo in her ear. The elastic band that had held it all together had perished and split apart by the look of the torn ends. The plastic insert that held the pens and circular cogs had become separated from the box. Johanna frowned at the spread contents; there was something that didn't belong: a white, dirty sock, half balled up at one end was amongst the debris.

"Err ... right, okay," she mumbled, but she had no idea what she'd just agreed to. Her focus had gone completely. Then she added, "I'll be in first thing tomorrow. See you then." She didn't wait for a reply as she ended the call and knelt to get a better look. The fluffy sports sock was too big to be hers even now. On closer inspection, the redy-brown stains were in odd places. Not on the underside and heel, where you would expect them to be on a well-worn sock. It didn't look familiar at all. It certainly wasn't on the floor earlier. She would have seen it when she came in.

She stood to grab a pen from the desk and used it to prod the infiltrator, not wanting to touch someone's smelly, old sports sock with her bare hands. She then slipped the pen into the sock, lifting it up, turning it over, and grinding clinks came from it. There was something moving around inside.

The browny-red stains were more prominent on the other side diluted to a pinky-red. Was it blood? What was a bloody sock doing at the bottom of her Spirograph box?

Johanna tilted it further to encourage the contents to shuffle out across the floor. It was broken whatever it was. Transparent plastic; flat, circular sections, indentations on the edges. She pushed the sock away, and it took her a moment to piece it together as she moved the plastic parts around with the end of the pen. It was a large Spirograph cog, the missing Spirograph cog from her set. The whole reason she'd stopped using it was the missing cog. Had it been hidden underneath all this time. Why? Simon first came to mind. Had he broken it and hid the evidence? Why would he leave it in the box, in a dirty sock? It didn't make any sense, but who else could have done it?

She carefully placed the items back in the bottom of the box and replaced the lid, but she couldn't resist sending a quick probing text to her brother. Then she needed to get her head back in the game, get back to Bath and prepare for her meeting tomorrow; she wanted to gen up on any information Travis had sent on this potential new client before meeting them in the morning. But before she did that, she sent another text message to Lucy:

Hi Detective, I had a really great time yesterday. Been called back into work for a day or two. Can we meet up when I get back?

She placed her phone down, ready to begin packing, surprised when her phone chimed almost straight away. A fizz began in her stomach as she read Lucy's reply.

Me too. So they can't survive without you after all. Call me when you get back.

CHAPTER 27

AMY BELL, August 20th 1988

Amy flopped onto the sofa as she glared at the TV. Her mood had been souring all morning. She didn't need to see the stain in her underwear to know what was going on; she hated her time of the month. Since when was it a good idea for teenage girls to have periods? She knew he'd be pissed off too. It meant he couldn't do what he wanted when he wanted. She'd wait till he said he was leaving for the supermarket tell him. They'd developed a code now. She didn't even need to say it out loud anymore.

He liked playing the dutiful father every Saturday, doing the weekly shop – it would just be one more thing for him to pick up – and she couldn't wait for him to leave the house. He was always in, always in her face, wanting her company, pawing her, breathing on her. She couldn't stand it sometimes.

Right on cue, he came trotting down the stairs, grabbing his jacket from the newel post at the end. "Right, I'm off. I need to take the car to the garage, so I'll be a bit longer."

She grunted, trying to avoid conversation with him, but she felt him move closer.

"Do you think you could do a bit of cleaning or put the washing away while I'm gone? When you've finished watching kid's TV, that is."

She hated his sarcasm, especially today of all days. She turned to scowl at him, twisting her nose to let him know exactly how annoyed she was with him, as he turned to leave, she called him back.

"Paul, I need something from the chemist." She waited for the penny to drop. Her lips twitched with satisfaction as he blinked before looking at her.

"Again, already? Amy, you need to go on the pill and stop all this shit."

"Yeah, and where does a twelve-year-old girl get those without drawing attention?" It was the same argument every month. Pointless. "God, just do it will you," she moaned and looked away, not wanting to see the bitter look on his face any longer.

Heavy footsteps thudded on the carpet as he eventually walked away, but she knew she'd pay for it later. Then the front door slammed, allowing her to finally breathe a sigh of relief. Settling back on the sofa, she closed her eyes, pulled the hot water bottle back onto her stomach, and the waves of pain started to ebb away ... until a knock at the door made her jump. Surely Paul wasn't home already.

She dragged herself off the sofa, mentally preparing herself for another round. Christ, why didn't he just use his bloody key?

A second knock sounded as she neared the door.

"Alright," she murmured as she reached for the lock.

She yanked open the door and was surprised by the visitor on the other side. He was breathing hard as if he'd run all the way, he looked scrawny as he rubbed his left hand on his jeans as his wide eyes scanned her. His oversized t-shirt draped on his small frame, no doubt a hand me down from Barney.

"Dan!"

She really wasn't in the mood for visitors, and Dan certainly wasn't a regular.

"Hi." He looked down, unable to meet her glare.

Amy leaned against the door frame. "What's up? Not gone to that Judo thing then?" Barney had been going on about his stupid competition all week.

"Nope." Dan shoved his hands into his jeans as he looked past her into the house.

Amy frowned. She really didn't have the patience to deal with this right now.

"What're you up to?" Dan asked.

"Just watching TV. My dad will be back from shopping soon." She hoped that might change his mind.

"Can I borrow a tape?" Dan asked, still unable to meet her eyes.

"A tape. A music tape?" she asked, confused. Dan wasn't much of a music buff, but he gave an awkward little nod and she had no option but to let him in. "Okay," she told him, leading the way to the main room, hoping she'd be able to get rid of him as soon as possible. "What are you after?" She had a rather good collection, even if she did say so herself. It was her thing. Well hers and Johanna's.

"Umm." He shrugged his shoulders. "Don't know."

"What's going on, Dan?" she asked. He'd barely set foot in her house since she'd moved there. Why had she even let him in?

Dan silently stared at the carpet, wringing his hands in front of him before eventually saying, "I want to help you."

"What!" She snapped. She was even more confused now as she turned her attention to the shelf of tapes.

And then he said the words that made the life drain from her body and she knew that nothing would ever be the same again.

"I saw you and your dad the other night."

"What are you talking about?" she answered and tried to sound casual as she continued to scan the titles of the cassette tapes, but the lettering on the tape spines began to blur. She felt his eyes on her as she stared straight ahead and everything began to clench. *How could this happen?* She thought back to everything that had happened over the last couple of days, searching for anything that someone might have seen, but she came up empty.

"I saw what he did to you!"

A cold sweat broke out on her skin. They were so careful. How had he seen anything?

"What? Who?"

Dan continued to look at her, his bottom lip wobbled as fear stretched his face. "Your dad," he said softly.

"What are you talking about?" Her tone was aggressive as she turned to stare him down, willing him to say the words. She wanted to hear them out loud.

"He's making you do things. I saw you." Dan finally looked away. "And him."

"What did you see?" she asked, prodding at the festering wound that had become her reality. When she'd started this new life, she never thought it would come to this, being found out by a ten-year-old boy. A scraggy boy that thought he could save her from herself.

"I saw bad things. Out the back the other night." Dan pointed to the back of the house. "You don't have to do that anymore."

Anymore? How could he be so stupid? Amy grinned at his lack of understanding. He didn't have a clue. She thought back to the other night. He must have seen them when Paul came home from work.

"How did you see us?" she asked. More importantly, who else saw? "I was on the other side of the fence going home for tea."

A fresh wave of panic filtered through her. "Was Barney with you?"

"No." He shook his head.

Amy's shoulders relaxed a little. She knew full well Barney would never be able to keep his mouth shut if he found out. "Who have you told?" she asked summoning tears. They always worked with Paul. She covered her face with her hands, sniffing loudly. "I don't want anyone else to know."

"No-one," he reassured her, "but we need to go to the police or ... or ..."

She peeked through her fingers to see Dan clasping the sides of his body, his eyes fixed on the street outside. Was he looking for Paul? Terrified for his return. It dawned on her then that he didn't have a plan at all. He was just a kid playing at being the hero. He'd never fill Barney's t-shirt let alone his shoes. Amy abandoned the tears and straightened her slumped frame. "Let's play some music," she told him and walked over to the tape player, turning it on.

Dan reached out to touch her arm. "No, Amy, we need to go," he pleaded, but she shrugged it off. She had nowhere to go. She'd run away from home to be with Paul. She had nothing without him. The thought of Dan telling everyone her hardest kept secret made her sick inside. Paul would know what to do. She just needed to wait for him to come back.

She selected one of her mixtapes, dropped it in and pressed play. Bananarama blared out of the small speakers.

"Amy!" Dan urged, moving closer. "We need to leave before he gets back," he added and marched over, pressing at several buttons on the stereo to make it stop. "We need to go!"

Silence filled the room for a second, but Amy quickly pressed play again, clicking off the record button. She didn't want to hear anything Dan had to say. Instead, she began jumping up and down, bopping to the music. She closed her eyes, hoping Dan would simply disappear.

"Amy, please, I want to help you," Dan tried again over the noise of the music, and Amy felt a hand rest on her arm.

"Get off me!" she snarled and pushed him away. Stepping forward, she shoved him again. "Don't touch me!"

Dan fell back awkwardly on the sofa. His mouth gaped open with shock as he slipped down onto the carpet "Amy. He'll be back soon," he pleaded.

Amy turned her back, focusing on the beat of the music and tried to remember the words of the song. It was so familiar, she'd heard it hundreds of times, but her mind was blank as she jumped to the beat.

"Amy, your dad's hurting you!" he begged.

Dan's voice filled every inch of her head. She tried so hard to blot it out, to listen to her music, she only had to wait for Paul to come home. But he wouldn't shut up, she heard him calling her name pleading again, on and on it went with his weedy heroics, as if she was a delicate flower that needed to be saved. She felt a hand on her arm again, it was as if it was crawling under her skin, she had to do something, she couldn't stand it any longer.

"Shut up!" she screamed and threw herself on top of him slamming her hand down over his mouth. She'd seen his brother do the same thing countless times. He fought her, but Amy had the higher ground and locked her arms in place, pressing down on him with all her weight. Closing her eyes, she felt moisture on her fingers. His feeble skinny limbs struggled as her nails dug in securing him in place, it was easy, too easy. She pressed harder as he continued to mumble under her hands. Dan's t-shirt rode up his bony body exposing his frail frame.

Tears streamed down her hot cheeks, her throat thick, preventing her from shouting her reply, but what could she say? Tears continued to fall as her body trembled, and she closed her eyes, blocking out the sight of him. "He's not my dad." She finally mumbled, confident she would never let anyone have that kind of power over her.

Dan's body stilled beneath her. Opening her eyes, she saw his wide-eyed stare.

Her body crumpled under his scrutiny, shame weighed heavily on her shoulders she removed her hands from his face. Blood covered her fingers. She must have split his lip or bloodied his nose in the struggle. She wiped her hands on her pyjamas as she climbed off him, wrapping herself into a ball. Her limbs ached from the exertion. She clenched her fists. How had it come to this? Paul had propositioned her that day, almost demanded his way with her when he came home. It was a private moment. Dan had no right to watch them. Anger grew inside her.

Dan wiped at his face as he tried to sit up. "W-who is he Amy?" His face twisted as the words left his bloodied lips.

She had no choice now; she needed to shut him up. A stack of clothes piled up on the armchair waiting to be put away caught her eye. She made a grab for something, anything to shut him up, and threw her full force on top of him again, easily overpowering him. She straddled his tiny hips, one hand pressing on his shoulder while the other covered his mouth not wanted to hear anything more, she glanced up at his fear-stricken eyes just visible above her hand. She'd laughed and joked with this boy, been tortured by his incessant drivel, no more she couldn't risk it. She moved her knee up to his shoulder freeing her hand then she forced the scrunched-up sock into his mouth, covering it with her hand. His mumbled words turned to tortured whines as his chest heaved under her weight. She wanted to silence him forever.

CHAPTER 28

JOHANNA WALKED past her assistant's desk on the way to her office and offered a friendly wave as Gail was occupied with a phone call. She groaned when she saw the pile of paperwork she had to catch up on before the meeting with the new clients later.

"Hey there, stranger," Gail offered by way of a greeting as she stepped inside Johanna's office. "Time off certainly suits you."

Johanna smiled. She was only back because of Gail's call yesterday. She didn't plan on staying any longer than she had to.

Gail stepped closer to her desk. "He wants your job, you know." Her voice had dropped an octave as if she were worried someone would overhear her words. "Travis," she added in the same tone.

What! She owned the company; how could he take her job? "What do you mean?"

"He wants to be in charge."

Johanna simply raised her eyebrows. She knew Gail would have more information. Besides, Travis was practically in charge in many ways while she was out of the office. He'd even brought in the new client, which could prove very lucrative if it worked out.

"I heard him in the kitchen, talking to Myles."

"I see." Johanna tried to hide her surprise. "I'll keep that in mind."

"Don't let him push you out. It's your company."

"Don't worry, I'll stand my ground." She saw the look of concern in Gail's eyes. Johanna's phone vibrated across her desk. Reaching out, she checked the screen, hoping to find Lucy on the other end. Instead, her brother Simon's name flashed on the screen.

"Sorry, I need to take this," she said, meeting Gail's eyes.

"Of course." Gail made her way to the door. "Coffee?" she asked before leaving.

"That would be great. Thank you," she said then accepted the call and brought the phone to her ear. "Hey, called to finally own up have you?" she said. Simon had failed to reply to her accusatory text she'd sent yesterday.

"What! No way, it wasn't me." Simon's tone was jovial.

She smiled at the easy way they fell into familiar sibling grooves. "Oh, really. Well, all I know is it's broken and I didn't do it."

"You were so freakishly obsessive about that thing."

"I was not," Johanna huffed, knowing he'd landed a solid blow.

"Trying to follow all those impossible patterns, making up weird pictures."

Johanna balked at his words. He was right about that; they were impossible.

"Amy probably broke it. She was as crazy about it as you were," he replied, raising his voice over the banging in the background. Typical Simon tactic: shift the blame onto someone else.

"You don't know anything about a bloody sock in the bottom of the box either I suppose?"

"A what?" His question was quickly lost amidst the loud thumping in the background.

"Where are you?" she asked, flinching at the noise.

"At work, where do you think? We can't all just take time off when it suits us."

Johanna saw no point in correcting him. He wrote the book on hard-done-by working fathers. No doubt he was tucked away in a comfy little heated office; hardly the construction coalface he often made it out to be.

"Anyway, what's it like staying in your hometown after all this time?"

"Weird. Keep thinking I've seen people from school, but I can't place them. You should have come to the wake. Mark Evans was there. He's really changed."

"Yeah, Mum said."

Johanna rolled her eyes. Simon always did have a hotline to their mother. No doubt she'd told him about the slap. Her hand went to the side of her face. Thankfully, the pain had mostly gone. She'd only needed a little makeup to hide the fading bruise.

"Right, well, I'd better get back before they totally fuck up this job."

"Okay. Well thanks for finally coming clean." Johanna couldn't resist one final dig. She joined in when she heard him laughing into the phone.

"My money's on Amy. You lent it to her all the time," Simon replied before ending the call.

Did she? How had that slipped her mind? She sat back in her chair, trying to remember if she'd lent it to Amy before going on holiday with her grandparents.

———

"DS Fuller," Lucy blindly answered as she brought her desk phone to her ear.

"One of the boys at the house on Grove Lane where that man died was Tyler Lloyd." The voice was flat and devoid of emotion.

Lucy grabbed a pen as she checked the small screen on her phone. The number was unavailable. *Shit!* "Can you give me your name please, sir?" she asked, but the line went dead before she'd even finished her sentence. If she didn't know any better, she'd have sworn it was John Cole on the other end, she thought as she put the phone down. It certainly explained the funny looks he was giving his wife during her last visit with the CCTV. They knew who one of the boys was all along. Her visit to West Heath yesterday to see if Laxton and Springer recognised the youths had been less than fruitful, but maybe things were starting to look up. They still had the option of releasing the footage, but that was a last resort for now.

Lucy got to her feet, heading straight for Barrel's office. If the tip panned out, she hoped this might go some way in reconciling their relationship; he was still standoffish towards her and she didn't like it. His mind had been elsewhere when she'd updated him earlier, considering his last brush-off she didn't feel it was her place to ask again. Disagreements went with the job, although, as she reminded herself, she'd done little to rebuild bridges, let alone dare to mention the Dunderdale case.

She knocked before stepping inside the open doorway.

"Boss, just got a tip on one of the boys seen at the Booker house."

Barrel looked up from his computer. "Who from?"

"Not totally sure. They didn't want to leave a name, but I think it was the neighbour, John Cole."

Barrel raised his eyebrows. "Who'd he point the finger at?"

"Somebody by the name of Tyler Lloyd."

Barrel shrugged. "Never heard of him. Check it out, see if he fits our CCTV footage."

"Yes, boss."

Lucy returned to her seat and looked across at Tanner. He was currently on the phone. She couldn't help tapping her pen as she waited for him to end his call. She wanted to know how the Coles knew this Tyler Lloyd. He had referred to him as a 'boy', but it was hard to tell the age, let alone the ethnicity, of the people they had on CCTV; they could be anything from fifteen to twenty-five.

Before Tanner's phone hit the cradle, she asked, "Hey, did you find out the employment history for the Coles?"

"Err … yeah." Tanner riffled through some papers. "They worked at the same school. He was a caretaker and she was a classroom assistant. Both retired just over two years ago."

That had to be the connection. "Which school?"

Tanner checked his information. "Guilford House."

"Really?" It was a good school from what she knew, located on the outskirts of Oldbury. Lloyd had to be a pupil, or recent ex-pupil, considering they had been retired two years. "Can you give them a call, see if a Tyler Lloyd is or was a pupil there?"

"Who's Tyler Lloyd?"

"Just had a tip-off that he was one of the boys at the Booker house," Lucy replied as she tapped at her keys to run Lloyds name through the system. Of the two listed, one had a date of birth in 1971 and the other in 2001, she clicked on the later. Young Lloyd had the beginnings of a criminal record too, cautioned for graffitiing three months ago.

"You jammy fucker!"

A screwed-up ball of paper bounced off her computer screen. Lucy turned to look at Tanner, eyebrows raised.

"I've just been trawling through CCTV for the past two days to get a decent picture of them, and someone just calls you up and drops a name."

Tanner's disbelief was fuel for her fire. "What can I say, Tanner? You've either got it or you aint." She returned to her screen, ignoring his mumbles.

The photo on Lloyd's record made him look incredibly young. He'd turned eighteen since, but she doubted that he'd matured a great deal in that time. She read the brief details of the caution; Lloyd had been caught with the rucksack containing cans of spray paint. He also had paint on his hands that matched the graffiti. First offence, they went easy on him.

Lucy made a note of Lloyd's address in Kingsford and put a call in to the arresting officers from West Heath. Maybe they knew who Lloyd hung around with.

According to PC Hancock, Lloyd was one of a gang of four that they'd chased that day, and he was the only one they caught. The rest had made their escape on bikes. Lloyd had refused to give their names. Hancock thought he recognised one of them as a Dale Saxby, local kid, but Lloyd wouldn't say. Lucy finished her notes before checking to see if Saxby had a record: nothing.

"Well." Tanner stretched his back as he appeared next to her desk, mug in hand. "The secretary at Guilford House would only confirm that Tyler Lloyd was a pupil till he left in May two years ago after sitting his exams."

The timelines fit; they were at the school at the same time. "We can follow that up later with the school and the Coles," Lucy told him and stood, offering him her empty mug. "I think we've got enough to pull him in. I'll see what the boss says."

Lucy tapped on Barrel's half open door before stepping inside. "Boss." Barrel was staring at his computer screen, although his focus was far from present. She thought he'd dropped off for a moment till he looked up a little surprised by her appearance. "Tyler Lloyd, eighteen years old." She handed him a copy of the photo from his record. "Got an address for him on Elcot Avenue in Kingsford where he lives with his mother."

"Anything?" Barrel asked without looking up from the paper she just given him.

She figured he was talking about any previous. "He was cautioned three months ago for graffitiing a railway bridge. I spoke to the officer from West Heath Station that gave him the caution. He says Lloyd was part of a group of four they caught in the act. He was the unlucky one that got picked up."

"Hung out to dry by his friends?" Barrel asked his tone held more interest now.

"They had bikes, apparently. We also found a link to the Coles. They both worked at the same school that Lloyd attended. So if it was Cole on the phone with the tip, we know how their paths crossed."

"Also, according to Booker's gas supplier he barely used it. He must have used the electric heaters instead, there was one in his bedroom and the front room." It hadn't escaped her notice that Booker's body had been found in the hallway, away from either of the electric heaters.

"What are you thinking?" This time there was malice in his tone.

She didn't want to have to spell it out again. "Don't know yet? It's odd though isn't it?"

"Agreed." Barrel nodded. "Good work." He sat back in his chair studying the photo. "So we like Lloyd as a suspect for something at least. Let's pick him up, see if we can find anything that links him to the scene."

"Yes, boss." She smiled at the complement. At least they were making progress.

"And get that call traced, see where it leads."

Lucy sat in the passenger seat, clipping her seatbelt into place. She didn't bother with the sat-nav, confident she could direct Barrel to the Lloyd house, until he drove in a totally different direction.

"Boss, Elcot Avenue's the other way."

"I know that. We're going to pay the Coles a visit first." He took his foot off the clutch, making the car jerk. "I want to make sure we're not wasting our time. Get uniform to keep an eye on the Lloyd house."

"Okay." She made the call. Jesus, would it kill him to let her in on their plans?

The one good thing about Barrel driving was they got there fast, not comfortably or safely, but fast. The car jolted to a stop outside the Coles' house. The vehicle in the driveway indicated that at least one of them was in.

"Okay." Barrel turned to her. "I'll do the talking as they've bluffed you already."

Lucy was just about to protest when Barrel got out of the car. Annoyed, she almost shouted across the top of the car towards him when she joined him. Taking a breath, she used her inside voice instead. "They lied to me; they didn't bluff me."

"Same difference," Barrel snapped as he stalked up the drive to the front door and knocked rapidly.

Lucy rushed to catch up. She wanted to see their faces when they lied again, considering what she knew now. The mild welcoming smile dropped from Heather Cole's face as she eyeballed them both stood on her doorstep.

"Hello again." She directed her words to Lucy.

"Mrs Cole," Lucy drained any warmth from her words. "This is DCI Barrel," She wasn't about to let Barrel ridicule her in front of a witness despite his earlier warning. "Can we come in for a moment?" She said stepping forward to place her foot on the doorstep.

Lucy watched as additional lines appeared between Heather Cole's eyes.

"Of course." Mrs Cole stepped aside.

Barrel brought up the rear closing the door as they made their way into the sitting room. Lucy stayed on her feet despite Mrs Cole's gesture for them to take a seat.

"Mrs Cole, do you recognise this person?" Lucy offered her the police photograph of Tyler Lloyd. She could feel Barrel's eyes boring into her as she took the lead, but she needed to step up.

Mrs Cole glanced at it before looking away. "No, I don't think so."

Lucy nodded. "Do you know a Tyler Lloyd?"

"Tyler Lloyd? No. I-I don't know–"

Lucy continued to pen her in. "Mrs Cole, we know he was a pupil at the school you and your husband worked at." Lucy pulled out her phone. "I can call the school to see if you worked with him if you like, if that will help."

"Oh." Heather Cole stepped backwards to sit on the sofa. "He-he's not a bad kid. He just mixes with the wrong people."

"Lying to the police is a very serious offence, Mrs Cole," Barrel added from behind.

"I'm sorry." Heather Cole pulled a tissue from her sleeve. "I just don't think he did it. He's just not like that."

"That's not for you to say, Mrs Cole. If he's innocent, the evidence will show that." Lucy replied taking over again.

"Will it?" Heather Cole questioned.

Was that what this was all about? "You didn't know he was involved when you phoned the police that night?" Lucy felt Barrel's eyes on her, but she needed to know.

"No." She closed her eyes for a moment. "He was the last one out. The kitchen light was on. He went back in to turn it off. He's so easily led. I worked with him for a couple of years. I know him; it's just not in his nature to do that to another person."

Lucy let out a frustrated breath. She looked away, scanning the rest of the room and focused on several statues on the top shelf of a bookcase in the far corner. They looked like trophies of some kind.

"Did your husband make a call to DS Fuller earlier today indicating that Tyler was at Mr Booker's home that night?"

Lucy turned back at Barrel's question.

Heather Cole frowned. "I don't know. I haven't seen him since this morning."

"Are you willing to make a new witness statement confirming Tyler Lloyd's presence at the house on the night of the incident?" Barrel asked, sounding a little too forceful still, and Lucy hoped Barrel's pressure on their eye witness wouldn't come back to bite them in the ass further on down the line. But the Coles had impeded the investigation by nearly a week, which gave the offenders ample time to dispose of any evidence.

Heather Cole nodded, the strain on her face evident.

"Thank you, Mrs Cole." A crack of a smile filtered through his stern expression. "I'll send round an officer to take your new statement."

CHAPTER 29

Lucy knocked on the front door, snatching a glance at the two uniformed officers that they'd requested to the scene. Searching the property would be easier with more bodies, but Barrel had asked them to wait outside till they were needed to keep the situation calm.

"Tyler Lloyd?" Lucy asked, watching the nonchalant grin drop from the young man's face when he opened the door. His eyed darted to the identification held in their hands. For a second, she thought he might bolt, but thankfully he didn't.

"Police. Can we come in for a chat, Mr Lloyd?" Barrel asked as he placed a hand on the doorframe.

Tyler looked even younger in real life. She would easily have mistaken him for a school kid had she not seen his record. He stepped back from the door, his t-shirt sagged against his thin frame seemingly too shocked to react, and Lucy shut it behind them, blocking the way as Barrel headed further into the house. Lloyd was forced to follow Barrel as Lucy walked towards him.

As they entered a small, open-plan living room, Barrel moved towards the stairwell, looking up to the next floor. Lucy glanced around the room, finding several cans of energy drinks and empty crisp packets littering the coffee table.

"Is your mother here?" Lucy asked, hearing movement at the back of the house.

Tyler shrugged struggling to make eye contact. "Work."

Lucy quickly stepped towards the noise. Glancing through the kitchen window, she saw somebody flipping over the back fence. *Shit!* Pulling out her radio, she called to the uniformed officers outside. "Round the back, we've got a runner over the fence. IC1 male, black beanie hat, grey bottoms, green top." She didn't hold out much hope. "Who's your friend?" she asked Lloyd.

He simply shrugged his shoulders before burying his hands in his tracksuit bottoms.

"Are those your shoes, Mr Lloyd?" Barrel nodded to the trainers next to the sofa as he came back into the room.

Lucy looked down at the grey socks on Tyler's feet then back to the white and red trainers Barrel was pointing towards. She knew they didn't belong to the guy who'd done a runner; he'd been fully dressed when he hopped the fence.

Barrel crouched down; he indicated for her to take a closer look, pointing towards the edges of the soles, and as she stepped closer, the thin, dark-red tide line around the rim was clearly visible.

The crackle of her radio prevented Lucy from confirming her suspicions.

"He's long gone," the officer panted into the radio.

"Okay. Head back here for the search," Lucy replied as she turned to face Tyler Lloyd. He looked wide eyed but said nothing.

Barrel got to his feet. Their suspect barely reached his shoulders. "Mr Lloyd," he demanded, "can you tell me where you were on the night of the twenty-fifth of October?"

"Here." Tyler's strained one-word answer was less than convincing.

"Is there anyone that can confirm that?" Barrel pressed, clearly not in the mood to be fobbed off, considering their earlier visit to the Coles'.

Tyler shrugged.

"Arrest him. Let's get the search team in," Barrel said over his shoulder as he walked away.

Lucy reached for Tyler's arm and said, "Tyler Lloyd, I'm arresting you on suspicion of murder...."

Lloyd looked dumbstruck as she handcuffed him before sitting him on the sofa. His docile demeanour hardly made him a threat, but she wasn't about to give Barrel any more ammunition to use against her. "Under the Police and Criminal Evidence Act, we have a warrant to search the premises for evidence related to the crime."

As soon as the other officers arrived, she asked one of them to get Tyler some different shoes and bag the potentially blood-stained trainers., Barrel insisted on transporting the suspect in his own car to speed up the process. They left the scene to be thoroughly searched on the way out, Lucy asked an officer to wait at the house for the mother as she was due home from work.

As they turned a corner too sharply, as usual, a group of figures on the side of the road looked up at their squealing tyres. A woman with two kids moved back from the road. Lucy saw the woman's shocked face was severely scarred from something on one side. The reddened skin flowed down her neck, disappearing beneath her coat.

Was that her, the woman Johanna had seen at the wake? It had to be. The chances of two women like that in the same town were slim to none. She could ask Goff, see if she knew who the woman was, put Johanna's mind at rest. Lucy watched in the side mirror as the woman manhandled the children, her manner was half way between firm and aggressive as they moved as a group across the road behind them.

Barrel disappeared upstairs as soon as they arrived back at the station. He was still giving her the cold shoulder, despite their progress. The fuck-up with the Coles weighed heavily, nevertheless, she was determined not to be the first to give in and back away from the Dunderdale case.

She booked in Tyler Lloyd with the desk sergeant, then went off to find him. They needed to talk strategy for interviewing Lloyd if he wanted to close this case, although the evidence was building, eyewitness account, CCTV and hopefully forensics would be able to place him at the scene.

As she approached the stairs, she spotted PC Goff down the corridor.

"Hey," she called and headed towards her. "You were at the wake in the Croft the other day, right?"

"I was. Did you hear about the–?"

Lucy cut her off, figuring she was going to give a blow-by-blow account of the infamous slap. "Do you remember a woman there with burns all down one side of her face?"

"Yeah. Err ... Mia I think. I didn't get her surname."

"Shit!" Lucy had wanted a softly-softly approach to this.

"But I did take down the registrations of all the cars in the carpark."

"Excellent," Lucy beamed as Goff handed her a black notebook, opened to a list of numbers and letters. Lucy pulled out her phone and took a picture of the page. She checked there weren't any more on the next page before handing it back to Goff. "Thanks, you've been a great help." She figured she at least had a legitimate reason for running the plates. If anyone asked, she could say she was looking for anyone connected to Compton Way.

"Any news on the Booker case?" Goff asked.

"Hopefully. Got a tip. Just brought someone in for questioning."

Goff's eyebrows rose as she nodded. With nothing more to add Lucy offered her thanks again before climbing the stairs.

Barrel was on the phone when she got to his office. She was just about to walk away when he waved her in. From the sound of it, the crime tecs were sure the trainers that they had found would fit the prints from the Booker home. And the crowning glory was the hooded top with stripes on the sleeves had been found crammed down the back of his wardrobe.

Barrel looked at her as he ended the call. "You did well with the Cole woman, stomped all over her feet I'd say."

Stomped all over her feet? She looked back at him in confusion for a moment before realising she'd used the same words to Barrel when talking about her initial involvement in the Dunderdale case. Honesty forced the next words from her lips. "I knew something was going on but I couldn't figure out what it was."

"Don't let witnesses fob you off in future, press them." He raised his hand. "Delicately of course but press them."

"Yes boss." She offered a tight smile. Maybe he was finally over his mood, it had to be something at home or maybe ACC Kirby was still pressuring him.

"That's what I need to see from you, squeeze every last ounce of information from what you have in front of you, witnesses, evidence and everything else in between."

"Yes boss." *Wasn't that what I did with the Levin footage?* She shook the thought from her head, now wasn't the time to burn anymore bridges.

"Right. Let's leave Lloyd to stew for a while before the first interview."

"Yes, boss. He's asked to call his mum and for the duty solicitor, so it could be a while." Lucy backed out of the room, hoping she had time to run the plates Goff had given her.

Returning to her desk, she keyed in the details. After several duds, the fifth plate came good. A white SUV registered to an Amelia Hunter, although the date of birth was a little off, a few years older than Johanna. If they were at school together, they certainly weren't in the same year.

Johanna had seemed so convinced she knew the woman; what if it wasn't from school but something else? An old neighbour for instance, Amy Bell. She'd changed her name before; maybe she'd done it again.

She squinted at the photo on the DVLA site. It could be her. But the scars were too distracting. Lucy searched her desk for the photo Johanna had given her. Holding it up to the screen, she blocked out the scars with the edge of the photo, but it wasn't clear; too much time had passed between the photos. Frustrated, she dropped the photo back in her drawer.

Just then, Barrel stormed out of his office. "Fuller. Let's go."

Lucy was confused for a moment then got to her feet. "Boss." She was fully aware they hadn't even discussed an interview strategy yet. "What's the plan?"

"Follow my lead," he told her as he gave her a laptop to carry. That was it. That was the strategy chat out of the way.

"But–" she began, but he cut her off with a glare as he marched down to the interview room. Once inside, everyone took their seats and Barrel carefully introduced everyone before taking the laptop from her and setting out his paperwork.

The duty solicitor was one she hadn't seen before. He was young, in his thirties, she guessed. The creases in his white shirt, visible beneath his suit jacket, matching those around his eyes.

"Mr Lloyd, do you understand why you've been arrested?"

"No." Tyler Lloyd shook his head as he sat slumped in his seat. Although there was a slight tremble in his torso as his leg jiggled beneath the table.

Barrel looked at the duty solicitor then back at Lloyd and said, "You've been arrested on suspicion of murder, Mr Lloyd." He waited a moment before continuing. "Can you tell me where you were between the hours of ten p.m. on Thursday the twenty-fifth and one a.m. on Friday the twenty-sixth of October."

The duty solicitor leant forward, delivering a brief word in Lloyd's ear.

"No comment," Lloyd mumbled in reply.

"Do you know where Grove Lane is?"

"No comment."

"Tyler, can I call you Tyler?" Barrel softened his tone.

Tyler Lloyd nodded but didn't speak.

"You need to speak for the audio recording." Barrel pointed to the recording contraption.

"Okay," Tyler croaked.

"I want to show you something, Tyler." Barrel reached for the laptop, opening it before turning it around for Tyler and his solicitor to see. "We have CCTV footage of you and three others in the area of Grove Lane on the night of the twenty-fifth." Barrel played the footage.

Lucy studied Lloyd. His eyes drifted to the screen only briefly. The duty solicitor made notes as he watched.

"A man was brutally attacked at a house on Grove Lane that night," Barrel continued as he shuffled his paperwork, looking for something. "We searched your room after you were brought down here."

Lucy studied Tyler's face to gauge his reaction, but his gaze was now fixed on the corner of the room.

"As you know, during the search, we found a pair of trainers that we're currently testing to see if they match footprints found at the house where the man was attacked. We're also testing them for blood."

Again no reaction, nothing from Tyler. He didn't seem surprised at all, and there was no immediate denial. It only said one thing to Lucy: they had the right man.

"An item of clothing was also recovered from your bedroom: a dark blue hoodie found in a bag stuffed down the back of your wardrobe. This hoodie has white stripes down the arms, just like the one in the CCTV. We're having it tested for blood."

Tyler leant forward, resting his head on the table.

"My client would like a break," the duty solicitor said, placing his pen down.

"Are you okay, Tyler? Would you like a break?" Barrel asked.

Tyler's head moved across the surface of the table as he nodded.

"Interview suspended at fifteen seventeen."

"Can I have something to eat?" Tyler asked without even looking up. No doubt, his change in circumstance had forced him to skip lunch.

"Sure, I'll sort something out for you, Tyler," Lucy replied. "Don't worry, we won't let you starve."

Tyler finally looked up, meeting her eyes.

Lucy heard her phone bleep as she read the initial report on Tyler's mobile phone. She wasn't entirely sure what role Tyler had to play that night at the Booker house; forensics would be the key to finding out exactly who did what, and they'd have to wait until tomorrow for more information on his location that night.

Half-distracted, she grabbed her phone, checking the message. It was from Johanna.

Are you free for dinner tonight? I could bring something over.

That got her full attention. She wanted to see Johanna more than anything but didn't want to sound too desperate.

Sounds good, she started to type. *How about 8ish? I'll call if I'm held up.*

Lucy knew from experience that Barrel liked to call it a night around then when they had someone of Lloyd's age in custody.

Johanna replied almost immediately, bringing another smile to Lucy's face.

Great, can't wait to see you.

"Right, Fuller, we're back in," Barrel bellowed from the doorway. "He's asked to talk. I've got a good feeling about this."

To Lucy, this meant he wanted to come clean, at least she hoped so.

She waited for Barrel to leave the room before stopping by Tanner's desk and placing a sheet of paper in front of him.

"Can you run this name for me?" she asked. "She attended the wake at the Croft Hall the other day. I think she might be my missing resident."

"No shit!"

"And, Andy, keep it between us for now, in case it's nothing." She walked away then something occurred to her. "Also find out if the DVLA have a record of any earlier photos of her before her accident. She renewed her licence a few months ago. See if we can find something earlier, we can ID her with."

She then walked off to catch up with Barrel, without waiting for a reply.

With all the interview formalities completed, the duty solicitor pulled out a sheet of paper.

"I would like to read out a statement on behalf of my client," he said.

Barrel made an approving hand gesture. "Go ahead."

"My client was in the area of Grove Lane on the night of the twenty-fifth of October. After watching somebody leave a property on that road, he assumed it was empty as the lights were out. He then went to the back of the property where he broke the glass in the back door to gain entry. On finding the man on the floor, my client panicked and fled the scene. My client strongly denies any part in the death of the man he found in the property."

Lucy looked at Tyler in surprise. He'd just copped to virtually everything they knew for sure so far, except the murder, that is.

"Thank you for that, Tyler." Barrel sat back in his seat.

Lucy knew Barrel would let Tyler stew for a moment or two, let the weight of the situation sink in, and Tyler bit straight away.

"I didn't do anything. He was already dead." Tyler sucked in his bottom lip.

He was cracking under the pressure, Lucy's grip loosened on the pen in her hand.

"Okay, Tyler, let's start from the beginning."

"I was on duty on the corner."

"On duty? What does that mean?" Barrel asked.

"I had to look out for the right place."

Had to look out for the right place. Was he working for someone? Lucy made a note for her own curiosity.

"Right place for what?" Barrel asked sounding equally as curious.

"It was my turn. I had to break in and take something from inside."

Had again. Was he being forced to do this?

"What do you mean, Tyler? You had to take something from inside?"

"To join the gang. They wouldn't let me till I stole something from a house."

Lucy thought back to Barrel's words at the Booker scene. He had said something about there being a string of burglaries with little taken from the scenes, just like the Booker place. One for each of them?

"That's why you were there that night?" Barrel asked.

"Yeah. Someone came out of the house, walked off down the street. There were no lights left on. I thought the place was empty."

Barrel sat forward. "When you say left the house, did you see which door?"

Tanner was going to have to revisit the CCTV see if this mystery man existed.

"Front door," Tyler replied.

"What did he look like, this man you saw?"

Tyler shrugged. "I don't know, old guy. He had a big coat on and one of them old-fashioned hats like they wear in the movies."

"What sort of hat?"

Lucy thought back to the crime scene. There was a coat rack by the front door. A selection of coats were hanging there but no hats.

Tyler shrugged at the question.

Barrel pushed a pen and paper in front of him. "Draw it for me."

Tyler leaned forward. Grabbing the pen, he made a few sharp squiggles before throwing it down. Barrel pulled the paper back without taking his eyes from Tyler. He glanced at the image before offering it to Lucy, who added it to her pile of papers.

"A trilby," Barrel speculated.

Tyler shrugged again. "He had a limp too."

"Anything else?"

Lucy caught the sarcasm in Barrel's question but doubted Tyler had picked up on it, he just shrugged in reply.

Barrel picked up the pen Tyler had used. "Was the man carrying anything in his hands?"

"No."

Lucy made a note to ask Dr Sharma about Booker's appearance during his most recent visit to the surgery for his flu jab.

"What time did the man leave?"

"Don't know, about eleven-thirty. I waited for a bit to see if he came back."

Lucy noted the time. It fitted with the pathologist's report. It was bang in the middle of his time window.

"Then what?" Barrel prodded.

"I went around the back, smashed the window."

I not *we*. He was still protecting his friends, even though they had footage of all four of them from that night.

"Any reason why you chose that particular house?"

Tyler shook his head. "Thought it was empty."

Lucy jotted a note for Barrel. She knew from experience he hated it when she interrupted. She subtly pushed it towards him.

"Was the heating on when you entered the house?" Barrel asked.

Tyler shrugged. "Don't know."

Barrel let out a breath. "Was it warm inside the bungalow?"

"Yeah, boiling."

Whoever left that house flicked the heating on before they left, possibly unaware it was out of the ordinary for Booker.

"Where was the man when you went inside the house?" Barrel continued.

"In the hallway. He was covered in ..." Tyler looked at his hands. "I ran straight out of there."

But he hadn't, had he? Lucy reminded herself. She recalled Heather Cole's words. Tyler was the last to leave. He'd even gone back to switch off the kitchen light. Despite that, Lucy still found herself believing Tyler's story.

"Now, the thing is, Tyler, we know you weren't alone that night. You've already seen the CCTV we have of you with three other individuals. We also have a witness that saw you with three others when you left the house. If they can corroborate your story, then you're off the hook, aren't you."

Tyler didn't reply.

"We know you sent a text at eleven twenty-three to someone by the name of Sax." Barrel pulled a piece of paper from the pile in front of him, pushing it across the table for Tyler to see. "The text, as you can see, says, 'All clear'."

Tyler leant forward, but his eyes merely grazed the paper in front of him.

"Can you give me the full name of the person that text was sent to?"

Tyler's solicitor leaned forward to quietly say something. "Can't remember."

It was an unregistered burner phone, but Lucy would have put money on it belonging to Dale Saxby, one of the youths that had escaped when Tyler was caught graffitiing the railway bridge. Maybe he was also the white male that did a runner from Lloyd's home earlier.

"Would that be a Dale Saxby?"

Barrel shuffled his paperwork in front of him. "We're currently looking at your phone to determine your locations throughout that night. We'll have access to all of your past texts, calls and photographs, even the ones you've deleted."

Again, nothing.

"Is there anything else you want to tell me about that night or the incident?"

"No," Tyler replied. His voice was small in the room as he looked down at his hands.

"Okay, I'm going to suspend the interview for now, Tyler, let you get some more food and rest."

In the hallway outside the interview room, Barrel turned to her, "What do you think?"

Lucy blinked back her surprise that he was seeking her opinion, she let out a long breath. "I don't think he's a murderer."

Barrel looked at her for a long moment before answering. "Agreed."

"Do you believe the story about the man he saw leaving the Booker place?"

Lucy raised her eyebrows. "I'll believe it when I see it on CCTV."

Barrel cracked a smile. "Spoken like a true cynic."

Lucy leant back against the wall. "The cell site report on his phone should be back in the morning. So we should have more for the next interview."

"Good. Get Tanner to look for our mystery man on the CCTV. And see if we can identify Saxby from the night of the incident."

"Yes, boss," she told him, and she hoped Tanner could handle it; she had plans after all.

"Let's leave him to stew overnight. We know he's fucked, but he needs to realise it before he'll give us the names of the others. We'll charge him in the morning."

Lucy glanced at the time on her phone. It was after seven. They had until tomorrow lunchtime to interview him again before they had to apply for an extension. Hopefully, forensics would be back by then.

She was just about to follow Barrel up the stairs to the office when someone called her name. She turned to see the desk sergeant heading towards her.

"Tyler Lloyd's mother's been on the phone, wants to talk to him or whoever's in charge," he said, waving a Post-it note in the air.

Shit! So much for getting out of there at a decent hour. She still had paperwork to tie before she could leave, too.

Lucy held out her hand for the Post-it. She knew Lloyd's mother wasn't entitled to speak to her son again, but she would try and placate her as best she could for the time being.

"Here!" Barrel's voice echoed from above as he came back down the stairs. "I'll call her. I'll let her know you're going to visit her first thing tomorrow with the CCTV footage, see if she recognises any of Tyler's friends."

CHAPTER 30

A FAMILIAR FRIZZLE of excitement circled in Johanna's stomach as she walked past a familiar car on her way up the steps to Lucy's flat. She'd missed being around the last few days. Grinning, she climbed the stairs, and the plastic handle of the takeaway bag wrapped itself around her fingers.

She wanted to tell Lucy about the bloody sock. It might have no importance at all, but it worried her. She couldn't live with herself if she held back a vital clue that might shed light on what happened to Dan. Explaining exactly how it came into her possession was another issue all together. Her brother had given her a little insight into that, pointing the finger at Amy Bell, but in truth after Dan they spent so much time at her grandparents she lost track. And why in the world why Amy Bell be involved.

Johanna knocked on the door and heard the faint thud of footsteps approach. "Evenin' all," she offered as the door opened.

Lucy rolled her eyes, nodding for her to come in. "Any idea how many times my dad has said that whenever they visit?"

Johanna appraised the woman in front of her, dressed in shorts and a t-shirt. Her hair was still wet at the ends, from the shower, she presumed. She gave her an appreciative smile before feigning hurt as she stepped inside. She was thankful she'd had time to stop off at the hotel to shower and change before heading out to pick up the takeaway.

"Please don't tell me my humour has slipped to dad jokes already."

Lucy closed the door. Turning, she levelled her eyes at Johanna. "It's a well-known fact that Police officers cannot lie." Her expression was firm, with only a hit of humour in her eyes.

Really? That sounded like something she'd need to test out later.

Despite the dim light in the hallway, Johanna could see the dark patches hovering under Lucy's eyes. "I promise I'll get better. I'm probably just hungry or something, low blood sugar. And I brought dinner, so ..." Johanna held the bag aloft, so Lucy could see the name of the restaurant on the side.

"You remembered." A wide smile brought Lucy's weary face to life.

"I did," Johanna grinned and slipped her shoulder out of her jacket, prompting Lucy to take it from her. The hallway was narrower than she remembered, and Lucy only had to stretch across the small space to deposit her coat on a free peg before she returned her attention to Johanna, who quickly raised her hand to Lucy's cheek, her thumb tracing the line of fatigue.

"You look tired."

"Long week," Lucy told her as her eyes settled on Johanna's. "It feels like ages since you were here."

Johanna continued to cup Lucy's cheek, enjoying the connection. "If you're too tired, I can go," she said, but regretted the offer as soon as she'd made it.

"No way," Lucy told her and stepped closer, almost pinning her to the wall.

Johanna's gaze fell to Lucy's parted lips, and the fresh scent of her floral shower gel filled her nostrils. She was just about to close the remaining distance when she pulled back. "You missed me!" she said. It was more of a statement than a question.

Lucy's lips twitched as she nodded.

She really couldn't lie.

Lucy's hands curled around her hips as she said, "Can you stay over?"

"Yes." Johanna leant forward as her hand trailed down Lucy's neck. Skimming over the soft t-shirt, her fingers found a nipple and circled it before rubbing her palm over it. Lucy wasn't wearing a bra, which also meant she probably wasn't wearing any underwear. The frizzle in her stomach grew exponentially as their lips touched. The kiss was soft and slow as Lucy leaned into her. Johanna parted her lips, deepening the kiss. A small moan of approval escaped Lucy's throat as she did the same.

Lucy pressed her thigh between Johanna's, bringing a welcome pressure as the seam of her jeans pressed against her pulsing clit. Johanna's head swam with desire; she wanted this, wanted to touch every inch of Lucy's skin, feel the throb of her sex as she came under her hand. Lucy's fingers then found hers as they clutched at the take-away bag. Tugging the plastic from her hand, she turned, placing it on the table behind the door and leaving Johanna with the immediate loss of her warm body. She couldn't remember the last time someone had managed to press her buttons so proficiently.

"How do you feel about cold Chinese?" Lucy asked as she moved closer again.

Johanna tilted her head and said, "I love it." With two free hands, she took the opportunity to turn the tables. Grabbing Lucy's hips, she switched their positions, pressing her firmly against the same wall as she kissed her again. Their lips parted at the same time, their tongues battling for control as Johanna pushed her own thigh between Lucy's and trailed her hands lower, under the waistband of Lucy's shorts. Edging closer, she cupped her buttocks as she pressed against Lucy's firm body and gently rocked her hips. Enjoying the aching need it sent through her, she pulled away from Lucy's lips to catch her breath. A low moan echoed around her as Lucy kissed her exposed neck.

"I want you, now," she whispered against Lucy's ear, unable to delay it any longer.

"Not here," Lucy replied as she pulled at Johanna's hand, which had been occupied cupping her bottom, and led the way through the flat to her bedroom, depositing Johanna at the foot of her bed before busying her hands to undo Johanna's shirt buttons.

The room was lit only by a bedside lamp, but it was enough for

Johanna to be able to see Lucy's darkening eyes. Unwilling to wait, Johanna pulled the shirt over her head at her first opportunity, earning a grin from Lucy as she dropped it to the floor. Lucy replied in kind, removing her own t-shirt. Before she could stop herself, Johanna cupped Lucy's exposed breast. She gasped at the warmth radiating from her flesh as she circled the same nipple that had been hidden by the thin material earlier with her thumb.

Lucy stepped closer, undoing the button and zip of her jeans. Johanna pushed them down her thighs as far as she could, taking her underwear with them, desperate for their skin to touch.

"Sit down," Lucy whispered.

Johanna complied, settling on the end of the bed, as Lucy knelt in front of her, pushing Johanna's jeans down her calves and over her feet, along with her shoes. She watched as Lucy tugged down her shorts before getting to her feet and letting them drop to the floor.

Johanna quicky stripped off her bra before she settled back on the bed, regarding Lucy as she knelt on the bottom of the bed. She watched in awe as Lucy slowly manoeuvred up the bed on all fours, and her breathing hitched as Lucy, wearing only a bold expression, skimmed her hands along the top of Johanna's legs, edging closer until her thigh brushed against Johanna's sex.

Lucy's hands continued their journey north, over the flare of her hips, along her straining rib cage that only just managed to contain the force of her hammering heart, toying with her nipples before lightly gripping her shoulders and finally planting themselves firmly on the mattress above Johanna. Now she hovered above her, her hair falling forward, a marker to their separation. Johanna pushed herself against Lucy's thigh, seeking more contact, but Lucy didn't react. She was toying with her.

Johanna strengthened her resolve; she wasn't about to be kept at bay. She stretched out her arm, pushing her hand between Lucy's parted thighs. Her fingers slipped between delicate, silky folds. She watched for Lucy's response as thick, molten fluid covered her searching fingers.

Lucy's eyes narrowed and her mouth fell open at the minor intrusion as Johanna continued her exploration, her fingers coated in Lucy, then upwards, finding her swollen nub and circled it slowly, eliciting a gasp from Lucy. Her hips jerked at her touch as Lucy began gently rocking against her fingers.

Slowly, maintaining eye contact, Johanna removed her fingers and slipped them straight into her mouth, her tongue sucking them clean. Lucy's reaction was instant. Leaning forward, she captured Johanna's lips before she'd finished feasting on her fingers. The taste of Lucy was intoxicating, driving her on, as Lucy wrapped a hand around her wrist, securing it above her head against the pillows as she rearranged her body, draping it over Johanna's.

Johanna groaned at the pressure against her clit and Lucy gasped as she rocked her hips, eliciting wonderful sensations as the pressure grew between Johanna's wet thighs. The warmth and weight of Lucy's body felt perfect against her skin and Johanna wasted no time spreading her legs, encouraging Lucy closer, their thighs slipping perfectly together. The slick friction stoked her fire as Lucy ground down firmly against her, rocking her hips. She pushed her own hips forward, meeting Lucy's frantic pace.

Johanna reached out, bringing their lips together for a crushing kiss. As Lucy pressed against her, she had to break away to catch her breath.

"God, I'm so close," she panted as her climax grew in time with Lucy's thrusts. The movement sent her over the edge within seconds, and her body involuntarily shook as her orgasm swept through her.

Lucy's body jerked forward as she released a long shuddering breath, her face buried against Johanna's neck as her hips slowed their vigorous pace. Moments later, Lucy rolled onto her back, her breathing heavy as she lay back against the mattress.

The cool air sucked at the moisture and heat on Johanna's skin. "And I thought you were tired," she mouthed.

"I thought I was too till you sucked your fingers."

"Oh. So you *were* teasing me earlier."

"What?" Lucy said, turning her head to look at her, half smiling, "I don't know what you're talking about."

"Hey. I thought police officers couldn't lie."

Lucy rolled her eyes. "Damn it. This is why I don't date smart women."

Johanna hoped the dim light hid any surprise at Lucy's use of the term 'date'. "You think I'm smart?" she asked, deciding to take this in a different direction.

"Oh, yeah."

Johanna turned on her side. The sight of Lucy's ruddy cheeks brought a wide smile to her face. She trailed her hand over Lucy's stomach as it rose and fell in quick succession. She then moved her hand lower, letting it fall between Lucy's parted thighs as she leant forward, sucking her pert nipple. It was warm and bulbus against her tongue as she toyed with it, and she felt Lucy's body react with a sharp intake of breath as she pushed her chest against her lips. Johanna then pulled back, releasing the moist nipple, and blazed a trail of kisses up Lucy's chest and neck. Edging her body half on top of Lucy's, she captured her lips as her fingers dipped lower. Separating wet folds, the pads of her fingers once again found Lucy's hardened clit. She circled the nub as Lucy pulled her closer, wrapping a hand around the back of her neck, tangling in her hair.

Johanna used her thigh to generate more pressure, and Lucy gasped as she plunged her finger into the wet heat. Removing it, she added a second as Lucy's hips spread wider, giving her greater access, and she struggled to ignore her own desires as Lucy's hips brushed against her own sex.

Johanna maintained her ministrations with her fingers as she edged lower, rearranging her body over Lucy's parted thighs. The sound of her fingers thrusting in and out of Lucy made her clit throb all over again.

The musky scent was intoxicating as Johanna moved closer and nibbled at the glossy folds before searching for the hardened nub her fingers had skirted over earlier. She used the flat of her tongue to find her target.

"Fuck!" Lucy whispered.

The tight muscles fluttered around Johanna's fingers as Lucy released a low moan. Johanna's tongue circled her clit before sucking it deep into her mouth. Lucy came undone almost immediately.

Johanna hummed her appreciation as Lucy's hips began to thrust wildly, and she stilled her fingers when flutters became throbs, Lucy's body shaking as the orgasm ripped through her. Johanna lapped at the Lucy's hot centre as the throbbing slowly ebbed away.

"Jesus, are you trying to kill me?" Lucy puffed out between breaths.

"I don't know what you mean," Johanna grinned as she climbed back up Lucy's panting body.

"You will."

"Really?" Johanna challenged as she settled above Lucy. "Big talker." She heard the whisper of a snigger before she was thrust onto her back.

"Really."

Lucy hovered above her for a second before ducking down and kissing her firmly. The taste of Lucy still swirled around in her mouth as their tongues battled. Johanna relaxed back against the bed, enjoying the attention as Lucy slowly made her way down her body.

The heat from Lucy's mouth almost brought her to climax before she'd even touched her, and she felt Lucy spread her open before plunging her warm tongue deep inside. Johanna gasped as she held on. Gripping the sheets, she raised her hips to meet Lucy's agonising, pleasurable rhythm.

Lucy's focus then moved higher as warm lips toyed with her clit before she sucked it into her mouth. Johanna was becoming hoarse from panting; her heart was beating out of her chest as the pressure built in her body. Seconds later, her body took over, releasing her from the hold it had over her, vibrating with ecstasy as Lucy lapped at her folds until her body melted into the mattress beneath her. She struggled to catch her breath, wiping at the sheen of sweat on her forehead as Lucy crawled up her body, settling between her open thighs.

Lucy rested her weight on her arms as she kissed Johanna's neck and whispered, "You make the most amazing sounds when I go down there."

Lucy dropped one hand to gently cup her mound, creating a wonderful aftershock down her thighs.

"You must be doing something right," Johanna said, between breaths.

"I hope so."

Johanna moved her hand to grip Lucy's bicep it was rock hard under her touch, and said, "Trust me, you are. Why do you think I didn't leave earlier? I nearly slapped myself when I made that ridiculous offer."

Lucy grinned. "Oh, so it wasn't just the thought of leaving the food you brought."

"Speaking of food," she smiled up at Lucy. "Do you think it's suitably cold yet?"

"Definitely," Lucy grinned, dipping her head lower, dragging her lips across Johanna's. "I think we've worked up a decent appetite."

"So ..." Johanna balanced her plate of food as she took her seat on the sofa next to Lucy. "Dare I ask how the case is going?"

"Slowly," Lucy said between mouthfuls. "I'm working on something else at the moment."

"Oh." *Shit.* That was meant to be her way in to telling her about the sock she'd found.

"Old guy, battered to death in his own home," Lucy continued.

"Gross," Johanna replied as she toyed with her food. "I think I heard something about that on the news."

"How was your trip home? Was it nice to be needed?"

Johanna jerked her head up at the swift change in subject. She forgot she'd told Lucy about her work situation. Good memory. A detective's trait, she figured. Or maybe Lucy remembered because she was genuinely interested. Johanna hoped for the latter.

"We picked up a new client. I say *we*; I mean my manager, Travis, he did all the work really."

"That's good, right."

"Umm." Johanna looked up to see Lucy was looking right at her. Was she reading her mind or something? "My assistant's convinced he's after my job."

"Isn't it your company?"

"It is," she nodded. Why was she even talking about this? Steph was never interested in her work.

Lucy frowned. "Then what's he planning on doing?"

"I don't know. The only thing he can do is buy me out, I guess."

"Is that something you want?"

"I don't know. Maybe." She wasn't exactly missing it while she was away, far from it, she considered as she fidgeted on the sofa, before her thoughts returned to the case, knowing she'd left it long enough. Pushing the rice around on her plate, she finally placed her fork down and said, "I need to talk to you about something."

"I knew it," Lucy said without looking up. "You ate the extra dumpling."

She recognised the hint of sarcasm in Lucy's words. "No. I promise I didn't eat it," she replied with a grin.

"But I always get five in an order."

"You do? Has he got the hots for you or something?"

Lucy balked at her words as she finished chewing her last morsal. "God no! Have you seen him? He's like seventy years old and barely able to see over the counter."

Johanna smirked as she tilted her head. "I didn't say do you have the hots for him, did I."

Lucy placed her fork down and reached for her glass of wine. "Oh, so you think I get special treatment."

"Possibly," Johanna smirked and placed her plate down on the coffee table in front of them.

"Umm. Next time order it in my name."

Next time. Johanna wasn't quite sure how to reply. She wanted to think it was possible. She hoped whatever *this* was between them, it wasn't just a fling, that it could be something more.

"So, what did you want to tell me?" Lucy asked, eyebrows raised as she picked up her fork again.

Johanna took a deep breath as she settled back on the sofa. "I want you to know before I tell you, I didn't know anything about it. I only dug it out of storage at my parents' house that night I met you outside the hotel."

"The night you walked in front of traffic?" Lucy replied with a grin.

Johanna rolled her eyes. Was she ever going to live that down? "They kept a load of our stuff from when we were kids packed in tea chests above the garage."

"Okay, now I'm getting a little worried." Lucy's fork was piled with rice, stationary, halfway to her mouth. "What did you find?"

"It's a box, a Spirograph set. Well, most of it. I hadn't opened it or anything else in the tea chest for years. I took it with me for sentimental reasons, I guess. I was a bit of an addict as a kid."

Lucy raised her eyebrows. "I see. I was always more of an Etch A Sketch kid myself."

Johanna resisted the urge to ask if she was mocking her. Everyone knows you can't do curves with an Etch A Sketch. "Anyway, I knocked it onto the floor in my hotel room the other day before I went back to Bath."

"Okay."

"There was something inside, underneath," she clarified.

"What?" Lucy put her piled up fork back down on her plate.

"A sock. I think it might have something on it, blood maybe I think."

Lucy frowned. "Blood? Who's blood?" She placed her plate on the coffee table.

"I don't know. But Amy and I were always playing with it. And I spoke to my brother the other day and he reminded me I was always lending it to Amy when I went on holiday. I was away most of the time till we went back to school in September." She let out a long breath. "I don't know it's just weird."

"You think it's got something to do with Daniel?"

"I don't know." Lucy shook her head. "I just don't understand why it would be in there. I vaguely remember shoving the box back in the wardrobe when I found one of the big cogs was missing." She waved her hand in front of her. "You need them to do all the different patterns."

"Whose sock is it?" Lucy asked, pulling her out of her reverie.

"I don't know. It's not one that I recognise. It's big." Johanna made a size gesture with her hands, hoping it would help. "Adult sized, I'd say. White sports sock, stripes around the top."

"What did you do with it?"

"Nothing," Johanna said before quickly correcting herself. "I put it back in the box. It's still in my hotel room."

"Okay." Lucy took another drink of wine as she stared straight ahead. "Why don't you bring it into the station? I'll try and get forensics to take a look, see if it's relevant."

"Okay," Johanna agreed as she let out a breath. "The weird thing is, the missing cog was also in there, broken up inside the sock."

Lucy swivelled her head to look at her, a frown knitting her brow. "Bring it into the station tomorrow."

CHAPTER 31

THE FOLLOWING MORNING, Lucy's visit with Tyler Lloyd's mother was a total washout. Mrs Lloyd claimed she couldn't identify anyone on the CCTV and spent the entire time claiming Tyler was innocent. Lucy didn't enlighten her regarding her son's recent confession. She was oblivious as she walked back into the station until her name was called she turned to see Laxton further down the corridor.

"Decided to see what a real police station looks like?" she quipped on the way to the stairs.

Laxton appeared next to her. "You look like crap," he told her. "What have you been doing or should I say *who* have you been doing?"

Lucy raised her middle finger in reply as she walked up the first flight. She figured no reply was better than a lie. She was beginning to wish that she was anywhere other than the station when Laxton said something useful.

"I've got some names for you."

Lucy stopped and turning to look at him. Raising her eyebrows, she indicated for him to go on.

"I was speaking to Hancock yesterday about your boy, Lloyd. He gave me the names of the lads he saw cycling away that day at the railway bridge." Laxton handed her a slip of paper from a notebook. "He's had dealings with them before."

"Thanks."

Lucy took the offered paper and scanned the names. Saxby was on the list, along with a Dean Collins and Jason Potter.

"I'll check them out."

"Mine's a pint next time you're in The Lion."

"Least I can do," she smiled, before skipping up the remaining stairs to the office. Tanner was nowhere to be seen when she got there – she was still waiting for the info from the DVLA on Hunter – so she settled at her desk, woke her computer and checked her emails. The initial forensics report was back on Tyler's clothing. The stains on the trainers were blood and they were a match to the victim. The tread also matched a set of footprints from the kitchen. Fine glass shards were found on the right sleeve of Tyler's hoodie, which were a match to the glass that had been smashed in the back door to gain entry. According to Dr Reed, the killer would have been covered in blood spatter, but there was nothing to link him to the body, except the blood he'd stepped in. One of his friends could be responsible or, as Lucy suspected, the mystery man that Tyler had seen leaving the house that night was the real perpetrator.

Barrel's door was shut, and she decided to call Dr Sharma's surgery before checking in with him. Her call was answered on the third ring.

"Hi, my name is DS Fuller from Woodley Police Station. Can I talk to Dr Sharma please?"

"He's with a patient at the moment. Is it urgent?" The woman on the other end of the phone had a sharpness to her voice.

"Just ask him to call me back please," she told her and added, "He has my number," before ending the call.

Barrel's door opened as she sat back in her seat, and she watched as he started to walk out into the main office, but something on his phone changed his mind. Turning around he hovered in his office doorway. He looked like shit, with heavy bags that had settled under his eyes over the last week. His shirt was creased as though he'd slept in it. He moved further inside cutting off her view of him.

Lucy got to her feet and headed for his office, knocking lightly on his door. She pushed the door open without waiting for a reply, he was sat behind his desk now, his focus on the phone in his hands.

"Boss, have you seen the forensics report?"

He placed his phone on the table but left it face up as if he was waiting for a reply. "Yeah, places Lloyd at the scene, but not much else."

Lucy nodded. "His mum was a waste of time, convinced he's innocent. Wouldn't give me any names of friends or even look at the CCTV."

"Close the door for a minute," Barrel replied without looking up.

Shit! She heard the tension in his voice. Did he know about her extra-curricular activities with Johanna Hale? Lucy reached for the door, quietly closing it. She'd been waiting for this moment for days, for Barrel to finally come clean about his foul mood. Maybe the case had gone awry, she hoped that was all it was but her mind raced with fear and the possibility of dismissal or reprimand if he knew about Johanna. "Something wrong, boss?" she asked, turning to face him she fought to make eye contact. He could end her career if he wanted to.

"You could say that." He sat back in his chair but didn't offer her a seat. His desk was covered with paperwork and plastic cups from the coffee machine.

Barrel looked down at his hands as they rested on his desk in front of him. "My wife..." He let out a long breath. "She err she died last week, cancer," his voice cracked on the final word. "Ex-wife, I should say, as she got remarried, I guess."

There was an edge of bitterness as he finished, she figured it wasn't his idea to get divorced let alone remarried. She blinked in surprise. "Oh. I'm so sorry, boss. I had no idea."

Barrel rarely talked about his homelife, only mentioning his son on occasion. It certainly explained his so-called extended time required in court and his ability to somehow get away when he was needed on the case.

"We weren't that close anymore. We kept in contact because of our son really."

Barrel rubbed at his face. His usual stubble had developed into a light beard.

Despite his words, Lucy got the impression Barrel hadn't quite let go of his wife.

"How old is your son?" she asked. She felt for any child losing a parent, regardless of their age.

"Twelve," He sighed as his phone buzzed, he glanced at it before meeting her eyes again. "He's not taking it too well."

Lucy nodded. "Understandable."

"Anyway." Barrel cleared his throat, back to work mode. "I wanted to apologise for the other day." He nodded towards the main office. "You were doing the right thing pursuing the Dunderdale case."

"Don't worry about it. It's forgotten," she told him and stepped closer to his desk. The relief she felt at being let off the hook was quickly covered with guilt all over again. "Maybe you should take a bit of time off," she suggested.

He shook his head. "No. I've told the chief I need to be here, keep busy."

Lucy nodded. "Okay." Maybe they could get back on track with the Dunderdale case with both of them back.

"I'm guessing you didn't just stop working on it?" Barrel asked, eyebrows raised.

Lucy shrugged her shoulders. "I may have done a little work out of hours."

Barrel grinned. "If you're not careful, Fuller, I might start to respect you. Update me later," he said, his voice was lighter than it had been in days as he indicated towards his computer screen, "because Tanner has found our mystery man, so we might have caught a break on this one."

"No shit!" Lucy stepped around the desk to get a look. The image wasn't great, but the figure was virtually as Tyler Lloyd had described: big coat, hat. "Does he have a limp?"

Barrel pressed a key on his computer. The figure subtly limped along a short stretch of road, his head down the entire time, giving them nothing.

"Can we see his face in any of the footage?" she asked, figuring he must be on more than one camera.

Barrel shook his head. "He disappears completely three streets away."

"Shit! Do you think Lloyd's telling the truth?" she asked, but before he could answer, there was a knock at Barrel's door. Tanner popped his head inside.

"Lucy, phone."

"Thanks."

Lucy returned to the outer office and picked up the handset lying on her desk.

"DS Fuller."

Dr Sharma's calm voice greeted her.

"Thanks for calling back, Dr Sharma. I just had a few questions about the last time you saw Mr Booker."

"Okay."

"Can you recall if he was wearing a hat of any sort when he came in?" She purposely left the question open in terms of the type of hat.

"Err ... yes, he did, like the ones worn in the fifties. My grandad wore one. Mr Booker's was dark brown, I think, with a darker band around it."

Lucy made a note. "And did he have a limp at all?" She waited, pen poised.

"Well, sort of, yes. He suffered with arthritis in his knees, so he often had a limp. He was a stubborn type though, refused to use a stick."

Perfect. "And do you have any CCTV in the surgery or outside?" If they could get an image of Booker, they could at least compare it to the footage they already had of the mystery man.

"We do, but I'd have to check to see how long we keep it for."

It was worth a try. "That would be a great help, Dr Sharma."

"No problem," he assured her, and at that moment, the desk sergeant appeared in the room. Barrel was out of his office talking to him She watched the interaction Tyler Lloyd must have asked for something or someone.

"Are you there, DS Fuller?"

"Sorry, yes, thank you so much for your time, Dr Sharma. I'll need you to make a statement confirming Mr Booker's appearance and we'll need a copy of any CCTV you find too."

"No problem. I'll dig it out for you and give you a call back."

"Thank you Dr Sharma." She replaced the phone.

"Boss. Sharma just confirmed the hat. Dark brown, he says. And the limp, arthritis in his knees. He's going to check how long they keep the CCTV and send through anything he finds from Booker's last visit."

"Good. Lloyd's asked for his solicitor. Apparently, his night in the cells might've had the desired effect."

Tanner reappeared in the office, his eyebrows raised as he caught Lucy's eye. "Boss, Cell-site reports back."

Barrel leant on the nearest desk. "Let me guess: it confirms Lloyd's story that he was in the area for the times he's given us."

"Pretty much," Tanner said as he handed Barrel the report. "We've also got the details of a handful of phones active on the same masts at the same time as Lloyd's."

"Okay, so providing they're not burner phones, we might be able to link them to possible suspects."

"Hopefully," Tanner replied as he moved back to his desk.

Lucy waited for Barrel to disappear into his office to devour the report before approaching Tanner. He replaced the phone that was in his hand as she stopped next to his desk.

"Anything on that name?" she urged. She wasn't quite ready to reveal everything to Barrel yet. Tanner pulled a sheet of notes from under a pile of files.

"Okay. You're gonna like this." Tanner beamed back at her. "Amelia Hunter was reported missing in July 1986, aged fourteen, from her parent's home in Northampton. Suspected runaway, left a note saying she was going to London. Clothes and money were taken. Parents never heard from her again."

"Jesus, another missing kid." But was Amelia Hunter really Amy Bell? And how was she going to prove it? "Anything back from the DVLA yet?"

"Nothing yet. I'll chase it up."

"Thanks," Lucy nodded as she smothered a yawn. It wasn't even eleven o'clock and she felt like she'd already done a week's work. She slowed her process along the corridor, recalling Tanner's words: *Northampton*. Wasn't Bellamy stationed there before transferring to Oldbury?

With the duty solicitor stuck in traffic, Lucy took the opportunity to chase up any newspaper reports on Amelia Hunter's accident. The archives assistant at Oxford Central Library was reluctant at first, but she managed to talk him into sending her a link to the Newsquest digital newspaper archives for Oxfordshire.

She clicked off the home screen to the list of publications available. Finding several for Banbury, she selected the *Banbury Evening News*. According to the DVLA, Amelia Hunter's previous address was in the Oxfordshire market town. Local papers were always the best source of archived information, especially when you're out on a limb. Right now, she needed to find out more about the incident that had scarred Amelia Hunter for life.

She selected what she thought was the right timeframe as she didn't have access to Amelia Hunter's medical records. However, she did know Amelia had changed her address sixteen months ago. Using that as a starting point and taking into account healing time in the hospital, she set the search parameters for two years ago. After twenty minutes of searching she was just about to adjust the time-frame when a red-top tabloid headline splashed across the screen in front of her. *Brave mum brutally burned saving her children*. This had to be it. According to the paper, *Amelia Hunter, 41, suffered third degree burns over almost twenty percent of her body while trying to save her two children after a fire broke out at her home on the night of Wednesday 23rd March.*

She did the calculation; it was just over eighteen months ago.

Emergency services were called to Chapel Lane in the early hours of the morning after being alerted by a neighbour. Ms Hunter had only recently moved to the house after separating from her partner, Jarred Young the previous month. She woke struggling to breathe. Opening her bedroom door, she found fire and heavy smoke filling the hallway. Moving through the house on her belly, she managed to grab her two children aged four and six years old.

The fire was centred at the front of the house, forcing Ms Hunter to shield her children as they escaped via the back door. Ms Hunter suffered severe burns to her face, neck and arm during their ordeal. Her children escaped with minor burns and smoke inhalation. All three were taken to the John Radcliffe Hospital in Oxford.

The accompanying photograph showing the remains of the devastated house was shocking. Amelia and her kids were lucky to be alive.

The last line of the story caught her eye: *Fire investigators are currently examining the source of the fire.* The fact that they hadn't already identified the cause sounded suspicious.

Lucy tried to pick up the story in later editions. Scanning the editions for the following week, she found a smaller headline: *Arson is suspected at Chapel Lane fire. After an investigation by fire officers, arson is suspected as the cause of the fire, which seriously injured a mother and her two children. An accelerant was found on the floor and wall of the hallway inside the property. Oxfordshire police have made an appeal for witnesses.*

Lucy sat back in her seat. Somebody had it in for Amelia Hunter. Jilted lover maybe? There was no mention of her ex-partner in the later report at all. If it had been her case, that would have been her first line of inquiry.

Tanner approached her desk, paperwork in hand and a smile on his face as he handed her a piece of paper.

"This photo was used to update Amelia Hunter's licence when she was –" he checked his notes – "thirty-six years old. Must be a few years before her accident."

Lucy did the calculations. "About five years maybe." She studied the image. Amelia Hunter had long, blonde hair, and her sharp facial features made her stand out from the crowd. Lucy pulled the group photo from her desk again to do a comparison.

"This one was used ten years before that," Tanner said, offering her a second piece of paper. "Nothing earlier."

"Nothing?" Lucy queried. Most teenagers couldn't wait to get a driver's licence. She included herself in that generalisation. Why not Amelia Hunter? Unless she had a licence in a different name. Lucy stared at all three photos; the shape of the mouth was the same, the line of the nose too. The older photo of a twenty-six-year-old Amelia Hunter clinched it.

"You think it's her?" Tanner asked.

"I do," Lucy confirmed.

"Fuller, we're up," Barrel said as he made his way across the office.

The duty solicitor was finally on-site. Lucy was curious as to what Lloyd was going to say. Evidence was building, yet she still didn't believe he was responsible for the death of David Booker. Taking a breath she settled in her seat as the solicitor cleared his throat.

"My client is prepared to give you the names of the other three people present on the night in question. He is also willing to admit to breaking and entering. But as per our previous statement, my client continues to deny any involvement in the death of Mr Booker. In return for his cooperation, he would like you to recommend a reduced sentence for his crime."

Barrel sat back in his seat. "If the names your client provide pan out, I'll put your request to the CPS."

The duty solicitor leant towards Lloyd. Their whispers were barely audible, so she had no chance of listening in.

Barrel pushed his pad and paper in front of him. "Can you write the names down for me, Tyler?"

Lucy studied Tyler as he hesitated to pick up the pen. She was a little surprised at how quickly he'd crumbled, but maybe Mrs Cole was right; he didn't have it in him to commit the murder, and his solicitor was just trying to shake of the possibility of a murder trial with a lot of evidence pointing in his direction.

Tyler picked up the pen and began writing. It only took him a few seconds, and he pushed the pad back to the middle of the table.

"Thank you, Tyler," Barrel said and grabbed the pad as he got to his feet, indicating for Lucy to follow.

They were silent till they were in the corridor outside the interview room.

Barrel handed the pad to her.

"Get uniform to pick them up. Let's see what they have to say."

Lucy glanced at the list of names. Dale Saxby was on the list, as she'd expected, along with Dean Collins and Jason Potter.

"Yes, boss."

CHAPTER 32

INSTEAD OF GOING BACK to her room after parking up outside The Fox, Johanna decided to take another walk on the marsh, taking advantage of the crisp October air. She had plenty to think about with Lucy, the bloodied sock and the possibility of her manager's plans to buy her out of her own company. She always found it easier to mull things over when her body was occupied with something else. With so much to consider, she took the longer route skirting across the bottom on Compton Way before taking a right onto Marsh Lane.

The roar of an approaching car from behind forced Johanna onto the thin grass verge, and she looked up as a white SUV sped past her. The driver slammed on the brakes soon after as they neared the end of the lane, and the boot automatically rose as the driver got out. The sound of children laughing drew Johanna to look more closely as the woman picked up a child's scooter from the roadside before walking to the back of the car and dropping it in boot, much to the children's enjoyment by the sound of it. Johanna was transfixed, she caught the smile on the woman's face as she passed the rear window of her car. It was her, the woman with the scars on her face. Despite the twenty or so metres between them, she could clearly see the discolouration on the woman's skin, not to mention her short, dark hair.

The boot closed as the woman got back in the car, reverse lights flicking on immediately. A wave of panic filtered through Johanna. She was leaving. She'd been too surprised to say anything while the woman was in earshot. Now it was too late. Johanna needed to know how she knew this woman, but before she could wave a hand to catch her attention, the woman quickly reversed into the small housing estate next to the marsh.

Johanna continued along the road, slowing as she came to the turning to look for the SUV, it was parked in the driveway of one of the end properties. She watched as two small kids barrelled out of the car towards the house. Instead of following, Johanna walked towards the marsh, slipping through the spring-loaded gate. She pulled out her phone as she made her way towards the canal and sent Lucy a quick message.

Hey, you can call off the search for the scarred woman. I know where she lives now.

She ambled along the canal while she considered what to say to the mystery woman. The more Johanna saw her, the more she was convinced they knew each other. Her mother had said her name was Mia, but she couldn't recall anyone of that name. There was something in the back of her mind, but she couldn't quite see it, like one of those optical illusions that you can only see when you're not looking directly at it. A blemish on a wall, a glimmer of light that you can only see out of the corner of your eye when you look away. Turning on her heels, she retraced her steps to the woman's house, the white SUV still parked in the driveway. She realised then that it was the same house she'd seen when she was in Lucy's car, the figure in the front window drinking tea was Mia.

The boot was open now, and there was movement at the back of the car. A gaggle of suitcases sat nearby, was she leaving?

Johanna stealthily moved up the driveway, keeping an eye on the windows facing her. Approaching the house, she cupped her hands to get a better look inside the large bay window. It was well lived in, with toys and books scattered across the floor. If they were leaving, they weren't taking much with them. *Jesus Christ! What was she doing spying on this woman, maybe she didn't even know her at all. No. She stomped down that thought, she knew her, somehow.*

"Johanna Hale!"

Johanna flinched. Her name had been stretched, as if she were being introduced as a TV host. She turned towards the voice, the scarred woman stood no more than three feet away, her hands welded to her hips.

"Amy Bell?"

She posed it as a question, but every second she stood in front of this woman told her she was correct. The idea had started like a sneeze that she couldn't stop; now she felt justified in her actions to find this woman.

"So my disguise didn't fool you," Amy's face twisted awkwardly as a sour cackle followed her words.

Johanna frowned in confusion. Would she really do that to herself to escape her past? Before she could ask, a small boy appeared around the side of the house.

"Mummy, when are we –?" The words died in the boy's throat as he spotted Johanna.

Amy raised her hand at the boy. For a moment, Johanna wasn't sure if was an act of protection or anger.

"Go back inside, Archie. I'll be there in a sec."

Amy's tone was soft. Johanna couldn't recall her ever using that tone, even with her, and she had once considered her a best friend.

"Come inside so we can talk. I'm guessing that's why you're here," Amy said over her shoulder as she followed the boy.

Johanna reluctantly followed. Her skin prickled, Amy had always had a hold over her. But she had little choice if she wanted to find out what had happened to her one-time best friend to scar her for life. Passing the back of the SUV, she noted the boxes and bags in the back. "Going anywhere nice?" she asked.

"Just taking the kids away for a few days."

Not a hint of annoyance echoed in Amy's reply, but half term was over, wasn't it?

Johanna dodged several carrier bags littering the floor as she entering a small kitchen diner through the back door, which was just as untidy as the other room she'd spied through the window. Drawings and papers held on with magnets covered almost every inch of the once-stark-white fridge. Worktops were littered with electrical appliances and household debris, which seemed wholly impractical to Johanna and far removed from her own home.

Amy cleared away books and plates from a round, wooden table, stacking them as best she could on the busy worktops.

"Have a seat if you like," she offered as she pulled out the nearest chair.

"Thanks."

The dried cereal stuck to the table made her decision less than appealing, and Johanna kept her hands firmly in her lap as she sat down.

"So, I hear you're doing well," Amy began, keeping her hands on the table.

Johanna was thrown by the comment. How did she know anything about her life now? She studied the woman opposite. She looked so unfamiliar. It wasn't just the disfiguration; there was a coldness to her features. Had she changed her eye colour too?

A thumping sound began to emanate from the other room, but Amy didn't react. Johanna realised as a warm smile took over Amy's face, altering her features entirely, as her attention was drawn to something behind Johanna. She turned to see a young girl stood in the doorway. Her bright blonde hair was below her shoulders. Sharp features gave her a strong resemblance to Amy as a young girl. She looked wide eyed at Johanna as she moved towards her mother.

"Can I have a juice?" the girl asked.

"Yes, sweetie."

Amy got to her feet. Pulling two plastic cups from a cupboard, she moved to the fridge and poured a tiny splash of orange juice into each one before adding a generous amount of water. Turning, she handed them to her daughter.

"Take one for your brother too."

The girl nodded before shuffling away, her whole focus on carrying the two drinks.

"I never imagined you with kids," Johanna told her. The kindness they seemed to bring out in Amy surprised her.

"That's Bobby and the drummer in there is Archie."

A high hat was being thrashed to within an inch of its life as she spoke. This wasn't what she came here for. She wanted answers.

"What happened to your..." She let the question hang, not wanting to spell it out. Amy had always been the pretty one in the group, she liked it that way, liked the attention.

The single eyebrow raised on Amy's face. "Oh, you mean my new face." Her hand raised to gingerly touch her branded skin. "This what happens when someone sets fire to your house and you're asleep in bed with your kids."

Christ! Johanna was floored by her answer. The kids at least hadn't been scarred physically from what she'd seen. "I'm sorry." Was the only reply she could muster.

"Why? You didn't do it did you?"

Johanna felt compelled to answer despite the absurdity of the question. "No." The word was lost in the drumming emanating from the other room. She waited for Archie to take a break before continuing.

"How's your dad?" She asked hoping to find some more stable ground.

Amy shrugged. "Wouldn't know, haven't seen him since I left home."

Johanna lowered her eyes to her hands, she was getting nowhere here. She tried a different tack.

"I found a bloody sock in my Spirograph box," Johanna's nerves frayed as she rushed the words out worried another flourish from Archie would drown them out.

Amy didn't react, and for a moment she thought she should have said 'bloodied sock' to clarify her statement.

Amy settled back in her chair, a serene look on her face.

"Took you long enough. I don't even know why I put it in there really."

Finally an acknowledgement that she wasn't totally crazy for coming here. The woman opposite was emotionless, but what had she just accused her of exactly. "Is it Dan's blood?" The prickle across her skin surfaced again as she looked back at Amy.

A smirk pulled at one side of Amy's lips creasing her face. For a moment Johanna was taken back to Little Mark and his unfortunate sneer.

"What do you think?" Amy challenged.

Johanna rifled through what she'd learned over the last week. "I think you tried to put the blame on someone else, again," she replied, remembering the bird incident. She was older and wiser now, no longer the underdog she once was.

A knowing smile appeared on Amy's face. Despite the scarring, the sneer was more familiar now. "I heard you talking to Barney."

Did Barney recognise her?

"Another victim of your charm," Johanna half questioned. "Like me."

Amy swiftly sat forward, studying her. "I see Barney's wife can pack a punch."

She tried not to react, even though Amy had landed a solid blow, much like Samantha Dunderdale.

Amy crossed her arms in front of her. "You would have made a pretty good suspect back then."

"What!" Johanna choked out as the heat drained from her face. "Why would I hurt Dan?" She floundered. She had no frame of reference for this conversation.

The smirk was back. "Don't you remember how angry you were with him for dobbing you in to the guy from the woods?" Amy chuckled again. "I saw the way you looked at him."

"You really think I could have done that to him?" Heat returned to her face. Her skin felt like a radiator. It was true, she was angry at Dan, but she would never have hurt him. Not like that.

"Anyone can if they're pushed hard enough, trust me."

A shiver ran down Johanna's spine at those words. Was she speaking from experience?

"Maybe an act of revenge that went too far. It's easily done."

Is it? Johanna wanted to ask but was fearful of the answer.

"To be fair, it might have worked if you'd have come home when you were supposed to. Your mum was out of it when I came around to drop off the Spirograph set, probably doesn't even remember me being there."

Johanna frowned as she released a breath. She couldn't take it all in. She hadn't realised how lucky she'd been. If her mother hadn't put her grandfather off that day, told him to not to drop them off back at Compton Way … She didn't want to finish that thought.

"Why, Amy? Why Dan? He was our friend."

Amy's gaze immediately turned cold. "He wasn't my friend and I didn't do anything." Her voice rose considerably. "It was your mum that ran him over." Her words held a familiar tone as if she were scolding Mark Evans for his poor speech.

Johanna sat forward, blinking at the words. "What-what the hell are you talking about?" Her voice roared, she was on her feet, hands flat on the table in a second, she leant towards Amy. It didn't make any sense. Her mother didn't even drive back then. She barely drove now. Her frustration boiled over. "Why are you saying this crap, to hurt me is that it? Do you ever take the blame for anything you do?"

"See what I mean, its easily done."

Amy's smug grin took some of the wind out of her sales for a moment. She retook her seat. Her hand went to her mouth smothering her words. "How…Why would you say…"

"You should really ask your mother about it," she said and rose to her feet again. "Juice?" she offered. Her voice had once again lost its icy chill.

Johanna was unable to reply. Her mind fogged. How could it possibly be true? Surely another attempt at deflection. It made her begin to question everything, couldn't it be just one of Amy's cruel games. "Were we ever really friends?" she asked.

Amy returned to the table with two glasses, placing one in front of Johanna. Amy's eyes drifted up to hers. "We were, although you were a little too young back then."

Johanna felt the jab. She'd known it all along. Amy was always the sophisticated, cultured one out of the two of them. That was her draw, that's why she liked her, despite her cruelty.

"Tell me what happened," Johanna demanded quietly.

Amy held the glass up to take a drink but placed it back on the table again. "Your mum was reversing your dad's car out of the garage and hit Dan. He was such a weed; she probably didn't even notice at first. Dan was wedged under the car. That's probably why no-one saw what happened."

Blood rushed in Johanna's ears. She couldn't think straight. She felt a laugh rise in her chest. Clenching her hands together, she waited for it to pass. She wanted the truth, not this. She grabbed the glass in front of her and downed the juice in two gulps. Wiping her mouth with the back of her hand, she placed it back on the table and said, "Why are you saying this? I don't understand." Dan had been found in a well. She looked back at Amy. "Why? How did she know about the well?" she questioned.

"Paul, my dad, helped her."

He moved the body. Lucy had been right all along. The killer was local.

"Why would he do that?"

"Well, that's another story. You see, my dad wasn't exactly my dad, if you know what I mean."

"Your dad?" No, she didn't know. Johanna felt her jaw slacken a little as she spoke. Was there alcohol in that juice? Her neck felt like jelly, like it couldn't support her head anymore. She hadn't thought it through, hadn't expected any of these words to come out of Amy's mouth. Now she couldn't think straight or put her thoughts in order.

"I'll be honest, I don't know how we got away with it. That street was as quiet as the grave that Saturday," Amy smirked. "Most people were on holiday, I guess, but–"

Johanna cringed at her words. "A boy …" she began, then corrected herself. "Our friend died and you're making jokes." Her voice sounded odd, heavy.

"He wasn't my friend," Amy scolded her again.

The sock; the bloody sock that's what had started all this, why did it have blood on it? She tried to ask the question that had formed in her head. "Why…the sock, covered….blood?"

Johanna brought her hands up to her face, rubbing her eyes, and the room began to spin as a queasy sickness rose in her throat. It felt like someone was pushing her eyes shut. As she rested her elbows on the table, she slurred, "W-wha-what have you …?" The words made no sense to her as her head fell forward, hitting the surface of the table.

CHAPTER 33

GILLIAN HALE, 20th August 1988

Gillian Hale stilled the paintbrush in her hand, convinced she'd heard movement from the front of the house. She hoped it wasn't her father arriving home with the kids. Turning her wrist, she checked the time. It was too early; he wouldn't have set off before taking a final walk along the beach with them. Besides, he always called when he got back home to give her a heads-up before driving them back here. Nevertheless, she carefully rested the paintbrush on the paint tin lid, walked through the dining room to the front of the house and peered through the front window. Her father's car was nowhere to be seen and the gates were still shut, so she pulled the net curtain to one side, looking for the source of the noise. The street was quiet, she'd need to open the gates soon, to make it easier for her father to drop them off, and that bloody Moody dog better not think of leaving a calling card on her lawn again. Gillian returned to the task in hand. She figured she had a couple of hours at least before they were due.

With everyone out of the house, it was the perfect time to repaint the downstairs windows, less chance of finding fingerprints everywhere. The burn-off from the fields was also expected in the next few weeks, and she'd wanted to get it done while the weather was good.

As much as she liked painting, she hated cleaning up after and sighed as she opened the garage door to grab the white spirit. She switched on the light and scanned the end of the confined space, but it was nowhere to be seen. Space was certainly at a premium in the Hale garage, and David's insistence on parking his precious car in the garage was a continued bone of contention, especially when she needed access to items that were discreetly packed away at the back, behind his bloody car. She'd asked him to move it out earlier before he left, but as usual, he'd forgotten.

She stood at the mouth of the garage, judging the space; the driver's side looked to be the best bet. The passenger's side was far too tight to the wall. She held her breath as she did a sideways crabwalk along the narrow space between the car and the junk-lined wall. Halfway down, she cracked her head on a ladder hanging on the wall. She swore under her breath as she continued, rubbing at the sore spot. She spent the next few moments gauging the conversation she would have with David when he returned from his stupid work thing. Agreeing to help a mate with his extension on a weekend when the kids were away? If she didn't know any better, she'd think he didn't want to spend time with her.

She rounded the bonnet of the car, still unable to lay her eyes on her target. No doubt her bloody husband had squirreled it away in the cupboard. She then squeezed her legs between the bumper and the workbench David had installed, frowning her annoyance; he'd covered the top with yet more boxes of odds and sods. Bits of wood and copper pipe poked out the top preventing her from opening the old kitchen wall unit. There was nowhere to put anything even if she could move it. She'd have to move the car; there was no other option. She'd never hear the end of it if she scratched it.

She returned with the car keys, feeling her frustration rise at the situation, and squeezed into the driver's seat, slamming the door behind her. Pushing the key in the ignition, she familiarised herself with the controls. She rarely drove. David always did the driving. He preferred it that way. She pushed out her legs, resting her feet on the pedals as she started the car, jamming the stick into reverse. The gearbox complained at her actions. Annoyed at its criticism, she pressed hard on the accelerator, and her head jerked back against the headrest, surprised at the sudden movement. Reversing always sounded like a chore for this car.

A dull thud a split second later jolted her body against the driver's seat. *For Christ's sake! What now?* Shock quickly turned to anger, this simple job was quickly turning problematic. *I must have knocked something off the bloody wall and driven over it. Typical, it had to happen when I was at the wheel. Why couldn't it be David?* She prayed there wasn't too much damage.

In her anger, she'd managed to move the car most of the way out of the shelter of the garage. She quickly opened the driver's door, careful not to catch it on the side of the garage. Once she was on her feet, she circled the car, looking for damage. Nothing obvious stood out. Her hands shook as she breathed a sigh of relief, until her eyes landed on something poking from under the car. A shoe, a child's white trainer. Johanna? Simon? Did one of them have a pair of white trainers? She couldn't think straight. Were they back already? They weren't meant to be back yet. What was it doing next to the car?

She stepped closer, seeing a sock-covered foot protruding from underneath. Her body shook as a cry escaped her. Her hand shot to her mouth as she dropped to her knees. Reaching out a shaky hand, she grabbed the foot. It was warm, Jesus! Who was it? What were they doing in the driveway? She started to pull them out, desperate to see who it was, but stopped, fearing she would hurt them more, and threw her body to the floor, daring herself to look under the car, fearing what she was about to see. She knew it couldn't be unseen. It would stick with her forever, tattooed on her mind.

It was a boy, but not Simon. Even in the shadow of the car, she could see the hair was black. They were on their front, face pressed to the driveway floor. The split-second relief was replaced with horror. How could this happen?

He wasn't moving.

Tears streamed from her eyes as she scrambled to get a better look. Twisting her body, she could see he was familiar. It was Daniel, Janet and Steve's boy from the top of the road. God, how the hell was she going to face her after this? How was she going to tell them she'd killed him, she'd killed their son? How could she? How could this happen? She covered her eyes, and the darkness closed in around her.

She'd go to prison. She'd lose everything. Who'd look after her family then? Her mind swirled with panic as tears spilled down her cheeks.

She looked up as footsteps approached her from behind.

CHAPTER 34

WITH A LULL in the Booker case while uniform rounded up the three suspects, Lucy tried to call Johanna for the third time. She'd only just picked up her earlier text about finding the scarred woman, a woman Lucy was now convinced was Amy Bell. It sent a chill through her. She prayed Johanna hadn't done anything stupid. The last time they spoke this morning, they'd agreed that she would bring in the Spirograph box to have its contents tested for DNA and fingerprints.

There was still no reply. She'd already left two messages. She didn't want to leave a third.

She grabbed her keys and slipped out of the station. She cared for this woman the thought of anything happening to her brought a panic to her chest. She drove a little faster than usual, ten minutes later, she parked up outside Amelia Hunter's address. The small estate was modern, the houses like shoeboxes with no space to swing your arms, let alone a cat. She scanned the number plate of the white SUV in the driveway and purposely left her car in front, blocking its exit.

Opening her boot, she grabbed a clipboard with a few crime prevention leaflets attached. She eyed her stab vest but decided to leave it, then marched up to the front door and knocked before fishing her credentials out of her pocket. No answer. She tried again. If no-one came this time, she'd already decided to go around the back. Her last message to Johanna was for her to call her back as soon as she got the message. She glanced at her phone. Nothing.

Suddenly, the front door opened.

"Yes." The scarred woman glared back at her. Her face was flushed a film of sweat visible on the edge of her brow, she looked harried.

"Hi there, I'm DS Fuller." She held up her credentials. "We're investigating a burglary in the area. Have you got a few minutes?"

Mia Hunter held onto the door. "What do you want?"

"Just a few questions about the burglary. Advice on crime prevention." It hadn't escaped her how dishevelled the woman looked, her shirt was untucked and bellowed in places. What had she just been doing? Where was Johanna? She scanned the outside of the building. "I see you have an alarm. Do you use it regularly?"

"I'm just about to go out," Mia snapped, and her grip on the door tightened.

"It'll only take a couple of minutes. Then I'll leave you in peace."

Lucy didn't want to have to force her way in, but she would if she had to.

The door swung open and Lucy painted a smile on her face as she followed Mia Hunter through the house. The door on her immediate right was pulled to. The sound of a kid's TV programme filtered under the door. She was going to have to do a security walk through to get a good look around. They ended up in a small kitchen. It was untidy but nothing looked out of place. Was she overreacting? Had she made a mistake coming here?

"Going away?" she asked, noticing a collection of bags near the back door.

"Just taking the kids away for a few days."

"Well, it's a good job I stopped by. Your neighbours were burgled while they were away." Lucy tried to sound upbeat as she placed her clipboard on the table to retrieve her notebook, continuing the ruse. "Have you lived here long?"

"A year or so."

Mia pointed to a chair on the opposite side of the dining table as she took a seat.

"Thanks," Lucy said, noticing that Mia had placed herself next to the units, nearest any potential weapons. "It's Mia, isn't it?" Lucy probed. "One of your neighbours said earlier."

Mia nodded, a slight frown crossing her brow, although she offered no more information.

"Must be pretty quiet down here with the marsh on that side," Lucy said and nodded towards the open fields only a short distance away.

Mia nodded. "The railway at the back can be a bit noisy sometimes."

Lucy looked down at her notebook. "Umm one of your neighbours said the same thing. Do you use your burglar alarm?" she asked again, aware she'd avoided the question earlier.

"No, I don't. Tea?" Amelia offered as she got to her feet. She watched Mia as she moved around her small kitchen. The house seemed quiet considering she'd had two kids with her the last time she'd seen her, that tv programme must be extremely engrossing.

"That would be great," Lucy answered. She had no intention of drinking it, but she wanted to prolong her stay to keep this woman talking for as long as possible. She had to find Johanna. "Sorry, could I use your bathroom?" she asked. "I've had quite a lot of tea today."

"Sure. Top of the stairs." Mia's tone was strained as she waved an arm behind her in the direction of the doorway.

"Thanks."

Lucy got to her feet and headed out of the room, pulling the door closed behind her, taking the opportunity to get a look around while Mia was occupied in the kitchen. She ducked her head in the front room on her way to the stairs, finding two kids asleep on the sofa, one at each end with the TV on low in the background. She carefully retraced her steps, taking the stairs two at a time. Four rooms led off the landing, all of which were in proportion with the small footprint of the building. And all were empty.

In the bathroom, Lucy spotted the white plastic container sitting on the tiled windowsill as she quietly closed the door. She picked it up, knowing immediately it was for contact lenses. She opened the bathroom cabinet where she saw a small stack of identical white boxes.

Replacements, each one had the same code on the side. She picked up the top box, noticing the lens's colour shade: honey brown.

It would be easy to change your eye colour from blue to brown, get a bit of distance from Amy Bell to Mia Hunter. The question was why did she *still* need to do that? Was she running from the person that scarred her for life? Perfectly reasonable considering what he did to her last time. Or was there another reason her ex hadn't surfaced yet apart from being wanted for questioning. Was she hiding from Paul Bell, did she know he was dead? Or was it her voice the neighbours heard that night?

Lucy flushed the toilet before returning to the kitchen. Rounding the bottom of the stairs, she saw the end of a piece of clothing sticking out between two narrow louvered doors. It looked like a cupboard of some kind, how had she missed that on the way to the bathroom. The clothing was familiar. A tea spoon clinked against a mug in the kitchen only a few feet away. Crouching down in front of the doors, her fingers toyed with the ends of the grey, silky fabric. It was Johanna's scarf. She gripped it between her fingers hoping it would give under the pressure, it didn't. Something was attached to the other end. *Shit!* She swallowed hard knowing full well she needed to find out what it was.

Getting to her feet, she clenched her teeth as she carefully gripped the small round handles praying the hinges wouldn't squeak. Dread filled her chest as she opened the doors, unsure of what she would find. A spoon clattered against the draining board making her jump.

Several coats appeared as the doors parted along with numerous empty hangers. It was a cloakroom. Lucy glanced down as a muddy walking boot on its side came into view. Was it Johanna's? She couldn't say for sure. Her eyes scanned the lower space as she ducked down slightly, a leg appeared from the boot wearing jeans. *Fuck!* Lucy fell on her knees. A body was slumped against the back wall, legs pressed against their chest to make them fit in the small space. She knew immediately it was Johanna even though she couldn't see her face. She quickly cleared the long coat obscuring her view. Lucy's heart raced as her hands immediately went to Johanna's face and neck, checking for signs of life. A faint gurgle emanated from the crumpled figure as she moved her head to face her. Her eyes tried to flicker open. There were no obvious signs of injury.

"Johanna," Lucy whispered. "Johanna, I need you to open your eyes for me," she urged as her fingers skittered over Johanna's neck to check for a pulse. The relief was overwhelming as she found it, and it was firm, but was it too fast? Her own was through the roof, her breath coming in gasps as her mind tried desperately to piece it all together. Drugged, she figured.

Lucy managed to manhandle Johanna's body into what she hoped was a more comfortable position, straightening Johanna's legs to allow her to breathe more easily. She could hear movement in the kitchen as she pulled out her phone to call Tanner. He was talking in her ear before she even got a word out.

"Barrel's looking for you."

"Forget that" Lucy said as quietly and clearly as she could. "Get uniform and an ambulance round to Amelia Hunter's address on Templers Way. Now." She hung up before Tanner could question her further, then looked back at Johanna's limp body, praying it was some form of sedative and nothing more. Her thoughts then drifted to the kids she'd seen asleep earlier. She stepped into the next room, trying not to tread on any of the toys littering the floor. Lucy's hand quivered as she held it near the young girl's face, breath pushed against her palm. Lucy released a sigh of relief, leaving the room and stepped back into the kitchen.

"Sorry about that. Had to take a quick call from a colleague," Lucy offered as she retook her seat. The bags that had been by the back door were now gone, the key ring swinging in the back door lock, Mia had used her time alone wisely. Had she locked them in? She felt a little sick as she tried to focus on the mug that had been set down in front of her. Was she attempting to drug her too. Pushing it away, she rested her elbows on the table as she focused on the woman opposite, her hands hidden under the table. She noticed a tea towel in front of Mia, bunched up, as if hiding something underneath, and swallowed hard. She'd made a mistake not wearing her vest and she knew it, but she just needed to keep Mia talking until uniform arrived, keep the situation as calm as possible with two kids in the house and an unconscious woman stuffed in a cupboard.

Mia's glare was unfaltering. "You won't stop me from going away you know."

Lucy frowned at her wording, '*you* won't stop me'. "I'm sorry."

"You'll need to move your car." Mia continued.

She was getting lost in this conversation already, nothing made sense. "Of course." Although she made no move to do so, she had no intention of letting her escape. Lucy picked up her clipboard and flicked through the pages biding her time.

"This place is rented, I don't care if it gets broken into."

The nonchalance of the words made Lucy look up, it was an immature statement for a mother in her forties to make. Mia's face had formed into an ugly twist. "I see, but I'm sure the owners will care, insurance and all-."

Mia huffed in reply cutting off any further lecturing. "Must be expensive renting out here?"

"I wouldn't know a friend rents it for me."

"Wow, I wish I had friends like that." She noticed Mia had made no move to drink her tea either, what was occupying her hands in her lap.

"They offered to help me get back on my feet."

Lucy nodded. She'd love to know who that friend was. "I see you wear contacts. I could never get used to them," Lucy lied. She wanted to see her reaction.

"Oh." Mia looked a little surprised. "Yes. Took me a while, but I eventually got used to them," her hand went to the scarred side of her face. "I couldn't wear glasses for a while after ..."

Lucy watched her, letting the statement hang between them, and Mia's eyes glared back at her in challenge, but she refused to comment. It didn't change who or what Mia Hunter was. Instead, she looked away to slowly flip through her notebook this time.

"So, who was burgled?" Mia asked as she puffed out a breath.

"Your neighbour round the back there."

Lucy pointed in the vague direction of the row of houses behind. "Did they take much?"

"Not really. Opportunists, I think. They tend to make more mess than anything else." Lucy looked up, meeting her gaze.

"Do you ever catch them?" Mia challenged, her eyes not straying from Lucy,

It was a minor jab and one that Lucy was more than used to. "If you don't mind me asking, what happened to you?" She wanted to hear it in Mia's own words.

"Someone tried to burn me out of my home, instead they burned me."

It wasn't quite the truth or what Lucy was expecting.

The smirk was back on Mia's face. "You didn't catch him either."

Him. Before Lucy could reply, a loud knock emanated from the front of the house. Mia aimed narrowed eyes across the table and said, "Have you brought friends?"

"You should probably get that." Lucy replied. There was a hint of something that she hoped was resignation on Mia's face, but she still didn't move.

A second knock came from the front door, suddenly Mia was on her feet her chair clattered against the kitchen floor behind her. She had a knife in each hand. She must have been keeping them in her lap.

"Police! Can you come to the door please?" Another thud echoed from the front of the house. The officers tone was more insistent this time.

Lucy slowly got to her feet, with her hands aloft she edged out from behind the table that separated them. Her sideways shuffle took her in the direction of the back door, which was currently Mia's only exit.

"I told you." She pointed the largest of the knives in her right hand towards Lucy. "I'm fucking leaving!" Mia's face scrunched up in agony.

Her bellow reverberated in Lucy's ears. She glanced around for something to defend herself with, spotting a kids coat on the worktop she grabbed it and wrapped it around her right arm. Fear gripped her throat as she tried to speak. "Y-you don't want to do this Mia. Think of your kids in there." She pointed towards the other room hoping it would make her see sense. If it was her Achilles heel, she had to play on it.

"You go near my kids, and I'll fucking kill you!"

Mia instantly lashed out with her right hand creating an arc forcing Lucy to step back. Her foot stumbled on something on the floor, she braced herself on the cabinet to her right.

"Police! Can you come to the door please?"

Christ gain entrance already for fucks sake. She wanted to call out to the officer but the words died in her dry throat.

Mia launched herself at her throwing her left hand out, the smaller knife caught her on her neck, ducking away she dodged the second one as it swiped towards her.

The faint sound of a police radio outside the kitchen window filtered through the madness as a shadow partially blocked the light. Then a knock on the window.

"Police! Come to the door please?"

"Officer in need of assistance." Lucy managed to squeeze out of her chest, while keeping her eyes fixed on Mia, trying to gauge her next move. A series of thumps radiated from the back door only feet away.

A split-second later Mia was on her, she dropped the smaller of the knives as she pushed her down, her head smashed against the cupboard door as she hit the floor. There was no time to regroup, the glint of the blade forced the air from her chest as she tried to brace her arms against it. The clothing wrapped around her arm took the brunt of Mia's fury.

She managed to grab hold of Mia's right hand, smashing it against the cabinet forcing the knife from her hand. She wasn't sure if the shriek that came out of Mia's mouth was from pain or anger. Lucy was breathless as Mia moved away groping for the knife.

Lucy kicked out, her boot colliding with the back of Mia's torso. She toppled to the floor like a sack of spuds bringing one of the chairs down with her. Lucy scrambled to get the higher ground like her life depended on it.

Mia was on her front, Lucy grabbed for the cuffs attached to the back of her belt, straddling Mia's hips she tried to secure one of her wrists as it flailed about.

The back door finally gave way to the uniformed officer. A blur of florescent and black moved across the room pinning Mia to the floor. The two officers took over cuffing Mia before lifting her to her feet.

It took a moment for Lucy to catch her breath, she gingerly touched her neck, she was relieved when only a trickle of blood appeared on her fingertips. Glaring at the woman now struggling in cuffs she took a step closer. "Amelia Hunter I'm arresting you for assaulting a police officer. You have the right to remain silent. Anything you do say can be used against you in a court of law..."

More feet rumbled into the house, from the front this time. A flash of green entered her peripheral vision. *Christ, Johanna.*

"Check the two kids in the front room first," she yelled towards them. "I think they've been drugged. I've got an adult female back here too." She pointed towards the open cupboard, seeing the tears on her jacket sleeve she pushed it up revealing two long cuts on her forearm, she hadn't even felt the knife go in.

"Don't you fucking touch them!" Mia's volume dial was already at eleven.

One of the paramedics tried to placate her as he passed her on the way to the sitting room, but she shrugged him off.

"Do you really think I would harm my own kids?" She screamed, her eyes wild with anger as she fought with the uniformed officer holding onto her upper arm. Her eyes bore into Lucy as she made her way back to check on Johanna.

CHAPTER 35

JOHANNA RUBBED AT HER FACE. She still felt dizzy.

"What did she give me?"

The female paramedic knelt next to her. "Ketamine, it's tasteless so you wouldn't have been able to tell."

"Shit!" she said quietly to herself as she clenched her eyes shut. "It must have been in the juice." She should have known. She looked up from her prone position on the floor to see Lucy standing against the wall watching her. Her face was hard to read. She wanted to smile in her direction, but she couldn't bring herself to do it. Not now.

"It only lasts for about an hour or so, depending on the dose. No lasting effects, so you should be fine."

Johanna didn't feel fine, she felt about as far away from fine as she'd ever been. Her mind was struggling to fit the jigsaw puzzle together. Nothing seemed to be the right shape. Her own mother had taken a life. How had she managed to hide that all these years? She turned her head to see what she was resting on. A zip dug into the side of her ear. Had someone tried to make her comfortable? Was that Lucy? Had she found her?

"What happened?" Her question was aimed at no-one in particular.

"You were found shoved in this cupboard," the paramedic offered with a stretched arm.

Johanna craned her neck to look at the two narrow doors hanging open, revealing the shallow space beyond. How on earth had she fitted in there?

"You should come to the hospital so we can check you over," the paramedic continued as she checked her pulse. Johanna tried to focus on the lamp shade hanging from the ceiling as the paramedic wrote notes across the back of her gloved hand.

"Amy." The words came to her before she could stop them. "She ... she ..." The words died in her throat as she recalled what Amy had told her, and her hand covered her mouth to smother the sob that bubbled in her throat.

"Can you give us a minute?" Lucy asked from the edge of the room.

"Sure."

The paramedic got to her feet, leaving them alone.

Johanna wanted to sit up, but just the thought of it alone was a struggle. Her limbs felt like lead.

Lucy crouched on the floor next to her. A small smile pulled at the edge of her lips. Reaching out, she took hold of Johanna's hand. "I'm glad you're okay."

"You found me?" she asked, although she already knew the answer. The text must have alerted her, but how did she know where to find her? "How –?"

Lucy nodded towards the cupboard. "Your scarf was poking out between the doors."

Johanna frowned. It didn't answer her question. "But –"

Lucy cut her off. "How did you know she was Amy Bell?"

Johanna closed her eyes. "I didn't to start with, but then she was right in front of me and I-I knew." She should never have come here. Her determination to know what happened now threatened every-thing she thought she knew and could trust. Now she was stuck with Amy's sour words going around and around in her head. How could it be true, her own mother? She prayed it was one of Amy's lies, a fabri-cation of reality to suit her own story. Just like the dead pigeon.

Johanna sniffed as a tear slipped down the side of her face. "Where is she?" She needed to know if Amy had told anyone else.

Lucy used her free hand to wipe at the tear. "It's okay, we've arrested her. You're safe."

Johanna felt her chest tighten. She wished Lucy had been too late, that Amy had escaped her clutches, taken her horrible secret with her. Dad, did he know too? Another tear slipped out. "I'm sorry."

"It's okay." Lucy smiled as her thumb rubbed over Johanna's knuckles. "What did she say to you?" A series of lines developed across Lucy's forehead as the skin pinched.

"Not much. It's a bit of a blur," she mumbled, trying to fob her off, hoping she'd let it go, at least for now. She didn't have long. Amy would soon be revelling in spreading her cruel words. She noticed a smear of blood on Lucy's neck, before she could ask her about it she was faced with another question.

"Did she say anything about Paul Bell or Daniel?"

She thought for a moment before saying, "Something about her dad not being her dad," and swallowed back the lump in her throat. She couldn't bring herself to tell Lucy the full story, not yet.

But Lucy didn't react to the news. She already knew. What else did she know?

"The kids!" Johanna blurted as she tried to sit up. The image of the little girl carrying the cups came back to her. They'd had the same drink.

"Whoa!" Lucy reached out her free hand to still her movement.

Lightheaded by the action, Johanna cupped her forehead.

"They're fine. Paramedics have checked them over. Maybe you should go to the hospital," Lucy soothed and moved her hand to the side of Johanna's face, tucking hair behind her ear.

Johanna ignored the request. "She drugged them too?" Was Amy going to leave them behind? She found that hard to believe when she recalled how sweet she'd been towards them? "Why would she –?"

"Probably just to keep them quiet while they made their getaway."

She wasn't abandoning everything, just escaping, although her scars would have made her easy to find, unlike her mother, who'd hidden in plain sight for thirty years, if Amy was telling the truth. "I think I need some fresh air."

"Are you sure you're ready to get up?"

Johanna made a move, answering Lucy's question as she got to her feet, despite the wobble in her legs. Lucy held onto her as they made their way through the house.

"I'll take you outside," she said.

Johanna squinted at the daylight jabbing at her eyes. The paramedic that had treated her earlier approached her other side, taking over from Lucy.

"I'll speak to you in a bit," Lucy offered as they parted.

Johanna offered a weak smile in reply as she was led to the ambulance.

Lucy glanced out of the front window of Amelia Hunter's house for the third time. Johanna still hadn't moved. She sat perched at the back of the ambulance between the open doors, a blanket wrapped around her. One hand drew the blanket tighter while the other moved to cover her mouth. She needed to speak to Johanna again now. She looked far from alright. She wanted to pull her into her arms, to comfort her, but the surrounding officers were making that impossible. If they saw anything, it could make her job difficult, which was exactly why she shouldn't have got involved with a witness. That once-grey area of witness or not had been cleared up and outlined in thick permanent marker after today's events. Lucy closed her eyes for a moment as she tried to eradicate any thought of Barrel's wrath.

Something was definitely strange about Johanna. It wasn't just the shock; she was guarded in a way that she had never been with her. Something was wrong – beyond the obvious. She was hiding something and Lucy needed to know what it was.

Lucy pulled down the sleeve of her jacket, covering the bandage the paramedic had used to dress her wounds. Ignoring the din of the house search going on around her, she made her way out of the room.

Tanner was stood in the kitchen, he looked up at her as she stood in the doorway.

"You were lucky." He said nodding towards the knife lying on the floor.

"I know." It had barely sunk in yet her focus was already elsewhere. "We need to find out who rents this house. Hunter said a friend rents it for her, I want to know who that is."

"Okay." Tanner replied as he pulled out his phone but she didn't wait for any further discussion.

Lucy left the house by the front door, she walked towards the ambulance and nodded to the paramedic as she approached, noting his pursed lips as he moved to the front to talk with his colleague. Someone was being a difficult patient.

"Hey. How're you doing?" she asked. It was a terrible opener but she didn't know where else to start.

There was no response. Johanna's eyes were locked on the ground near her feet. Lucy knelt in front of her, trying to get into her line of sight. "Hey," she said softly, looking up at her, but her dazed expression didn't change. She quickly checked around her for prying eyes before reaching out to place a hand on Johanna's knee. "You know if we weren't surrounded by all these people, you would be in my arms right now."

There was a flicker of movement in Johanna's eyes as they met hers before she finally broke her silence. "Can you take me home?" she asked, her voice pitiful.

Lucy breathed a sigh of relief, but it wasn't what she wanted to hear. "Back to the hotel? I can take you to the hospital."

Johanna shook her head and the blanket slipped from her shoulder. Lucy stood as she reached out to secure it, lightly gripping Johanna's shoulder. "I'll get someone to drive you."

"Can't *you* take me, please?" Johanna pleaded as a tear slipped down her cheek.

Lucy knew she couldn't really leave the scene during the search, despite wanting to, but the desperation in Johanna's eyes made it impossible for her to refuse.

"Sure. I can do that." It wasn't asking much considering what she'd just been through, and it would give them some time alone.

Lucy pulled out her phone, letting Tanner know she was leaving the scene and would be back in ten minutes before hanging up, then said, "Let's get you out of here," and placed a hand on Johanna's shoulder, guiding her to her feet. "Did you walk here?" she asked, scanning the road beyond the ambulance for Johanna's car. She turned back to see a slight nod as Johanna pulled the blanket tighter.

Lucy pulled out her key fob and unlocked her car. Wrapping an arm around Johanna's shoulder, she guided her into the passenger seat then slipped into the driver's side, realising how narrow the road was. With all the other vehicles parked up, she'd have to do a twelve-point turn to get back out of here.

"Good job I'm driving you," she said, trying to fill the deafening silence as she manoeuvred her car. "My boss is a terrible driver. I could probably make a claim for whiplash most weeks." With no response, she decided to live with the silence.

"Can you take me to my parents' house?" Johanna mumbled as they reached the junction at the end of the road.

"Are you sure?" Lucy glanced across at Johanna, her skin was still pale. Why would she want to go there of all places, could they give her the comfort that Lucy was more than happy to provide? Maybe she could see her later once they had finished at Hunter's house.

Johanna only nodded in response.

"What did she give me, ketamine?" Johanna stated a few moments later as her hand rubbed at her eyes.

"Yeah. It was given to her as a pain reliever for her burns. The paramedic thought it might be to help her sleep," Lucy answered, but Johanna didn't reply. Concerned, Lucy looked across to Johanna as she pulled up outside the Hale residence. Johanna's posture was rigid in the passenger seat, her focus firmly on the front of her parents' house.

There was no car in the driveway. Maybe they weren't even in. From what Johanna had said about their relationship, she doubted Johanna would even have a key.

"Hey." She reached across, placing her hand on Johanna's thigh. "Are you sure you don't need to go to the hospital? You seem –"

"No."

There was a coldness in Johanna's voice she hadn't heard before. It was unfamiliar, considering the warmth they had shared only a few hours ago.

"Johanna," Lucy tried, keeping her voice calm as she stretched out her hand to find Johanna's clamped between her thighs. "I care about you; I'm worried about you."

Johanna glanced back to look at her. The frown on her forehead seemed to force the tears from her glassy eyes.

"Hey," Lucy whispered as she leant closer, pulling Johanna into her arms.

It took a few moments, but Johanna's body finally relented and her body shuddered as gasps were released.

"It's okay. You're safe," she whispered as she held Johanna close. She wanted to tell her how much she'd grown to care for her, but something told her it wasn't the right time.

Reluctantly, she let Johanna pull away. Her face was wet with tears. Using the sleeve of her tattered jacket, Lucy gently wiped at the reddened skin and cupped the side of Johanna's face, pressing her lips to Johanna's. It was brief, but it was a connection, and she hoped Johanna felt it too.

"What happened?" Johanna held her arm with one hand while the other pushed up the slashed sleeve revealing the bandage.

"It's nothing, Mia was a little reluctant to be arrested." She saw no reason to distress Johanna more than she already was. It was only just beginning to dawn on her exactly how lucky she'd been in Hunter's kitchen.

"Jesus. Did she do that too." Johanna's finger pushed open her collar.

"Umm." Lucy pulled at the rear-view mirror to get a look at the wound. A thin angry red line was all that remained, it was a little tender but nothing more.

Johanna sucked in a breath. "I'm sorry. It's all my fault-."

She turned to see tears brimming in Johanna's eyes again, the strain evident on her face. "No, it's not. No-one could have predicted her reaction." She reached out cupping Johanna's face again.

"Can you come in for a minute?" Johanna whispered as her hand found Lucy's.

"Are you sure?" Lucy knew she'd be missed from the scene soon.

"You need to hear this."

Hear what? Lucy felt the ground shift, her hand slipped to Johanna's thigh. "What's going on? What did Mia say to you?" She tried to keep her voice calm, but what the hell was she walking into?

"Please. I'll tell you inside," she pleaded and the desperation was back in her eyes.

Lucy got out of her car and followed Johanna up the driveway to the front door.

CHAPTER 36

Paul Bell, 20th August 1988

Paul Bell breathed a sigh of relief as his house came into view. The shopping bag had been knocking into his leg for the last thirty minutes. He should never have bought so much stuff with his car in the garage. Why the fuck couldn't they fix it while he waited? Now he'd have to leave early on Monday to pick it up before work.

He glanced at the house, hoping Amy was in a better mood. She could be such a cruel bitch sometimes, even when it wasn't her time of the month.

The Hale's garage door was up. He wished he'd taken Dave up on the offer to go with him after all. Anything to avoid Amy's moods. But he knew from experience that if he ignored her for a few hours she'd be more amiable, loving even.

He struggled to unhook the gate, pushing it open with one shopping bag to allow him to pass through the opening, he considered knocking for Amy to let him in, then thought better of it. Instead he shuffled the shopping bags into one hand to pull the keys from his front pocket, opening the front door he pocketed his keys and kicked the door closed behind him. The TV blared in the front room as he made his way to the kitchen. Paul bit his tongue at the noise as he placed the shopping bags on the kitchen floor. Then a sob behind him, over the noise from the TV, got his attention. Turning, he was faced with a dishevelled, crying Amy.

"Where have you been, Paul!" she screamed as she came closer.

She was using his name. Why was she using his name? If somebody heard … It was dangerous, she knew that. How many times did they need to have that conversation? They couldn't have people questioning any part of their relationship as father and daughter.

He stepped closer to silence her, convinced it was just another period mood swing, and she gripped at his torso as he held her. He'd never seen her this emotional. Then she pulled away, grabbing his hand and pulling him towards the sitting room, dropping it again as they rounded the dining table. She continued walking backwards into the room. He watched as she stopped in her tracks, pointing to something on the ground hidden by the armchair. Tears streamed down her face and she covered her mouth, smothering a sob.

"What?" Paul asked, his frustration beginning to surface at the lack of communication. He was expecting to see a puddle of something spilled on the carpet, probably the ridiculous coffee she'd started drinking lately.

He moved around the armchair but stepped away just as quickly when he finally saw the object of her distress, his hands moving to his face and then to the back of his head as the full horror settled into the pit of his stomach. It was a boy. He looked so small sprawled on the carpet next to the sofa, arms roughly by his sides, his mouth bulging with something white. He couldn't quite make out what it was. He turned away, but the image remained in his head, of the bright red blood staining his bottom lip, his eyes closed. He wasn't moving.

With his head in his hands, Paul's heartrate soared to a thunderous beat in his ears. How could this happen? What was the boy doing here in his house?

"What's happened?" he finally managed to say. "What did you do, Amy?" His voice shook as a creeping fear filled his chest.

"He-saw-us-together-the-other-day!" she shouted at him.

The noise from the TV grated on him, but he knew he couldn't turn it off. No-one could hear this conversation.

"Is he ...?" he started and turned to glimpse the boy as he attempted the question but was unable to finish. Then his attention returned to Amy. "What are you talking about?" he asked, gritting his teeth.

"Out the back, in the evening. He thought you were abusing me, wanted to save me," she sobbed, edging forward, touching his arm. "I didn't have a choice; he was going to tell everyone."

Paul gripped her by the arms, his fingers tightened as he stared down at the boy. He looked familiar, from further up the street. One of the Dunderdale kids. Jesus, he could imagine the fallout this was going to bring. They'd worked so hard to fit in. Now it was all fucked up.

"Christ, Amy, what have you done?" he bellowed, but before he could do anything, the boy sprang to life. He was on his feet, climbing over the sofa and heading for the front door.

"Stop him!" he yelled and sprang into action while Amy just stood there, perhaps too shocked to move. But he couldn't let him go, couldn't let the truth get out. The boy's version of reality would be much worse than his. They wouldn't understand; they'd look down on him, look down on them both. He'd seen the suspicion in his colleagues faces before in Northampton. He couldn't let that happen again, so he pounced, but he was too slow. His leg, always his leg. He dodged around the sofa as he tried to reach him before he got to the front door, lurching forward to grab the boy's t-shirt, but it passed through his fingertips as the boy flitted away, leaving the door ajar behind him.

Fuck! The last thing he needed was a scene on the street as he tried to talk the kid round. They'd built a life here; he didn't even have his car. How were they going to get away? Away from all the hateful looks.

A heavy squeal quickly followed by a thud sounded from around the corner as Paul threw himself outside. He stumbled, reaching out a hand to the brickwork to stop himself as he got to the corner of the garage, and discreetly peered across the front of the two joined garages. The Hale's car had been reversed out of the garage. That accounted for the noise he heard a few seconds ago. He had a horrible feeling about what the other noise was, but he couldn't see anything past the low fence. It was Gillian who exited the car; he'd never even seen her drive before. She then staggered around the back of it, her mouth gaped open; she was saying something but he couldn't hear what it was. She collapsed on the ground next to the undercarriage.

He ducked back around the corner, hiding himself from view. Turning his head to the street, he scanned the nearest houses. Nobody was in sight. Swallowing hard, he knew he had to find out what was happening; control the situation. A weight settled on his chest as a wistful thought sank in; he was hoping for the death of a young boy to save them, to save his skin. He quickly pushed it away as he heard a muffled howl and moved back to the corner of the garage. Stepping around into the sun, he felt the warmth of the August day on his skin.

"Gillian, are you okay?"

Her head and shoulders were just visible over the low fence separating their driveways.

He braced his hand on the brickwork again as he stepped over the fence. Gillian was crouched next to the undercarriage of the car. He couldn't see what she was pawing at, but he had a good idea.

"Are you hurt?" he asked.

"Ambulance," Gillian mumbled. She looked overcome.

He rested a hand on her shoulder and said, "It's okay, I'll call them." He then placed a hand under her arm to lift her up, but she wasn't having any of it. "Let me help you," he said, stepping between her and the car, he scanned the street again, looking for movement: nothing. The fence and gates shielded them from most onlookers. He needed to know if the boy was dead. Maybe this whole situation could be put down to a tragic accident. An accident he had no involvement in.

He fought his duff leg to get down onto the floor next to the car. He didn't want to move Gillian in case she freaked out, alerting the neighbours. She'd done this. He needed to make this her fault. More importantly, she needed to know it was her fault.

The space between the car and fence was tight, preventing him from getting on his belly to get a good look. Instead, he stretched out a hand under the car, feeling for an extremity, his palm scraped along the rough concrete of the drive. She continued to sob next to him as he lowered his body as best he could. Stretching, he finally found something, clothing, then a leg, and swallowed his own fear as he pushed his hand along the tiny limb, the jeans brushing against the back of his hand. The skin was warm as he moved his hand back down. There was no shoe to hinder his progress. He knew from first aid training on the airbase that you could take someone's pulse on their foot, and he pulled down the sock, feeling for the toes, making his way to the top of the foot. His fingers trembled as they slid across the skin, stopping every few seconds. He tried to picture the position of the artery in his mind as he searched for the right place. Eventually, a faint throb pushed against the pads of his fingers. He was alive. *Shit!* He closed his eyes for a moment to try and put his ragged thoughts in order.

A vague outline of a plan came into view.

"I'm sorry, Gillian, he's gone. There's nothing we can do," he told her and removed his hand from the boy, placing it on Gillian's arm. "It was just an accident; you didn't mean to do it."

Tears flooded her cheeks as her lips trembled. "I've killed ... I thought it was Simon-I-I didn't see him." Her hands went to her face. "I didn't know he ..." she cried and collapsed, pressing her head against the side of the car.

Paul moved his hand to her shoulder. He needed to move fast if he was going to remedy this situation. "It's okay, I won't tell them how quickly you reversed," he said, keeping his voice low. "They don't need to know that bit," he continued, aware that time was a factor. "They'll probably send you to prison though. You'll lose everything."

"I killed-I kill–" Gillian's words filtered between her fingers as her breath came in short bursts. "It was my fault."

"He was such a lovely kid," Paul told her, keeping the pressure on as he pretended to wipe away his own tears. "His mum and dad ... God, what are you going to tell them?"

"I don't-I can't ..." Gillian looked up, struggling to get the words out.

Paul leant closer and finally said in a soft tone, "I can make this all go away," hoping it would filter through her sobs.

Gillian looked up, meeting his eyes, her mouth twisted out of shape as she continued to shake.

"I can help you," he added. "No-one will know what happened here." He moved closer to her, turning the screw a little more. "Think about your family," he said, resting a hand on her shoulder. "They need you here, not rotting away in prison."

Gillian froze, a heavy frown appearing on her brow. "How can–?"

"I'll need to borrow your car; just for a while. I won't be long. I'll put it back in the garage when I get back." He wasn't about to give her details. The less she knew, the better.

Gillian just sat there, motionless, her scrutiny solely on the boy's foot, just visible under the car. Taking her silence as confirmation. Paul reached out, struggling to his feet, he stepped around the car. The keys were poking out of the ignition.

"Okay," he said to himself.

He stepped around the front of the car into the cool garage. He needed something to move the body in. He looked blindly around the space, hoping something would jump out at him. In truth, he was struggling to distance himself from the situation. Looking for something suitable to transport a small dead child was not the best way to do that. But he wasn't dead yet, was he. He saw a pair of work gloves tucked behind a ladder and immediately slipped them on. There were boxes stacked on a unit at the far end of the garage; maybe he could use one of them. The brimming contents of the first one changed his mind. He ripped a large rubble bag from the roll in the top box, shaking it open. He just hoped it was big enough for the body; he couldn't think of him as a boy, a living person with a home and parents waiting for him to return. If he did that, he would lose everything. He needed to do this one thing, then they would be okay. It would all be over. They could disappear out of sight when it all died down, start a new life together. At thirty-one years old he deserved that, Amy was older now she could look quite grown up when she made an effort. People wouldn't look twice at them now, he gripped the bag as he held onto that thought.

Gillian was still on the floor when he returned. He stepped back beside her, keeping her to his right so she would shield what he was about to do, and avoided her eyes. He didn't want to give her a reason to change her mind.

"Turn away," he said softly as he clutched for the ankle underneath, but she made no movement. "Gillian, please," he said, a little louder.

Eventually, she complied. He crouched lower. Reaching under the car, he pulled at the stray limb and dragged it towards him. He opened the thick rubble bag, drawing and shoving the boy inside. Noticing a slight tremble in the boy's arm, he swallowed back his fears, if the boy woke up now it was all over. Gillian would force him to get help. He moved his own frame to shield her from his actions, thankfully there didn't seem to be much blood. On closer inspection as the boys head came into view his matted hair told a different story in contrast to the blank expression covering his face. Guilt devoured Paul's insides as he jostled the bag to sit upright the contents now hidden. It was a bag of rubble now, nothing more, not if he wanted to get through this.

He left the bag next to the car to open the boot and moved back to Gillian. Her hands trembled as they held a small white trainer.

"Let me take that," he said. Everything needed to be gone, no trace left behind.

Gillian handed it over without looking up, and he dropped it into the rubble bag, twisting it closed as best he could. He wanted nothing to spill out. He struggled to lift it with one hand but tried to look casual in case of unwanted onlookers. Just as he placed it carefully in the boot, a whaling voice came from behind him. With his heart in his throat, he shut the boot before turning abruptly. The young girl opposite was chasing after their bloody dog again. There was a reason they'd put up gates and fences.

Relieved the body was now secured and hidden, he needed to get Gillian inside and away from prying eyes. A distressed woman on the street would raise questions. He carefully moved towards her.

"You need to go back in the house and wait for me to come back. I won't be long," he said, trying to put her mind at ease. He knew from his conversation with Dave that their kids were away, and that they were coming back today. "When are your kids back?"

There was no response.

He tried again. "Gillian, what time are your kids arriving back?"

"I ... err ... I." Gillian turned her wrist to check the time. "I-I don't ... soon, I think."

Paul encouraged Gillian to get to her feet, leading her inside her house, and sat her at the dining table while he searched the kitchen cupboards, hoping to find some form of alcohol. If this was going to work, Gillian needed to snap out of it. He found a bottle of whisky in the top cupboard, grabbed a glass and poured a generous amount.

"Here, drink this," he said and wrapped her hands around the glass, offering it up to her.

She blindly complied, taking a large gulp, and it seemed to ground her a little as she looked up at him, although her focus still looked a little off.

"Can you put off the kids coming back?" he asked.

There was no reply.

He tried again. "Gillian, can you put the kids off, get them to come back tomorrow or something?" At least then she'd only have to deal with Dave, and he wouldn't be home for hours yet.

"What?.. I …" She took another drink. "I killed him. It was Daniel, wasn't it? I killed him."

He saw no need to confirm her fears. "Gillian, I'm trying to help you. We can't go back on this now." He needed to be firm. His neck was on the line too.

"I'll-I'll say I'm ill when-when he calls."

Her gaze was fixed on the drink in front of her. He didn't want to question who *he* was, her father maybe as they were on holiday with her parents. He poured her another drink and said, "I'll need you to open the garage door when I get back."

She nodded as she clutched her glass, a quiver still visible in her hands.

"I'll be as quick as possible."

Paul quietly left the house, reversing Dave's car out into the road, looking back at his own house. Amy was in her bedroom window. Her face was unreadable as she stared back at him. He was doing this for her, for both of them, he told himself and sped off.

He had an idea of where he was going; overhearing a friend talking about a job he was doing this morning had given him the perfect location. He just hoped it was far enough from the immediate area that it wouldn't be scrutinised.

Paul pulled the visor down as he drove out of the estate, it was relatively quiet a couple of people washing their cars, no-one looked twice at him. Yet he felt everyone could see the awful truth of what he was carrying in his boot as he passed them. Being on the edge of town worked in his favour as he headed onto the small road that led to the farm. No-one passed him, he saw nobody as he approached the entrance.

He sat there in the car for a couple of minutes to make sure there were no approaching spectators. The overgrown trees in the driveway should obscure his presence. At least he wasn't in his own car if anyone did spot it.

With the coast clear, he got out and quickly moved to the back of the car. As he pulled open the boot he could see the boy had moved. He was coming around. He closed his eyes, it wasn't over. He'd thought the boy might just lose consciousness, prayed he would but now, he sucked in a breath as he opened his eyes. As he watched, there was more movement; a limb moved under the crinkling plastic, sloshing in the blood puddle at the bottom of the bag, the darkened liquid painting the inside. If blood spilled into the boot, he was done for, they were all done for. He couldn't let that happen, not ever.

He had no choice now.

Eyes closed in a squint, he felt the surface of the blue plastic with a gloved hand, and his fingers soon located a head, then a profile. He clenched his teeth at the size of it, how it fit into his hand, then pressed down, keeping his palm and fingers firmly in place. Turning away, he tried to ignore the sounds of flailing movement in the plastic. Life drained from his own body as it did the boy in front of him, nothing would never be the same again. It seemed to go on for ever, the plastic stretching under the strain of the small figure trapped inside.

And then silence fell, but he was reluctant to remove his hand. He opened his eyes, focusing on the scene in front of him. He concentrated on the plastic, looking for any movement. It was done. His secret was safe.

The bag was motionless as he removed it from the car with both hands, sweat rolling down the side of his face. The weight of the task, of what he'd done, was heavy on his soul as he trudged through the field behind the farmhouse. But if the body wasn't found, what could they prove? He held onto that thought as he approached what he hoped was the perfect hiding place. It was almost midday; he prayed his mate was as reliable as ever and already in the pub after cutting the metal to seal up the well.

A patch of bare soil set into the ground came into view. As he got closer, he could see the hard lines of something underneath the edges of the thin soil. He set the bag on the ground as he knelt next to the edge of the freshly cut metal and pushed hard with gloved hands. His feet dug into the grassy ground beneath him as the top slowly moved, exposing the darkness below. He took a moment to catch his breath, but he couldn't go back now, and without giving himself time to think, he lowered the body into the void below, swallowing hard as he released it to fall the final distance. With the rubble bag still on the grass, he swore under his breath. He wasn't about to take it back with him. Splitting it open, he threw it down on top of the boy. Maybe if it was ever reopened, he would be hidden for a while.

He moved to the other side of the cover and pushed it back into place.

CHAPTER 37

THERE WAS no car in the driveway as Johanna stomped towards the house, which meant her father was out. At least she had that to be grateful for. She knew her mum was in, though; she always was. No doubt, she was planning another ridiculous memorial service to absolve herself of her guilt.

"Let's go around the back. The door will be open," she told Lucy as she made her way down the narrow walkway between the garage and the fence. The trees from next door's garden were overshadowing them, making it gloomy despite the bright autumn day.

"Please tell me we're not breaking in." Lucy's voice came from the darkness behind.

Lucy, she'd been so sweet to her since finding her with Amy or Mia, whatever her fucking name really was. If she hadn't been so focused on her task, she might have cracked a smile.

"She'll be in," Johanna replied as she stepped into the bright back garden, glancing at the brickwork her father had been working on the last time she had been out there. He was such a kind man; she couldn't even process the thought that he'd been involved in this mess too.

She'd been so determined, but now, as she approached the back door, her fingers rested on the metal handle; it was cold in the palm of her hand as she gripped it. She was stuck. She wanted to know the truth but was scared to hear the words fall from her mother's mouth.

"You okay?"

Lucy's soft words were filled with concern, but Johanna didn't dare turn around to face her, fearful of what she might say in reply. "Yeah," she mumbled and let out a long breath before pushing down the handle, feeling the catch release the door to swung open. She hesitated a moment before stepping inside, but the kitchen was empty, the glasses and plates in the sink the only evidence of recent use.

"Mum?" she called as she looked around the familiar space, and then she was off, charging through the kitchen and out into the hallway, still calling out to her. She pushed open the door to the front room and finally saw her mother sitting on the far end of the sofa reading the paper, the TV on low in the background. Her mother looked genuinely shocked when she twisted to look at her, not surprising considering her intermittent visits.

"Johanna! Are you okay? You look terrible?" The paper fell into her lap. "Whose blanket's that? It looks like a hospital blanket."

Johanna did her best to ignore the questions. She was here to get answers of her own. "Where's dad?"

Her mother was on her feet now, the paper discarded on the sofa. "He's dropping the boys back off at Simon's." She tilted her head to one side. "Why? Who's that with you?"

Johanna stepped further into the room, giving Lucy a better view. She needed her here, reaching out to touch Lucy's arm. "This is my friend, Lucy." They were, of course, more than friends, but with no discussion on their developing status, she kept it simple.

"I know you. You're police, aren't you?"

Before Lucy could answer, Johanna cut off the conversation between them. She didn't want any distractions now. "Mum, I need to ask you something."

"Ooookay." She stretched the word out as she continued to frown at Lucy.

"I am a police officer, Mrs Hale," Lucy confirmed. "We met a couple of weeks ago."

Her mother's focus returned to Johanna. "Is everything alright? Are you hurt?"

Johanna bristled at the distress in her mother's words. If what Amy had said was true, how dare she show any concern for her wellbeing? She racked her brain for her mother's response to Daniel's disappearance. Nothing came. She glanced at Lucy. She wanted to acknowledge her by-the-book honesty, how grateful she was that Lucy had agreed to come with her, but all she could think about were Amy's cruel words.

She shrugged off the blanket as she swivelled her head to look back at her mother.

Gillian Hale looked old as she frowned back at her. That was the problem with intermittent visits; her parents seemed to age uncontrollably in-between. One minute they were fit and active, the next they were struggling to climb the stairs. The words died in her throat as she opened her mouth. She noted the shake of her mother's hands. Did she already know the question? How could she even ask this of her own mother, it all seemed too unbelievable, but now Amy had put the scenario in her head she couldn't let it go.

She tried to form the words. "I need to know.....did-." She couldn't finish her question. Sucking in a breath she tried again. "Did you hit Daniel with dad's car?"

Her mother stepped back. "What? Who told you that?"

"You know who told me. Amy's with the police now. It's all going to come out, Mum. Tell me!" Johanna pleaded, her voice rising.

"Johanna?" Lucy called from the corner of the room.

Ignoring her, Johanna pressed on. "Mum, I need to know the truth."

"I don't know what you're talking about."

"Stop lying to me, Mum!" Johanna demanded and stepped forward, taking her mother's shaking hand in hers. "Please," she begged and the impact of her words and the strength of her emotion were clear on her mother's face as tears began to bubble in the older woman's wide, grey eyes before they looked down at their joined hands.

Finally, when she was able to speak, she said, "It was an accident." Her words were barely above a whisper.

Johanna closed her eyes. *Amy wasn't lying. God, how can this be happening?* She felt the weight of her stomach as the dizziness returned. Movement behind her made her turn. Lucy stretched out a hand to steady her wobbly frame, but the expression on her face was unreadable.

"After, I-I was in shock. I didn't know what to do," her mother whispered.

Johanna struggled to accept her mother's ridiculous statement. She shook her head wildly, her eyes wide. "If it was an accident you could have called for help! Maybe he could have been saved?"

"He wasn't moving. I thought he was dead." Tears streamed down her mother's face as her free hand moved to cover her mouth.

"What! You didn't check?" Johanna couldn't hide the distain from her voice.

"Paul did. I-I was so scared. I couldn't think straight."

She was a mother and a human being; she was meant to nurture and care for people, not toss them aside to be thrown into a hole.

"I thought about you and Simon, how it would destroy our family. Who would look after you all if I went to prison?"

Johanna opened her mouth but couldn't form any words.

"Please, you have to believe me. He came out of nowhere." She gripped at Johanna's hand. "I didn't know he was there. I didn't see him."

Johanna frowned as she tried to picture the scene that day. "What was he doing there?"

"I don't know. I-I thought he was coming around to see you."

"Why would you think that? I wasn't even there."

"He had a thing for you." Her mother's voice had regained some of its strength.

"No, he didn't. He had a thing for Amy." Johanna blurted out. "And why the bloody hell was Paul Bell helping you?"

"What?" There was genuine shock in her mother's voice.

"There's more: Paul wasn't Amy's dad. They were, well, I don't know what they were," Johanna realised as a listlessness took over her fuzzed mind.

"What are you talking about? That's –"

"It's true. She told me." The warmth had evaporated from Johanna's voice.

"But-but she…I-I didn't-."

"Is that why you've hated me all these years, you blamed me for Dan being there that day…" She looked at the ground unable to hold her mother's gaze. "I thought it was because I'm a lesbian but…"

"What. No-I I, Johanna. I don't hate you. I hate myself, what I did." Her mother reached for her hand. "I'm so sorry."

Lucy stepped forward. "Gillian Hale, I'm arresting you in connection with the murder of Daniel Dunderdale. You have the right to remain silent. Anything you do say can be used against you in a court of law…"

Johanna felt the ground shift under her. It was out of her hands now.

"I'm sorry, Johanna. I don't have a choice."

She turned to meet Lucy's eyes, briefly nodding her understanding. She'd brought Lucy with her for support, yet part of her knew she would also do the right thing where she could not.

She let the grip on her mother's hand fall away as she watched Lucy lead her from the room. The front door opened and closed. Alone with the gaping void of reality in front of her, Johanna held onto the back of the sofa as her legs threatened to give way. Footsteps in the hallway followed, then Lucy reappeared in the room. She was confused for a moment, but when she glanced out the front window, she saw a uniformed police officer escorting her mother to a police car. When did they arrive? What else had she missed today?

"Did I do this?" Johanna asked as Lucy shuffled further into the room, before quickly corrected herself. "I did this!" The words were out before she could stop them. She'd pulled at a loose thread, unravelling it until it revealed the ugliness behind the thirty-year-old, dusty curtain. She'd searched Amy out, forced the truth from her spiteful mouth.

Lucy moved to put an arm on her shoulder, blocking the doorway in front of her. "No you didn't," she soothed and moved into her line of sight. "We were closing in on Amy. It was just a matter of time."

Tears stung Johanna's tired eyes. "How could she keep something like that inside for so long?"

Lucy stepped closer, pulling her into her arms, but said nothing.

After a moment of comfort, a question burned at Johanna's insides. She pulled back to look at Lucy. "Why did Paul help her? Why did they hide it?"

Lucy took a deep breath before answering. "I don't know," she said, holding Johanna close. "Is it okay if I send someone to pick up the box and sock from your hotel room?"

Johanna nodded before burying herself in Lucy's embrace. She'd meant to do it earlier, but the day had gotten away from her. Then another thought assailed her. Her dad. How was she going to explain any of this to him?

Lucy kissed the side of her head. "I know it's going to take you some time to process all this," she said, "but if you need to talk about it, or anything, please call me. Anytime."

"Thank you."

Johanna reluctantly let Lucy pull away as the sound of a car pulling up outside drew her attention to the front of the house.

"Your dad's back," she said. "Do you want me to talk to him?"

Johanna wiped at her eyes. "No, it's okay." She gripped Lucy's hand as she moved to the front door. "I'll do it."

CHAPTER 38

LUCY SAT AT HER DESK, staring blankly at Johanna's statement in her hand. Her head was still reeling from the day's events. The only case she half expected to tie up today was David Booker's. In her absence, Barrel had interviewed all three lads that Tyler Lloyd had named. Each one had more or less the same story. Initial reports from forensics after searching their residencies had given them nothing. Their mystery man seen leaving the property was looking like the most likely culprit for the still motiveless crime.

She rubbed at her eyes, trying to rid them of the starey tiredness. Christ, she felt for Johanna, for what she'd put herself through to find out the truth. But at what cost? Selfishly, she hoped Johanna wouldn't pull away. The time they'd spent at her flat the previous night felt like a lifetime away.

"Fuller."

Lucy looked up from her paperwork. "Boss."

Barrel nodded his head, indicating for her to come into his office. She kept the paperwork in her hand as she headed in. He'd barely said anything about the fact she'd made two arrests in the Dunderdale case since her return.

"How's the arm?" He asked taking his seat.

"Its fine." Luckily, she'd had a clean shirt in her locker.

"I want you to do the interview with Amelia Hunter," he said as he sat back.

"Boss?" She hadn't been expecting that. She figured she'd be his wingman but nothing more.

"You deserve it. You've worked hard on this case, done most of the legwork, and I know I haven't been around much lately. It's only fair that you get to do it. Take Tanner in with you."

Lucy opened her mouth to protest, but Barrel raised his hand to stop her. Maybe all the hard work she'd put into this case had finally paid off.

"You'll be fine," he said firmly as he placed his hand down on his desk. "What are you thinking?"

She figured he was asking for her interview plan. Lucy took a breath before launching into what she knew so far. "According to Johanna Hale's statement, Amelia Hunter admitted to being Amy Bell as confirmed by the DVLA photos we have. She also said that Gillian Hale was responsible for the death of Daniel Dunderdale when she reversed her husband's car out of her garage hitting Daniel. I've contacted Dr Chadwick, giving her the circumstances and the make and model of the Hales' car at the time to see if Daniel's injuries are consistent with being hit by a car. I'm waiting to hear back."

"Okay." Barrel picked up a pen and tapped it on the desk.

Lucy took another breath as she considered whether to bring up the bloody sock. She decided to wait till the forensic result came through.

"I was present when Gillian Hale admitted to her daughter that she had hit Daniel with their car. She claimed it was an accident."

"It's going to be hard to prove otherwise now," Barrel added.

Lucy nodded. "Amelia Hunter apparently also said that Paul Bell wasn't her father. We already know she was a fourteen-year-old runaway from Northampton, which happens to be where Paul Bellamy was working at the time."

"Ran away together?"

"Possibly. She was underage, so ..." She let the statement hang in the air. "As we know, Paul Bellamy – Hunter's boyfriend slash father –

died in nineteen-ninety-five possibly in suspicious circumstances. And he disposed of Daniel's body."

"Why? Why cover up for Gillian Hale if it was just an accident?"

"Exactly." That's precisely what she planned to find out. She had an idea, but she needed to hear it from Amelia Hunter. If Daniel Dunderdale was the squealer everyone thought he was, what did he know that meant he had to die?

Lucy dropped her paperwork on the table as she took her seat. She waited for Tanner to get settled before going through the process of introducing everyone in the room for the recording.

"So," Lucy began, looking up, eyeing the woman sat opposite. Her face still held the smug expression she'd seen earlier. Her lips twisted upwards for a second, Lucy wondered what had caught her attention, looking down she noticed her bandage was poking out of her replacement shirt. Refusing to pull it down Lucy looked up meeting her glare. "What would you like to be called? Amelia? Amy? Mia?" She just managed to remove the sarcasm from her question.

"Mia is fine. I've got used to it."

Like the contacts. Lucy settled back in her seat as she went through the interview strategy in her head. "Just to confirm, you don't want a solicitor present at this time."

"No. I haven't done anything wrong, so." Hunter shrugged. "Do you know what Mia stands for? M.I.A. Missing in action," she continued.

Lucy picked up her pen as she studied Amelia Hunter. She'd made a big decision at the age of fourteen that had changed the direction of her whole life.

"I've been missing in action since I ran away at fourteen," Hunter added and stretched out her arms on the table before bending them and lacing her fingers together in front of her.

"Is that when you met Paul Bellamy?" Lucy gambled on the fact that Hunter seemed to be forthcoming at the moment.

"Bellamy." A smirk broke out across Hunter's face. "Yeah."

"Can you tell me how you met Paul?" She'd considered a few possible scenarios in her head.

"He worked at the airbase in Croughton. My parents ran the village pub, The Plume and Feathers. I used to help out collecting glasses on the weekends." Hunter shrugged. "He was a regular, we got chatting."

Grooming came to the front of Lucy's mind as Bellamy was almost thirty at the time. "How long did you know Paul before you ran away?"

"I don't know," Hunter said and rubbed the pads of her thumbs together. "Four months maybe."

Lucy made a note but purposely didn't mention the age gap or, more specifically, that she was underage. Amelia Hunter must have known that more than anyone, hence the need for them to run away.

"Paul was being transferred to Oldbury, so we arranged to meet a couple of days after he left."

Lucy knew he'd requested the transfer. Was it to force Hunter's hand? "You moved to Compton Way, Kingsford in August nineteen eighty-seven with Paul Bellamy?"

"Yes."

"You were living there in August nineteen eighty-eight when Daniel Dunderdale went missing?"

"Yes."

"Do you know what happened to Daniel?" Lucy pushed her luck a little more.

"Paul killed him."

Lucy tried not to let the surprise show on her face. It certainly wasn't the story she'd told Johanna a few hours ago.

"You're saying that Paul Bellamy killed Daniel Dunderdale? How do you know this information?"

"He told me." Hunter almost sounded blasé. "And well, I heard and saw some of it."

"What exactly did you hear and see?" Lucy asked. Out of the corner of her eye, she could see Tanner's pen had barely left the paper with all the notes he was taking.

"Daniel came round on the Saturday morning. He told me he'd seen us together."

"On Saturday the twentieth of August, the day he went missing?" Lucy confirmed. "Do you know what time he came round?"

"About ten o'clock." Hunter took a drink from her water. "He'd seen us."

Lucy waited, biding her time. Could this finally be the motive for Daniel's death? She had a gut feeling Daniel had seen something he shouldn't have, hence the need to hide away in his room.

"Kissing!" Hunter confirmed and let out a long breath. "He must have been spying on us through the back fence, little pervert." Hunter's mouth made an ugly shape as she finished her words. Lucy recalled Johanna saying you could walk up the entire street behind the tall farmers fence completely unseen.

"Daniel told you what he'd seen?"

Hunter nodded. "Wanted to save me, said he could help me get away. He wanted us to go to the police station."

Not an option, considering Amelia Hunter was a runaway living with a man twice her age out of choice. "What happened?"

Hunter seemed to bristle at the question, and Lucy prepared herself for the inevitable shutdown. She'd seen it before when suddenly people realise the gravity of the situation and what it means for their near future.

Hunter laid her hands flat on the table, her focus on her spread fingers. "What is it about men, always thinking you need saving or something?"

Lucy watched as Hunter's gaze landed firmly on Tanner. She felt sorry for young Daniel Dunderdale, so unfamiliar with the twisted dynamics going on in the Bellamy household. Not to mention the fact that Hunter's current appearance told a different story. Had she suffered at the hands of a different man that had wanted to do anything but save her?

"Are you okay to continue?" Lucy asked in a soft voice.

Hunter nodded. "Paul was out shopping when he came round."

Lucy bit her tongue, not wanting to prod. Amelia Hunter seemed less sure of herself for a moment.

"When Paul came back, he got up and ran like shit off a stick straight out the front door."

"He was unharmed?" Lucy asked.

"Yes." Hunter nodded, she took another drink. "I don't know where he was running to. Down the gardens I guess, so he could skip the fences easier like the Moody dog."

Nothing so far accounted for the blood on the sock, yet Hunter had mentioned it to Johanna, even admitted putting it in the box. She needed the lab results before she could question her about it. If it was Daniel's blood there were questions to be answered.

"What happened then?" She wanted to hear Hunter's version, although there was little chance of corroboration with Bellamy dead.

"I heard a thump," Hunter continued. "Johanna's mum was reversing their car out of the garage. Paul went to find out what happened. He said he thought Daniel was dead to start with, but then he found a pulse."

"But he didn't call for help?" Lucy questioned.

"No. He told Gillian that Daniel was dead, talked her into letting him help her hide it all."

It corroborated what little she knew of Gillian's version of events. More than anything, Lucy noted the offhanded way Mia Hunter delivered her information.

"Why do you think he did that?"

Hunter shrugged. "I don't know. So she wouldn't go to prison and lose her family I guess."

That tallied, but there was clearly another angle to consider, besides the fact that Gillian Hale had created her own prison. "And so no-one found out about your true relationship with Paul Bellamy," Lucy added.

Hunter glared back at her. "I guess. Paul told me he killed him, smothered him with his hand while he was in the boot of Gillian's car when he went to dump the body."

Dump the body. Lucy tried not to react to the emotionless, matter-of-fact statement. Instead, she focused on the latter part of the information as it plugged a hole in the events of the day.

"Paul used the Hale's car to move Daniel's body" *How had nobody seen that?*

"Yeah. His was in the garage being fixed."

Lucy tried to recall what Bellamy's statement had said about his car. Ironically, at the time, it would have ruled him out in some ways as Daniel had not been found in the immediate area, despite the extensive searches. "What was wrong with Paul's car?"

Amelia Hunter shook her head. "I can't remember. Something he couldn't fix himself."

Lucy nodded. "Did he tell you why he killed Daniel?"

"He did it for us, to protect us." Amelia Hunter fiddled with the plastic cup in front of her. "Once he started, I guess he couldn't stop."

"Protect you from what?" Lucy didn't want any surprises further on.

"People like you." She pointed to Tanner. "Looking down on us, telling us we're filth."

"Did that happen?" Lucy asked, wondering why no-one else had said anything at the time.

Mia Hunter picked at the skin on her fingers. "Paul lived in fear of it every minute of the day. He was so strict about how we could act, what I could say all the time."

"That's not what you told Johanna Hale earlier." Lucy stated. Now she had an outline of the so-called full story, she needed to press a little harder.

Mia smirked. "I wanted to piss her off, with her perfect little family and perfect little life."

Lucy made no comment. She imagined most of Mia Hunter's life had bordered on shitty until she met Jarred Young, then it went downhill from there. Still, she couldn't stop herself from asking the question. "And when Daniel's disappearance was linked to David Levin?"

Amelia Hunter looked up from her hands to glare back at her. "Paul said we couldn't say anything, didn't want to stir things up again. We'd left the area by then."

Lucy matched her scowl. "You thought it would be better for his parents to think Levin had killed Daniel rather than it being a simple accident?" She felt Tanner's eyes on her and she willed him not to say a word to break the spell between them.

Mia Hunter was quiet for a moment before looking away. "Paul was never the same after that. Wouldn't shut up about it."

Lucy ignored the dismissal of her initial question. "What do you mean by that?" she continued to press, although she already had a fairly good idea, as the post-mortem on Bellamy had indicated a history of alcohol abuse.

"Started drinking, a lot," Amelia Hunter sighed as she folded her arms tight to her chest.

"Is that why you left him?"

"He used to get angry, so he drank. The more he drank, the angrier he got. Until I couldn't stand it any longer."

"I see." She nodded perfectly understandable how killing an innocent child might change a man. "Can you tell me how he knew about the well being covered up on Combe farm?" It was the last piece to the puzzle.

"He played darts with a guy who laboured on the farm sometimes, remembered about the old man having it covered it up after he lost a sheep down there or something."

"Dog," Lucy said. "It was a dog he lost down the well."

"Anyway." Amelia Hunter waved a hand. "He thought that no-one would ever find him down there."

He was right. Well, almost. "When did you last see Paul Bellamy?" Lucy asked.

There was a slight change in Hunter's posture as she tried to sit a little more upright.

"When I moved out, years ago."

Lucy studied the smug look on Amelia Hunter's face. She needed to disrupt her thinking. "You don't like weakness, do you, Mia? Correcting Little Mark's speech, bludgeoning injured birds to death."

Hunter rolled her eyes before a smug grin filled her face. "That bird was going to die of starvation. Barney could have stopped me, took the wood off me any time he liked. He wanted to see what would happen just as much as me."

What would happen? Wasn't it obvious? Lucy tried not to let her revulsion show for this woman. Was that what happened to Paul? He got weak after killing Daniel so she put him out of his misery too. She needed more evidence before venturing down that road.

Hunter smashed her hand on the table, her persona changing in an instant. "I need a break, now!"

Lucy felt Tanner's eyes on her once again as she picked up her pen and papers ready to leave the room.

Lucy hugged the paperwork to her chest, waiting till Amelia Hunter was out of earshot before turning to Tanner. He looked as tired as she felt.

"What do you think?"

Tanner blew out a breath. "It's all circumstantial. We can't prove much either way without Bellamy or any forensic evidence."

Lucy nodded. He wasn't wrong. "Well, we've got two people telling us more or less the same story." She wanted it to sound better than it did. She didn't even know which one was true at this stage. "We need to talk to Gillian Hale."

"Okay," Tanner nodded.

She was just about to head towards the stairs when she turned back to Tanner. "Was Hunter even questioned when Bellamy was found dead?"

"Don't know. I'll find out."

Lucy pursed her lips. "Let's take a quick break, check in with the boss. Then we'll talk to Gillian Hale. Oh, and find out if Jarred Young has surfaced anywhere yet."

Tanner frowned. "Who's Jarred Young?"

"Mia Hunter's ex-partner, the one who might have set fire to her house while she was in bed along with her kids."

CHAPTER 39

Gillian Hale looked every bit the broken woman as she sat in the interview room, wrapped in the blanket from her cell. She gripped at it, hugging her shoulders, her blanched fingers standing out against the dark material. Her duty solicitor, on the other hand, looked calm and collected as he sat, pen poised over a legal pad.

"Would you like a hot drink?" Lucy asked as she sat down opposite.

Gillian Hale remained silent as she glanced up from the floor, her eyes red rimmed.

Lucy turned to Tanner, silently asking the question. He nodded, placing his paperwork on the table before leaving the room. She checked through her notes while she waited for Tanner's return, and her thoughts drifted to Johanna and how she'd fared at explaining the arrest to her dad. After a few minutes, the door swung open, pulling her back to the task in front of her.

"It's from the machine, I'm afraid," Tanner offered as he pushed the half-filled plastic cup across the table towards Gillian Hale.

Lucy waited a beat before introducing Tanner, herself and Gillian Hale. She looked at the duty solicitor, indicating for him to do the same for the benefit of the recording. Gillian Hale slowly stretched out her knobbly, pale fingers to reach for the cup of what looked like murky tea.

"Mrs Hale, I need to remind you that you are still under caution."

Gillian Hale nodded, glancing at her solicitor before returning her attention to the tea.

Lucy continued. "I need you to go over the events that led to Daniel's death."

Gillian Hale closed her eyes for a moment. Lucy considered calling the doctor to ensure she was fit to be interviewed. The last thing she wanted was to fuck it all up at this stage. Before she could voice her thoughts, Gillian Hale met her eyes.

"I was ..." she began and sniffed loudly. "I was painting the window frames. Like I said, I needed the white spirit from the garage to ... err ..." She waved her left hand in the air. "... to tidy up the brush, my hands. I couldn't find it. There was always so much ... stuff in there. The car was in the way. I couldn't get to the cupboard where David kept it."

Lucy waited for her to continue, not wanting to interrupt her train of thought.

"I went to get the keys to move it ... I didn't really drive, but I just needed to move it back a bit. I thought it would be fine. It should have been fine." Gillian Hale was getting flustered now.

"You had to move the car," Lucy clarified, giving her time to breathe.

Gillian nodded. "Yes."

"Do you know what time that was roughly?" Thirty years was a long time, but Lucy figured this particular day had been hard to forget.

"Mid-morning I think. There was no-one around on the street. The gate was shut. I just don't understand where he came from. Johanna –"

"The gate?" Lucy asked, cutting her off. She needed her to focus on back then, not what Johanna had told her. Gillian looked back at her blankly. "You said the gate was shut."

"To the driveway," Gillian mumbled.

It was an accident, a terrible accident. Until the likes of Paul Bellamy and Amelia Hunter put their spin on it.

"I just ..." Gillian continued. "I asked David to get it out of the garage for me but he forgot, so I had to."

"Okay." Lucy made a note.

"I was so worried I'd damage his precious car. I looked in the mirror as I reversed. There was no-one there." Gillian wiped at her nose. "Maybe I did go too fast, but there shouldn't have been anyone there."

Lucy frowned for a second. There was something about the way Gillian spoke made Lucy think that someone had already sewn the seed of doubt for her.

"I felt the bump. I thought I'd hit something hanging on the garage wall, but-but when I got out, there was nothing. Then I saw the shoe on the driveway ... the foot," she added and dissolved into tears.

"Maybe we should take a break?" The duty solicitor finally broke his silence.

Lucy felt for this woman. First Daniel then Gillian Hale; both victims of the Bells' twisted secrets. She pulled a clump of tissues from the box on the side and offered them across to Gillian Hale. "Are you okay to continue?"

"Yes." Gillian took the offering, covering her nose with the tissues. "I need to ... I thought it was all a dream," she continued. "There was nothing, no proof of what had happened, what I'd done. But the moment I saw Paul again, I knew it was real."

"Can you explain that to me?" Lucy asked, trying to bring her back on track.

"He must have heard it and came out to see what ... Daniel was under the car, I thought ... Paul checked for a pulse. He said it was too late, he was gone."

Paul Bell made sure Daniel kept his mouth shut. "What did Paul say when he came to help you?" Lucy gambled.

Gillian nodded. "He said I'd reversed too quickly, that I'd lose everything if we went to the police. He said he could make it all go away."

"How was he proposing to do that?" Lucy would have loved to have been a fly on the wall for that conversation, if you could call it that.

"I, err ... It's all ... mixed up." Gillian tapped the side of her head.

"He put Daniel in the boot of the car so no-one would see. I still had his shoe." Gillian held out her hand as if she were holding something. "He took it off me, said I needed to forget all about it. He took me inside, gave me a drink. He took the car to move Daniel."

"Do you know how long Paul was gone?" She knew the distance to Combe Farm was only about seven miles. Adding in the time it took to put Daniel in the well, he could have been gone for less than an hour.

"No." Gillian shook her head. "I don't remember. I was drinking ... the shock, I-I."

"Okay," Lucy nodded. "Did you know where Paul took Daniel's body?" She was careful to use the past tense, as she had an idea Gillian Hale had found out at some point.

"No." Gillian shook her head again. "He didn't tell me till they moved away."

Lucy nodded. Nice leaving present. "Did you have any contact with them after that?"

"No."

"I just have a few more questions." Gillian looked a bit more stable now, but Lucy informed her anyway.

Gillian Hale nodded. "Okay."

"Were you aware that Mia or Amelia Hunter is Amy Bell?" Lucy confirmed before going any further.

Gillian Hale nodded. "Yes." Her voice was raw. She drank the last of her tea.

Lucy waited a few moments before continuing. "When did Amy Bell get back in touch with you?"

"Just after Christmas." Gillian's voice had almost returned to its usual timbre.

Lucy thought back to the timeline of Hunter's house fire. She'd been out of hospital for a few months by then. "How did she contact you?"

"She turned up at my house with her children. I didn't recognise her at first, then she started talking about Daniel," she answered and brushed away a stray tear with her right hand.

"What did she say?"

"She said they needed somewhere to live. Her ex-boyfriend had tried to kill them all in a fire. They'd lost everything." Hale looked down at the table. "She told me Paul was dead. I-I looked it up on the internet after they left. I had no idea."

Was Hunter really running in fear from her ex? Or just desperate? "She asked you to help her?"

"She said if I didn't, she'd tell everyone about Daniel." Gillian Hale's lips trembled.

"You rented the house on Templers Way near the marsh for her," Lucy asked and silently scolded herself for her impatience. They'd already requested a copy of the contract from the rental agency after finding paperwork with Gillian's name on during their search of Templers Way.

Gillian Hale nodded. "She picked it, said the kids would like it there."

Lucy had a feeling it hadn't stopped there. "Did she ask for anything else?"

"Money. She said she couldn't work with her … injuries." Gillian fumbled for the right word. "She wanted me to give her money." She used her fingers to wipe at more tears escaping down her cheeks.

Lucy placed the box of tissues on the table between them and watched as Gillian plucked two from the box, almost pulling the box over in the process. Tanner's hand stretched out to rectify the situation. Lucy waited a second before continuing.

"Did you give her any money?"

"I sent money to her account every month."

Lucy made a note to acquire Gillian Hale's bank records to confirm the payments. Maybe they could get Hunter for blackmail. "How did you hear about the development planned for Combe Farm?"

"David told me. He's part of the conservation group thing. He said some of them were going to try and stop the build, something about newts on the land."

Lucy could see the fatigue pulling at Gillian face as she spoke. They had several things to check up on now before the next interview.

"Why don't we take a break, let you get a decent cup of tea?" Lucy offered. She was looking forward to hearing what Amelia Hunter had to say in her second interview.

Lucy sat in the interview room, checking through her paperwork while she waited for Amelia Hunter to be escorted back for another interview. She looked up as the door swung open. Tanner led the way, followed by an obviously pissed-off Hunter. Lucy tried not to smile at her twisted face. She was probably expecting to have been released hours ago, especially considering how forthcoming she'd been already.

Hunter slumped down heavily in the chair opposite and said, "How long are you going to keep me here? I need to be with my kids."

Lucy knew her two children were safely with social services, who were in the process of assessing their living arrangements after Hunter's decision to drug them prior to being arrested.

"We just need to ask you a few more questions, Mia. Shouldn't be too long now." She waited for Tanner to settle in his seat before starting. "Can I confirm that you do not require the presence of a solicitor, Mia?" Lucy asked, looking at her expectantly.

"Yes," Hunter replied a little too loudly.

"Okay."

Opening her folder, Lucy pulled out a copy of a photograph. "Mia, do you recognise the item in this image?"

Hunter pulled the piece of paper closer. Her face twisted again as she glanced down at the image.

"For the benefit of the tape, I am showing Amelia Hunter a photograph of a white, adult-size sports sock." She waited for Hunter to answer.

"Okay. It's a sock." Sarcasm dripped from her words.

"Do you know who that sock belongs to?" Lucy asked using her pen to point to the item.

"No." Hunter pushed the paper away.

Lucy nodded. "This sock was found in the bottom of a Spirograph box by Johanna Hale." She omitted the word hidden from her statement. "Do you know how it got there?"

Hunter let out a frustrated breath. "Did *she* tell you I put it there?"

Lucy made no comment as she waited for Hunter to continue.

"Okay." Hunter threw her hands in the air. "*I* put it there to make her look guilty. I was just a stupid kid." She rolled her eyes. "She didn't bloody come back anyway, though, did she."

"I see." Lucy nodded, purposely leaving the photograph in view. "Johanna Hale returned home the following day," she confirmed. "Can you tell me how the box came into Johanna Hale's possession?"

"It was hers. She always bloody left it with me when she went away. She thought I liked it as much as she did. I put the sock in there to get rid of it. I took it around to her house after Paul left with the body, *Daniel*."

Lucy noted the correction. Hunter was starting to fray at the edges.

"Her mum was crashed out on the sofa. She'd been drinking. She didn't even see me come in. I put the box under Johanna's bed and left."

That certainly cleared up one chain of events and confirmed Johanna's statement. Lucy pushed back the photograph towards Hunter. "Do you know what those stains are on the sock?" She'd already asked the lab to compare the samples with Daniel Dunderdale's DNA profile.

"No!"

A simple one-word answer, Lucy pushed some more. She moved the photograph directly in front of Hunter. "Did something happen while Daniel was at your house that day? You've already said you put the sock in the spirograph box to make Johanna Hale look guilty, what is the significance of the sock? Is it Daniel's blood?"

Hunter closed her eyes. "I was just trying to shut him up, I put my hand over his mouth. He got a split lip that's all." She wiped at her eyes.

"He had a split lip." Lucy repeated. "And the sock?"

"It's Paul's, Daniel used it to wipe his mouth." Hunter rubbed at her eyes before pushing the paper away again.

"He wiped his mouth."

Hunter sat back in her seat. "Yes! I told you he had a split lip." Her annoyance surfaced again.

Lucy nodded. "When you were trying to shut him up." Lucy was careful to use Hunter's own words. It was hard to believe someone would choose a random sock to wipe their blood on as opposed to their hand or clothing. In discovering the last moments of Daniel's short life she'd ended up reliving them with him, and it made her crave justice, she prodded Hunter a little more firmly. "When did you move back to Kingsford?" she asked, moving onto another subject. She had an idea of the timeline but wanted Hunter's input.

Hunter eyeballed her for a few seconds before answering. "After I got out of hospital."

Lucy frowned. "Why Kingsford of all places, considering what had happened before?" Her move back to Kingsford was hardly far enough to escape an ex-boyfriend's clutches if he was still in the area.

"I just wanted somewhere safe to bring up my kids. Jesus, do we need to do this now? I need to be with them." Hunter's voice rose with each word. She was on her feet now, leaning across the table, getting into Lucy's personal space.

Lucy did her best not to flinch at her actions.

"Sit back," Tanner warned her.

Lucy looked into Amelia Hunter's eyes. They'd turned black. She still wore the tinted contacts, but behind them, her eyes were like black holes, dead space. It reminded her of a nature documentary she'd seen on sharks. Maybe she needed to bait the water a little more.

"Sit back!" Tanner repeated as he got to his feet.

Hunter complied, giving Tanner a smirk as she returned to her seat.

"Who pays for the house on Templers Way where you're living with your children?" Lucy asked.

"A friend." Hunter's tone was dismissive.

"Why do they pay for it?" Lucy pressed.

"They offered to help me, us."

Lucy made a show of checking her notes. "According to Gillian Hale, she's paying the rent on that house."

"So? Can't she be my friend!"

"Gillian Hale, the woman that hit Daniel with her car thirty years ago." Lucy laid it out. "Are you blackmailing her, Mia?"

Hunter sat up a little straighter. "No. Is that what she said?"

Lucy ignored her question. "Does she help you out in other ways too?"

"No comment."

Finally, a question she didn't want to answer. Lucy pressed on. "Do you know who set fire to your house in Banbury?"

"No, I don't. I figured it was my ex." Hunter pursed her lips.

Lucy flicked through her notes. "Your ex-partner, Jarred Young? You told the police you thought Jarred Young was responsible for the fire at your home."

"Yes, he is, and yes he did this." She indicated to her face with both hands as she let out a frustrated breath. "Why are we even talking about this?"

Lucy poked a little harder. "Do you know where Jarred Young is?"

"No, I don't. I haven't seen him."

"When was the last time you *did* see him?"

Hunter rolled her eyes. "I don't know, a few weeks before he set fire to my home and tried to burn me alive."

Me not *us*. It was all about Mia Hunter. "You haven't seen him since the fire? He hasn't tried to see his children?"

"No." Hunter placed her hands flat on the table. "I think I'd like to see my solicitor now."

"Do you have a solicitor?" Lucy questioned, knowing full well she'd finally touched an angry nerve.

"I do." Hunter sat back in her seat. "Thomas Bridger from Bridger and Co."

Lucy grinned as she gathered her paperwork while Hunter reeled off her solicitor's number. Who has her solicitor's number memorised? "I'll pass your request on to the duty sergeant."

Lucy sat at her desk as she checked through the Proof of Life enquiries that had been carried out for Jarred Young. His passport had run out two months ago, and there'd been no request for a renewal, he'd not registered with a new GP or contacted any NHS service across the UK since the initial enquiries had been made after the fire. She knew from her recent research that when someone goes missing, or on the run in Young's case, they usually want to maintain certain aspects of their life, like staying in contact with immediate family to provide access to money if nothing else. His friends and family had been contacted, but no-one had seen him since the twenty-first or twenty-second of March 2017, a day or two before the fire had occurred. His phone records were the same; no activity since the twenty-second, the day before the fire. The phone had either run out of battery or been turned off at that point.

Despite being the victim of the arson attack, Amelia Hunter was not coming off well according to Young's family and friends, most of whom weren't convinced he was guilty at all, but at least two people were of the opinion that if he did do it, she probably drove him to it. There was animosity after they split up regarding his access to the kids; she was reluctant to let him have anything to do with them, claiming he was physically abusive towards her.

Next, she checked through Young's previous. There were several driving offences for no insurance, not wearing a seatbelt and no MOT. Then six months before the fire, he was cautioned for possession of class-C drugs. She scanned further down. Young was arrested three years earlier after a brawl in a pub carpark and accepted a caution for ABH. Maybe Young did have violent tendencies after all.

Lucy looked up from her screen as PC Goff entered the office. She looked nervous as she made a beeline for Tanner's desk.

A mumbled conversation ensued to her right before Tanner appeared out of the corner of her eye.

"The number that your anonymous tip came through on was traced back to a pay phone in Oldbury," he said.

Lucy nodded, knowing Andy had more than that judging by the paperwork in his hands.

"I asked PC Goff to check through CCTV in the area around the payphone, see if anyone we know cropped up."

She knew what was coming but let him continue as Goff was still hovering.

Tanner placed a slightly blurry image of a man on her desk. "And we have a Mr John Cole on the street within a minute of the call taking place." He placed a second image of the same man walking away. "And leaving three minutes later."

"Excellent." She looked past Tanner, offering Goff a brief nod and smile of appreciation.

Tanner cleared his throat and said, "Gillian Hale's mobile records have also come through. She was the woman that called the ecologist about the survey. Also, there were lots of calls and texts between her and Hunter's number too."

Lucy replayed the conversation she'd had with the ecologist.

"The estate agents sent through a copy of the rental agreement for Templers Way signed by Gillian Hale on the twenty-third of January. Her bank records show regular payments going out of her account from the start of February."

"And into Mia Hunter's, the master manipulator." Lucy thought back to the bunched-up tea towel on the table in Hunter's kitchen.

"She's clever. None of her texts are menacing," Tanner said as he looked through the remaining paperwork in his hand.

"She saved that for their face-to-face meetings." Lucy was beginning to get a feel for Mia Hunter's devious nature. "I've been looking through the Proof of Life search on Jarred Young. Something doesn't feel right. He's either super cautious to the extent that he turned his phone off the day before the fire or ..." She waved a hand in the air.

Tanner frowned. "What are you thinking?"

"I'm not sure, but what if she killed Young to get him off her back or maybe there was an argument that got out of hand, I don't know." She was grasping at straws and she knew it.

"Then she sets the fire herself to point the finger at Young, which goes horribly wrong." Tanner sounded sceptical.

"Maybe." Or horribly right in Hunter's eyes, as it makes her the perfect victim. "Makes Young the perfect villain that we're apparently still searching for."

"Jesus!" Tanner's eyes widened.

"I'm just not sure what we can prove right now." Lucy sat back in her chair and looked over to Barrel's office. "The boss is contacting the CPS about the confessions. We might not have a choice soon."

Barrel had never wanted this case in the first place. He couldn't wait to get rid of it.

"But –" Tanner protested.

"It's just a theory." Lucy cut him off. She didn't want to let it go any more than he did.

EPILOGUE

LUCY TURNED OFF THE SHOWER, a split second later she heard her phone ringing from the other room. She stepped out, grabbing a towel along the way she jogged into the bedroom in search of her phone. She found it on the small table next to the bed, she would have been hard pressed to lose it in the pokey little hotel room she'd been landed with to attend the conference.

Tanner's name flashed on the screen. Releasing a groan under her breath, she accepted the call as she sat down on the edge of the bed. She prayed it was something that could wait till after the weekend. She was too tired to drive back to Oldbury now.

"Hey." Tanner's voice echoed down the phone. "Look, I know you're busy at your conference thing, but I thought you'd like to know I just took a call for you from a DS Pete Laker from Bristol."

"Okay," Lucy said, confused as to where this was going. She couldn't think of any recent cases that had links to Bristol.

"He wants to talk to you about the Booker case. He thinks it might be linked to one they had down there with a similar MO and maybe some others he's found."

"Sounds interesting." There had been no movement on the Booker case for months, not since the four lads had admitted the break-in. No evidence was ever found to charge them with anything else, and their search for the mystery, limping man had continued but proved fruitless when he disappeared from CCTV several streets away. Still no weapon had been found. Licence plates had been checked for cars parked up or passing through the area, but nothing had budged. The case was in danger of being moved into the reactive phase with no action until new evidence was found. Maybe this was the breakthrough they needed, a pooling of information.

"I'll call him first thing when I get back. Thanks, Tanner, have a good weekend," she said ending the call.

Lucy flopped back on the bed, covering her torso with the towel to fight the chill. She took a deep breath and sank in to the mattress, the last couple of days at the Policing Theory and Research conference had wiped her out. She couldn't help thinking it was some form of punishment Barrel had picked her out for after closing the Dunderdale case.

She was just dropping off when her phone rang again, jumping she lifted the phone to her ear fully expecting Tanner to give her more information on how the Booker case linked to Bristol. "Tanner, why are you call-."

"Lucy?"

The voice cut into her train of thought waking her weary head. She blinked several times trying to get her mind straight. "Johanna."

"Sorry, did I wake you? I didn't realise, is it late?"

"No." Lucy sat bolt upright, grabbing the towel just before it slipped to the floor. "No, its fine. I-err. How are you? Is everything okay?"

"Yes. Yes, fine."

Lucy released the breath she hadn't realised she was holding. "Good." Her shoulder hunched as a chill shivered through her body. She needed to put some clothes on, looking around she saw the jogging bottoms and t-shirt thrown on the chair she'd wore to slum around her room. Trapping the phone between her ear and shoulder she pulled them to the bed and struggled into them. "I tried to call, but…" She couldn't find the words to finish the sentence.

"I know." A long breath sounded down the phone. "I'm sorry, I.."

Three months to return a phone call was she being too harsh on her.

The silence dragged between them. She was flying blind here, she had no idea how this woman felt about her. She was just about to break the silence when Johanna beat her to it.

"I'd really like to see you. I-I wondered if you were free to meet for a drink?"

Lucy was too stunned to speak for a second, she'd waited to hear those words for so long and now she didn't know how to respond. She got to her feet and paced the length of her tiny room. "Oh. I'm-I'm in Trowbridge right now for a work conference."

"Trowbridge. Oh, it doesn't matter I just-."

"I-err. I'll be heading home tomorrow." Bath wasn't exactly on her way, but it could be. "I could stop off in Bath on the way if you're free, maybe in the afternoon." She stood by the window, pulling back the curtain to see the picturesque view of the back of the hotel in the near darkness.

"Really." There was a familiar spark to Johanna's voice. "That would be great."

Lucy smiled despite herself. "Where would you like to meet?" She wanted to give Johanna the choice, she hoped it would help her decipher the context of their meeting.

"There's a great café on the outskirts, I could send you the address?"

"Okay." She tried to hide her disappointment, was there a reason they weren't meeting at her house. Neutral ground maybe. "I'll give you a call when I'm nearby."

"Great. I'm looking forward to it."

Lucy said her goodbyes and hung up. *Was she looking forward to it, am I looking forward to it? Was it the brushoff she'd been expecting, but face to face.*

She'd had a brief taste of something; a taste of Johanna before it was ripped away. They hadn't argued or had words. Arresting the mother of your lover for murder wasn't exactly the best way to ingratiate herself with the Hales. Johanna's lack of contact despite Lucy's efforts had or so she thought, made it clear that she wanted nothing more to do with her, but now she didn't know what to think.

The fallout from the Dunderdale case continued to send ripples through people's lives.

Johanna marched along the footpath the chaos in her stomach threatening to bubble over, still she moved with purpose, determined to make up for her three-month tardiness. She hoped she hadn't given Lucy too much time to rethink their chances of embarking on a relationship. She wanted to be with her, there was such a firm connection between them. She'd even felt it during their brief phone call, despite Lucy's guarded approach. She'd thought of little else since, fearful Lucy would call it off last minute.

The cold felt good against her skin, being inside stifled by central heating always made her feel claustrophobic this time of year especially when her father kept shutting any open window he found. He'd been staying with her for almost a month now, so he could work on her new studio, or so he told himself. Johanna had a sneaking feeling he didn't want to be alone and she couldn't blame him for that.

She pondered the events that had brought him to her home, the one positive outcome was that the Dunderdale's finally had the answers they'd been seeking after all these years. She could only admire their resilience and desire to move on, or so she'd read in the press. Johanna had considered calling Barney but shied away from the prospect, the guilt for her mother's actions still too strong.

The café appeared on the opposite side of the road ahead, her stomach fizzed as she glanced at the large windows. Had she waited too long to return Lucy's call? At first she'd needed a bit of distance from it all, for it to sink below the surface a little. Then Christmas was upon them, it was a difficult time for her father, he struggled with the separation. With her father a little more settled she needed to know if the connection was real between her and Lucy.

Rocky's Café had become her local despite the distance from her home. She automatically scanned the parked cars to see if Lucy had arrived yet, nothing. Entering the café she recognised the young woman behind the counter from her frequent visits. A hot beverage at the midpoint in her walk was the perfect fuel for her journey back home. Ordering a hot chocolate she took a seat at a table near the window hoping to spot Lucy's arrival. She'd already checked her phone several times, making sure she'd sent the address of the café to the right number even though Lucy had already replied to her message.

Johanna glanced around at the other patrons as the clattering of spoons and plates created an acceptable din, no one looked familiar but then she rarely stayed when she came here preferring a take-out to keep her hands warm on the way home.

The café door swung open jingling the bell. She looked up to see Lucy scanning the café, realising she must have arrived from the opposite direction, Johanna stood raising her hand to wave her over.

Lucy had a warm smile on her face as she approached; her hair was loosely tied up, it was longer than she remembered highlighting the time that had passed. The collar of her black pea coat was up but the front was unbuttoned revealing a dark maroon top underneath, her blue jeans looked loved and comfortable. Casual attire suited her almost as much as formal wear.

It had taken only a couple of seconds for Johanna to realise she was still very attracted to Lucy Fuller, she just hoped it was mutual.

"Hi. Would you like something?" Lucy pointed towards the counter.

Johanna looked down at the marshmallows floating in her mug realising she should have waited for Lucy to arrive before ordering. "Err I'm okay, thank you."

"Have you been here long?" Lucy asked as she returned to take the seat opposite.

"No, not long." She smiled as she studied Lucy, she looked tired but that wasn't unusual.

Rain lashed at the window next to Johanna making her jump. "Looks like you made it just in time." Her hands tightened around her mug to fight the sudden chill. They were quiet for a moment, Johanna wasn't quite sure where to start.

"So, how have you been?" Lucy broke the silence.

"Good. Well, okay." She conceded offering a small smile. Johanna's mind was half rooted in the future, a future she hoped would include Lucy. While the other half was still stuck in the past, on that street in Compton Way where her mother had taken a life. "I've decided to take a more permanent background role in my company."

"Really." Lucy took a sip from her drink, coffee by the aroma drifting across the table. "Diversifying?"

"Sort of." Johanna grinned. "Well on paper I'll still the owner, but I'm leaving all the day-to-day running in the hands of my management team." For which they'll receive a suitable pay rise. It was a decision that had been made easier after her mother's arrest, as it allowed her to support her parents through the next few years. "Don't laugh. I'm taking up pottery."

"Oh." Lucy's eyebrows raised in amusement.

Steam pumped from the coffee machine behind the counter punctuating Lucy's one-word reply.

"I really enjoyed it at art college, so I thought I'd give it a go. I enrolled on a course and joined a local group."

"You have been busy."

Was that a dig? Johanna looked down at the table, she couldn't avoid the elephant in the room any longer. "I just needed to get out of the house and do something different for a bit." Lucy's hand appeared next to hers on the table, her fingers stroked the back of her hand.

"Sorry." Lucy whispered.

"I can't help thinking my mother came off the worst." Suddenly realising her words she quickly added a caveat. "Apart from Daniel of course." Paul Bell had gotten exactly what he deserved in her mind. She tried to blink away her embarrassment. Her mother's conviction was largely because she was driving the vehicle that hit Daniel, although according to the investigation there wasn't enough evidence to support manslaughter.

"I think you're right." Lucy placed her coffee back down. "Unfortunately, the CPS were determined to prosecute even though the evidence was largely circumstantial, the confessions were solid regardless of the thirty-year timeframe and lack of forensic evidence."

"She was the driver though." She sighed conceding the point.

Lucy nodded. "Although the pathologist couldn't say definitively that Daniel had died because of the impact with the car, Hunter's statement implicated Paul Bellamy in the actual murder."

Resulting in her mother receiving a lesser charge of causing serious injury by dangerous driving. The CPS had then decided to add further charges regarding the concealment of Daniel's body. The delay in the find had resulted in lost evidence, preventing the suspected perpetrator from being brought to justice.

"I made a point of putting your mother's state of mind at the time of the incident in my report."

Johanna looked up meeting Lucy's gaze. "I know, thank you. Our solicitor told me." She recalled him saying something about her mother's *actions being born out of shock and panic*. The concealment of the body was the final straw, exasperating the grief and distress to Daniel's family. Her mother received a two-year prison term and would be eligible for parole after nine months. "Considering she's been in a prison of her own making for the last thirty years, I guess she got off lightly in some ways."

"Have you visited her?" Lucy asked.

"A couple of times." Her mother's sentence had proved a shock despite its leniency. At first their conversations during visits had been stunted, but they had found a new understanding of late. It was strange to think how the truth coming out had made them closer. Her mood soon changed to one of anger when she thought about how Amelia Hunter had escaped a custodial sentence, not to mention Paul bloody Bell.

"It was always going to be difficult to get Hunter, due to her age at the time and the circumstances that had brought her there."

Johanna was grateful that Lucy was willing to talk about it. "Grooming, they said."

Lucy nodded. "That's what she claimed, combined with her age at the time and the fact that she wasn't involved in the concealment of Daniel's body."

Johanna frowned. "What about the sock?"

"Well," Lucy raised her eyebrows. "Forensics came back with Daniel's DNA with both blood and saliva, which, in the words of the forensics experts, was consistent with it being forced into Daniel's mouth. But Hunter stuck to her story that Daniel had wiped his mouth several times, which, although questionable, still supported Hunter's version of events."

Bitch. She had a feeling Amelia Hunter had far more involvement that she'd made out.

"She's free for now?" Lucy sighed.

"What do you mean?" She asked, as far as she knew everything was cut and dried.

"I have a feeling I'll be seeing her at some point in the near future." Lucy looked around her for a moment then back at Johanna. "I think she might have been involved in the death of Paul Bellamy and possibly the disappearance of her ex-partner but I can't prove it. Not yet."

"She even got away with blackmailing mum!" Claiming she was suffering trauma from the house fire and was trying to escape a violent partner, resulting in her preparation to escape Kingsford before she was caught.

Lucy nodded. "The thirty-month suspended sentence will allow us to keep an eye on her, and she'll be monitored by social services for drugging her kids, at least until she's managed another vanishing act."

"I sometimes think the justice system has it all arse about face."

Lucy sniggered. "Tell me about it."

"Paul bloody Bell." Johanna pushed away her mug. "He seemed so," she shook her head picturing the man in her mind, "harmless. Especially with his limpy leg, it used to make us all laugh, even Amy. I felt sorry for him sometimes, but he was the worst of us, look at what he did to Daniel, Amy and my mum."

"I know." Lucy placed a hand on her arm, she felt the warmth of her touch under her shirt as it pressed against her skin.

"I'm sorry, I really didn't come here to talk about all this."

"It's okay, it's better to talk about it."

Johanna nodded. "Thank you. So enough about me, how are you doing?" She'd managed to get side tracked from her initial task.

"Good."

"Lots of new cases I imagine."

"Yeah, there's always something going on."

As usual Lucy was tight lipped about her work. "I'm so sorry I didn't call you back. I wanted to but I-I just needed a bit of time, then it was Christmas and my dad -."

"Johanna, stop." Lucy interrupted. She placed her hand over Johanna's.

She looked up seeing the creased brow of Lucy's forehead. "I don't want you to think I didn't want to or I didn't think about you I-."

"It's okay." The warm smile returned to Lucy's face. "So, what did you want to talk about?"

A perfect opening. Johanna glanced at the clock behind the counter, god was it nearly four already, she had another cooking lesson with her father this evening. She wasn't ready to leave yet. "Would you...." She hesitated for a moment. "Would you like to come to lunch or dinner next weekend if you're not busy." She could have done this over the phone, but she wanted to gauge Lucy's feelings towards her first.

"Are you cooking?" Lucy tilted her head frowning.

"Don't worry it won't be burnt toast." She hoped. "I've been in training over the last few weeks. Don't expect Wan's Palace but I'll certainly rustle something up." She had no idea what, yet.

"You do make it sound tempting."

There was a humour to Lucy's words that settled the worry in her chest. "In fact I'm going to be late for another lesson."

Lucy placed her hands flat on the table. "Right, well we can't have that, not with your skill level. I don't want to get food poisoning."

She pursed her lips at Lucy's retort. "So you'll be my first victim, I mean you'll come for dinner?"

"I will. Thank you, I think." Lucy sniggered.

The waitress hovered nearby she hadn't realised they were the sole customers in the café, when did everyone else leave. Lucy pulled open the door for Johanna to go first, the rain had continued but was now a fine spray. The February gloom settled around them as they stepped outside.

"Where are you parked?"

"Oh I walked, I thought I'd get a bit of fresh air on the way." It was always her best time for thinking.

Lucy stood under the café's awning. "Can I give you a lift then. Save you getting soaked."

"Thanks, that would be great."

"It's the safest option after all, don't want you wondering in front of any more lorries."

She sniggered at the quip, slipping her arm through Lucy's edging closer as she urged Lucy to start walking. "That was a one-time thing."

"Glad to hear it. You'll need to give me directions, I don't know the area that well."

Yet. You will Detective Fuller, you will. "I can do that."

They turned a corner and Lucy's car came into view. Settling in Johanna rattled off several directions before they drove off.

"You walked all this way?"

"You know me I like a bit of a walk."

"I do." Lucy replied snatching a glance at her.

"It's just there." They slowed to a stop at the side of the road.

"Thanks for the lift." Johanna glanced at her house, the hallway light was on illuminating the stained-glass panel above the front door.

"No problem."

The dim light of the car made it easy for the words to spill from Johanna's lips. "I've missed you." She placed her hand on Lucy's thigh. "I'm sorry I waited so long to return your call."

She saw Lucy's hands flex on the steering wheel.

"I'm just glad you did." Lucy slowly turned to face her as she sat back in her seat.

"Really?" She half questioned to be sure.

"Yes. Definitely."

Johanna took the initiative, leaning across she pressed her lips to Lucy's. The kiss was soft, Lucy's hand cupped the side of her cheek holding her in place.

Lucy pulled back slightly but remained close. "Definitely." She repeated as her thumb caressed her cheek.

Johanna couldn't stop the smile from overtaking her face as she sat back in her seat. "I'll be expecting you next weekend detective." Without waiting for a reply she slipped out of the car, dashing towards her front door to escape the rain. Unlocking the door she realised

Lucy's car had yet to pull away. She turned smiling as she waved good bye, seeing movement in the car before it slowly drove off.

Johanna closed the door, the smile still plastered to her lips. As she shook the sides of her coat her father appeared in the hallway, she was only slightly late. He stood with his hands bunched in the front pocket of his apron.

"You got a lift." He half questioned. Had he been watching her.

"I did." She wasn't ready to reveal exactly who had given her a lift yet.

"I could have picked you up."

"I know, but you didn't have to." She placed her keys on the small table.

He took her coat, shaking it before draping it over the post at the bottom of the stairs.

"Ready for your next lesson?"

Absolutely." She needed to be able to cook something by next weekend.

Lucy pulled over parking up on a side street, she'd been looking forward to this all week. The text messages had been thick and fast after their meeting in the café which had served to stoke her feelings for Johanna. She'd truly missed her brief presence in her life.

She stepped out onto the pavement turning up her collar to the icy wind. She bypassed the front door walking towards the back of the house, knowing full well where the occupant would be. She hovered near the side door to the garage, and a faint whirring mixed with chattering voices met her ears. She imagined the woman inside occupied by her task.

"Police! Open up! You're surrounded!" she called out and the whirring suddenly stopped.

"You'll never take me alive, copper," came the chuckling reply, quickly followed by "It's open."

Lucy opened the door, surprised by the rush of heat that drenched her as she stepped inside. The interior space was no ordinary garage;

the internal walls and floor were clad with timber, not to mention the small wood burner to her left kicking out a moderate heat.

"Hey there. This is a nice surprise. I wasn't expecting you so early."

Johanna was on her feet, legs planted either side of the potter's wheel in front of her. Her blue boiler suit was covered with splashes and finger marks, sleeves rolled up beyond her elbows.

Lucy smiled. "I managed to slip out a bit early." The benefits of attending a conference in Trowbridge in your own time.

Johanna dragged one leg over the seat of the wheel to get closer and stood a few inches away, her hands wiggling as she held them up. They were covered in wet clay.

"Don't even think about it," Lucy warned as she leant forward to place a kiss on Johanna's lips.

Johanna just smirked as she walked past her to the Belfast sink set on a low breeze block wall under the window.

Lucy glanced back to the potter's wheel. "What are you working on?"

"What does it look like?"

Lucy stepped closer to the potter's wheel. The turned clay was slightly unruly in shape. "Umm. Well, it could be a bowl or a vase?" She turned to see Johanna staring back at her a wide grin on her lips.

"I'm just practicing pulling," she replied with a flash of her eyebrows.

"Oh. It looks … pulled." She had no idea what she was talking about. Instead, she looked around the large garage space. David Hale had turned it into a great potter's studio for his daughter. "Your dad's been busy."

"He's even insulated the walls and floor for me as well as the little stove."

"How is he?" Lucy asked. She was nervous about the answer, but she needed to know.

Johanna blew out a breath. "I think he's still in shock, to be honest. This was just something to take his mind off it for a while."

"I'm sorry." She wondered if Johanna had told him she was coming over.

"It's not your fault," Johanna said and slipped her hand into

Lucy's. "She should have come clean at the time; Dan could have gone to the hospital. He could have been saved ..." Johanna looked down at the floor. "We'll never know," she added sadly then looked back up, meeting Lucy's eyes. "I'm glad it was you that arrested her."

Lucy frowned for a moment, confused by her words.

"I knew you'd be more than fair with her."

Lucy wasn't so sure her boss was happy with the fact that she'd managed to prove him wrong. She'd found the truth after thirty years, except the murderer had managed to escape the justice he deserved. She regretted the impact it'd had on Johanna's life, but she had little choice when it was presented right in front of her.

"Let's go inside," Johanna said, pulling at their joined hands, leading the way out of her studio, flicking off the lights as she opened the door.

"What about the stove?" Lucy asked.

Johanna pulled a small bunch of keys held together with string from her pocket. "It'll be fine."

With the door locked, Johanna clung to her as the icy wind blew across the short path to the kitchen door located on the side of the house. Once unlocked and inside, Johanna kicked off her baseball boots before continuing to undress. Pulling at her overalls, she slipped them from her shoulders, exposing a navy vest top below. Lucy noticed a slight smell of cooking in the air, a little spicy maybe. She remembered one of Johanna texts saying her dad was trying to teach her to cook.

Johanna released her hand as she moved towards the sink. Steam rose from the tap as she soaped up. Rinsing her hands and arms, Johanna grabbed a towel and turned to face Lucy. "I'm glad you're here."

"Yeah?" The word was out before Lucy could stop it.

"Definitely." Johanna threw the towel onto the worktop as she edged closer. "I've really missed you."

Relieved, her reply was barely above a whisper as she stepped forward. "I've missed you too." Her mind flashed back to the scene in Johanna's hotel room as they did their little mating dance. Things were different now. She placed her hands on the discarded parts of Johanna's boiler suit, using it as leverage to pull Johanna's body firmly towards her own.

The corners of Johanna's lips lifted as she looked back at her.

Lucy ignored the freckles of clay that covered Johanna's left cheek as she tilted her head to bring their lips together. She had wanted to do that since walking into the garage earlier. Johanna's lips were as soft as she remembered, and the tip of her tongue skirted along her bottom lip, a hopeful promise of what was to come.

Lucy pulled back. "You've got some ..." She picked up the towel from the worktop. Finding a damp patch, she wiped away the tiny splashes of clay.

"Thanks."

"You're welcome." Lucy spotted the large, lidded pan on the stove as she placed the towel back on the worktop. "Have you been cooking?"

"Well, sort of. I'm still in training, apparently. Dad made a chicken curry for us."

"Us?" Lucy questioned. "He knows about ...?" She let Johanna fill in the blanks.

"He does."

"And?" Lucy held her breath.

"He doesn't blame you." Johanna looked away for a moment. "She did it. Well, Bellamy did." She met Lucy's eyes again. "I think he likes you."

"Really?"

"Really. Not as much as me, obviously." Johanna grinned back at her.

"Obviously." Lucy slipped her hands around Johanna's waist as she leaned in to kiss her again.

Johanna leant back to pull a scrap of paper from her front pocket. "He's even left me notes on how to cook the rice." She dropped the paper on the worktop before moving back towards her.

The kiss was slow, soft at first. Lips slowly parted as tongues mingled, igniting a generous heat below Lucy's stomach. Johanna moved her hand to the back of Lucy's neck, deepening the kiss.

Breaking away to catch her breath, she pressed her body against Johanna.

"I wanted to see you so many times over the last few months."

Lucy's heart fluttered with relief at Johanna's words as she nestled into her neck, breathing in her familiar, floral scent.

"Me too," she whispered and Johanna's hand stroked the back of her neck as they stood in silence for a moment. "I was trying to give you some space." In the hope that she would come back to her.

"I know you were." Johanna smiled as she moved her hand to cup the side of Lucy's face. "I'm grateful for that."

Johanna edged closer, bringing their lips together again. Her lips parted almost immediately. Lucy was quick to respond as Johanna's tongue sought her out, a small groan escaping her throat at the contact.

"Where's your dad?" Lucy asked before they went any further.

"Worried he'll walk in on us?" Johanna chuckled to herself. "He's staying with my brother for a while, sorting out his garden."

"Good." Plenty of time to work up an appetite.

Dear Reader

Thank you so much for reading *Obscured* I hope you enjoyed it as much as I enjoyed writing it. If so please take a few moments to write a review. Getting feedback from readers is amazingly useful, it will also aid other readers in deciding whether this is a book they might enjoy.

Thank you.

ABOUT THE AUTHOR

Charlotte Mills was born and bred in the south of England, after studying Fine Art at Loughborough University she has made the Midlands her home for the last twenty years, where she lives with her long term partner.

Her career has bridged several different fields including the arts, education and construction.

When she is not writing she enjoys watching films and daydreaming about living in the middle of nowhere without any neighbours in earshot.

Connect with Charlotte Mills
Email: charlottemills863@gmail.com
Twitter: @CMills_author
Website: charlottemillsauthor.com

Made in the USA
Monee, IL
05 March 2023

29249746R00229